JASMINE CRESSWELL

PAYBACK

MIRA®

ISBN-13: 978-0-7783-2487-4
ISBN-10: 0-7783-2487-7

PAYBACK

www.MIRABooks.com

Printed in U.S.A.

For Alexander, always in my heart…

One

Luke Savarini took a second bite of the lobster ravioli, just to be sure he hadn't judged too hastily. He'd been right the first time, he decided, letting the flavors dissolve on his tongue. There was too much oregano, and the sauce splashed over everything was weighted down with excess cream.

Anna, his sister, watched his reaction and then gave a crooked smile. "Not up to scratch, huh? My veal is okay, but not spectacular. Want to taste?"

"I'll take your word for it." Luke put down his fork, pushing away his heaped plate. With all the food there was in his life, he avoided eating anything he didn't completely enjoy. His waistline and his taste buds both thanked him.

"Why did you insist on bringing me here, Annie? You're not usually a fan of second-rate Italian."

"The restaurant is owned by Bruno Savarini. He's a

cousin of ours, sort of. His grandfather and our great-grandfather were brothers."

Luke rolled his eyes. The most remote and fragile twigs of the family tree all made perfect sense to his sister, whereas he had his work cut out simply keeping track of the names and birthdays of his six nieces and nephews.

He mentally reviewed the vast clan of Savarini cousins. "Okay, I'm working hard, but I can't place a Cousin Bruno."

"He's Great-Uncle Joe's grandson. You must have run into each other at a wedding."

Luke grinned. "Yeah, but that's almost the same as saying I've never met him. Can you ever recall a Savarini wedding with less than two hundred relatives milling around and at least half of the men singing 'O Sole Mio' at the top of their lungs?"

Anna returned his grin, tacitly acknowledging the cheerful mob scenes that passed for family gatherings in the Savarini clan. "Bruno had his sixty-fifth birthday last month. He's short and stocky, with brown eyes and an olive complexion—"

Luke laughed. "Well now, that narrows it right down. Short, stocky, brown eyes. I guess only ninety percent of Savarini men fit that description."

Anna tried to look severe. "Just because you're a six-foot, gray-eyed genetic freak, there's no need to get snooty. Anyway, I brought you here because Bruno plans to retire as soon as he can find a buyer for his restaurant. He has crippling arthritis and he only comes into the restaurant occasionally nowadays. You'd be astonished at how much better the food tastes on the days when he's here."

"I wouldn't be astonished," Luke protested. "I'm a chef, remember? I know just how much difference it makes when you have somebody talented in charge of the kitchen."

"The restaurant is in a fabulous location," Anna continued as if he hadn't spoken. "The decor is attractive and the kitchen is state-of-the-art. And Bruno has plenty of loyal customers. Look around you. The place is full. That's pretty good on a Wednesday, especially since we're eating late."

Far from looking around the restaurant, Luke's gaze fixed on his sister with suddenly narrowed focus. "Wait. I must be slow on the uptake tonight because I've only just realized why we're here. You want me to buy this place, don't you?"

Anna had the grace to blush. "Well, you're a chef. You own restaurants. Bruno wants to retire and he's our cousin. It seems a natural fit."

Luke felt a surge of affectionate exasperation. It was a familiar sensation in Anna's vicinity. She was a brilliant physicist, working for a government agency that she claimed was part of the Department of Education, although he'd believe crayfish grew on trees before he believed that. He loved her more than any of his four other siblings, which was saying a lot. But whereas she found quantum mechanics and string theory simple concepts, the economics of running a family business had always dangled far beyond her ability to grasp.

He took a sip of Chianti and then toasted his sister with the glass. "I appreciate your good intentions, Annie, but I can't just randomly acquire restaurants all over the country. I live in Chicago, remember?"

"News flash. Have you noticed there must be thirty flights a day between Chicago and Washington, D.C.? A thousand miles isn't so far."

Luke laughed, genuinely amused. "From your perspective, maybe. That's what comes of working all day with astronomers who consider Alpha Centauri to be practically banging on the back door because it's only a billion miles away—"

"You're missing several zeroes," Anna said. "And it *is* banging on the back door as stars go."

"Yeah, well, that's my point, Annie. A billion or a gazillion, it's all in a day's work for you. However, when you're running a restaurant, a thousand miles is a long way. You need to be on the spot so you can keep an iron grip on quality control, not to mention you have to be on hand to step in whenever there's a crisis."

His sister wasn't ready to give up. "But you have three restaurants in the Chicago area already, and you can only be in one of them at a time. And they're doing so well…"

Luke mentally crossed his fingers; he was superstitious where his restaurants were concerned. "You're right, Luciano's is succeeding beyond my wildest hopes. And part of the reason the restaurants are doing well is *because* they're all in the Chicago area. Where I live." *And where he was already working a minimum of sixty hours a week.*

She sighed. "I hoped that the lure of opening a restaurant in the D.C. area might be enough to tempt you to visit more often. I miss you, Luke, much as I hate to admit it, seeing as how when we were growing up you were a totally annoying snot."

He raised his eyebrow. "Me? A snot? You must have me confused with one of your other brothers. Tom, maybe. He has major league snot potential."

She shook her head. "Uh-uh. No confusion. I'm talking about you."

"How quickly good deeds are forgotten." Luke gave an exaggerated sigh. "What about the time I saved you from being discovered with the captain of the baseball team in Mom and Dad's whirlpool tub? When you were both naked, no less. I figure that ought to have earned me at least a decade or two of gratitude."

"My God, Robert O'Toole and the hot tub." Anna's expression was suddenly arrested. "I'd forgotten about that."

"If Dad had found the two of you, trust me, it would be one of your more vivid teenage memories."

She chuckled in wry acknowledgment. "Love is weird, isn't it? For two whole months I was convinced my life would be over if Rob didn't ask me to the senior prom. And I haven't given him a single thought since the day I left for college."

"He would be devastated to hear that," Luke said dryly. "Rob definitely fancied himself."

She gave a nostalgic grin and her gaze became wistful. "Damn, I miss you, Luke. Are you sure you don't want to reconsider buying Bruno out?"

Luke quelled a moment of temptation. "I wish, Annie, but I'm already stretched way too thin, time-wise. I'm sorry."

She gave a resigned shrug that didn't quite conceal her disappointment. "Oh, well. It was worth a try."

He leaned across the table and briefly rested his hand on his sister's. The movement shifted his perspective and his gaze happened to land on a couple seated at the table closest to the entrance. The man's back was turned toward their table, but as Luke watched, the man laughed and reached out to put his arm around the woman's shoulder so that Luke glimpsed him in profile. The man listened to his companion for a moment, and then laughed again at whatever she had said. A sudden lull in the noise allowed Luke to hear the sound. It was teasing and low, a throaty chuckle. It was also eerily familiar.

Shock momentarily froze Luke in his seat. Then he jumped to his feet, grabbing his chair just in time to prevent it toppling over. "Be right back," he told his sister, moving swiftly toward the couple.

"Luke, what's wrong? Where are you going?"

He didn't answer, partly because he was having a hard time catching his breath, partly because he was focused with hypnotic intensity on the couple by the door. The man must have sensed that he was being observed. He glanced up and his head jerked in visible shock. He immediately rose to his feet, putting his hand in the small of his companion's back and hustling her toward the exit. She followed without a word of protest, oddly compliant.

A waiter carrying a heavy tray crossed Luke's path, obscuring his view. He wished he could push the waiter violently aside, the way they did in the movies, and to hell with the food arrayed on the tray. But the habit of deferring to a server carrying dishes was ingrained and Luke skirted the waiter, losing another crucial few seconds in his journey toward the exit. He had to excuse himself twice to an oblivious woman whose chair stuck far out from the table, forming an impromptu barricade. When he'd negotiated that obstacle, he squeezed past the two final tables separating him from the hostess station and reached empty floor space. The man and his companion were nowhere in sight.

Luke ran outside, cursing himself for having wasted too much time being polite. Why hadn't he just elbowed and shoved his way across the dining room, and to hell with flying dishes? Unfortunately, the parking lot was crowded and he couldn't immediately spot the couple. Dammit, surely there hadn't been time for them to drive off?

The lot served several specialty stores in addition to Bruno's restaurant, and there were at least a dozen people strolling around, as well as a van pulled up to the curb, collecting trash. Although the lot was rimmed by lights, the humidity was high and there was a slight mist hanging in the night air, making it frustratingly hard to see. Luke finally picked out his quarry simply because the man was running, his companion jogging awkwardly in his wake, hampered by her high heels.

"Stop!" Luke yelled, ignoring the interested stares of passersby. "Stop, for God's sake! Ron Raven, is that you? Ron, stop!"

The man didn't answer. If anything his pace got faster. The woman, indifferent to the damp pavement, tugged off her shoes and ran barefoot across the lot.

Luke tore down the aisle of parked cars, catching up as the man clicked the car locks with his remote and slid behind the wheel of a silver-gray Mercedes. Ron, or his look-alike, didn't even wait for his female companion to get into the car before turning on the ignition. He was already backing out of his parking space before she closed her door, and long before she could have latched her seat belt.

Luke gave a final burst of speed and caught up with the couple. He stood behind the car, waving his arms. It was impossible for the driver not to have seen him, but the car continued to back up.

Jesus! The guy was going to run him over if he didn't move, Luke realized with a flash of total incredulity. At the last minute, he had no choice other than to jump to one side. Without a backward glance, the driver swung around on squealing tires and dashed for the exit.

"That man sure was in a hurry." A middle-aged woman stared at the disappearing Mercedes, her frown disapproving. "Crazy drivers. He could've killed you. If he keeps driving like that he's going to cause an accident for sure. You okay?"

"Yes, thanks." Luke realized just in time that if he could get the license plate number, the police would have a way to track down the owner. "Excuse me. Really, I'm fine."

He squeezed between two parked cars and dashed into the next aisle where he had a better view of the Mercedes racing toward the exit. It was a Virginia plate, he saw, with the license number AB7 4K3. Or maybe it was 4K8. He squinted, trying to confirm one number or the other, but the plate was dirty, the night dark, and the car was rapidly receding. The Mercedes sped down the block and made a sharp left turn at the first corner. Luke was a fast runner, but he knew he didn't have a chance in hell of catching up with it. He reached into his jacket and pulled out his Palm Pilot, jotting down the license plate numbers before he could forget them.

When he realized he'd been staring at the empty road for a full minute, he walked back into the restaurant and wove his way around servers and crowded tables, returning to his sister. His legs felt surprisingly shaky and he slumped into his seat, breathing hard. Anna started to lecture him, but changed her mind when she got a good look at him.

"What is it?" she asked. "For heaven's sake, what happened just now? Are you okay?"

"I'm not sure." He reached for his wineglass and then pushed it aside and took a gulp of water instead. He put the incredible truth into words. "I think I just saw Ron Raven."

Two

"**W**ho is Ron Raven?" Anna's forehead wrinkled in puzzlement and then she gave a jolt of surprise. "You mean *the* Ron Raven? The guy from Raven Enterprises who bankrolled your first restaurant and then turned out to be a bigamist?"

"Yes, that's who I mean." Luke tried not to sound impatient. "I just saw him. He was over there, eating dinner with some woman."

Anna's eyes widened in shock. "But you can't have seen him—he's dead! He died in Miami this past spring."

"Supposedly."

"What does that mean, *supposedly?* Ron Raven was murdered, and so was the woman who was with him in his hotel room the night he disappeared. We talked about the murder a half dozen times already. Good grief, Luke, you can't have forgotten! There was a ton of stuff about Ron Raven on TV. It turned out he had one wife in Chicago and another in Idaho—"

"Wyoming," Luke corrected.

"Right, Wyoming. He also had three kids. Two with the Wyoming wife, and another with his wife in Chicago. They're all grown-up, of course."

"Anna, I know all this stuff—"

"We talked about seeing his children on TV." Anna shoved a swathe of shiny, dark brown hair off her forehead, oblivious to Luke's answers. "They were all disgustingly attractive, although they didn't look much like one another. And one of his children was in the news recently. Ron's son. I don't recall his name, but he's a celebrity lawyer in Denver."

"Liam Raven. I wouldn't exactly call him a celebrity, although he's tried a couple of notorious cases."

"I didn't mean *he* was famous," Anna clarified. "I meant he works for famous people. He defended the mayor of Denver's wife when she was accused of murdering her husband. That was just a couple of months ago, wasn't it?"

Anna's sense of time, like her sense of distance, worked better on the astronomic scale, but in this instance she was more or less correct. "Yes. The mayor of Denver was murdered back in August."

"I watched some of the TV coverage because of the connection to Ron and your restaurants. Liam Raven got the charges against the mayor's wife dropped before she ever came to trial."

"Liam must be good at his job. Ron was good at his job, too." Luke gave an ironic shrug. "I guess professional competence runs in the Raven family."

"You can't get away from news items about the Ravens these days." Anna leaned back in her chair, nursing the last of her wine. "I saw a picture of Ron's Chicago wife in a magazine at the dentist's office last week."

"Avery Raven."

Anna wrinkled her nose. "Avery *Fairfax*. That's the name she goes by these days, apparently. She was attending an opera performance to benefit abused wives, which struck me as somewhat ironic given her personal situation."

"Or perhaps just very brave," Luke suggested.

"Maybe." Anna sounded unconvinced. "Avery's beautiful, but I saw her interviewed on *Larry King* and she struck me as a real snob. The sort of woman who has her initials embroidered on her underwear and would never leave the house without wearing her pearls."

"Is that how she struck you? In the clips I saw of her after Ron died, she looked pretty much shell-shocked to me."

Anna shrugged. "That, too, I guess. Anyway, the point is you must have been mistaken about seeing Ron Raven." Her voice took on a hint of amusement. "He's six months dead, which kind of rules out the possibility that he was eating dinner here at Bruno's."

Luke suspected he was being foolishly stubborn, but he fought against Anna's simple logic. "The cops never found Ron's body, or the body of the woman who was in the hotel room with him. Who's to say he's really dead?"

"The entire world, except you." Anna frowned, amusement vanishing. "The only reason the cops didn't find any bodies is because the killer took a boat miles out to sea and tossed them into the Atlantic. You saw those chilling security videos of the murderer using a dolly to wheel the bodies onto a yacht. The video was on every TV channel and in every newspaper. You couldn't avoid the clips even if you wanted to."

Luke shrugged. "Those videos never struck me as proving very much. All you saw was a masked person— you couldn't even determine male or female—pushing something onto a boat deck."

"Not *something*. The guy was clearly wheeling body bags."

"Okay, body bags. But they were zippered shut, for heaven's sake! They could have contained anything from dirty laundry to the Russian Imperial crown jewels."

"Yep, you're right, they *could*," Anna said crisply. "But the cops believe those bags contained the bodies of Ron Raven and the woman who'd been with him in the hotel room and they're most likely right. After all, the cops found traces of blood in various places on the boat and you yourself told me a reputable lab used DNA testing to confirm that the blood belonged to Ron Raven. DNA matches don't lie, Luke."

"I understand that. I'm not disputing that the DNA evidence confirms the blood on the boat deck was Ron's."

"Well, there you are."

"The fact that a lab established the blood was Ron's doesn't tell us anything about how the blood got onto the boat," Luke pointed out. "If I took a vial of your blood and dripped it across the floor of my bedroom, it doesn't mean you're dead or even that you were in my bedroom. A DNA match would simply prove that the blood on my bedroom floor was yours."

"And this is relevant to Ron Raven's murder because…?"

"Because we have no clue if Ron was dead or alive when his blood ended up on the deck of that stolen yacht."

"What exactly are you suggesting?" Anna's gaze focused on him with new intensity. "That Ron and some unknown woman faked their deaths convincingly enough to persuade the entire Miami police force they'd been murdered? Good grief, Luke, get a grip."

"I just saw Ron, so that's what must have happened." Luke knew he sounded as stubborn as he felt. "It would have been easy enough for Ron to cut himself and sprinkle blood to fake a shooting."

"It wouldn't have been easy at all." Anna shook her head. "There was a *lot* of blood. We're not talking about Ron pricking his finger. We're talking lots and lots of blood, in a spatter pattern that suggested he'd been shot."

"If Ron had a good reason to disappear—and presumably he did—he might have been willing to sacrifice a pint or two of blood."

"You're forgetting something important—the police identified his murderer."

"Yeah, so they did." Luke's voice was heavy with sarcasm. "And we all know the cops have never pinned a murder on the wrong culprit."

Anna turned her left hand palm up and wiggled her fingers. "Okay, on this side we have weeks of intensive professional investigation and a ton of forensic evidence suggesting Ron Raven was murdered in his hotel room by a man who'd already committed other murders." She turned over her right hand. "On this side we have the fact that you saw somebody who looks like Ron Raven eating dinner in Cousin Bruno's restaurant."

She tilted her head in exaggerated perplexity. "Hmm…let's see. Which theory should we go with? Is Ron dead or alive? Gee, I can't imagine."

Luke leaned across the table. "Stop being a smart-ass and explain to me what we know about Ron Raven's disappearance that makes it impossible to believe the guy faked his own death."

"I thought I just did that, but I'll do it again." Anna ticked off on her fingers. "There was enough blood in Ron's hotel room to suggest he was seriously injured. Ditto for his female companion. In that same hotel room, the cops found DNA from a convicted felon who'd already spent years in prison for murdering two other people. So we have two bleeding victims and a known killer in the same hotel room. Plus there's been no activity at any of Ron's bank accounts since the day he disappeared. If he faked his own death, he walked away from a load of money. Why would he?"

"Because he was a bigamist and his life was getting complicated?"

"He'd been a bigamist for decades," Anna retorted. "Neither of his wives suspected anything."

"Maybe he left for financial reasons, then."

"He wasn't under any unusual financial pressure. Everyone agrees Raven Enterprises was profitable at the time he disappeared."

Luke pushed back his chair, giving in to a burning

need to do something more productive than argue the odds with his sister. Or maybe he just didn't want to acknowledge the logic of his sister's viewpoint. "I need to talk to the server who waited on Ron Raven."

"The server who waited on Ron's look-alike," Anna corrected.

He ignored her reproof. "Sorry, Annie, I won't be more than a minute or two. Choose something decadent for dessert, okay?"

Luke made his way across the room and stood quietly while the young woman served entrées to a party of five businessmen. He stopped her as she hurried back toward the kitchen, glancing at her name tag as she whisked past.

"Hey, Merrie, I'm sorry to delay you, but my name's Luke Savarini. Bruno Savarini is my cousin." He nodded across the room toward Anna. "And that's my sister, Anna. You might recognize her since she's one of your regular customers."

"I'm sorry. I'm new here." The server smiled, trying not to look as impatient as she undoubtedly felt. "Anyway, it's great to have you with us, Mr. Savarini. I hope you and your sister are enjoying your dinner."

"It was delicious, thanks." Luke usually had a difficult time lying about food. This time, he barely noticed. "You're the server for this table near the door, aren't you?"

Merrie glanced to the empty table he was indicating and nodded. "Yes, why? Is there a problem?"

"Not at all." She already seemed on the defensive, Luke thought. He needed to reassure her that she wasn't about to get into trouble. "The thing is, I believe I saw an old friend a few minutes ago. He'd been eating at this table but he left before I managed to catch his eye."

"I'm afraid I can't help—" Now that she knew she wasn't facing a reprimand, the server was visibly itching to get away.

Luke stepped in front of her, debating whether a healthy tip would make her more forthcoming. He decided against the tip, afraid it might be such an obvious bribe that she would clam up even more. "My friend and I lost track of each other when he moved to the D.C. area six months ago. I wondered if he was a regular here at the restaurant."

"I wouldn't know. Sorry, Mr. Savarini. Like I said, I'm new. I only started last week and I'd never waited on him before, that's for sure."

"Did he pay by credit card? If so, could you tell me his name? That would help me to confirm it really was my friend."

Merrie wasn't stupid. Her smile vanished. "I'm sorry, sir, but I can't give out personal information about one of our customers. As it happens, though, the guest you're inquiring about paid in cash. In fact, he left without even waiting for his check. He just dropped a bundle of twenty-dollar bills on the table, but it was more than enough to cover his bill. Now, if you'll excuse me, we're really busy and I need to get back to work." She walked away before Luke could ask any more questions.

"Well, that got me precisely nowhere," he said to his sister, sliding back into his seat. "The server admitted the guy didn't wait for a check. He simply left a stack of twenty-dollar bills on the table to pay for his meal.

As the owner of three restaurants, I can tell you that almost never happens."

"Let it go, Luke." His sister handed him the dessert menu. "The reality is that Ron Raven is dead and you saw somebody who looked like him."

"The man recognized me," Luke said. The more he replayed the incident in his mind, the more convinced he became that he'd seen Ron Raven, not some look-alike. "He knew I'd recognized him and he bailed without even waiting for his check. Then he damn near ran me down in the parking lot in order to avoid talking to me. If it was somebody who just looked like Ron, why was he so anxious to avoid me?"

"Because you made him nervous the way you were obviously pursuing him?"

"No." Luke gave a decisive shake of his head. "He ran because he recognized me. Then he dropped a pile of cash on the table to cover his bill because he hoped to get out of the door before I caught up with him. And it worked."

Luke knew he was being obstinate, but the sound of Ron's laughter and the tilt of his head had seemed familiar even before he'd glimpsed the man's features full face. A stranger might happen to look like Ron. What were the odds that the same stranger would also sound like him and have similar mannerisms?

Anna was silent for a moment, finally giving real weight to the possibility that her brother had seen what he claimed. "If that man was Ron Raven and he recognized you, that means he hasn't lost his memory...."

"I agree."

"But if Ron isn't suffering from memory loss, he's

deliberately hiding. That can't be good, especially for his families."

Luke shrugged. "His wives and children already know Ron was a liar and a cheat. How is it worse for them to know he's a live scumbag as opposed to a dead one?"

"Maybe it's not," Anna conceded. "But I sure as hell would think long and hard before I went to either of his previous wives and informed them that I'd just seen their supposedly dead husband eating dinner in my cousin's restaurant. Their most likely reaction is to have you arrested for harassment."

"Don't they have a right to know?" Luke was unsure how he would answer his own question.

"Know what, precisely?" Anna demanded. "That you think you *may* have seen a man who looks like Ron Raven, but he left the restaurant before the two of you exchanged a single word? Wow! There's news to set the blogosphere humming."

"I wouldn't be telling his families I saw a man who looked like Ron Raven," Luke answered quietly. "I'd be telling them I'm pretty much one hundred percent sure that I saw Ron Raven, alive and in the flesh."

Anna drew in a sharp breath, taken aback by his conviction. "You were simply a business acquaintance of Ron's, not an intimate friend. You probably didn't meet him more than a couple of times."

"Try at least a dozen. Usually one-on-one, and sometimes for meetings that lasted as long as three or four hours. Ron Raven was a hands-on type of investor."

"Even so, it was six years ago and you've been leading a hectic life ever since then. Memories blur. Impressions get distorted. Plus, you have no idea what sort of people his wives and children are. Do you have the right to mess with the lives of people you've never even met?"

Luke was silent for a long time. This was what came of stubbornly clinging to the notion of privacy in a family where if one person sneezed on Tuesday, by Friday every sibling and ten percent of the other relatives would have called to find out how the guy's cold was progressing.

"I have met Ron's family," he said finally. "Or at least his Chicago wife and daughter. I know them quite well, in fact."

Anna stared at him. She was thirteen months older, which meant that she'd known him for the entire thirty-four years of his existence. Apparently something in his voice had alerted her to the fact that his meetings with Avery and Kate Raven involved more than socializing with the family of the man who'd provided him with investment capital.

"Define what you mean by knowing them *quite well,*" she said, in an ominous, older-sister tone of voice.

Luke cursed silently. If he hadn't been thrown for a loop by the glimpse of Ron Raven, he would never, ever, have laid himself open to this sort of sisterly scrutiny.

He tried to speak with brisk indifference. "Kate…Ron's daughter…is a pastry chef. She was a member of the U.S. team that competed in the Coupe du Monde de la Patisserie last year. The design concept for their chocolate torte was Kate's and their team took the bronze medal. The French team won, of course—they always do—but the U.S. has never even placed in that competition before. These days, Kate is working as head pastry chef for La Lanterne, the finest bakery in Chicago."

He was rather pleased with his casual summation of Kate's life. All professional accomplishment and nothing personal. Anna, unfortunately, was not deceived. "How long have you been dating her?" she asked. "And how the hell could you have kept quiet about her all those times we discussed Ron's disappearance?"

"I'm not dating her." Under his sister's unrelenting gaze, he expanded his answer. "Not anymore. We broke up a while ago."

"Before her father was murdered?"

"Yes. A few weeks before, in fact." To be precise, not long after their argument as to whether Luke respected her professional ambitions enough to take time off from the opening of his newest restaurant to fly to Lyon and watch her compete in the most important contest of her professional life. The preparation and endless hours of practice for the Coupe du Monde were so arduous they had both known Kate would be unlikely ever to enter the contest again. Seven months after their breakup, he was finally able to admit that his decision not to fly to France had probably contributed to the chain of events leading to their final, hideous confrontation.

Anna looked hurt. "Quite apart from all the times we discussed Ron Raven's murder, why didn't you ever tell me you were dating somebody special?"

Because he'd worked his ass off to keep the affair quiet. Because while he and Kate were dating, he'd been desperate to develop the relationship minus the analysis of his parents, his five siblings and all the assorted in-laws and cousins who might decide to stick their noses into this latest interesting piece of Savarini family gossip. Ironically, the spectacular emotional storm that ended his relationship with Kate had taught him the hard lesson that there were far more ways to screw up a relationship than subjecting it to benevolent interference from a close-knit family.

"There was no point in talking to you about Kate. It wasn't serious and we didn't date all that long." Eight months wasn't very long, he soothed his conscience, so he wasn't exactly lying. Luke hurried on, dodging more sisterly questions. "The thing is, I do know Kate and her mother well enough to be fairly sure that if Ron Raven is alive, they would want to hear about it."

A gruff, rumbling voice greeted them from across the room, saving him from further cross-examination. *Thank you, Jesus.*

"Anna, *mia piccola, come stai, carina?*"

"Bruno! *Che sorpresa piacevole! Sto bene, grazie. E tu?*"

"*Eh, cosi, cosi.* No, no, don't get up, Anna." Cousin Bruno squeezed her shoulder. "What a treat to find you here! I'm glad I decided to stop by the restaurant after my daughter dragged me to the movies. We saw this horrible, boring movie about blowing up cars. If there was anything more to the plot, I must have missed those two lines of dialogue."

Anna laughed and stood up to hug him, ignoring his command. "Bruno, stop complaining. You know you love movies with lots of car chases."

"Yes, providing there's a plot squeezed in between the chases." He patted her shoulder. "You should have told me you planned to eat here tonight. I would have skipped the movie and been here to welcome you both."

"I wasn't sure what our plans would be. Luke's only in town for twenty-four hours. By the way, do you remember my brother, Luke?"

"We never met." Bruno shook hands. "But I ate at your restaurant last year when I was in Chicago. Luciano's on Chestnut. I inquired after you, Luke, but the sous-chef told me you were at one of your other places that night. You can be very proud of what you've achieved with Luciano's. The meal my brother and I ate was spectacular."

"Thank you. It's a relief to know you were there on a night when we didn't screw up."

"Somehow, I get the impression that you and your team don't screw up very often." Bruno pulled out a chair and sat down. "Well, I can't compete with Luciano's—we don't even try to cater to that level of sophistication—but I'm proud of the desserts we make here. What can I get the two of you? Our tiramisu is made from an old family recipe handed down by my grandmother, and it's the best ever, if I do say so myself. The panna cotta with caramel sauce is mighty fine, as well. We use buttermilk in addition to the cream and it's not as bland as the traditional recipe."

"I love your amaretto ice cream," Anna said. "It's my personal favorite."

"Then amaretto ice cream it shall be for you, *cara*." Bruno gave her hand a fatherly squeeze. "Luke, how about you?"

"The panna cotta would be great," he said. "I've never made it with buttermilk and it sounds interesting."

Their desserts arrived along with tiny cups of aromatic espresso and Luke chatted politely with his cousin, who seemed both a kindly man and an experienced chef. Maybe the ravioli has just been an unfortunate exception to generally good food, Luke mused. The panna cotta was certainly first-rate, and the buttermilk made for an intriguing variation on an old standby.

Bruno excused himself to have a word with his staff, and Anna worked hard to keep Luke from reverting to their previous conversation about Ron Raven. Since Luke was working equally hard to prevent her picking up their conversation about Kate, the atmosphere around the table was unusually strained. They were both relieved when Bruno returned after a few minutes and sat down across from Luke.

"Merrie, one of our servers, asked me to give you this," he said, handing Luke a thin, crumpled credit card receipt. "She said you were inquiring about a couple that was seated at one of her tables. Apparently, they left this behind."

Luke picked up the flimsy slip of paper. "I appreciate Merrie thinking of me. But she told me that couple paid their bill in cash."

"They did. This isn't one of our charge slips," Bruno said. "If it was, I couldn't pass it on. But Merrie found it tucked in among the stash of twenties they left behind to pay their bill. She was about to toss it away when she saw me ordering your desserts and realized you really are my cousin. Since this charge slip is nothing to do with us or the meal they ate here, and there's no way to return it to the couple, I figure there's no harm in handing it over to you. Merrie says you were interested in this man."

There was a definite question in his cousin's voice and Luke repeated his story about seeing an old friend he'd lost touch with. "I'm not sure if I'm enthusiastic enough to track him down through a credit card bill, but I appreciate Merrie's gesture. Tell her thanks from me, will you?" He deliberately downplayed his interest, since he could only imagine how Bruno would react if Luke repeated his claim to have seen a supposed murder victim eating dinner on the other side of the dining room.

Bruno seemed satisfied with Luke's explanation, and left to go back to the kitchen after another profuse round of good wishes and goodbyes.

Luke smoothed out the charge slip, scrutinizing the scanty information as he and Anna made their way back to her car. The charge of forty-three dollars and change had been made earlier in the day at an establishment called Sunrise. There was no indication of what sort of establishment Sunrise might be.

"What's the name on the charge slip?" Anna asked, clicking her key to spring the locks on her car.

Luke held the slip up to the light. "Stewart M. Jones."

"You see!" Anna looked relieved. "I *told* you the man you saw wasn't Ron Raven. Now you can relax and stop obsessing about seeing dead people. I feel as if I spent the past hour living in an outtake from *The Sixth Sense.*"

The fact that the name on the charge slip read Stewart Jones proved nothing at all about the identity of the man Luke had seen in Bruno's, as his sister must realize. If Ron had faked his own death, he wouldn't be opening charge accounts under the identity he'd just been at great pains to get rid of.

Anna must be afraid that he was seeing visions of Ron because he was hung up on his failed relationship with Kate, Luke decided. As it happened, his sister was way off the mark. He wasn't fixated on Kate—far from it. Their affair had ended in nothing less than misery and he sure as hell wasn't wasting any time regretting its end. Kate might be beautiful and sexy and have the same career interests as he did, but their personalities were polar opposites. Not to mention the fact that her concept of faithfulness bore no relationship to his.

He realized now that their character differences had mattered almost as much as the betrayals. As their affair started to unravel, their differences worked to the surface, causing unbearable friction. His frustrations had boiled over into the sort of noisy Italian explosiveness he'd spent most of his adult life learning to control. Kate had reacted to each of his displays of temperament with a deeper and deeper retreat into icily silent WASP disapproval.

Even the memory of those last few weeks was enough to make Luke feel slightly sick, quite apart from the horrors of the final denouement. Allowing his sister's comments about the real identity of Stewart M. Jones to slide past unchallenged, Luke tucked the charge slip into his billfold and took his seat next to Anna in the car. He returned the conversation to family, food and the imminent birth of their youngest sister's first baby and made sure he kept it there.

For all his silence, Luke's conviction that he'd seen Ron Raven remained strong. But six months had already passed since Ron disappeared, and Luke decided he could afford to wait until he got back to

Chicago before notifying the authorities that, far from moldering in the depths of the Atlantic Ocean, Ron Raven was alive and well, and seemingly enjoying life in one of the more prosperous suburbs of Washington, D.C.

Three

The Miami police department didn't even bother to be polite when Luke called to inform them that he'd seen the supposedly dead Ron Raven eating dinner in Herndon, Virginia, a week earlier. Dismissed by a bored clerk—his call never made it as far up the hierarchy as a real cop—he tried again with the Chicago police.

Smarter this time around, he directed his call to a detective sergeant whom he'd met eighteen months earlier when Luciano's was being remodeled. The cop had been assigned to find out who was stealing construction materials from the restaurant site and Luke figured the two of them had a good rapport.

Their rapport apparently didn't extend far enough for the cop to believe Luke's claim to have seen Ron Raven. His tale was received with greater politeness, but with the same bored disbelief demonstrated by the police department in Miami. The bottom line was that cops in both places had fielded hundreds of reports alleging that Ron Raven was alive, and the fact that Luke described himself as an old friend and business acquaintance of the deceased carried no particular weight.

"Has it occurred to you that maybe you've received so many reports because Ron Raven *is* alive and people really *are* seeing him?" Luke finally asked, no longer bothering to hide his frustration.

"No," the cop responded baldly.

"That's it?" Luke asked, incredulous. "Just *no?*"

"What do you want me to say?" The detective sighed. "We receive reports like this every time there's a murder that attracts a lot of TV coverage. And when there's no body to be buried, you can guarantee that half the weirdos in the state are going to claim they've seen the deceased."

It was sobering to realize that from the detective's point of view he was simply one more wing nut craving notoriety. "But you've dealt with me before!" Luke protested. "You know I've met Ron Raven because it was right in your report about the thefts from the construction site. You needed a record of who was providing financing for the restaurant and I told you then—almost three years ago!—that I had a revolving line of credit with Ron Raven."

"That's true." The cop's voice added a layer of impatience to existing boredom.

"And it isn't as if I'm calling you when Ron Raven's disappearance is being hotly reported by the media. They moved on to fresh meat weeks ago. Months ago, in fact."

"I'm sure you believe what you're telling me, Mr. Savarini—"

"But you don't believe me, and you have no interest in conducting any sort of follow-up investigation."

"No, I don't." In view of their past acquaintance, the cop relented enough to expand on his reply. "Look, here are the facts. I pulled up the case notes while you were talking and I'm reading them right off my computer. In the three months the investigation was on active status, we took reports from a hundred and twelve people claiming to have seen Ron Raven. Do the math. That's around ten supposed sightings a week. Miami police have taken hundreds more. On top of that, six callers told us they'd committed the murder, and another three identified themselves as the woman who'd been in the hotel room with Mr. Raven. We followed up on all six confessions and interviewed all three women who claimed to have been in the Miami hotel room. Our detectives concluded the closest any of those people had come to seeing Ron Raven was via the TV screens in their living rooms. That was your tax dollars at work, Mr. Savarini, from May until the end of July. A complete waste of time and police resources. Be grateful the case has been put into inactive status. Except for the warrant outstanding against Julio Castellano, of course. Now, if you thought you'd seen him, I'd be more interested."

"The fact that crazy people like to confess to murders they didn't commit proves nothing about whether I saw Ron Raven in Virginia last week."

The cop no longer sounded bored, only impatient. "We have forensic evidence that proves Julio Castellano, a twice-convicted murderer, was in Ron Raven's hotel room," he snapped. "We have bullets and blood-spatter patterns in the hotel room, in the exact places forensic experts would expect if the victims were shot while they were running from the bed. We also have security video of two bodies being wheeled onto a yacht. Based on discrepancies between the ship's log and data collected from the yacht itself, experts have calculated that the boat traveled a total of thirty-five nautical miles that night without knowledge or permission of the owners. Trust me, Mr. Savarini, we know exactly what happened to Ron Raven the night he disappeared. He was murdered. He's dead and his body— what's left of it—is at the bottom of the Atlantic Ocean."

It was depressing to hear Anna's arguments repeated more or less point by point. Luke realized that announcing he had the number of the car in which "Ron Raven" had driven away from the restaurant was going to get him nowhere. The chance of the Chicago police department agreeing to run the numbers was somewhere south of zero. He cut short what was clearly a useless exercise by thanking the cop for his explanations and hanging up.

It was approaching 11:00 a.m., almost time for him to leave for work, and way past time for him to stop obsessing about a sighting that apparently nobody cared about except him. He was sweaty after his morning run, and he retreated to the bathroom to take a shower in preparation for the long hours ahead. He'd be lucky if he was back in his Lincoln Park condo before two or three in the morning, and that was assuming the night produced no major crises at any of his restaurants.

Luke let the water pound in a scorching stream over his head and body. The cops were convinced they had the case of Ron Raven's disappearance wrapped up, despite the minor detail that they hadn't actually managed to arrest the alleged murderer. Who was Luke to persist in the claim that he'd seen Ron eating dinner in Herndon, Virginia, when the rest of the world was happy to accept that the guy had long since become an all-you-can-eat buffet for the Atlantic fishes?

Even if he was right and the rest of the world was wrong, he had no good reason to hurl himself against the brick wall of police indifference. The eight months he'd spent dating Ron's daughter didn't justify sticking his nose into Raven family business months after his affair with Kate had ended. God knew, he had enough problems within his own family to keep him occupied for the next lifetime or two. He sure as hell didn't need to take on anyone else's family problems.

But, dammit, he'd seen Ron Raven! The annoying conviction remained, despite his efforts to wash it down the shower drain. Luke reminded himself of all the reasons why this was a totally lousy time for him to set off on some idiotic quest to convince the world that Ron was alive. The sous-chef at his newest restaurant in suburban Winnetka had sliced open his thumb yesterday, which meant that Luke would be putting in ten long hours of intensive labor tonight, instead of merely checking in for a couple of hours before transferring to his flagship restaurant in downtown Chicago. The Food Network had called yesterday and asked him to tape a show for their upcoming series on America's most exciting new chefs. Somehow, his already crammed schedule for next week had to be expanded to include eight hours of interviews, with a camera crew trailing him while he cooked and the network expert analyzed everything from his fall seasonal recipes to his underlying technique.

Luke turned off the shower and shook water from his body. Clearly, he didn't have time right now for pursuing ghosts, literal or metaphorical. Nevertheless, he found himself grabbing a towel and padding wet-footed back into the spare bedroom that served as his home office. Tucking the towel around his waist, he grabbed his Palm Pilot and retrieved a phone number for George Klein, a private detective he'd hired over the summer to identify a dishonest Luciano's employee.

George greeted him warmly, a soothing change after the indifferent cops. "Luke, it's good to hear from you again. How are you?"

"I'm fine, but I need your help. Nothing to do with the restaurants, thank God. Either the security systems you put in place are working or I've managed to hire some really loyal and honest employees. I hope it's the latter."

"I do, too. There's nothing I like better than to install protective systems that never get activated. So, how can I help you?"

"I'm hoping you can run a license number for me. It's a Virginia plate, and I need to know who the car is registered to. Do you have any contacts in Virginia?"

"A couple. Hopefully, they'll come through for me. Give me the plate number and I'll give it my best shot."

"I'm not sure of the final digit. I was reading the license in the dark and I couldn't see whether it was AB7 4K3, or AB7 4K8. What I want to know is the name and address of the owner. The car was a silver gray Mercedes coupe, by the way. I don't know if that makes a difference."

"Absolutely. It's a big help." George Klein was far too discreet to inquire why Luke wanted to track down a Virginia license plate. "I'll have both sets of numbers run through the DMV database, and if my contacts are still good, I should be able to get names and addresses for you before the end of business tomorrow."

George called early the following afternoon, tracking Luke down at the smallest and least formal of the three Luciano restaurants, a trattoria in Oakbrook. He informed Luke that the vehicle registered as AB7 4K3 was a Hyundai, owned by a woman. Her name was Jennifer Parker and she lived in Reston, Virginia.

"Based on your description of the vehicle as a gray Mercedes, I assume that's not the person you're looking for," he said.

"No, I'm trying to trace a man," Luke said. "He's an old friend and we…um…lost touch."

George Klein was kind enough to ignore Luke's lame attempt to justify his snooping. "The vehicle registered as AB7 4K8 is a Mercedes CLK 550 coupe," he said. "The color is listed as Evening Pearl. That sounded more like the vehicle you're looking for."

"Yes, it sure does."

"Apparently it was sold last week. The system caught up with the change of ownership only a couple of hours before I checked, so we got lucky. It's currently registered to a Mercedes dealer in Arlington, Virginia. I figured you'd want to know the name of the previous owner—"

"Yes, I sure do."

"It was a man called Stewart M. Jones."

Luke's breath caught at the now-familiar name. It might be sheer coincidence that Mr. Jones had sold his car right after Luke chased him down in the restaurant parking lot. But the hasty sale could also mean that Ron Raven was so determined not to be traced that he'd been willing to part with an almost-new Mercedes to avoid discovery.

"Do you have an address for Mr. Jones?" Luke asked the detective.

"I do. Mr. Jones gave his place of residence as McLean, Virginia—2737 Elm Court to be precise."

"Thanks, George. I really appreciate the swift service. Can you do one more thing for me? Find out if Stewart Jones is still living at Elm Court."

"I figured you might want that information." George Klein sounded pleased with his forethought. "I already checked with the owners of the building. According to them, Elm Court is a short-term rental place but it's pretty upscale, mostly catering to diplomats and international businessmen. Unit 6, which is where Mr. Jones was living when he registered his car, rents for five thousand bucks a month, furnished, weekly maid service included. That's not out of sight for the D.C. area, but it's obviously not cheap, either. Mr. Jones stayed there for only one month and left three months ago, with all his bills paid up. From the point of view of the management company, there was nothing in the least remarkable about his stay or his departure. They screen all tenants, of course, and Mr. Jones passed the screening without a hiccup."

If Ron Raven were alive and wanted to conceal that fact, then Washington, D.C. would be an ideal city for him to hide in, Luke reflected. Nobody noticed strangers or transients in the D.C. area because the city was full of them. From Ron's perspective, there were few cities in the United States that would offer better prospects for lucrative business deals, combined with plenty of comfortable places to hide.

The fact that "Stewart Jones" had passed a standard credit check didn't surprise Luke in the least. Ron Raven had been running background checks on prospective clients for three decades and he would certainly know all the danger points he needed to protect himself against. On top of that, he'd been concealing his bigamous lifestyle for twenty-eight years. Never confiding fully in anyone, procuring duplicate documents and spinning stories to obscure the truth would be second nature to him. Now that he thought about it, Luke realized Ron Raven was almost uniquely qualified to disappear and reemerge with a new identity.

Unfortunately, the more convinced Luke became that Stewart Jones and Ron Raven were the same person, the more difficult it became to imagine how he was going to track the guy down. On top of that, he would soon have to consider the issue Anna had raised last week: Would he be doing the Raven family any favors by telling them he'd seen Ron? Or would he be heating up an emotional pot that had just started to cool down from the traumatic news of Ron's death?

"I suppose it's too much to hope that Mr. Jones left a forwarding address," he said to George Klein.

"He left an address, but it's in Australia. In Adelaide, to be precise. I haven't followed up. I figured I'd talk with you first before going to that expense."

"Stewart Jones's forwarding address is in *Australia?*"

"Yes. You sound surprised."

"I am."

"I take it you didn't know that Mr. Jones is an Australian diplomat?"

"An Australian diplomat?" Luke stared blankly at the contract with a seafood vendor that he'd been reading before he picked up the detective's call. Ron Raven clearly had acting abilities his family didn't know about if he'd managed to pass himself off as an Australian.

"Luke? Are you there?"

"Sorry, you surprised me, that's all. I assumed…Mr. Jones…was an American."

"Perhaps he is. If you're a person trying to hide, adopting a foreign identity is a great first step."

"Why's that?"

"Because superficial identity checks in the States are all set up around social security numbers. An Australian diplomat doesn't have an American social security number, meaning that credit checks are a lot more difficult. Not to mention more expensive."

"And that would make it harder for somebody to identify Stewart Jones as a fraud," Luke said.

"Absolutely," George agreed. "But if Stewart Jones isn't really Australian, we can soon find out. Do you want me to check the Australian address he gave the rental company?"

Luke's first instinct was to stop this investigation right now. What the hell was he trying to achieve by chasing a chimera across thousands of miles of Pacific Ocean? In the end, though, he couldn't quite let go.

"It can't hurt, I guess, since we've come this far so quickly. Thanks, George. Some information about Mr. Jones's forwarding address would be useful. Can you dig deep enough to find out if we're talking about a mail drop or a residence?"

"Sure thing. I could also check with the Australian foreign ministry and confirm whether or not they have a Stewart M. Jones on their diplomatic roster."

"That would be great. Although Mr. Jones passed the background check conducted by the Elm Court management company, so I'm not sure that we're going to unearth any discrepancies without going to a lot of trouble."

"You'd be surprised—make that alarmed—at how easy it is to pass a standard credit check. I'll just peel back a couple more layers and see what we uncover." George paused. "It would help if I knew what I'm trying to find out."

"For now, I'd prefer just to tell you that you're right, and I think Stewart M. Jones is a stolen identity someone has adopted." Luke gave up on the unrealistic pretense that he was conducting a simple search for an old friend. "If the Australian authorities acknowledge they have a diplomat called Stewart Jones, could you get a description of him? That way, I can compare the man I saw with the Stewart Jones employed by the Australian government. I don't want to make any accusations or leap to any wild conclusions until I'm sure I didn't just see a hardworking Australian guy who happens to look like somebody else."

"I'll do my best. In fact, if I tell the Aussies that I'm investigating a suspected identity theft, they'll probably be quite willing to cooperate."

"Thanks for all you've done so far, George. I'm very grateful."

"Glad I could be of help. I'll hold off on sending you a bill until I've contacted the Australian authorities and traced this address in Adelaide." The investigator's voice took on a tinge of laughter. "If I give you the damage in one fell swoop, you'll only be shocked once."

Luke avoided thinking about Ron Raven for the rest of the night, which wasn't hard, chiefly because the pressures of serving top-quality food in three crowded restaurants, one with an injured sous-chef, occupied every scrap of his attention. He assumed George would take at least a couple of days to get back to him and he was almost glad of the delay. However, he'd underestimated George's efficiency. Luke opened up his e-mail the next evening and found a note from the detective already waiting for him.

Thought it might be easier to put this in writing, instead of interrupting your work schedule. Mr. Jones's forwarding address in Adelaide turns out to be for an abandoned warehouse. I've attached an aerial picture of the site, which as you can see is surrounded by a chain-link fence and appears deserted. I spoke to a local cop (local to Adelaide, that is) and he assures me that any mail forwarded to this warehouse from the States during the past six months would have been returned to sender or delivered to a dead-letter box, since the ownership of the site is in dispute between two companies.

I checked again with the superintendent of the apartment building in McLean, Virginia. He has no memory of any mail either being forwarded to Stewart Jones or being returned from Australia. It seems likely, therefore, that no first-class mail for Mr.

Jones ever arrived at Elm Court after he left there in late June.

I also contacted the Australian embassy in Washington, D.C. I informed them somebody might be fraudulently using the identity of a supposed Australian diplomat, Stewart M. Jones. The embassy informed me that there has been no diplomat of that name serving in any capacity in the United States for the past two years. They wouldn't comment on whether they have a diplomat of that name assigned elsewhere.

The management company for the Elm Street rental properties at first declined to share with me how they checked the credentials and references for prospective renters. After some persuasion, a clerk parted with the information that all applicants are required to provide a security deposit equal to three months' rent. If the applicant's check clears, the rest of the credit check is cursory. Renters are required to provide a work phone number, and this number is always called. However, since applicants provide the work number themselves, they—in this case, Mr. Jones—have complete control over how the call is answered. Mr. Jones could pretend that a caller had reached the Australian embassy, and then provide himself with a glowing reference. Child's play for anyone with experience in setting up a scam. Sometimes I wonder why anybody in this country bothers to be honest, when deception and fraud are so easy.

Bottom line: Anyone wanting to rent accommodations at the Elm Street location could use almost whatever name they pleased with little risk of having their alias exposed.

Let me know if you need to investigate further. Sincerely, George Klein.

P.S. Invoice attached.

Four

Tim, one of the sous-chefs at Luciano's on Chestnut, stuck his head around Luke's open office door. "There's a woman waiting to see you in the main dining room. Says she arranged to meet you here."

Luke glanced up from the stack of vendor accounts he was checking, one of his least-favorite chores. "Is it Mrs. Fairfax?"

"Could be. Something like that. Sorry, you know me and names." Tim, who happily obsessed over the most obscure herbs and heirloom vegetables, and agonized over precise details of recipes, had only a perfunctory interest in the humans who would eventually consume his dishes. He gave Luke a casually apologetic salute and moved on to the kitchen.

Luke made his way into the dining room, breathing in the faint aroma of freshly chopped herbs. The restaurant was closed at this early hour of the morning, the tables shrouded in starched gray linen cloths, waiting for the stemmed water goblets, silverware and signature damask napkins that would be added later.

Even now, five years after the grand opening of his flagship restaurant, Luke's heart still beat a little faster each time he walked across the stylish dining room. This morning he was especially aware of the fact that his success would have been impossible without Ron Raven. His requests for financing to start his own restaurant had been turned down by half the banks in Chicago. He was too young, the bankers said, not even thirty, with grand ideas but insufficient practical experience. Besides, restaurants were a notoriously risky investment.

And then he catered a meal for Raven Enterprises and everything changed. Ron agreed to underwrite the first Luciano's to the tune of a quarter million dollars in exchange for twenty-five percent of the equity. The restaurant had been a success almost from opening night, and plenty of banks had fallen over themselves to finance Luke's next two ventures. But the undeniable bottom line was that without Ron, there would have been no Luciano's.

Luke had wrestled with the question of what he owed Ron for several days before finally placing his call to Avery Fairfax. In the end, he'd decided this couldn't be about gratitude toward Ron; this had to be about honesty owed to Ron's wife and daughter.

He pushed lingering doubts aside and smiled a greeting at the slender, elegant woman waiting by the door. "Avery! It's great to see you again. Thanks for making the trip across town."

Avery Fairfax turned to him, her classic features

warmed by the friendliness of her smile. "Luke, how are you? It's been much too long. I've missed you."

He shook her hand since Avery wasn't the sort of woman who invited random hugs. "I missed you, too." He was surprised at how true that was. "Can I get you something to eat? A croissant? Some coffee? Juice?"

"Thank you, but I only finished breakfast a few minutes ago."

"Then let's go into my office. We have more hope of being left alone there." Luke escorted her through the dining room and pulled out a chair across from his desk as soon as they reached his office. Avery sank into the seat, managing to look entirely comfortable without slumping, crossing her legs or disturbing the perfect lines of her tweed skirt.

"You look very well," Luke said truthfully.

"I feel well, too. Or perhaps *energized* would be a better word. October is always my favorite month and the weather's been heavenly for the past few days, don't you think?"

"Perfect, especially in contrast to the rotten summer we had this year." The phone rang. Luke ignored the ring and pressed the button to switch his calls through to voice mail. "Did you manage to escape from the city during those hot spells back in June and July?"

"Only for the odd day, now and again. I was too busy selling the penthouse. Fortunately, we managed to find a buyer before the real estate market totally tanked. The new owners are a couple from India who've just moved to the States and they were eager to buy a lot of the furniture, too, which suited me very well. So it was a successful transaction all around, with happy buyers and a contented seller."

Luke hoped the sale of the penthouse had left Avery financially secure. She undoubtedly needed the money. Even if Ron had made a will and left her a decent share of his estate, Luke doubted if she would see a penny of her inheritance anytime soon. There would surely be years of litigation over the disposition of the estate, even if all the parties tried to be reasonable. The tabloids had mentioned something about a three-million-dollar debt hanging over the heads of Ron's Wyoming family, so it seemed safe to assume both wives had suffered major financial blows when Ron disappeared.

"Have you decided where you're going to live now the penthouse is sold?" he asked Avery, wondering how the complicated Raven family finances would ever be unraveled if Ron was officially declared alive again. Just contemplating the potential legal nightmare of getting the estate back out of probate had Luke questioning his decision all over again.

"At first, I thought about moving back to Georgia," Avery said. "Then I realized that would be silly. It's so long since I've lived anywhere other than Chicago that my roots are here now. So I'm about to move into a small house in Wicker Park."

"That's one of my favorite neighborhoods." It was where Kate lived, too, so Avery was moving away from the superexpensive lakeside and closer to her daughter. Wicker Park was a younger, trendier neighborhood than the only-millionaires-need-apply Gold Coast.

"I like my new neighborhood better the more I explore. Actually, I'm rather excited. Not just about the house, but about my prospects generally. I've started a small business and discovered that I very much enjoy being gainfully employed."

"That's great, Avery!"

Her smile turned into an outright laugh. "You should never play poker, Luke, you'd be wiped out in a couple of hands. I know everyone thinks I'm a useless social butterfly with all the management skills of a potted plant, but I'm actually quite efficient."

"I'm sure you are."

"You're not sure at all." Avery seemed amused by his doubts, not offended. "I'm like a lot of other Southern women of my generation, a great deal more competent than I look. We were brought up to hide our capabilities and defer to our husbands and flutter our eyelashes if any of the gentlemen discussed politics or money at the dinner table. But the truth is, I've raised millions of dollars for art galleries and museums and homeless shelters over the past twenty years. I've personally organized more benefits and charity balls than most people attend in a lifetime. When Ron died, and I was trying to think how in the world I should spend the rest of my life, it occurred to me that I already had all the training I would ever need to become a professional event planner. So that's what I've started doing, and I'm loving every minute."

Luke smiled. "That's a brilliant career choice, Avery. It's the perfect niche for you." If anything, she was understating the number of important fund-raisers she'd planned over the past decade. "You already know the best venues in Chicago for every conceivable type of event, and you have a Rolodex full of outstanding caterers, florists, musicians—anything your clients could want or need for the perfect party."

She laughed, drawing a sleek gray PDA from her purse. "Actually, I now have a BlackBerry as well as a Rolodex. Kate finally persuaded me it was time to take a few tentative steps into the twenty-first century, and I discovered technology is great when you understand it. I even know how to access my e-mail account while sipping coffee at Starbucks. I can send instant text messages, too. I can't quite bring myself to sign off with a smiley face, but I'm getting there!"

"Congratulations." Avery's pleasure was infectious and Luke smiled back at her. "In addition to becoming a techie, you're always so polite and serene that even the most neurotic client will calm down simply knowing you're in charge. You're going to be hiring extra staff and turning away customers before you know it."

"Thanks for the compliments, Luke, I really appreciate them. Especially the bit about being serene. From my perspective, viewed from the inside, I'm a nervous wreck. Still, I don't seem to be having any difficulty finding clients, especially since I don't want to get overwhelmed before I have all my ducks in a row."

"I suspect your ducks are already lined up and waiting to swim off into deep waters."

"Perhaps." Avery's cheeks flushed with a mixture of excitement and pride. "I just finished putting together a wedding for the daughter of an old college friend. She gave me a bare four weeks' notice and the ceremony was last weekend. Everything seems to have gone rather well, if I do say so myself. And I'm working on two new projects right now. One is a business conference next month and the other a coming-of-age celebration for a young woman who has fabulously wealthy parents, both remarried to other partners. They apparently hope that if they spend enough money on the party, their daughter will forget they ignored her for most of the past eighteen years."

"That sounds like the very best sort of client." Luke grinned. "There's nothing like a double dose of parental guilt to shake loose a deluge of money."

Avery pulled a wry face. "Ah, yes. Parental guilt, the gift that goes on giving. I've certainly experienced a full dose of that these past few months. Although Kate is a kind person and she's almost managed to convince me that I wasn't utterly foolish not to have realized the truth about her father."

Luke drew in a deep breath. Avery had opened the door and there was no way to put off discussing Kate any longer.

"How is Kate?" he asked, hoping he didn't sound as stiff and awkward as he felt. He was alarmed that even now, months after their breakup, he still felt a tightening in his chest at the mere mention of her name. Dammit, he must have some deep masochistic streak that he felt this crazy tug of yearning for a woman who'd made the final weeks of their relationship something pretty close to a living hell. Not that he'd exactly been a prince, he admitted silently. But, God knew, their final breakup had been caused exclusively by Kate, with zero assistance from him.

"Kate's well," Avery said, her voice cooling just a little. "Busy, of course. She spent a month in Vienna this summer, working with Torsten Richter. She found him as terrifying as his reputation, but she said the terror was worth it. According to Kate, Torsten can do things with chocolate that are somewhere between obscene and heavenly."

Luke quelled an irrational surge of jealousy toward Torsten Richter, who was known as one of the finest pastry chefs in Europe. Pathetic as it was, it seemed he still craved Kate's professional approval. "Is she planning to compete in the Coupe du Monde again next year?"

"No." Avery didn't expand on her answer. Perhaps she thought Luke didn't deserve any insights into Kate's professional plans, given that she believed their relationship had foundered on the rock of their demanding and incompatible schedules.

He hesitated for a moment. "I wrote to Kate in May," he said finally. "After Ron…after her father disappeared."

"I know. She showed me your note." Avery's voice was dry. "It was a very polite letter. Emily Post would have been proud of you."

Luke didn't misinterpret the seeming compliment. "I realize it was a lousy letter, Avery. But Kate and I broke up a month before her father disappeared and I had no clue what to say. We'd both made it clear that we didn't want to see each other ever again, so it seemed wrong to get too personal." He noticed he was drawing circles all over his vendor invoices and tossed the pen aside. "In the end, platitudes seemed better…no, not better. They seemed less bad than any of the alternatives."

Avery relented slightly. "It was a difficult situation," she conceded. "And the consequences seem never-ending. I'm getting so tired of the constant fallout." She stopped abruptly, visibly chagrined to have lapsed into the sort of complaining she would consider bad manners.

And he was about to make the situation more difficult by several orders of magnitude, Luke reflected. Seeing Avery in person, he wondered why he'd been so sure he was entitled to disrupt her peace. She was poised on the brink of putting her life back together in a pattern that clearly pleased her. Why force her to confront the possibility that her bigamous husband might not be dead? After all, Ron had lied and cheated for the entire twenty-nine years of their relationship. Why would she care if the son of a bitch was alive?

It would certainly be kinder to Avery to allow Ron to remain buried. Kinder in the short term, he reflected, but maybe not right?

"You have your poker face on again, Luke, and it's still not working." Avery's gaze didn't waver and it was disconcertingly perceptive. "You're agonizing over something. Why did you ask me to come here today? Is it something to do with Kate?"

"No, or at least it's only indirectly about Kate." It dawned on Luke with sudden, piercing clarity that it was precisely because Ron had deceived his family for almost three decades that he owed Avery the truth. She was an intelligent, mature woman who didn't deserve to be lied to, even if the lies were supposedly for her own good.

He spoke quickly, before he could lose his resolve. "There's no easy way to break this news, Avery, so here it is. Earlier this month I was having dinner with my sister at a restaurant in suburban Washington, D.C. While we were there, I'm fairly sure…scratch that. I'm *confident* I saw Ron in the restaurant. He was with a woman about my sister's age, mid- to late thirties. Ron and this woman were eating dinner, but when Ron realized I'd seen him, he quickly got up and left. To be frank, it seemed to me that he ran away."

Avery's body stilled, all movement so controlled that even her breathing was invisible. When she finally spoke, after several seconds of utter silence, her voice sounded husky. "Did Ron look ill? Injured?"

"No, he looked well." Luke realized she was the first person to ask him about Ron's well-being, as opposed to launching into an instant denial of the possibility that he might be alive. "He was thinner than when I last saw him, which was at the birthday dinner he threw for you in early March. He looked fitter and more tanned, but unmistakably Ron."

"You say he ran away when you tried to speak to him?"

"Yes, he did. I'm quite sure he wanted to avoid me." Luke once again decided against cushioning the truth with a comforting lie. There had been more than enough lies already, most of them perpetrated by Ron himself.

Avery looked up and her eyes were no longer tranquil; they were now a tormented, storm-tossed gray. "Are you telling me Ron ran away because he recognized you and didn't want to be confronted?"

Luke winced inwardly. "I'm sorry, Avery, but that's exactly what I think happened."

She made a distressed sound, hastily suppressed. She stared for several long moments at her hands. Then she turned to him, her ghost-pale face a silent plea for help. "I'm embarrassed to admit I have no idea what I should do next. Tell me, Luke. What must I do? Should I go to the police?" She gripped the edge of his desk, the white-knuckled intensity of her grip all the more devastating because she was trying so hard to hide the signs of her inner turmoil.

"I wish I knew how to advise you, Avery. I've already tried to inform the cops, here and in Miami, but they didn't believe a word I told them and they had zero interest in reopening the investigation into Ron's disappearance. I'd be amazed if you get any help from them. In fact, if you want to ignore what I've just told you, nobody will care. Not the cops, that's for sure."

"How can I ignore something so important just because the authorities aren't interested? Ron might be in trouble…."

Luke resisted the urge to say Ron hadn't looked troubled to him. In fact, the bastard had looked as if he was thoroughly enjoying his meal—and the company of the woman eating dinner with him—at least until Luke brought their cozy night to a swift end.

"Most people will advise you to pay no attention to my story, you can be sure of that," Luke said flatly. "It's definitely what the police would tell you."

"Perhaps, but I'm not really interested in the opinion of the police." Avery's voice picked up a healthy note of anger. "The Miami detective in charge of the investigation formed his theory of the case the moment they identified one of the blood stains in the hotel room as coming from that Julio Castellano person. Castellano was an illegal immigrant and a convicted murderer, so the police essentially ended their inquiries at that point. Radio talk show hosts raged about illegal immigrants committing crimes for a few days. Then the media attention moved on, and so did the attention of the police. I don't think the Miami cops even looked very hard for Castellano, despite the fact that he was their chosen suspect. They assumed he was in Mexico and left it at that."

"You sound as if you've never accepted the cops' theory about what happened to Ron."

"I did at first." Avery hesitated for a moment. "Later, I changed my mind."

"Any special reason for the change?"

She hesitated again and Luke got the strong impression that she was choosing her words with care. "Did you know that Adam, my youngest brother, has met Julio Castellano?"

Luke was astonished. "No, I had no idea. You mean your brother met Castellano *before* he was accused of murdering Ron? That's an amazing coincidence. Is Adam sure it's the same man, not just the same name?"

Avery shook her head. "No, that isn't what happened. My brother met Castellano this past summer. Ron had been missing for several weeks by then and Castellano was already the prime suspect in his murder."

Luke frowned. "But if your brother found Castellano, why in the world isn't the guy in custody?"

"It's a long story. The short version is that Adam flew to Belize on the trail of some money that was missing from Ron's estate. My brother traveled with Megan Raven, Ron's other daughter by his Wyoming wife.

Adam and Megan were married recently, so she's my sister-in-law on top of everything else." Avery paused after spelling out the ramifications of the relationship, as if, even now, she had trouble absorbing the reality of her supposed husband's double life.

She gave her head a little shake. "Anyway, it seems Adam and Megan were rescued from a life-threatening situation in Belize by Julio Castellano. Adam is anything but a soft touch, and yet he's convinced not only that he and Megan would have died without Castellano's help, but also that the man isn't a murderer."

"But Castellano's been accused of killing three different people," Luke protested. "And he's been convicted of the first two murders! I'm sure I remember reading that at the time the police in Miami named him as their only suspect."

"I know." Avery's shoulders lifted in a slight shrug. "According to Adam, Castellano claims the first death was an accident and that the police were covering up a crime by one of their own when they pinned the second murder on him."

"Well, yeah, Castellano would claim something like that, wouldn't he?" Luke didn't bother to hide his skepticism. "If you want to find a thousand innocent men all in one place, go visit your local prison." The idea that a convicted felon implicated in three murders might be innocent of all of them struck Luke as barely this side of absurd. Then he remembered that if Ron Raven was alive, Julio Castellano was categorically innocent of at least one of the crimes he'd been accused of committing.

"Has your brother informed the cops that their prime

suspect in Ron Raven's murder is hiding out in Belize?" He gave a wry smile. "Where the heck is Belize, anyway?"

Avery almost managed an answering smile. "I'm glad you don't know, either. I had to look it up myself. It's a tiny country that shares borders with Guatemala and Mexico."

"Is it one of those places where criminals go to hide?" Luke asked. "Is that why Castellano is there?"

"I don't believe so. It's a former British colony and the total population is around half a million, so it's not exactly a place where you can disappear into the teeming masses."

"So why would Castellano be there?" Luke found the story of Adam's encounter increasingly odd the more he heard.

"According to my brother, Castellano was born in Belize and the police here were mistaken when they identified him as Mexican."

"Can that possibly be right?" Luke shook his head. "Man, I'm willing to buy a certain level of police incompetence, but your brother is basically suggesting that the cops have the entire story on three separate killings screwed up in every detail, right down to the citizenship of the guy accused of the murders!"

"My initial reaction was the same as yours, that Castellano had every reason to lie to my brother. The police in Miami conducted a thorough investigation, so why not accept their conclusions? But Adam was pretty convincing. On top of that, you're telling me now that you may have seen Ron. If you're correct, that means Castellano can't possibly have murdered him. Since he isn't guilty this time around, it does give cause to wonder if the police might have been wrong on the previous occasions, as well."

"Even if Ron is alive, we don't know what happened the night he disappeared," Luke pointed out. "There's no reason to give Castellano a free pass. Ron might have managed to trick him and escape. In which case Castellano would be guilty of attempted murder at the very least."

Avery was silent for a moment. Then she shook her head. "If Castellano tried to kill Ron and didn't succeed, why is Ron still hiding? Why didn't he come home and identify Castellano as the would-be killer? Even if Ron was injured or suffering from amnesia for a while, it seems his memory is in full working order now. You yourself said that he ran away when you saw him. That means he recognized you and didn't want to talk to you. Why doesn't Ron want to be discovered? Who is he hiding from?"

"Castellano is the logical suggestion," Luke said. "He's a convicted criminal and his blood was in the hotel room, so there must have been a fight."

"Not necessarily. The fact that Castellano's blood was in the hotel room doesn't provide any information about why he was there."

"Why else would he have gone to Ron's hotel room if not for robbery or some other crime?"

"He might have been there for the simple reason that he was an accomplice of Ron's," Avery suggested. "If Ron wanted to disappear, what could be more convincing than staging a room to look as if he'd been fighting for his life against a known killer?"

Avery seemed as determined to believe Ron was alive

as the police were determined to believe he was dead. Luke found himself in the bizarre position of trying to rein in her willing acceptance of his own story. "But if Ron isn't hiding from Castellano, who is he hiding from?"

"His families," Avery said quietly. "Both of them."

"That can't be the explanation." Luke hoped he sounded convincing. "Avery, if Ron was tired of his families, why not say so? You don't go to the huge trouble of faking your own death just to avoid the hassle of getting divorced!"

"Most men don't go to the huge hassle of maintaining two marriages, two homes, two completely separate lives. Most men aren't bigamists. Ron apparently doesn't react like *most people*." With a sudden, jerky movement Avery pushed back her chair. "The more you try to dress it up and make it look pretty, the more convinced I become that Ron wanted out of his life—and so he ran."

"I don't agree with you," Luke said.

"Then give me a better interpretation of the facts."

"We don't have enough facts to speculate in any meaningful way. Right now, though, I suspect professional gamblers would say the odds are in favor of me being mistaken and Ron being dead." Luke felt obligated to provide Avery with that out if she wanted to take it. Hell, everyone else who'd heard his story had taken the route of assuming he was an idiot, so she was entitled.

She tilted her head back, searching his face. "You don't think you're mistaken, do you?"

He debated for a second and then gave her the truth.

"No. I'm sorry, Avery. I'm almost as certain as I can be that I saw Ron Raven."

"Then I'm grateful to you for telling me what you saw. Now all that's left is for me to decide how to deal with this. I just finished telling you how competent and self-sufficient I am. I need to prove it."

"Even the strongest and most independent person sometimes needs a friendly listener. Anytime you want to discuss your options with me, Avery, I'll be happy to listen and offer any advice I can. After all, I'm the person who opened up this can of worms."

"Right now, I've just about exhausted my capacity for rational discussion. I need some time alone to think. Thanks for the offer, though, Luke. Later on, I'll probably take you up on it." She got up and walked in the direction of his office door, bumping into the corner of his credenza as she passed by. For graceful, controlled Avery, the clumsy movement demonstrated a distress level that was the equivalent of a normal person tumbling flat on her face.

Luke escorted her to the restaurant door, his hand beneath her elbow. "You're upset. Let me call you a cab."

"Thanks, Luke, but I'd rather walk. Fresh air seems very appealing right now. Goodbye."

Luke watched Avery weave a not-quite-straight path to the corner of the block. When she turned out of view, he didn't even attempt to return to his office and his chore of checking invoices. Instead he made his way to the kitchens and silently began preparing a port wine reduction to garnish the beef tenderloin that would be on tonight's menu. Cooking was usually absorbing enough that he could lose himself in the process. But today, his brain remained disengaged from his hands. Despite the heavy weight in the pit of his stomach, he was fairly sure he'd done the right thing in contacting Avery. Unfortunately, doing the right thing apparently could leave you feeling like hell.

Perhaps he should call Kate and warn her that her mother… He cut off that insidious thought before it could carry him down any of the dangerous paths that led to Kate. He'd taken that walk too many times already, and he sure as hell didn't plan to take it again. He'd told Avery what he'd seen and his responsibilities in regard to Ron Raven's resurrection were now ended.

It was time to move on, leaving Kate locked safely in the past, where she belonged.

Five

Later the same day

Kate Fairfax—formerly Kate Raven—not only loved her mother, she'd always admired her. Her respect had been heartfelt, even during her teenage years when she'd been intimidated by her mother's unfailing elegance and exquisite taste. In self-defense, Kate had indulged in a few years of grunge dressing just to prove that she didn't give a flying flip about clothes or makeup. On her eighteenth birthday she'd reinforced her rebellion by getting a tattoo of a dragon on her butt, a gold ring threaded through her left nostril and multiple piercings in both ears.

Her efforts provoked a satisfactory bellow of outrage from her father, but unfortunately nothing much from her mother. After complimenting Kate's choice of earrings, Avery offered a mild comment to the effect that she'd always wanted to have a tattoo but was too much of a coward to endure the pain.

Since her mother didn't seem to care in the slightest

about the nose ring, and it was a major pain to keep the hole disinfected, Kate had given up on it within three months. By the end of her first semester in culinary school, she'd allowed half of the ear piercings to close, and by the time she graduated, she had acquired a fair-size wardrobe of clothes that weren't black, weren't denim and had no rips anywhere.

The tattoo, however, she'd never for a single moment regretted. Luke had christened the dragon Puff, and had woven several highly erotic fantasies that supposedly revealed the secret story of how Puff came to end up living on her butt. It was only after they broke up that she happened to hear the old Peter, Paul and Mary song and understand why he'd picked that name. It annoyed her every time she glimpsed the dragon in her bathroom mirror and realized that she was still mentally calling him Puff. There was also the problem of the tiny jeweled egg that she kept buried in a shoe box in her closet. This, according to Luke when he gave it to her, was the egg from which Puff had hatched several centuries earlier. The fact that she had neither given the egg away nor found the courage to display it on a shelf suggested an unhealthy level of neurosis about the ending of their relationship.

Her memories of Luke sometimes seemed impossible to shake, and Kate was frustrated by her inability to banish him to the trash can of past mistakes. She was twenty-seven, for heaven's sake, which ought to be old enough to recognize when a relationship had been doomed from the start. She constantly repeated the reasons why they had made a lousy couple and her brain was finally convinced by the mantra. Unfortunately, the rest of her was having a hard time getting with the program. A succession of dates in the past couple of months had merely reinforced the forbidden judgment that Luke Savarini was the world's most superlative kisser, bar none. Why couldn't he have been an arrogant, uncaring lover to match the rest of his arrogant, uncaring personality? That was one of life's more annoying puzzles.

Kate switched her thoughts back to her mother, which was a lot more agreeable than thinking about Luke. In the six months since her father had died, her lifelong admiration for her mother had blossomed into full-blown hero worship. She had learned how much more there was to Avery than a kind heart, a pretty face and a knack for selecting attractive clothes. She watched the bravery with which her mother set about rebuilding a life that had been shattered not only emotionally and socially but also financially, and she was torn between pride and an odd sense of role-reversal protectiveness.

Today, as she looked around the little house that her mother had just begun to restore, Kate's admiration was tinged by a dose of worry. The house was structurally sound, but it had been owned by an elderly couple for fifty years, and routine upkeep had clearly defeated them over the past decade. Avery had acquired the house for a rock-bottom price, despite the excellent location. Still, ten days of hard work had barely made a dent in what needed to be done.

The kitchen had the very latest in modern conveniences, circa 1973. The shag carpet looked as if it might date from approximately the same era, and the drapes seemed to be held together by twenty years of solidified grime. Last weekend they'd managed to clean the master bedroom and bathroom and get both rooms painted. On Monday, a new bed had been delivered, so Avery now had somewhere other than Kate's small row house where she could take showers and sleep. The rest of the place, however, was still a complete disaster.

Carrying a pail of steaming water, her mother returned from the kitchen just as Kate poked gingerly at an unidentified gray object on the decrepit living room sofa. "I think it was a cushion," Avery said.

"I'll take your word for it." Katie shoved the putative pillow into a giant plastic garbage bag, already half full of similar unidentified objects. The house should have been cleared out by the sellers, but pursuing them out of state to their retirement villa was more hassle than doing the cleanup themselves. "How much money have you set aside for hauling trash, Mom?"

"Sorry? What was that?" Avery set the pail by the fireplace and pulled on rubber gloves.

"I wondered if you'd budgeted enough money for hauling trash," Kate repeated.

"Oh, yes, I'm sure I have. I got several quotes, you know. It's less expensive than you'd expect. Or less expensive than I expected, anyway." Avery looked vaguely around the room, as if waiting for hard copy of the quotes to leap into her hand. "The men I contracted with are scheduled to come on Friday, and they've agreed to rip up the carpet, too."

"Good." Kate reviewed her mental checklist. "The hardwood gets refinished next week, right?"

"Hardwood?" Avery looked vague again. "Oh, yes, the floors. That's right. They'll take a day to sand everything down and then another day to apply the coating.

They promised to be done by the middle of next week, so I decided to hold off on getting any more of my new furniture delivered until then. Thank goodness, everything I ordered seems to have arrived from the manufacturers."

"Sounds like you have a plan. You seem preoccupied today, Mom. What's up?" Kate gingerly pulled out the sofa, afraid of what she might discover between the furniture and the wall. Dust bunnies frolicked in abundance, but there were no live critters, thank God.

"I am a little distracted, I suppose. I've…had some surprising news." The tension in her mother's voice was palpable. Belatedly, Kate realized that Avery had been on edge the entire afternoon. She would have noticed earlier if they hadn't mostly been working in separate rooms.

"Surprising *good* news?" she asked, straightening. Searching her mother's face, she shook her head. "No, it's bad news, isn't it?"

"I'm not sure." Avery's laugh was harsh, an astonishing fact in and of itself. Kate was even more astonished when her mother covered her face with her grimy hands and burst into tears. "Oh, God, how can I possibly say I'm not sure? I *loved* him! I did. Once upon a time I loved him. So what's the matter with me?"

Loved who? Kate put her arm around her mother's slender shoulders. "I could answer that better if you'd give me some clue as to what we're talking about."

Avery wiped her tears with the backs of her hands, leaving a streak of dirt. Not only that, she didn't immediately find a pure white tissue and remove the smudge. Kate wouldn't have been shocked if the world had shuddered to an immediate halt at such a betrayal of the accepted order.

"I saw Luke Savarini today," Avery said.

The name struck Kate like a blow. She stepped back, hoping her smile looked more natural than it felt. "Well, that would certainly be enough to reduce me to tears. I can't imagine why he made you cry, though. He's quite civilized in company."

Kate's feeble attempt at humor flew right past her mother. Avery drew in a short, shaky breath. "Luke was in Washington, D.C., with his sister a couple of weeks ago. They were eating dinner in a restaurant there. Luke says he saw…your father…eating dinner there, too. Right in the restaurant. In D.C. Well, a suburb, actually. But basically in the D.C. area."

Kate knew she couldn't have heard right. "Wait. I'm confused. Luke was in Washington, D.C., with one of his sisters and he claimed that he saw *my* father? He saw Ron Raven?"

"So he says. He seems remarkably sure of his facts."

"Did he speak to my father?" Kate realized she was shaking. Despite that, her voice sounded oddly controlled.

"No."

"Why not? Didn't it occur to him that it might be helpful to find out what the hell my father was doing alive in Washington, D.C., when everyone thinks he's dead in Miami?" She was still shaking and it was a lot easier to be sarcastic than to work out what she was actually feeling.

"It seems that your father…that Ron ran away as soon as he realized that Luke had recognized him. Luke tried to catch up with him, but he couldn't. Apparently, there was a woman with him."

Kate's brow wrinkled. "With Luke?"

"No, sorry. I'm not being entirely coherent, am I? Your father was with another woman. Quite a young woman. Luke thought she might be in her thirties. Early forties at most. But he definitely said that your father recognized him."

She was going to kill Luke, Kate decided. She was going to find some long, slow, agonizing way of causing his death and then she was going to stand over him and watch it happen. In fact, she wouldn't just stand passively and watch. She'd dance a celebratory jig as the lifeblood oozed out of him. For what conceivable reason had the stupid man found it necessary to share his delusions about seeing Ron Raven? Her father was dead, murdered in a Miami hotel room along with his companion, a still-unidentified woman. Luke must know how badly Avery had suffered from the media frenzy provoked by reports of Ron's bigamy, not to mention the sinister security video of the body bags being wheeled onto the yacht, presumably by the murderer himself. Why would Luke choose to open a wound that had been closed only with great courage and slow, painful effort on her mother's part?

"Obviously Luke was mistaken." Kate managed by some miracle to keep the rage out of her voice. Luke had no idea how lucky he was not to be anywhere within striking range of her supersharp chef's knives or he'd be singing soprano from now on. "Heavens, Mom, you're not paying any attention to his nonsense, are you? He must have sniffed a few too many of his own cognac fumes."

"Is that what you think? That Luke was imagining things?"

"Yes, that's what I think! Of course it is." Contemplating the alternative possibility that her father might be alive and deliberately hiding from his wives and children left Kate feeling sick to her stomach. She had assumed nothing much worse could happen than losing her father before she had a chance to confront him about the lifetime of lies and deception that he'd perpetrated. Apparently she'd been wrong. The possibility that he might be alive and in hiding was even more difficult than accepting his death. Anger lodged as a hot pain in her chest, making it difficult to breathe.

Avery turned and recommenced scrubbing the shelves built at the side of the brick fireplace. She spoke to the wall. "The thing is… Well, in an odd sort of way, what Luke said didn't come as a total surprise to me."

Kate stared at her mother's back. "I don't understand."

"After the initial shock of Ron's disappearance wore off, I was never as sure as everyone else that he was dead. I know his…other wife in Wyoming never doubted that he'd been murdered. But I…wondered."

"What are you telling me, Mom?" Kate forced herself not to shout as she struggled to keep her anger with Luke separate from the surprise caused by her mother's admission. "Why aren't you sure Dad was…is dead? The police seemed pretty certain of what happened that night in Miami."

"Yes, I know, but the penthouse was mortgaged, you see."

"You're going to have to spell that out more clearly, Mom. What has a mortgage on the penthouse got to do with Dad's death?"

"What happened to the money?" Avery asked. "That's what I kept asking myself after the initial shock wore off. Where is it?"

"Where is what money, Mom?" Kate was beginning to worry that her mother was losing it. Normally the most precise of women, right now Avery was making no sense at all.

"The money Ron raised with the mortgage," Avery explained. "We owned the penthouse free and clear, I'm sure of it. It's true that I never paid close attention to Ron's business deals—there were so many of them—but I was quite well-informed about our personal finances." Her voice flattened. "Or, to be more accurate, I was well informed about those parts of our personal finances that Ron felt safe to share with me."

Which left out a hell of a lot, Kate reflected grimly, given that her father had been supporting another entire family in Wyoming that neither she nor her mother had known anything about until Ron Raven was officially declared missing.

"There could be a dozen reasons why Dad needed cash," she pointed out. "Hundreds, in fact, given that he lied to both of us all the time. We haven't the faintest clue what was going on with his finances, or any other part of his life, if you get right down to it." After months of coming to terms with her father's betrayal, Kate managed to state the sordid truth without being overwhelmed by bitterness.

"That's true," her mother conceded. "But Ron never

expressed any need to mortgage the penthouse in the twenty years since we bought it. Why, two months before he disappeared, did he suddenly decide to take out a three-million-dollar loan? We weren't facing any unexpected expenses, and it's inconsistent with the way he'd handled our personal finances for the entire time we were together."

"Because he didn't consult you about the mortgage, you mean?"

Avery nodded. "In retrospect, I understand he wasn't really asking for my opinion when we discussed our personal finances, but he at least went through the motions. I had the illusion we were making decisions together, even if the reality was otherwise. But Ron never breathed a word about the mortgage on the penthouse. I only found out it existed after he'd disappeared. Why?"

It seemed to Kate that her mother was placing too much emphasis on a relatively trivial part of the myriad deceptions Ron Raven had perpetrated on them both. The penthouse mortgage might be the only financial deception Avery had uncovered to this point. That didn't mean it was the only deception Ron had engaged in, not by a long shot.

"Perhaps Dad wanted to put extra capital into his business?" she suggested. "Have you talked to Uncle Paul about it? That must be the answer, Mom. Raven Enterprises needed an infusion of cash for some reason, and Dad raised the money by taking out a mortgage on the penthouse."

"I've talked to my brother about the mortgage several times and he insists there was no three-million-dollar infusion of cash into Raven Enterprises. Besides, he says the business was in great shape, although the legal difficulties since Ron's disappearance have created problems for Paul going forward, which is why he hasn't been able to give me any cash from the business while we're waiting for the wills to be probated. The lawyers are controlling everything. However, according to Paul, at the time Ron disappeared there would have been no reason at all for your father to seek extra business capital."

"So how does Uncle Paul explain the mortgage on your home?"

"Well, he doesn't, of course. But you know my brother. He's a Southern gentleman of the old school and he's secretly convinced I'll get brain fever and go into a decline if he discusses money and finance with me. Paul insists the penthouse was always mortgaged and Ron simply refinanced at a better rate. He claims the documents I found weren't a new mortgage. They were refinancing papers that just happened to be signed a couple of months before your father disappeared."

"If Uncle Paul says there was no three-million-dollar payment into Raven Enterprises, then he must be right," Kate said. "He was Dad's business partner, after all. But that doesn't mean you're wrong about the mortgage on the penthouse. It just suggests Dad invested the three million elsewhere."

She needed to have a come-to-Jesus talk with her uncle, Kate reflected. Paul had been wise to protect his sister from unnecessary worries about finances in the immediate turmoil following Ron's disappearance and the discovery of his bigamy. However, six months had passed and it wasn't sensible for Paul to continue shielding her mother from every harsh reality. God knew, with all the details of their private lives that had been blazoned across the nation's TV screens, it was almost comic for her uncle to adhere to the quaint, 1950s custom of protecting the womenfolk from a clear understanding of their own financial situation.

"You're right," Avery said. "Ron must have invested the money elsewhere, because I'm sure there was no mortgage on the penthouse until very recently. But arguing with your uncle is so exhausting I just gave up." She looked chagrined by the admission, as well as the implicit criticism of her elder brother, mild as it was. "I'd have to search through boxes and boxes of papers to confirm my belief, and there's always seemed so many other, more useful ways to employ my time…."

"You're right. There were. There's no reason to sound guilty, Mom. Dad's financial affairs are one giant mess. Trying to pick apart one tiny thread of the muddle makes no sense. Between us and the family in Wyoming, we have what seems like a thousand lawyers and accountants already poking around in Dad's finances. You're smart to leave them to it and get on with your life."

"Maybe, except that once I'd talked with Luke this morning, it began to seem as if I might have been right to suspect the mortgage on the penthouse was significant."

"I'm not following, Mom. Why does it matter? Except that you're potentially three million dollars worse off, of course. But even if the penthouse had been free of all mortgages, wouldn't the proceeds from the sale have gone into probate, anyway?"

"I expect so, since nobody can decide which of Ron's wills is valid, if any. But if your father isn't dead…if he's alive…doesn't it strike you that there might be a connection between the sudden three-million-dollar mortgage on our penthouse and his disappearance?"

The meaning of Avery's comment hit Kate with the force of a physical blow. "Are you suggesting…" She needed to swallow before she could finish her question. "Are you suggesting that Dad mortgaged the penthouse so that he would have money to finance his disappearance?"

"Well, it certainly seems a possibility, wouldn't you say? I've…wondered about that over the past few months."

"If he's alive, I guess it's a possibility." Kate's mouth felt dry and her stomach tightened in a sickly knot. "I just don't see any reason to believe he's alive."

"Luke saw him. Isn't that a reason?"

"Luke *thinks* he saw him," Kate corrected.

Avery's scrubbing intensified as if she wanted to erase her own suspicions. She'd scrubbed so hard the shelves were beginning to show evidence of having once been white. "There's another thing about the money. Do you remember that your father also took out a three-million-dollar loan with Adam's bank, using Ellie's ranch in Wyoming as collateral?"

"Yes, I knew about that." Kate nodded. "It was the need to find out what had happened to the missing money that brought Adam and Megan together in the first place, and then sent them chasing off to Mexico in pursuit of the missing millions. Adam and I have talked quite a bit about the way Dad double-crossed him, of course."

The pursuit of the money, and the complicated reasons behind its disappearance, had interested Kate less than the fact that her mother's youngest brother had ended up marrying Megan Raven. Adam was her second favorite relative in the world after her mother and she'd wondered many times in the past few weeks how her father would react to the news that the daughter of his first wife had married the younger brother of his bigamous second wife. Kate saw a definite hint of ironic retribution tucked away in the fact of Adam and Megan's marriage.

Her mother turned around, her scrubbing brush dripping soapsuds. She spoke with careful lack of inflection. "Doesn't it strike you as oddly symmetrical that both Ron's so-called wives ended up three million dollars poorer than they might have expected? And in both cases because of loans that Ron took out using our homes as collateral?"

Kate felt a tiny shiver run down her spine. "Mom, you're seeing patterns that don't exist."

"The pattern exists," Avery said tartly, dumping her scrubbing brush into the pail of hot water with a decisive splash. "The only question for discussion is whether the pattern is a coincidence or deliberately planned."

Kate's heart started to thump uncomfortably fast. "The loan on the ranch in Wyoming was taken out a couple of years before Dad disappeared, not a couple of months."

"I'm well aware of that. It makes you wonder how long your father was planning his disappearance, doesn't it?"

Her mother's sarcasm was unprecedented. Kate pressed her hands against her stomach and drew in a long, deep breath. "Mom, let's get back to the earlier question. The important one. Forget the mortgages on the penthouse and the Wyoming ranch for a moment. Are you telling me that you think Luke might be right? That Dad really was eating dinner in a Washington, D.C., restaurant, and Luke saw him?"

Avery used a clean rag to mop up the soapy water pooled on the shelves. "All I can say is that Luke definitely believes he saw Ron. And Luke always struck me as a man with both feet planted firmly in the real world. You know him better than I do, of course. Does he strike you as a man given to fantasizing about dead people?"

"No." It was a measure of her turmoil that Kate didn't even think something rude about Luke, much less say it out loud. "If Luke is right, shouldn't somebody notify the police about what he saw?"

"Luke tried calling the police in Miami and here in Chicago, too. That was before he contacted me. He said they had no interest in taking his report."

Kate felt a surge of relief. "Well, Mom, doesn't that tell you something?"

"Yes," Avery said, the bite of uncharacteristic sarcasm still in her voice. "It tells me that police departments tend to be overworked and that since they have a suspect in Ron's death who is a convicted felon, they have no interest whatsoever in spending a lot of time revising their theory of the case."

Kate hesitated for a moment, but the question needed to be asked. "Okay, given that the police aren't likely to do much, if anything, do *you* want to reopen the case, Mom?"

"I don't know. I think so. I'm not sure." Avery tried to smile at her own hopeless indecision. She couldn't hold the smile. "What if Ron has lost his memory? What if he desperately wants to come home and doesn't know how to find us?" She leaned against the damp bookshelves, her face whiter than the shelves behind her. The pallor was less shocking to Kate than the fact that Avery still hadn't found a tissue and wiped the dust and dried tears from her cheeks. Even in the immediate aftermath of Ron's disappearance, when Avery had been battered by the news that her husband was a bigamist and their twenty-eight-year marriage didn't legally exist, she had never lost her composure this completely.

Her heart aching on her mother's behalf, Kate forced herself to speak gently. "Didn't you tell me the man in the restaurant ran away as soon as he saw Luke?"

Avery nodded. "Luke chased Ron...the man...into the parking lot, but he drove off before Luke could speak to him." Her voice became wistful. "I wish Luke had managed to catch up with...whoever it was."

From Kate's perspective, it was hard to imagine any way that her mother's happiness would be increased by tracking down the man who'd already seduced her, gotten her pregnant, deceived her through twenty-eight years of bigamous marriage, and now might be perpetrating the ultimate deception by pretending to be dead. A fresh surge of anger swept over her. Dammit, Luke shouldn't have gone to her mother and presented her with this terrible news!

Kate recognized that she was angry with Luke because that was a whole lot easier than being angry with her maybe-not-dead father, but that didn't alter the facts. Luke should have come to her with his stupid theories instead of destroying her mother's hard-won peace of mind.

Unfortunately, the genie was out of the bottle and there was no point trying to stuff him—or Ron—back inside again. She and her mother needed to decide what to do next. She saw only two viable choices: she could talk to Luke in the hope that he had sufficient information to enable a private detective to track down the man in the restaurant. Or they could ignore what they'd heard and carry on as if they'd never learned there was a possibility Ron Raven might be alive.

It wasn't in the least difficult to decide which option she preferred. If her father was alive and hiding from his families, as far as Kate was concerned he could stay lost forever. And that was before she contemplated the horror of having to meet with Luke Savarini again, an activity that ranked right up there with the joys of having a limb amputated without benefit of anesthesia.

Sadly, Avery's attitude made it clear that her choice would be to look for Ron and attempt to confirm whether her bigamous husband was alive or dead. It was a measure of just how much she loved her mother that Kate made the offer.

"Would you like me to talk to Luke and find out if there's any information he has that might help us to track down the man he saw in the restaurant?"

"Would you?" Avery's face lit up. "You wouldn't mind?"

"Not at all." She hoped her smile didn't look as sickly as it felt.

"Thank you so much, Katie." Avery sighed with visible relief. "I was so overwhelmed this morning that I really didn't ask many sensible questions at all. It might be impossible to trace the man Luke saw, but it would be nice to know that for certain, wouldn't it?"

"I guess so."

This might be a time of emotional confusion for Avery, but she was a sensitive woman and she wasn't self-absorbed enough to ignore Kate's lack of enthusiasm. "I'm being silly," she said quickly. "There's no reason in the world for you to question Luke if meeting him again makes you uncomfortable. Good heavens, I'm more than capable of asking him if he has any other snippets of information that he didn't share with me this morning."

Avery sounded determinedly brave and cheerful and Kate castigated herself for being a mean, selfish daughter. She knew how excruciatingly hard her mother found it to discuss Ron's multiple deceptions and criminal acts with anyone, much less someone she knew only as her daughter's discarded boyfriend. For goodness' sake, how tough could it be to have a brief, businesslike meeting with Luke?

"There's no need for you to talk with him, Mom. I'll track him down in one of his restaurants tonight and find out what other information he has, if anything."

"So soon?" Avery's face lit up. "Oh, that would be great."

"I'm grateful for the excuse to stop cleaning," Kate lied. "You're such a slave-driver, you'll have me working until midnight unless I take this chance to escape."

Avery shot her daughter a grateful glance, the only sign she gave of seeing through Kate's cheery facade. "I'll treat you to dinner first," she said, stripping off her rubber gloves. "We've both been working long enough. You get to pick the restaurant."

The way Kate's stomach was churning right now, cream of wheat struck her as about as daring a meal as she should risk. "Actually, Mom, if you don't mind, I'll skip dinner. Given the way Luke runs between restaurants, it might take me the rest of the evening to track him down. If I do manage to reach him, I'll get back to you tomorrow morning, okay?"

"That's fine. I suppose there's no real rush." Avery's voice became acerbic again. "Ron's been missing for six months. I daresay I can wait a few more hours to discover whether he's dead or moved on to greener pastures and a younger woman." She ruined the effect of her breezy indifference by walking out of the room at high speed.

Her mother was crying again, Kate reflected grimly. Damn Luke! And double damn Ron Raven. Her confusion finally gelled into certitude. She hoped her father was alive, she realized. That way she could have the pleasure of killing him as soon as she found him. Maybe she could build a bonfire and tie her loser ex-boyfriend and her loser father to opposite stakes. The way she felt about them right now, that would make a definite two-for-one bargain.

Six

It was late that night before Kate caught up with Luke at Luciano's II, his restaurant in Winnetka. Walking into the once-familiar surroundings, she was impressed all over again by the subtle welcome offered by the clever layout and the classic Tuscan decor. The damp October night turned the log fire burning in the brick fireplace into a cheery focal point. The ocher of the rough plaster walls blended soothingly with the rusty-coral table linens, and an inviting aroma of herbs and simmering sauces seeped out from the kitchen. Cilantro and garlic, Kate thought, and red wine. If her stomach hadn't been giving such an excellent imitation of a butter churn in full operation, she might actually have felt a spark of appetite.

The dining room was full, and the hum of conversation was loud enough to suggest everyone was having a good time without being intrusive. Luke had been working to upgrade the acoustics of the room at the time their relationship ended, and his investment had apparently paid off.

She hadn't called to let Luke know she was coming. Talking to him on the phone would be difficult in any circumstances, given the way their relationship had ended. She'd decided it would be impossible with Ron Raven as the subject of their conversation. Now that she was here, though, she wondered if a phone call might not have been smarter after all. At the best of times, thinking about her father tended to provoke the urge to scream with rage or sob inconsolably, and meeting with Luke Savarini was light years away from the best of times. Kate broke into a sweat just imagining the horror of bursting into tears when she was around him.

By a significant effort of will, she brought her feelings under control. She was cool, she was calm, and there was no reason to suppose she'd embarrass herself. Provided she didn't allow her fears about her father and her worries about her mother to bleed over into what should be a brief, polite conversation, all would be well. God knew, Luke was likely to be as anxious to end the discussion as she was. Neither of them had any interest in reigniting a flame that had caused burns of life-threatening severity without providing either warmth or light.

The hostess waiting by the door was new, which was a relief. Kate spoke her carefully rehearsed piece before her courage ran away and died. "Hi, I understand from the executive sous-chef at Luciano's on Chestnut that Luke Savarini is working here this evening. Would you tell him that Kate Fairfax would like to speak with him? I realize this is a busy time and I can come back later if that would be more convenient."

"Kate Fairfax, did you say?" The hostess smiled, giving no hint that she'd ever heard Kate's name before.

The TV coverage had been so blistering when her father disappeared that Kate still half expected to be recognized everywhere she went. The gradual return of anonymity was a blessing she appreciated every day.

"Yes, that's right. Luke and I are old friends." A slight misrepresentation, but she could hardly announce she was a former lover who, in normal circumstances, would prefer being locked in a small cage with a large crocodile rather than spend time with him.

"I'll let him know you're here."

"Thanks so much."

The hostess headed toward the kitchens and Kate gratefully stopped smiling. She picked up one of the heavy, leather-bound menus to check what was new since her last visit. She soon realized she was only pretending to read and put the menu down again. Her stomach continued to whirl. She strove to ignore it. For the past several months, it sometimes seemed that denial had become her default state of being.

The hostess returned. "Luke says he'll be right out. He asked me to bring you a glass of wine from the bar while you're waiting. Our house white is a Garofoli and the house red is a Valpolicella—"

"I appreciate the offer, but I'm fine, thanks." Sipping a glass of wine struck Kate as an invitation to disaster. She'd changed into dress pants, a cream silk blouse and a cropped, brass-buttoned black jacket before coming in search of Luke, and she hoped she looked reasonably put together. Sadly, the aura of a woman in charge of her life was sheer illusion. Unlike her mother, who had clearly been a princess in a previous incarnation, Kate often felt that her social graces were no more than a paper-thin layer stretched over a seething swamp of klutziness.

She heard a slight stir in the dining room and looked up. Luke had come out from the kitchen and was walking toward her, leaving little ripples of interested conversation in his wake. The seven months since she'd last seen him had clearly done nothing to dim his charisma. Kate accepted, almost with resignation, that her skin pricked and her nipples tingled in automatic response to his approach. Even her stomach stopped whirling long enough to clench with sexual tension.

She supposed she shouldn't be surprised by the instant tug of desire. Somehow, though, she'd managed to forget the power of Luke's sexual magnetism. Still, they hadn't broken up because they'd fallen out of lust, she reminded herself. Lust had worked well for them, right up to the end.

What the two of them had lost was mutual respect and any vestige of trust. Which made for a pretty comprehensive indictment of their relationship, she thought wryly. Her own final act of betrayal had simply been an exclamation point to punctuate the end of a relationship that had already died.

Luke was wearing the traditional starched white chef's jacket and black cotton pants. The jacket was pristine, presumably because he'd changed before leaving the kitchen. He'd discarded the mandatory head gear and his short-cropped hair stood up in a thick, dark crest above his tanned complexion and smoke-gray eyes. Despite spending twelve-hour working days inside various kitchens, Luke looked as if he made his living outdoors. She knew he started each morning, almost regardless of the weather, with a five-mile run along the lakeshore, which partly explained the permanent tan and the impressive physique. She admired his self-discipline, but even when they first started dating and the gloss was still pretty blinding, she'd wished he could be a little less perfect.

They'd needed to break up before Kate was willing to admit the extent to which she'd been intimidated by Luke's assets. He had so darn many, aside from self-made wealth and good looks: his warmth, his friendliness, his easy sense of humor and his ability to roll with the punches while still working at a fiendish pace.

Then there was his storybook Italian family. She'd loved hearing tales about his brothers and sisters, not to mention his ever-expanding crop of nieces and nephews. She'd envied him the casual camaraderie of his five siblings and the general aura of controlled chaos surrounding his family life, although toward the end of their relationship she'd begun to wonder why she'd never met any of his relatives face-to-face. She knew Luke well enough to realize that any girlfriend he was serious about would be required to get along with his family.

Even more than his family, she'd envied the ease with which Luke showed his emotions. If he was happy, he laughed. When he cooked for her, he hummed as he worked, completely indifferent to the fact that he was always off-key. When they made love, his passion was all-consuming, his attention totally devoted to her. If he was angry, he yelled. And when the anger passed, it was forgotten, with no lingering bitterness or need to prove he'd been right all along.

She'd been with Luke the night he learned that his

maternal grandfather had died from complications after supposedly routine surgery, and he'd cried as he heard the news. Apparently he'd never received the memo informing him that macho men were required to keep a stiff upper lip at all times. Kate's grandparents, Southern aristocrats who believed that gentlemen and ladies should avoid behaving like men and women whenever possible, would have been appalled by Luke's emotionalism. She had simply loved him more for his lack of inhibitions.

Luke's ability to grieve openly had haunted her in the aftermath of her father's disappearance. He had seemed to know instinctively how to integrate death and mourning into the natural order of his life. Kate, by contrast, had floundered. Her father's death brought nothing but unanswered questions and the hurt of issues left permanently unresolved. Her sadness at his loss seemed too complicated to grasp, let alone to express in something as mundane as tears.

Kate instructed herself to stop wallowing in the past and focus on coping with the present. Luke had paused to chat at several tables as he crossed the dining room, but now he was only steps away from the hostess station. Steps away from her. Kate wished she could greet him with a casual smile and a throwaway comment about…something. Unfortunately, when your last encounter involved the sort of brutal betrayal that left you internally bleeding, it was a bit difficult to come up with anything that didn't sound either snide or demented.

Luke halted a couple of feet away and simply stood there, saying nothing. She pretended to look at him but was actually careful to avoid meeting his gaze. Her brain was a blank, but eventually she managed to manipulate her mouth into a smile. At least, she hoped it was a smile and not a grimace.

She held out her hand. "Luke, thank you for meeting with me on such short notice."

He ignored her hand. "You're welcome." His icy tone belied the polite words. "I assume you're here to talk about your father."

"Yes, if we could." She let her hand drop to her side, her voice chilling to match his. If she'd expected the passage of seven months to heal the wounds of their parting, she had obviously been delusional.

"Let's go to my office." He turned without waiting for her to respond, not bothering to check if she was following as he wove a swift path to the tiny room set aside for him to make phone calls, pay bills and meet with vendors. Unlike the colorful dining rooms, or the shiny stainless steel of the spacious kitchens, his offices in all three restaurants were tiny, white-walled cubes. Small enough to be oppressive, and cold enough to form a suitably icy background for their conversation, Kate thought bleakly.

"I hope your mother wasn't upset by what we discussed this morning." Luke stood behind his desk and didn't suggest that either of them should sit down. If body language was anything to go by, his attitude to this meeting was several degrees less enthusiastic than her own.

"Of course my mother is upset." Kate bit back the urge to suggest he should refrain from making ridiculous statements. "Six months ago she found out that the man she'd loved for twenty-eight years was a bigamous, cheating liar. Then she was informed he'd been murdered. The next cheery little revelation was that her supposed husband had left far less money than anyone would have thought possible. What funds did exist went straight to probate, where the lawyers are having a grand time charging huge sums of money to unravel a quarter century of my father's carefully manufactured deceptions. In the meantime, my mother's been forced to sell her home of a dozen years and adjust to the fact that at least half her friends weren't actually friends at all, merely hangers-on, out for what they could get. Now you summon her to your presence so that you can pass on the news that—big surprise!—maybe Ron Raven is alive after all." She let out an exasperated breath. "How in the world do you think she feels?"

Luke's voice and expression both remained cool. "Right now I imagine she's teetering somewhere between overwhelmed and devastated."

"Your imagination is correct. I'm wondering what the upside of your revelation was supposed to be."

"The fact that Avery might be able to uncover the truth about what really happened to her husband?"

Kate made an impatient sound. "Where my father is concerned, truth is likely to remain unavailable however much we scrabble in the dust he left behind."

"It's clear you disapprove of my decision to tell your mother what I saw."

"Yes, of course I disapprove. In effect you told her that Ron Raven cared so little about her that he was willing to fake his own death to avoid ever seeing her again. Thanks so much for your comforting words!"

He winced at her sarcasm. For a moment, his

guarded expression broke down, revealing unmistakable self-doubt. "I felt I owed your mother the truth precisely because Ron lied to her for so many years."

Kate wasn't ready to acknowledge that Luke might have found himself in an almost impossible position. "You should have talked to me," she said tersely. "Not my mother."

Luke's smile was wintry. "Maybe, but I was never into masochism, Katie. Having my balls cut off and shoved down my throat comes way down on my list of ways I want to spend the morning."

Goose bumps erupted all over her arms when he called her Katie, even though the endearment was tucked inside a major insult. She reminded herself that her body was simply responding to ingrained sexual cues after months without sex. In her current celibate state, she could probably watch Patrick Dempsey making out with a TV lover and her hormones would provide the same knee-jerk response. And, watching Patrick, she'd get the sexual buzz without the added insult.

"For some reason, my mother believes your story about seeing Ron Raven might actually be true." She hadn't intended to sound so hostile, but Luke's presence suffocated her, destroying her good intentions. She struggled to moderate her tone. "My mother asked me to find out if you had any additional information we might be able to hand over to a private investigator in the hope that he would be able to track down the man you saw in Washington, D.C."

"Do you believe I saw your father?" Luke asked. His voice was unexpectedly quiet and the question seemed less of an attack, more of a genuine request for her opinion.

Kate hadn't yet summoned the courage to examine that question. She'd focused on her mother's state of mind and Luke's transgressions mostly because it let her off the hook in terms of her own reaction to the eerie possibility that her father was alive.

"I'm sure you believe you saw him," she said finally. Even when she'd first heard the news, she'd never doubted Luke's sincerity.

"That's not what I asked."

She shrugged. "You knew my father quite well. I'm assuming the lighting was adequate and you saw him reasonably close up?"

"Yes." Luke's hesitation was almost imperceptible. "I heard him laugh before I looked at him. I was talking to my sister when I heard this familiar sound and I thought, *My God, that sounds just like Ron Raven.* I glanced up, not expecting to see him, of course, despite the laughter. But there he was. Eating dinner with an attractive, dark-haired woman and looking as if he was enjoying himself. For a couple of seconds, I was literally too shocked to move."

The sickness in Kate's stomach returned with renewed intensity. Hearing Luke describe the incident gave her father's possible reappearance a reality it had previously lacked. An unwelcome reality, she realized. "There doesn't sound as if there's a whole lot of room for you to have made a mistake."

"No. Still, I never exchanged a single word with the man and never heard him speak to anyone else. Everybody's supposed to have a double somewhere in the world. Perhaps I saw Ron's."

She wished she could believe that, but her ability to

ignore inconvenient facts wasn't quite up to the task. "My mother said the man ran away when you tried to approach him."

Luke nodded. "He was sitting right next to the door, and I was across the room, tucked into an alcove, with at least half a dozen tables between me and the exit. I chased him into the parking lot, but there was no way to stop him driving off once he made it into his car. I discovered it's a lot more difficult to catch somebody than it looks in the movies."

"I guess you didn't manage to get the license number of his car as he drove away?"

"Actually, I did."

"You did?" She glanced up, startled. "Could we trace it, then?"

"I already had a private investigator track it down before I contacted your mother. The car was a brand-new Mercedes, and it was registered to a man called Stewart M. Jones."

For a second, Kate was puzzled. Then she realized that—of course—if her father wanted to avoid being discovered he couldn't go around calling himself Ron Raven. "If you have those vehicle registration details, my mother and I should be able to track the car's owner back to an address, shouldn't we? I assume you have to give an address when you register a car in Virginia?"

"Apparently, yes. But my investigator reported that Stewart Jones sold the vehicle the day after I chased him into the parking lot. What's more, the address given on the accompanying paperwork isn't valid."

"He gave a fake address?" Kate realized her surprise

was misplaced. "Well, of course he would have to, I guess, since he was trying to stop you tracking him down."

"The address wasn't fake in the sense it didn't exist. It just wasn't Mr. Jones's current place of residence. According to my investigator, somebody calling himself Mr. Jones lived at the address for a few weeks back in the summer. But he moved away from that particular location a couple of months ago."

She sighed. "In other words, the car is pretty much a dead end in terms of tracking down Mr. Jones."

"I'm afraid so."

"You clearly believe that Stewart Jones is simply another name for Ron Raven, and that Ron sold his car rather than risk being traced."

"Yes, that's what I think." Luke shrugged. "But take my opinion for what it's worth. Not much, according to the cops. They're convinced Ron is dead and that I'm a crime-scene junkie with delusions of seeing dead people. And they're the experts, after all."

She wished she could dismiss his story as the ramblings of a nutcase, Kate thought miserably, but his information was almost more compelling because he was so willing to provide her with reasons not to accept it. Luke was among the more down-to-earth people she knew, and she simply couldn't picture him disrupting an enjoyable dinner with his sister to conjure up imaginary visions of a dead man.

"I appreciate the effort you put into tracking down the man you saw," she said finally. "It sounds to me as if it really could be my father, so it's probably just as well you didn't manage to catch up with him." She forgot for a moment to hide her feelings and allowed bitterness to seep into her voice. "I don't see how it can bring my mother anything but grief to have proof that her lying, cheating husband is alive."

"Ron left behind three children as well as two wives," Luke said, his voice still quiet. "What does it say about his relationship with them...with you...if he's determined not to be found? Don't let him off the hook, Katie. You deserve better from him. For that matter, so do your half brother and sister."

The absolute last thing she wanted was for Luke to be kind or sympathetic. Kate could feel her composure fraying by the second, unraveled by his gentleness. This would be an excellent moment to make her escape, she decided. So far she and Luke had managed to avoid inflicting serious bodily harm on each other, which had to be a good thing. Not to mention a precarious thing. It would be smart not to tempt fate.

"You're right." She inclined her head in acknowledgment. "If my father is alive, he has a lot to answer for. Except that I'm not sure I care enough to ask the questions. Right now, I feel he doesn't deserve that much attention from me."

"What about your half brother and sister?"

"I don't know. I haven't found the courage to meet them yet. Fortunately for me, I was in Europe when Adam brought Megan to Chicago after they got married." She stopped abruptly. This was getting too personal again. "Anyway, thanks for all you've done, Luke. Sorry about the earlier hostility. I was worried about my mother and took out my worries on you."

She dredged up a bright, meaningless smile, just to

show that they were both grown-ups, and that this was a business conversation despite the intensely personal nature of the topic. "Would you give me the name of the detective you used to track the vehicle registration tags? If my mother should decide to pursue an investigation, it only makes sense to build on the inquiries you've already made."

She felt Luke's gaze rest on her face, but she avoided looking up. She was getting the same shaky, desperate feeling that had afflicted her in the weeks immediately after she learned Ron Raven had been murdered. She despised herself for still caring about her father, but she could only hide her emotions, not banish them. Luke had always been able to see through her protective barriers more easily than other men and that was a problem, given how badly she wanted to keep her feelings to herself. With all the evidence they already had of Ron Raven's deceptions and double dealings, it was humiliating to go to pieces over the fact that her father apparently cared about her even less than she'd previously realized. She didn't want Luke to know how…abandoned…she felt at this moment.

Thankfully, he made no more personal comments. "The investigator I used is called George Klein," he said. "George is ethical, efficient and easy to work with and I'm happy to recommend him. If you decide to go ahead with an investigation, let me know. I have a couple of other tips that might help. Or they might be completely useless. To be honest, my guess is that your father has already moved on to a different city. He most likely ditched the Stewart Jones identity at the same time as he sold the Mercedes. He's a man accustomed to planning ahead, so he would have had another identity already waiting for him to step into."

"I'm sure you're right." The restaurant business stayed afloat on illegal immigrant labor, and Kate was all too familiar with how easy it was to buy fake documentation. If dishwashers with no education and no English language skills could get themselves all the papers they needed, it would presumably be child's play for her father to acquire however many new identities he might want or need. Even in a post 9/11 world, as long as you weren't trying to get into a secure building or fly overseas, a fake ID could take you almost anywhere you wanted to go.

Luke pushed a pile of papers to one side and picked up a business card. "I intended to give your mother George's card this morning, but in the end it didn't seem appropriate. She was too upset." He held out the card and Kate concentrated on taking it without touching even the tip of his fingers. She tucked it into her purse, repeating her thanks.

She was so relieved that their meeting was over that she looked up to say her final goodbye without paying proper attention. She'd gone through their entire conversation without actually meeting Luke's eyes. And then, in the final seconds, she was careless enough to blow it.

His gaze locked with hers and he said her name, just once. She could have sworn she detected a note of yearning in his voice. They were separated by the width of his desk, but the space between them filled instantly with emotions woken from an uneasy seven-month slumber. The weight of issues left unresolved became heavier and more oppressive as they stood there, unable to look away from each other.

Like the rumble of distant thunder moving ominously closer, Kate realized that desire was fermenting beneath all her other feelings and had been ever since Luke walked out of the kitchen and into her line of sight. One wrong move on her part and the background rumble would become a crashing, foreground crescendo.

Luke saved her from making a move that she would inevitably have regretted later. "How is Michael?" he asked.

The thunder exploded directly overhead, flattening every last trace of desire and leaving her shaking with rage. "Michael is well," she said, surprised that her brain and vocal cords were capable of working in synch to produce coherent words. Actually, for all she knew, Michael could be dead. More likely, he was exercising his sexual charms on some blond wannabe starlet, his usual quarry.

"Thanks again for the information about my father. Goodbye, Luke." She turned and walked out of his office, almost running across the dining room to the safety of the exit. Were there really a hundred miles of carpet for her to navigate? It sure felt like it.

She knew she ought to be grateful for the salutary reminder of exactly why she loathed Luke Savarini. Give her a couple of hours and she'd undoubtedly get there. Right now, though, she wasn't sure what hurt more: the fact that her father might be alive, or the fact that her relationship with Luke was incontrovertibly, hopelessly dead.

The only thing she knew with certainty was that one way or another, this had been a hell of a rotten day.

Seven

He was a stupid, dumb fuck. And that was the polite way to describe himself, Luke thought bitterly. Ignoring the buzzer and the blinking lights that warned him a major crisis had just occurred in the kitchen, he tore through the dining room in search of Kate. He caught up with her outside, where she was handing her parking ticket to one of the valets.

"I'm sorry," he said, putting his hand beneath her elbow and propelling her away from the curious ears of the college kids working the valet station. "Katie, look at me, for God's sake. What I said—it was stupid. I couldn't handle the way I was feeling, so I made the first comment that came into my head."

"If that's supposed to make me feel better, it doesn't." Kate disengaged her arm and half turned so that she didn't have to look at him. "What does it say about us if the first thing that pops into your head is an image of me with Michael?"

She was so far off the mark Luke might have found

her misconceptions funny in different circumstances. The first thing that had popped into his head when he saw Kate tonight had nothing to do with Michael. Not a damn thing. His first thought had been simply that she was so beautiful it hurt him to look at her. His next couple of hundred thoughts had been variations on the theme of how badly he wanted to take her to bed. His question about Michael had been a desperate attempt to stop himself from doing something insane like lunging across the desk, grabbing the lapels of her sexy black jacket and kissing her senseless.

At one level, you could say his move had succeeded brilliantly. The chances of him and Kate ever having sex again had just sunk to several levels below the possibility that the Cubs would win two World Series in a row.

Hey, congratulations, moron! You won the pissing contest. Feeling good about your victory?

"I wasn't trying to hurt you." Admitting the truth was fairly easy since he had nothing much left to lose. "I lashed out at you to protect myself."

"I know. I do understand, Luke. I understand all too well." She tilted her head to look up at him, her spectacular blue eyes more sad than angry. "That's exactly why we should keep out of each other's way, because when we're together, that's what we do nowadays—we lash out and hurt each other. You look at me and all you see is one unbearable image—Michael…your best friend…lying next to me in bed. I look at you and see the man who always—*always!*—put work ahead of our relationship, however much I needed you."

Luke forced himself to shut up and think before

speaking. Okay, so Kate was equating two things that in his book didn't begin to balance out. Yes, he'd failed to put in an appearance when she was competing in an important culinary contest, but that hardly ranked up there in the sin department alongside her decision to have sex with Michael, former high school buddy and fabulously wealthy commodities broker.

For the first time since the two of them broke up, Luke recognized it was a zero-sum game to get dragged into an argument about who was more of a workaholic and who had been more at fault. He didn't change his opinion that Kate's betrayal had been worse than his, but he at least managed to avoid pointing out how despicable her infidelity had been.

How much her infidelity had hurt him, he finally admitted.

"We messed up in the spring, Katie, both of us. But that's past and there's plenty of blame to spread around. Right now, I'm thinking I'd like the chance to redeem my share of the screwup."

"How? By rolling back time?" Her question seemed sad rather than sarcastic. "That would be quite a trick if you can pull it off."

"If we concentrate on the future, the past doesn't have to control us."

"There is no *we*. We don't have a future, Luke."

"No, I guess we don't, not as a couple. But we have a shared interest in finding out who it was I saw in Herndon."

"Why do you care if Ron Raven is alive or dead? He's nothing to you."

"That's not true. Ron Raven is the man who made

my dreams possible. I owe him. And I'm the person claiming he's alive. I need to find out if I'm right." He reached out, the gesture instinctive. He was smart enough to let his hand drop without touching her. "Let me set up a meeting in George Klein's office and we can talk to him together. Bring your mother if you want, or not, if you would prefer the two of us to handle the nitty-gritty of the investigation."

Kate still didn't look directly at him. "It's my mother's decision whether to pursue an investigation, not mine."

"You never used to duck the difficult issues," he said softly. "Yes, it's your mother's decision, but it isn't hers alone. There's your father's family in Wyoming to consider. And then there's you." He wasn't entirely sure why he was pushing to get involved in the search for Ron Raven, but he had a gut-level feeling that fate was holding up a billboard-size placard informing him that there are no coincidences in life and that he'd seen Ron in his cousin's restaurant for a reason.

"Be honest about what's at stake here, Katie. Even if you're prepared to give Ron a free pass on his bigamous marriage to your mother, you can't ignore what supposedly happened in Miami last May. If Ron wasn't the victim of a brutal murder, then he almost certainly faked his own death. He sure as hell owes you an explanation for that."

"You think?" Kate's smile was ironic, but for the first time that night, he sensed it was also genuine. Her smile changed to a sigh. "You're right, I suppose. I can't just ignore what you saw. We need to find out whether my father's alive."

"I understand it's a messy situation that might be difficult to resolve. What I don't understand is why you're so reluctant to make the attempt. How is it better to live with the mess? Do you just keep walking around it and pretending it's not there?"

"You've no idea how tempting that sounds."

"Not long-term. Long-term, it's disastrous, because the mess grows bigger the harder you try to ignore it."

"You don't have my talent for ignoring messes. I've been coping for the past seven months by avoiding as many difficult issues as possible."

"And how is that working for you?"

"Not well," Kate acknowledged. "The truth is I've about run out of places to hide from my problems. Pretty soon, I'll bump into some monster-in-the-closet whichever way I turn."

"So this might be a good moment to change tactics and confront at least this one problem? Give it a try, Katie."

She gave a wry smile. "Couldn't we start with something a bit smaller? Like whether I need to add more brown sugar to my Christmas pecan torte."

"I'd say no, if it's the same torte you made for me last year. That was already perfect." Like everything else about the Christmas they'd spent together. Christmas Eve with Kate had brought back all the magic that had been missing since he was five years old and waiting for Santa. He wondered if she still had the dragon's egg he'd given her at midnight on Christmas Eve. Wondered if she had even a smidgen of a clue how erotic he found the dragon on her butt. Thought about how much he'd love to sleep just one more time with his hand resting comfortably over Puff.

Luke held her gaze and realized just looking at her was enough to make his heart race. He forced his thoughts back on track. "Trying to find the man I saw is the right decision, Kate, even if it's more difficult for you and your mother in the short term."

"I guess." She looked away and pressed her fingertips to her forehead. "No, you're right. I need to stop with the wishy-washy stuff. It's time for me to take a stand. We need to track this man down, even if he turns out to be just a look-alike."

"Great. We agree about something! Stick to your original recipe for the pecan torte and we've agreed about two things in one night."

She gave him a real, wholehearted smile. "Okay, I'll stop experimenting with the Christmas torte. How's that for eagerness to please?"

"It's amazing. I believe a major milestone in our relationship has just been passed." Luke decided to end the conversation while he was at least fractionally ahead. This was about as close to harmony as the two of them were likely to achieve, given everything that lay between them. "I'll get back to you as soon as I've arranged a time to meet with George Klein. Afternoons are still best for you?"

"Anytime after three," she agreed. As a pastry chef, she started work at dawn and went to bed early. As a restaurant owner, he worked late into the night. When they were dating, he had often gone to bed only a couple of hours before she got up.

"You'll need this." She reached into her purse and handed him a printed card. "My phone number's the same but I have a new e-mail address."

He stashed the card in the pocket of his work pants. "Thanks, I'll be in touch. It's misty tonight. Drive safely, Kate."

He left before she could change her mind about meeting with the detective. And before he could ask another of the dumb questions percolating in his pathetic, sex-addled brain. Something terminally dim-witted along the lines of *Are you and Michael still sleeping together?*

It was odd how much he wanted to ask the question, when he was quite sure he didn't want to know the answer.

Eight

Luke was surprised when Kate didn't bring her mother to the meeting with George Klein the following Monday afternoon. Instead she walked into the detective's sparsely furnished but spacious office on the arm of a tall, handsome man in his fifties. He recognized her escort as Paul Fairfax, Kate's uncle and Ron's former business partner in Raven Enterprises.

Kate seemed determined to set a brisk, businesslike tone for the meeting. Perhaps that was why she'd brought her uncle, Luke speculated. She acknowledged Luke's presence with a quick nod and an immediate introduction, neatly avoiding the need to say anything personal.

"Do you remember my uncle, Paul Fairfax? Uncle Paul, this is Luke Savarini. I believe the two of you met a few years ago when my father was financing the start-up of the first Luciano's."

The two men shook hands and Luke, in turn, introduced the Fairfaxes to George Klein. "I apologize for turning up like this unannounced," Paul said, gesturing to include both Luke and George in his apology. "I had conference calls with some business partners in Denver right after lunch. We're developing a major building project in the city, and the death of the mayor last summer has caused us a couple of minor problems. I wasn't sure I could break off in time to get here. However, the more I mulled over what Kate had told me, the clearer it became that I need to be part of this investigation. So I decided to cut short my phone meeting in order to get here. All very rushed and last-minute, I'm afraid. Hence no warning."

"I understand," Luke said. "In fact, it's good to have you here, Paul. I should have realized you have almost as much reason as Ron's wives and children to want to know if he's alive."

Paul winced at the mention of Ron's wives. Ron's bigamy still visibly roiled him and Luke could empathize. If some son of a bitch bigamously married one of his sisters, he'd have a hard time coming to terms with it, too.

Everyone sat down and George Klein delivered his standard spiel about needing a unanimous agreement concerning the goals of the investigation. Paul jumped in as soon as the detective finished speaking, not to clarify the goals of the investigation but to insist on taking responsibility for paying the bills.

"Ron was my business partner," he explained. "Attempting to discover whether or not he's alive is a tax-deductible business expense for Raven Enterprises, whereas it would be out of pocket for Kate and Avery, and for you, too, Luke. Besides, this is a small service I can perform for my sister and I really want to do it. I must insist. No arguments, please."

George took off his reading glasses and rubbed his eyes. "If you all agree that Mr. Fairfax should pay the bills, that raises another issue we should clear up before we get started. If you pay the bills, Mr. Fairfax, then you're the person entitled to receive my reports. From my perspective, there's no reason why you shouldn't be point man, so to speak. But just so we all understand the situation."

Paul gave an airy wave of his hand. "As far as I'm concerned, the fact that I'm the person paying the bills doesn't mean the reports have to come to me. However, as a practical matter, I might be easier to reach than Kate or Luke. They both have erratic work schedules, whereas I'm more likely to be in the office between eight and five, and at home in the evening."

"Just so long as you keep us updated, Uncle Paul." Kate's voice was teasing, but her expression warned that she was serious. "Don't pull one of your Southern gentleman tricks and decide to protect me and my mother if you don't like the information George digs up."

Paul flashed his niece an affectionate glance. "I wouldn't dare to hold anything back from you, Kate. I promise to share all of Mr. Klein's reports with you and your mother. Every last word. And if you want to keep Luke updated, that's entirely up to you. I have no objection, of course, none in the world. After all, if not for Luke, we wouldn't be here right now."

It was entirely logical for Paul Fairfax to pay George

Klein's bills, and equally as logical for him to be the person on the receiving end of George's reports. Luke ought to have been relieved that yet another item wasn't about to get added to his already overflowing agenda, and yet he felt dissatisfied with the arrangement. Probably because he was afraid that Kate would cut him out of the informational loop, he reflected wryly. He really didn't want that to happen.

Truth be told, finding Ron Raven was becoming somewhat of a fixation for him. As each day passed, he became more determined to track down the man he'd seen in Cousin Bruno's restaurant. He'd realized last night, tossing and turning in a quest for sleep, that even if he hadn't been afflicted with some weird hang-up about his failed relationship with Kate, he'd still want to know if the man he'd seen was Ron Raven.

Luke kept silent about the bill because there was no way to express his objections without revealing more about the state of his feelings for Kate than he cared to have on public view. George Klein, satisfied that the administrative details were taken care of, outlined the information about Stewart M. Jones that he'd already uncovered while working for Luke, and asked for feedback from Paul and Kate.

"I have a file of newspaper and magazine clippings concerning Ron's disappearance." Paul placed a thick folder on George's desk. "I only kept the least sensational accounts. I'm not sure how much of this material will be relevant, but it does provide all the background to Ron's disappearance that you could possibly need."

"Except for the information Adam picked up in

Belize," Kate interjected. "We need to tell George about that."

"True." Paul turned to the detective, frowning as he tried to order his thoughts. "This gets complicated. Kate is referring to the fact that my younger brother, Adam, was in Mexico and Belize on the trail of some money that went missing at the time of Ron's death."

Paul stopped short, shaking his head. "I suppose I have to get used to saying *at the time of Ron's disappearance.* I'm having a hard time absorbing the implications of what we're doing here. Anyway, while Adam was in Belize, he ran into Julio Castellano."

"The police have identified Castellano as the man who murdered my father," Kate explained for George's benefit. "When Adam returned from Belize, he told us that Castellano denied having anything to do with my father's murder—"

"Which we didn't believe, of course. At least, back in the summer." Paul sounded as if he was having a hard time changing his opinion about Castellano's guilt.

George Klein glanced up, eyebrows lifted in surprise. "Are you telling me that another member of your family has been claiming for months that Ron is alive?"

"Oh, no!" Kate and Paul exclaimed together.

"Castellano never hinted that my father might be alive," Kate explained. "He just claimed that he hadn't killed him."

"Naturally it never occurred to my brother that Ron might be alive," Paul added. "Adam was simply persuaded that somebody other than Julio Castellano had murdered Ron."

"We none of us believed Adam," Kate admitted. "In

fact, when he and Megan returned from Belize, I told him not to be naive, that Castellano was spinning him a fairy tale. But Adam insisted that Castellano had saved his life and Megan's, too, when it would have been much easier to let them both die. He insisted the cops were targeting the wrong suspect."

"Naturally I assumed gratitude to Julio Castellano was clouding his judgment." Paul directed an apologetic glance at Luke, massaging just above the bridge of his nose as if a headache was forming. "To be honest, I'm still having trouble accepting that the police in Miami have misread this whole case from the beginning. In fact, Luke, I wouldn't be pursuing this investigation if Avery and Kate weren't adamant that you're a reliable witness. But dammit, are you sure about what you saw? The cops didn't just pull Castellano's name out of the air! They identified his blood in the hotel room!"

Luke sympathized with Paul's skepticism. "Of course, I can't be a hundred percent sure the man I saw was Ron. We never spoke, and I only glimpsed him for thirty seconds or so before he realized I was watching him. At which point he ran like hell. But if it wasn't Ron, why did a perfect stranger rush out of the restaurant the moment he caught my eye? And why did this same stranger sell an almost-new Mercedes the day after he saw me writing down the license plate number?"

"It sure sounds suspicious enough to warrant investigation," Paul conceded grudgingly. "But if you really did see Ron, then I have to change my opinion about this Julio Castellano person. Apparently he told Adam the truth. He's a convicted murderer, he was in Ron's hotel room, his blood was smeared on the wall—and he didn't kill Ron. God, *listen* to what I'm saying! It's incredible! Truly incredible."

"There's one other thing," Kate added. "Castellano told Adam that the woman in the hotel room with my father that night was a relative of his, a woman called Consuela Mackenzie. Adam described Consuela to us as a woman in her late thirties, unusually tall for a native Belizean, but petite by American standards. She has thick, dark hair, very curly, which she wears long. She was, apparently, in love with my father, at least according to Julio. Does that description of Consuela sound anything like the woman you saw in the restaurant?"

"It sounds a lot like the woman I saw," Luke said. "I guess it only makes sense that if Ron Raven didn't die that night in the hotel, then the woman with him didn't die, either."

He wondered if Ron Raven could possibly have been crazy enough to fake his own death simply to start life with a new and attractive young woman. But how could faking your own death be easier than getting a divorce? In Ron's case, of course, he would need to get a divorce *and* shed a mistress he'd kept for twenty-seven years. Still, that would surely pose fewer problems than planning a double fake murder. For that matter, he could simply have left his wives, without any elaborate ruse or explanations.

"We're getting diverted here," George Klein said. "We can't get sidetracked into worrying about the identity of the woman Luke saw. We need to stay focused on the main item on the agenda, namely gathering information that will lead us to Stewart Jones. If

I can find Mr. Jones, a lot of other questions will be answered almost automatically. Once we know whether or not Stewart Jones is also Ron Raven, it should be child's play to discover the identity of any woman he might have living with him. Does that sound like a plan?"

"Yes, it does." Paul directed an approving nod at the detective. "Thanks for getting us back on track, George."

"You asked me to bring a few photographs of my father and I have them here." Kate unzipped a small leather portfolio and took out a plastic bag filled with a dozen or so pictures. She handed the stash to George. "Those were all taken in the last few weeks before my father disappeared. There are headshots and a couple of full lengths to give you an idea of his body build. My father was…is…he's just over six feet tall, with powerful shoulders and unusually thick hair for a man in his fifties. I have duplicates of all of the photos, so I don't need those copies returned."

"Excellent." George rifled through the pictures. "Yes, these will be great. A fine selection, thanks. I plan to take these to the apartment building where Stewart M. Jones was living in June and show them around, especially to the custodial staff. If I can get a positive ID, at least we know we are dealing with a man who looks very much like Ron Raven."

"Let's assume somebody at the apartment building makes the identification," Paul said. "What's our next step? From what you were telling us earlier, you've already run the car registration tags and come to a dead end."

"You never know in advance what tidbits you're going to turn up when you conduct an on-site investigation," George said. "Over the phone, rental agents and building superintendents are reluctant to share information. When you're asking questions face-to-face, it's surprising how much more you can learn. Look on the bright side. I'm actually not short of leads. I have an address where Stewart Jones lived for six weeks. I have the auto dealership where he sold his car. That car was a nearly new Mercedes and those aren't turned in every day of the week. There's a decent chance—more than decent—that I'm going to find somebody who remembers Mr. Jones and can direct me to his current whereabouts."

Paul still looked discouraged. "I hope you're right. The worst thing from my point of view…from all our points of view, I guess…is to have this issue looming over us, forever unresolved. It's hell not knowing for sure whether Ron is alive or dead. Frankly, the uncertainty could destroy my sister's peace of mind. And it can't be pleasant for Kate, either." He gave her knee a comforting pat as he spoke.

"I'll do my best to make sure you aren't left floating in limbo." George turned to look at Luke. "When you called to set up this meeting, you mentioned that you collected one other small piece of information at the restaurant the night you spotted our quarry. Could you share that with us now?"

"It's nothing dramatic, unfortunately." Luke opened the envelope he'd brought with him and extracted the credit card receipt Bruno had given him. He handed it to George.

"How is this connected to the man you saw?" the detective asked.

"He left it, by mistake, I'm sure. As I explained before, the man I saw in my cousin's restaurant not only appeared to recognize me, he was obviously spooked by the sight. As soon as he realized I was coming to speak to him, he seized his companion's arm and hustled her toward the exit. He hadn't paid for their meals, but he was in too much of a hurry to summon the waitress to ask for his check. He simply grabbed his wallet and pulled out a bundle of twenties, which he tossed onto the table to cover the bill. Since the restaurant is owned by one of my cousins, it was a bit easier for me to ask questions and get them answered than it would have been in normal circumstances. I told the waitress I'd seen an old friend and I was anxious to get in touch but I had no contact address or phone number. In response, my cousin brought me that credit card receipt. Apparently the server found it stuffed in the pile of twenties that had been left on the table."

Paul and Kate both looked skeptical, as if they couldn't imagine what use a stray credit card receipt might be, but George studied the flimsy scrap of paper with interest. "Stewart M. Jones went shopping at a store called Sunrise, which, according to the address, is located in the Reston Town Square shopping center."

"Reston's right next to Herndon," Luke said, not sure if George was familiar with the area. "They're both basically dormitory suburbs for the D.C. area."

"And the fact that Stewart Jones and his companion were eating in Herndon and shopping in Reston suggests that they might live somewhere in the general vicinity." George tapped the receipt. "This is a better lead than you anticipated, Luke. Hopefully, Reston Town Square will turn out to be a plaza with a bunch of shops and boutiques and cafés. I'll flash Ron's picture in every store. We might catch a break and have someone recognize him. If we get super lucky, someone's going to tell me they not only know who he is, they also know where he lives. Maybe he's a regular customer at Sunrise and they'll be able to provide us with his current address." He chuckled at his own optimism. "Well, we can hope."

Luke had noticed before that George was amazingly positive for a man who spent his professional life documenting the general sleaziness of humanity. Perhaps his optimism flowed from the fact that he was happily married and had two young kids he adored. He sent the detective a rueful smile. "I hope finding Mr. Jones turns out to be as easy as you're making it sound, George."

"Me, too." Kate leaned forward, her body language still tense. So far this afternoon, she hadn't cast a single glance in Luke's direction. "How long before you can leave for Virginia?" she asked the detective. "Luke told us you're always very busy, and it might be a few days before you could even start working for us."

George smiled at her. "Fortunately for you, I'm much more interested in finding out if Mr. Jones really is Ron Raven than I am in setting traps for dishonest employees and tailing cheating spouses. I'll turn my current caseload over to my assistants and I'll leave for Washington's Dulles airport on the first flight on Wednesday morning. I should be in Herndon by noon. I'll work through the weekend if need be, but I hope to get back to you with at least an interim report by Friday night."

"That's only two days after you'll arrive in Virginia!" Paul was clearly startled by the detective's speed.

George's polite smile changed to a grin as he handed over a printed form. "Be grateful I work fast, Mr. Fairfax. That's my rate sheet, and as you can see, I'm expensive. I'm also darn good at my job, if I do say so myself."

Paul glanced at the sheet. "Yes, indeed, you are expensive. But if you can confirm whether Ron Raven is alive or dead, believe me, I'll consider you worth every penny."

Nine

Avery stared at the phone with loathing. The phone stared right back, mutely accusing. This was a ritual that had been going on all day, and so far, the phone was winning. It was way past time to show some backbone, Avery decided, summoning a ferocious scowl. Kate would be arriving for dinner in less than an hour, so if she was going to call Ellie Raven in privacy, she needed to do it now.

It was humbling to consider what a hard time she was having placing a simple phone call. What in God's name was her problem? Ellie had demonstrated much more courage back in May. Within days of Ron's disappearance, she had flown from Wyoming to Chicago and confronted Avery in person. Without ever being rude, Ellie had asked all the questions Avery wanted answered but would never have found the gumption to ask.

It was past time to prove to herself that she wasn't a

total wimp. Avery reached out to lift the receiver, but once again changed her mind at the last minute. Maybe her reluctance to place the call was a warning sign that her decision to speak with Ellie Raven was inappropriate. Wasn't there something rather distasteful about Ron's bigamous wife forcing personal contact onto his legitimate wife? It was bad enough that her relationship with Ron had no legal status. She didn't need to compound the humiliation by being socially inept on top of everything else.

Avery gave an impatient shake of her head. Good grief, she needed to stop thinking like her mother. *Distasteful. Socially inept.* What gutless, limp words. She and Kate were trying to find out whether Ron was alive or dead and she was worried in case her behavior seemed *socially inept!*

Finally fired up, she smoothed out the piece of paper where she'd written down the number for the ranch in Wyoming, given to her by her brother, Adam. Inhaling deeply, she snatched the handset and dialed before her brief spurt of courage could desert her.

A female voice answered on the second ring. "Hello?"

Oh, my God, it was Ellie. It was too fast. She wasn't ready. Avery wiped her sweaty palm on her tailored, cashmere-blend slacks. Her clothes might be flawless but the rest of her was a mess. She cleared her throat. "Hello, this is Avery."

She'd planned to identify herself as Avery Fairfax, but the last name stuck in her throat, refusing to come out. Apparently it still hurt too much to acknowledge to the real Mrs. Ronald H. Raven that she, Avery Fairfax, had never been entitled to the name.

She forced the silly, painful thought aside, drawing on years of social training to keep her voice steady despite her inner anxiety. "Is this Ellie Raven?" she asked, just as if she hadn't recognized her rival's voice immediately.

"Why, yes, it is. How are you, Avery? This is an unexpected call. I hope nothing's wrong." Ellie gave a brief laugh. "Nothing more wrong than usual, that is." She sounded warm, kind and confident of her place in the universe.

"I'm not sure how to answer that." Avery paced the newly bare floor of her living room, careful to avoid the giant splinters sticking up out of the hardwood. She wished she didn't invariably feel so…shriveled…when she spoke to Ellie, like desiccated coconut in the presence of lush, ripe fruit. "Unfortunately, I'm afraid I'm going to cause you more worry, at least in the short term—"

"This isn't about Megan and Adam, is it?" Ellie's voice sharpened with anxiety.

"Oh, no! Not at all. They were fine when I spoke with Adam a couple of days ago. I'm calling about…about Ron."

"Oh, land's sakes. Now what? Have those dratted lawyers found something new to torment us with?"

"It's not the lawyers. There's no way to make this less shocking, so I'll simply cut to the chase. Luke Savarini, a good friend of ours, made a trip to Washington, D.C., last week. When he returned he told us that he'd seen Ron eating dinner at a restaurant in one of the D.C. suburbs. There was a woman with him. A woman in her late thirties. Luke knows Ron well—they worked together for a couple of years—and he was confident of his identification. According to Luke, the man he saw was either Ron, or Ron's living double."

Ellie drew in an audible gasp. "Oh, my heavens! Did your friend speak to Ron? What did he say?"

"No, they didn't speak. Ron left before my friend had the chance."

"Oh, well, that's a bit different, isn't it? I certainly appreciate the heads-up, Avery, but there doesn't seem any reason in the world to believe your friend is right, does there? A sighting in a restaurant doesn't seem much to stack up against the weight of evidence law enforcement has produced. I don't mean to sound flippant, but the police in Miami are quite sure Ron is dead."

"The police in Miami seem sure of a lot of things that other people have doubts about," Avery said tartly. "Luke Savarini isn't the sort of person to imagine things." She realized she was getting rather tired of hearing why the police must be right and everyone else wrong. "How sure can anyone be about what happened to Ron and…and the woman he had with him, when there are no bodies?"

"That's true, we can't be sure. But the other evidence all seems to back up the police theory that Ron and the woman are dead." Ellie hesitated for a moment. "Although, to be honest, this isn't the first time I've heard from somebody who thinks they've seen Ron. One of our cousins called from Texas a while back and insisted she'd seen Ron going into the Nieman Marcus store in Houston. We never passed on her story to you because the police convinced us we should ignore her. They said literally hundreds of people have claimed to see Ron in various places. On one particularly busy day in May, Ron was supposedly spotted in New Zealand, Tokyo and Miami—all within the space of about four hours!"

"Yes, that's exactly what the police told Luke, too. They informed him they'd received hundreds of reports and interviewed dozens of the most promising informants, but every single sighting proved to be without foundation. The thing is, though, I know Luke Savarini, whereas the police don't. Luke is a clear-headed businessman with a jam-packed working schedule and an active social life. He's much too busy to waste time imagining he saw Ron if he didn't."

"He sure sounds like a reliable witness. Still, it's a bit like all the reports of people seeing flying saucers, isn't it? Nowadays if a movie star or a politician is doing something they'd much prefer to keep private, you can guarantee there'll be some Johnny-on-the-spot with a camera, ready to record the misdeed for the world to snicker over. But when an alien spaceship flies into Earth's orbit—which truly would be amazing news— nobody ever manages to point their camera and get a clear shot of the dang thing."

"I'm sorry, I'm not sure I understand your point."

Ellie gave another rueful laugh. "Sorry. My children always tell me they hope it's less muddled inside my head than it seems from the outside! What I'm trying to say is, with all these hundreds of people reporting to the police that they've spotted Ron eating or shopping and so on, how come nobody ever manages to click the button on their cell phones and get a picture? Much less actually *talk* to him?"

"In Luke's case, the answer is simple—because Ron ran away."

Ellie was silent for a moment. "Your friend...Luke...is suggesting Ron ran away because he knew he'd been recognized?" she asked finally.

"Yes, I'm afraid so. But that's not all. Luke hired a private investigator before he mentioned one word to me about what he'd seen. He wanted to be sure there wasn't a simple explanation for what had happened, something that had nothing to do with Ron. Unfortunately, everything the detective turned up suggested that the man Luke had seen was extremely anxious to avoid being found. At the very least, at this point we can say for sure there's a man out there, calling himself Stewart M. Jones, who looks just like Ron and is taking a lot of trouble to hide his tracks."

Avery outlined the remaining details of George Klein's investigation and explained the reasons why she believed they needed to track down Stewart Jones and resolve the issue one way or another. "It's my feeling we can't ignore what Luke saw just because the police keep telling us that high-profile murder cases always attract dozens of fictitious reports," she concluded. "Luke insists not only that he recognized Ron, but that Ron recognized him, too. And then immediately ran away. I think that instead of listening to the police we need to take Luke at his word, at least to the point of investigating some more."

For the first time, Ellie seemed to acknowledge there was a possibility her husband might be alive. "Ron's cousin insisted the man she saw made a dash for an escape route the moment he recognized her. That's what your friend is saying, too." She gulped in an audible breath. "Their stories sound too much alike to be comfortable."

"Yes, there do seem to be points of worrisome similarity."

"At the time, we dismissed our cousin's tale as just another example of Tricia Riley being her usual ditzy self. Maybe we should have paid closer attention."

"Hindsight is always twenty-twenty," Avery offered. "I've comforted myself with that thought a lot over the past six months."

"Me, too." Ellie gave a dry little laugh. "Sometimes it even makes me feel a bit better. Although in this case, maybe we're off the hook for ignoring our cousin's report. The fact is, there would have been no way to follow up on her story, however hard we might have tried. She chased the man into Nieman Marcus, but she didn't see where he went and she had no idea where he'd come from, so there were no leads for us to pursue."

"It's different this time," Avery said. "George Klein, the investigator working for us, believes there's at least a chance he'll be able to discover where this supposed Stewart M. Jones is living. And once he does that, we'll know if Mr. Jones is merely a man who looks a great deal like Ron or if he is, in fact, Ron." Avery still felt a shiver running down her spine when she expressed that possibility, even though a week had passed since Luke first broke the news.

"If it really is Ron and he ran away, it means he's hiding from us." Ellie's voice roughened. "He's hiding from all of us. From you, from me and from his children."

The words stabbed and Avery's stomach swooped. "Yes, I'm afraid it does seem that way."

Silence once again stretched out at the other end of the phone. Finally, Ellie spoke again. "After I heard that Ron had most likely been murdered and that there had almost certainly been another woman in his hotel room when he was killed, I thought nothing much worse could happen. Then I learned about you and Kate—that he had another wife and daughter in Chicago, a whole life I knew absolutely nothing about. But it still wasn't the end of the bad news. To crown it all, when Megan and Adam got back from Belize, I realized Ron had lied consistently about the small part of his life he did share with me. Worse, my own brother was deeply involved in the lies. It's funny, but after all those betrayals—and, God knows, they aren't exactly small ones—it still hurts to think Ron would do something as cruel as allowing us to believe he was dead when he wasn't."

"I had the same reaction," Avery confessed. "I held up pretty well in the days immediately following Ron's disappearance, despite realizing I'd spent twenty-eight years living with a man who wasn't my husband. But last week, after Luke told me he'd seen Ron, six months after he was supposed to have been viciously murdered, I went home and cried for three hours straight."

She astonished herself by the admission. More astonishing still was how good it felt to acknowledge the truth—to Ellie Raven, of all people. There was something so unforgivably cruel about allowing people to mourn your death when you were actually alive. She felt sick every time she considered the implications.

Had Ron—her companion and lover for twenty-eight years—really been that vicious?

"If it's any consolation, after about two days, I realized I wasn't devastated anymore." Avery could never have admitted as much to anyone else, but she was emboldened by the knowledge that she was talking to the person in the world most likely to share her feelings. "Instead, I was angry with Ron. More angry than I've been at any time since he was reported missing. In my opinion, it's past time for both of us to stop blaming ourselves for what happened and start putting the blame where it belongs—with Ron. If he's alive, Ellie, he's not just unfaithful, he's cruel."

"I'm not sure how I feel about the possibility that he could be alive." Ellie gave a laugh that broke into a sob. "Totally confused would be about right, I guess."

"I hope you agree that we should at least try to track down this person Luke saw."

"Yes, I do. Absolutely. I appreciate that you've hired a detective and taken on the job. Most of all, I appreciate the fact that you called to let me know what was going on. It was kind of you. Thank you, Avery. I'm real grateful."

Ellie hung up the phone before she realized that she hadn't actually said goodbye. She hoped Avery wouldn't think she intended to be rude; nothing could have been further from the truth. She was just so *tired* of having her life constantly thrown into turmoil because of Ron that for a minute she'd forgotten her manners.

She choked back a broken laugh when she realized

the drift of her thoughts. She'd just been talking to Ron's bigamous other wife about the possibility that their mutual husband had faked his own death. It seemed safe to assume that the etiquette books had no section dealing with manners for such an occasion.

What in the world was she going to do if Ron was alive? They'd spent the past three months actively persuading the courts that he was dead. If that turned out to be untrue, the legal mess would be monumental. Still, leaving aside worries about the legal tangle, how did she *feel?*

In a moment of stark self-knowledge, Ellie confronted the astounding fact that she didn't much care whether her husband was alive or not. The bottom line was that she didn't especially want to see Ron again, although that lack of enthusiasm made her feel guilty, damn him! She forced herself to push the guilt away and face her lack of interest head-on. The dogs sidled up to her, instinct alerting them to her misery. She scratched the top of Belle's head with one hand, and Bruno's with the other, and they snuffled comfortingly against her legs.

Her eyes blurred with tears she refused to shed as she watched Harry Ford, the sheriff of Stark County and a friend since grade school, finish his self-appointed task of setting the kitchen table for their dinner. Thank God for Harry! She was so glad he happened to have been here when Avery called, even more glad that he was tactful enough to give her a few seconds of silence to pull herself together.

With cutlery, place mats and napkins all arrayed to his satisfaction, Harry crossed to her side, pushing the dogs out of the way with the ease of a man who'd spent his life around animals and enjoyed their company without getting sentimental about their place in the hierarchy.

"Was that Avery Fairfax on the phone just now?" he asked, his eyes narrowing, and the sun lines wrinkling on his forehead as he took in her worried expression.

She nodded, thinking how kind and dependable his craggy features always looked. He was nothing like as handsome as Ron Raven, but she considered him a thousand times the better man. "Yes, it was Avery."

"I hope it wasn't bad news. She's never called you before, has she?"

She looked straight at him, sharply aware that her feelings toward her missing husband had suddenly become clear at the very moment when the facts of her situation were murkier than at almost any moment since she learned Ron had been declared missing, presumed dead.

"I want a divorce," she announced with a fierceness that made her voice shake. "I don't care how difficult it is to arrange. I want a divorce *right now.*"

Harry went very still for a moment, then he touched her gently on the cheek, his mouth quirking into a smile. "Gee, Ellie, I don't know. I'm an old-fashioned kind of a guy. I'd always thought we would get married first before we moved on to the divorce stage."

She knew he was teasing her, of course, but she was so flustered at the mention of marriage, even in a joke, that she could only mumble something garbled about not talking about him but about Ron, all the while hoping against hope that her cheeks weren't as flaming-red hot as they felt. Good grief, she was fifty-three, not twenty-three!

"You know what?" Harry stroked his hand down her neck and let it rest on her shoulder. "I'm mighty sick of talking about Ron Raven. In my opinion, the whole world has wasted far too much time discussing him for these past six months."

"But we can't avoid talking about him right now." Ellie sighed. "Avery didn't call just to be sociable. She called to say there's a chance Ron may not be dead after all."

"What?"

"You heard right." Ellie gave a small smile. "One of Avery's friends claims to have seen Ron at a restaurant in Washington, D.C. This friend apparently isn't the type to be mistaken about something so important."

"Is there any reason in the world to believe this friend?" His gaze narrowed. "Did they speak? Ron and this friend, I mean."

"No, Ron ran away. He had a woman with him. At least, according to Avery's friend."

"If it's true that it was Ron and that he ran way, we have to accept that he doesn't want to be found." Harry made a dismissive gesture. "Count me in with the folks saying I hope he succeeds in staying hidden."

"I don't understand the way his mind works," she said tiredly. "Even if he's bored with me and Avery, why would he hide from his kids?"

"How do you want me to respond to that, Ellie? I'm betting you can think of all the same unpleasant answers I can. And he most likely isn't hiding from you or his kids. Based on everything we've learned since Ron disappeared, it's clear he led a pretty ramshackle kind of a life. Could be any number of folks he's hiding from, not just you and Avery."

She stared at the dogs, not yet ready to look at Harry. "It's incredible to think he's made such a mess of his life that he has to pretend he's dead! What can he have done, for heaven's sake?"

Harry shrugged. "Who knows? Heck, Ellie, the man I thought I knew and you thought you married didn't exist. And the real Ron Raven probably isn't a man either one of us would like all that much."

"I feel stupid," she said in a soft voice. "Stupid and betrayed."

"Well, you sure aren't stupid and Ron can only betray you if you care. Otherwise, whatever he does, however malicious, he's just pissing into the wind."

"And that's almost the worst of it. After all those years of marriage, I don't believe I do care about him anymore. That's why I want a divorce. While I was talking to Avery just now, I realized I'm done with Ron Raven. I'm done dancing to his tune. As far as I'm concerned, it's over. Finished. I want to get on with the rest of my life."

"Good for you." He touched his knuckles to her cheek. "I'm real happy to hear it."

"Ron and I…we were married for thirty-five years. I was eighteen, fresh out of high school and crazy in love." Ellie realized she was sad for the girl she'd once been, but not for the woman she'd become. "When I heard Ron was dead, I felt I owed him a couple of years of grieving, at least. Now that I'm not sure whether he's dead or alive, I realize I don't owe him anything. He's let us down one time too many." She spoiled the effect of this assertive speech by gazing up at him uncertainly. "Does that make me a bad person, do you think?"

"No. It makes you a mighty smart person not to allow Ron to ruin your life. He sure isn't worth it." Harry's eyes held a smile that warmed her clear through to her insides. He took her hands and pulled her close, his gnarled hands rough and yet soothing as they moved on her arms, ending up clasped around her waist. He was almost six feet to her five foot one and he had to tilt her chin upward to see her face clearly when he spoke.

"This may not be the right moment, but what the hell. Is it too soon, Ellie, to talk about us? You know I'm in love with you, don't you? Have been for years, in fact." His mouth twisted into a wry smile. "I wasted a heck of a lot of good fishing time over the past ten years, wishing you weren't married to Ron."

"You did?" Ellie wasn't quite sure she believed him, but it was obscurely pleasing to picture Harry sitting on a riverbank, trout swimming past as he pined for her.

"I absolutely did."

"Maybe I still am married to Ron. If he's alive, I guess I must be."

"Either way, whether he's alive or not, let's talk to Cody Holmann and get him working on a divorce. I've no idea how you set about ending a marriage when you don't know if one of the parties is alive or dead, but Cody will know."

"Cody's already drowning under the paperwork from Ron's estate."

"Who cares? If Ron's alive, the paperwork for his estate is irrelevant. If Ron is dead, Cody has wasted a few days organizing a divorce instead of sorting out the mess the son of a bitch left of his finances." Harry brushed his thumbs across her cheeks, his gaze tender. "Heck, Ellie, I'm willing to wait if you say you're not ready to start a new relationship. But it doesn't sound to me as if that's what you're saying. The opposite, in fact."

"I don't know, Harry. We've been friends for so long and you're really important to me, but I have to admit I'm a bit gun-shy where love is concerned."

He put his finger against her lips, stopping her excuses. "We're both fifty-three years old, we've known each other since grade school. What's holding us back?"

"Well, there's Megan and Liam to think of. Not to mention your twins."

"That's an excuse, not a reason. Our kids are grown and out of state and doing well, thank God. Yours and mine, both. My ex has been happily remarried for ten years, so that's taken care of. Why do we need to hang around, waiting for the old biddies at the church supper to decide that enough time's passed since Ron disappeared for us to move on? Marry me, Ellie. I promise to make you happy."

"You do make me happy."

His smile sent her heart racing. "Trust me, it'll be even better when we're married."

Without expending any effort at all, Ellie could think of half a dozen reasons why it was crazy to consider marrying Harry Ford, even though she loved being in his company. The truth was that as sheriff he probably shouldn't get entangled with Stark County's most notorious widow. From her point of view, there was the indisputable fact that her last marriage hadn't worked out too well. You'd have thought her experiences with

Ron would make her suitably wary about jumping into a new relationship when it was barely six months since her marriage had been revealed as a sham and a fraud from top to bottom.

And yet, she realized her hesitation in accepting Harry's proposal had nothing to do with her feelings and everything to do with her sense of what was right and proper for a middle-aged woman whose husband had disappeared in a cloud of mystery and scandal. Then the full absurdity of her reservations struck her with powerful force. Heavens above, she and the rest of Ron's family had endured weeks as the focus of a nationwide media blitz. It sometimes seemed like everyone in the entire world knew her husband had been a bigamist, with a fancy, socialite second wife in Chicago. At least half the folk in Stark County were secretly convinced Ellie must have known the truth about Ron's marital status. Quite a few people had made it plain they suspected she'd kept quiet because Ron had been rich and she liked his money. What were the gossips going to say that could be worse than what had already been said? In Stark County, everyone knew everyone else's business, anyway, so it wasn't exactly a secret that Harry spent most of his free time with her. Marrying him probably couldn't tarnish either of their reputations one bit more than they were already tarnished.

The decision to say yes left her breathless, terrified and excited in about equal parts. She rather liked the heady strangeness of the feeling. She gave him a shy smile. "You're a good man, Harry, and a kind friend, and I'd like to marry you. That is, if you think the sheriff of Stark County can survive being married to the local scarlet woman. I don't want you to lose the next election because of me."

"Ain't gonna happen." He grinned. "And if it does, I'll just have to apply for a job as security chief at the fancy new resort you're planning on building here with Megan and Adam."

"I don't think you'd much like rounding up drunken guests after being sheriff for the whole county."

"Heck, Ellie, I'm not worried. I'm guessing I can stay sheriff until I decide it's time to retire. Marrying you isn't going to change that, for heaven's sake!" His smile deepened. "The only reason folks are going to care if I marry you is because all the other bachelors will be jealous I was the one who managed to catch such a sexy woman."

She blushed, hoping he didn't really believe she was a sexpot. She was afraid nothing could be further from the truth. If she'd been any good in bed, presumably Ron wouldn't have needed a second wife in Chicago, not to mention yet another woman to keep him company in his Miami hotel room.

She shoved the dispiriting thoughts aside and gave Harry another smile, this one more confident. "Then let's do it as soon as Cody can clear up my legal status. And to heck with the old biddies."

If Harry noticed that she hadn't actually said that she loved him, he was wise enough to make no comment. He tightened his hold around her waist and bent to kiss her full on the mouth. His kiss was gentle at first, and Ellie felt awkward and embarrassed. Eager as she was to stop living in the past, it struck her as somewhere between immoral and embarrassing to be kissing a man who wasn't Ron. Even without Ron to worry about, it seemed to her that when you were fifty-three, it was indecent to be making out with a new man. Or if not indecent, at least a tad on the ridiculous side.

But Harry, it turned out, was really good at kissing. Something caught fire deep inside and Ellie's entire body suddenly felt hot. Not a hot flash, she thought in wry amusement. Good Lord, she was experiencing the sort of intense, pulsing desire she remembered from years and years ago when she was fresh out of high school and the whole world was a magic playground, opening in front of her eyes. It was, all in all, a mighty fine feeling.

She allowed herself to relax and returned Harry's newly demanding kisses with a fervor that no longer embarrassed her. Instead it made her want to rip off her clothes and his, too. Apparently Harry felt the same way. "Come to bed with me," he whispered. "Come now, Ellie."

Years of being sensible intervened. "There's chicken for dinner roasting in the oven—"

Harry reached behind him and switched off the oven, one hand still resting on her waist. "Not anymore there isn't."

He didn't ask her again, just took her hand and led her into the bedroom that had once been Liam's and was now a guest room. She and Harry had been friends for so long she didn't have to explain to him that she couldn't have sex with him in the king-size bed she'd shared with Ron. He knew, thank goodness.

Harry also seemed to know a few interesting secrets about what else he needed to do to prove to her that she was something of a sexpot after all. Ellie supposed that tomorrow she might be horrified at the intensity and uninhibited passion of what was happening between her and Harry on the guest room bed. But for right now, not only did everything about her body feel absolutely wonderful, it was also gratifying to know, beyond any possibility of doubt, that Harry was enjoying the experience every bit as much as she was.

He took a long time making sure she was ready, and when he thrust into her she was already soaring so high that she was the one who climaxed first. Harry followed quickly and for a few minutes afterward she was content to collapse into his arms and marvel about how easy and right sex could sometimes seem and how perfect it was on those occasions. She felt flushed, satiated and obscurely triumphant.

When they'd both caught their breath and come back down to earth, Harry propped himself up on one arm and looked down at her, his gaze loving in the gathering darkness. "You're an amazing woman, Ellie," he said. "Thank you."

"You're pretty amazing yourself." She was glad the light had faded, because it wasn't easy for her to put her feelings into words, even when they were talking about sex and not deeper emotions. Ron had so battered her self-esteem she wasn't sure that she knew anymore what it meant to tell a man you loved him.

Harry rolled out of bed, tall, rangy, naked, and unbelievably desirable. Good Lord, she couldn't possibly be thinking that she'd like to make love again. She was fifty-three, for heaven's sake, with the wrinkles to prove it!

"Let's go and eat dinner," he said, turning to smile at her. "Then maybe we can try that again. If you want to, that is."

She returned his smile. "Yes, please. I definitely want to." She stretched luxuriously, glad that long days on horseback and all the hard work of running a ranch had kept her body supple. She'd lost ten pounds since Ron died, and that was enough to make a big difference since she was so short. When Harry looked at her like that, she could almost believe she was beautiful. Well, not an old hag, at least.

He glanced down at her, his smiles fading into an expression that sent a thrill of excitement chasing down her spine. "What the hell," he said, getting back into bed and pulling her close. "Dinner can wait. Seems I can't."

Ten

October 19, 2007

"Uncle Paul!" Kate made her way around the bakery counter and greeted her uncle with a surprised smile. "Nobody told me you were waiting for me out here."

He leaned forward and gave her cheek a friendly peck. "I didn't want to interrupt. I know how busy you are as it gets closer to the weekend. Don't worry, I wasn't bored. I entertained myself buying some of your wonderful pastries. I chose some éclairs that looked worth an extra hour on the treadmill." He held up a box tied with La Lanterne's distinctive forest-green-and-silver ribbon. "You've finished for the day, right? I thought we could go and get a coffee."

"Sounds great. I could use the caffeine. I've been at work since five and I'm wilting." Kate passed through the door he held open for her, waving goodbye to the two clerks behind the counter. "I can't remember how long it's been since you stopped by the bakery, Uncle Paul."

He grimaced. "Work's been insane the past six months, as you can imagine. Carrying the load alone and surviving the scandal surrounding Ron's disappearance… Still, that's no excuse. Family should come first."

"You've always been there when we needed you. I know Mom really appreciates the help you've given her since Dad went missing." That was true, even if Kate sometimes wished her uncle would stop treating the pair of them as fragile blossoms in acute need of a strong masculine arm.

"Thanks for the kind words. I've wanted to do everything possible for Avery after your father… Well, anyway, your father is the reason I came to find you. I just received an e-mail from George Klein." Paul patted his pocket. "I have a copy with me. I'll give it to you when we get to Starbucks. I thought we should discuss what he has to say face-to-face."

Kate looked up quickly, her heart thumping. "Has George managed to find the elusive Mr. Jones?"

"No, but he's obviously been working hard. Luke was right to recommend him. I'm impressed with his thoroughness."

Kate's heartbeat slowed. She fished in her coat pockets for her gloves, which she had apparently left in her car. The early afternoon was gray and rain looked imminent, but they had less than a block to walk so she shoved her hands into her pockets and lengthened her stride.

"The wind's bitter today." Paul hunched into the collar of his cashmere overcoat. "So much for global warming. I swear winter starts earlier in Chicago every year. I remember when October used to be the best month of the year. Nothing but sunshine and clear skies. Now look at what we're enduring."

Kate murmured something noncommittal, not bothering to point out that it had been sunny up until yesterday. She wasn't about to get involved in a discussion of climate change with her uncle, since he was convinced global warming was a myth concocted by mad scientists and tree-hugging liberals to make life difficult for hardworking entrepreneurs like himself.

Even in mid-afternoon the coffee bar was busy, but Paul managed to spot a vacant table and they were soon sitting in a comfortable corner with their steaming drinks. Kate took a luxurious sip of her foamy mocha latte and leaned back against the wall, stretching muscles aching after a busy day. "You look grim, Uncle Paul. I take it George Klein sent bad news?"

Paul rubbed worriedly at his chin. "I can't decide. Realistically, his report isn't definitive enough to be good or bad." His mouth turned down at the corners. "Besides, do we want Ron to be alive or dead? What would be good news? Damned if I know." He gave an apologetic grimace. "Sorry, I know it's your father we're talking about and I ought to be more tactful."

"That's okay. Where my father is concerned, the situation moved way past tact months ago." Kate frowned. "I guess I've reached the point where I just need to know the truth."

Paul nodded his agreement. "Me, too. Still, I'm angry enough about how Ron treated your mother—not to mention you and me and all our colleagues at Raven Enterprises—that it might be better if I never get the chance to confront him in person. Anyway, here's the e-mail from George Klein. I printed it out so you can judge for yourself."

Kate read through the two single-spaced pages. Their investigator had clearly been busy. He'd visited Sunrise, and discovered that it was a boutique selling gifts from Central America, ranging from specialty coffees and candies, to pottery handcrafted in Guatemala. Unfortunately, the nature of the store meant that few customers were regulars and nobody had recognized the picture of Ron Raven.

George had enjoyed better luck at the Mercedes dealership. He'd shown around multiple pictures of Ron Raven, and after some hesitation, one of the salesmen had agreed the man in the photos might be Stewart Jones. The same salesman had further identified Mr. Jones as an Australian diplomat on temporary assignment to Washington, D.C. He confirmed that Mr. Jones had recently sold a three-month-old Mercedes to the dealership. According to the salesman, Mr. Jones told them he'd been transferred back to Australia for an unexpected promotion, so nobody had given the early resale a second thought. In fact, the salesman pointed out with pride, Mr. Jones hadn't lost much money on the deal, since Mercedes vehicles held their value so well.

Some heavy-duty persuading on George Klein's part had convinced the salesman to part with the dealership's last-known address for Mr. Jones. Not surprisingly, the address turned out to be the same as the one appearing on the car's title documents, the ones George had already traced for Luke.

George had inquired if Mr. Jones had a wife or companion with him when he sold the car. The salesman confirmed that there was a Mrs. Jones and volunteered that she was an attractive, dark-haired woman in her early forties. He even managed to recall that her name was Heather. She had seemed pleasant, but she hadn't said much. The salesman was adamant that Heather had spoken without a Hispanic accent and he didn't think she was foreign. George had pressed the point, but the salesman stuck to his guns. The woman had seemed like a regular American to him and her name, Heather, certainly wasn't popular in the Hispanic community. So much for the theory that "Mr. Jones" might be traveling with Julio Castellano's niece. The e-mail finished with the information that George planned to return to his wife and kids in Chicago for the remainder of the weekend, since there were no obvious leads to follow, and he would look forward to receiving further instructions when Paul and the rest of Ron's family decided how to proceed.

Kate looked up from the report and took a sip of her lukewarm coffee. "What are we supposed to conclude?" She tapped the printed pages. "Have you spoken to George since you got his report?"

Paul nodded. "We had a brief conversation a couple of hours ago. He hasn't managed to come up with anything really new."

"So what's his honest-to-God opinion, minus all the professional humming and hawing in his e-mail? Does he think there's still a chance this Stewart Jones person is my father, or does he think Luke made a mistake?"

Paul pressed his fingers against his temples, massaging a headache that was almost visible. "Bottom line,

I'm guessing George has major doubts about Luke's story. He didn't come right out and say that, mind you. After all, Luke is the person who recommended him in the first place, so we're dealing with some loyalty issues, as well."

"The woman—Heather—sounds like the one Luke saw, don't you think?"

Paul shrugged. "Kinda, sorta. Luke guessed the age of the woman he saw at midthirties. The salesman suggests Mrs. Jones was in her early forties. It might be two takes on the same woman. Or it could be two different women."

"Luke and the car salesman both described the woman as petite and dark-haired."

"And there can't be more than a hundred thousand women in the D.C. area who are fortyish, small boned and dark haired." Paul sighed. "The fact is, George Klein has put in a fair bit of work on our behalf and we've learned almost nothing that we didn't know before he left for Washington."

"We have a car salesman who identified a picture of my father as Mr. Jones," Kate pointed out.

Paul shrugged. "But we always knew the man Luke saw looked like Ron, didn't we? Otherwise Luke would never have suggested he'd seen him."

Her uncle was right, of course. Finding a car salesman who said Mr. Jones looked like a photo of Ron Raven didn't really take them any closer to uncovering the man's true identity. Kate shook off a cloud of depression. "Did George Klein recommend any new line of investigation when the two of you spoke?"

"He suggested it might be worth spreading the net wider—showing the pictures of your father to more people in the hope of snagging a current address." Paul scowled at his paper coffee cup. "I don't know.... It seems a bit pointless to me."

But if they had no other leads to follow, what were their other choices? Kate wondered. "Don't you think we should do everything we possibly can to find Mr. Jones? Even if it seems like going over the same ground with different players."

"Yes, I guess we should." Paul sounded less than convinced. "But we could have George Klein running around for weeks and in the end we might achieve nothing except to have our lives thrown into turmoil by the constant uncertainty."

"Then your conclusion is that we should end the investigation now?"

Paul winced and stirred the dregs of his coffee. "That would be logical, wouldn't it, in view of what I just said? But I confess I haven't a clue what to recommend. I've been puzzling over this for the past four hours and all I've done is give myself a headache. That's why I brought the e-mail to you in person instead of just forwarding it. What's your opinion? It sounds as if you believe we should push a bit harder."

Kate leaned back, staring abstractedly at the line of customers snaking their way toward the counter. "Yes, I guess I do think we should go the last mile. The possibility that Dad is alive—that's huge. I don't feel ready to call it quits."

Paul nodded in agreement. "I see where you're coming from. Still, I'm not sure what going the last mile would mean at this point. Since the leads we gave George Klein don't seem to have panned out, what do we do next? Our options are telling George to go over the same ground one more time, despite the fact that he's been more than thorough. Or he could ask questions in other stores near where Sunrise is located. Another possibility is to suggest he should switch his attention to this Heather woman. Although I haven't an idea in the world how we would set about tracing her."

Kate gave a bleak smile. "When you put it like that, we don't have much to hang on to, do we? Maybe George will have some brilliant new idea up his sleeve. Investigating is his profession, after all."

Paul raised his coffee cup in a toast. "I can certainly drink to that. Here's hoping George is full of brilliant ideas. He seems good at his job so far, so I'm willing to hope." He looked unconvinced by his own optimism. "In the meantime, why don't you share this report with your mother and see what she wants to do? We can only hope she has a strong opinion one way or the other, and that would let you and me off the hook in terms of deciding whether to forge ahead or call a halt. For right now, the best I can suggest is that you should discuss the situation with Avery over the weekend and then give me a call first thing on Monday. After that, we'll either talk to George Klein on the phone, or arrange another meeting. I do have to go out of town next week, but I'm flexible about when."

"Have you forwarded this e-mail to Luke?" Kate was annoyed to discover that she couldn't mention Luke's name without her cheeks growing hot. "Does he have an opinion about what to do next?"

Fortunately her uncle was busy stuffing his napkin into his empty coffee cup, ready to throw it away, and he didn't look at her. "I forwarded the e-mail, but I haven't heard back from him. Was that the right thing to do?"

"Yes, of course."

Her voice, apparently, wasn't quite as brisk as her words. Paul looked up, his gaze kind but concerned. "I know the two of you were dating a while back and I thought you'd prefer it if I kept Luke informed, rather than forcing you to get in touch. I suggested that if he had any comments, he should send them to me. But I don't want you to feel I'm cutting you out of the loop."

"Thanks, although there's no need for you to be so tactful." She forced a bright smile. "My relationship with Luke was never serious enough for the breakup to be a big deal." The lie came out sounding smooth, but inside her stomach knotted.

Apparently she'd done a better job of hiding her feelings this time and Paul seemed satisfied. "That's good, then." He pushed back his chair and rose to his feet. "Julia and I have a dinner party tonight, so I have to run or I'll be in her black books. Tell your mother to give me a call anytime if she wants to discuss the situation." He pulled a wry face. "I'll try to come up with something clever and insightful to suggest. But here's the bottom line, Kate, at least as I see it at this point. Despite our desire to uncover the truth, it's possible we'll have to accept that we'll never know whether or not Luke saw your father."

"Never know if Dad is alive or dead?" Kate's stomach plummeted. "That would be worst of all."

"Yes, it's not a very satisfactory outcome, to say the least." Paul patted her hand, clearly trying to reassure, but his smile didn't quite cover the worry in his eyes.

Kate pushed away the remains of her mocha latte, which was cold and flat. Pretty much the way she felt. "Say hi to Aunt Julia for me. Tell her to give me a call next time she's coming into the city and we'll get together for lunch or something. It's been ages since I saw her."

"Will do." Paul gave her arm another encouraging squeeze. "Don't get down in the dumps, sweetie. Enjoy your weekend and I'll wait for your call on Monday morning. Give your mother a hug from me, will you? Tell her not to work too hard on fixing up her house."

"I will, but she won't listen. She's anxious to get her office set up."

"I know, but that little business of hers can get off the ground just as well after Christmas as before."

Kate reminded herself that her uncle couldn't help being a dyed-in-the-wool chauvinist. There was no way he would ever take Avery's attempts to start her own business seriously. She should simply appreciate him for the good qualities he had instead of grumbling to herself about attitudes he would never change.

She felt a surge of gratitude for the amount of time and energy her uncle had spent on Avery's affairs since Ron disappeared. She walked arm in arm with him to the door and left him with an affectionate kiss on the cheek. "Drive safely, Uncle Paul. I'll talk to you on Monday."

Eleven

October 20, 2007

Kate smothered a yawn and tried to think of a tactful way to ask Will Fairchild to take her home before they ordered dessert. This was their third date, and she'd realized a couple of hours ago that she should never have accepted his invitation to dinner. Will was Chicago's youngest alderman and an aspiring congressman. He was also great to look at and seemed a decent-enough guy. Unfortunately, she'd run out of things to say to him somewhere in the middle of date number two. The truth was, she would never have come out tonight if she hadn't been busy convincing herself that seeing Luke Savarini hadn't caused even a minor blip on her emotional barometer.

Studying the menu with more attention than it merited, she acknowledged that Will didn't deserve to have his feelings hurt because she was a self-deceptive moron with major hangups about a dead affair.

Settling on a pomegranate sorbet for dessert, she

resigned herself to toughing it out for another hour at least. Unfortunately, since tomorrow was Sunday, she didn't even have the excuse of a 6:00 a.m. start at the bakery as a reason for putting an end to their date.

Her cell phone rang just as the waiter walked away with their dessert orders. Normally she would have ignored the call and switched off the ringer. But listening to Will explain the intricate details of the city council's recent vote on municipal water purification was a bit more than she could endure in her current restless state. She ignored his frown and checked her phone, gratefully taking the call when she saw it was from her uncle.

"Uncle Paul, this is unexpected. What's up? Did Mom call you about the investigation? She said she would."

"No, I haven't spoken to your mother, but I have terrible news. Just terrible. George Klein is dead."

"Oh, no!" It felt as if a fist had slammed into her gut. "My God, how did he die? Was it a car accident?"

"It wasn't an accident at all. It's hard to take in, but it seems he's been murdered. He was mugged in a parking garage at O'Hare airport. He was dead when the paramedics got there. The cops estimate he'd been dead for quite a few hours. His body was stuffed in a corner behind a pillar and nobody found it for a while." Paul's voice wasn't quite steady.

"Murdered? Oh my God! I can't believe it!"

"I'm afraid it's true. Talk about being in the wrong place at the wrong time. This is terrible. Just terrible."

Will was looking at her with a mixture of concern and disapproval. His politician's antennae had apparently been turned on by her mention of murder and he made no effort to pretend he wasn't listening to her call. Avoiding his gaze, she murmured an apology and headed for the lobby where she could continue the conversation in private.

"When did this happen?" she asked her uncle. "You said the police think he was killed several hours ago."

"Right, they're estimating late yesterday night."

"That would be when his plane got in from D.C."

"Yes, it would. His wife had already reported him missing this morning, but the police didn't do anything, of course. They never do until at least forty-eight hours have passed."

George Klein was an acquaintance, not a friend, but Kate realized she was shivering in shocked reaction to the news of his death. "Oh my God, that poor woman! They have kids, too, don't they? I saw pictures of two young boys on his desk when we were in his office."

"I don't want to think about his wife, much less his kids." Paul's voice cracked and he cleared his throat. "It's terrible," he said yet again. "Just terrible." Shock seemed to have reduced his vocabulary to a single stock expression of grief.

Kate recovered from her initial surprise enough to wonder how her uncle had heard the news. "Did you see a report about the murder on television? Is there any chance they've made a mistake?" Although it was hard to imagine what that mistake might be.

"No, I didn't see it on TV. The police called me. Unfortunately, there's no chance of a mistake."

"The police called *you?*" Why on earth would the cops call her uncle because George Klein had been killed?

The connection between the two men had been trivial, at least from a law enforcement perspective. "Good heavens, how did the cops even find out that we knew him?"

"The muggers took George's wallet and his money," Paul explained. "When his body was first found, the police tagged him as a John Doe. But when they stripped the body at the morgue, they found one of my business cards that had slipped through the lining of his jacket. Since the muggers had left no other identification, the police called me. They told me they didn't know who it was they'd found, just that a dead body had been found at the airport and he had my business card."

"Oh my God!" No wonder her uncle sounded so upset. "Did they ask you to identify George's body?"

"Yes, they did, since they had no other lead. That's an experience I never want to repeat." Paul broke off abruptly and then said nothing more for a few seconds. "The police drove me to the morgue a couple of hours ago. They took me right to where the body...to where they had him in a drawer. Now they're driving me home. I'm in a police car right now. And feeling a bit shaky, to be honest."

"I'm so sorry, Uncle Paul. Is Aunt Julia home? Will you be all right?"

"Julia's gone to visit our daughter, but I'll be fine." Paul tried, not very successfully, to sound upbeat. "It's just that I'd never seen a dead person before. Not in real life. Amazing, isn't it? I'm fifty-three years old, and I'd never seen a dead person. I guess that makes me lucky." His voice trailed away. Clearly, at this precise moment he was feeling anything but lucky.

"Are you sure you don't want company? I could come—"

"No, really, I'll be fine." He drew in a deep breath. "The experience was more draining than I expected, that's all. The morgue looks clean and impersonal, but the bottom line is that you know inside all those drawers are people who've died violent or unexpected deaths. People who had families and friends who love them. That's a brutal fact no amount of stainless steel and disinfectant can disguise."

Will came into the lobby and mouthed a silent question, inquiring if there was a problem. Kate shook her head, wishing he would go away. She spent another few minutes trying to console her uncle and was glad to hear him sounding a bit more cheerful when they finally hung up.

"What's happened?" Will asked as soon as she stopped talking. "Can I help?" He kept his expression scrupulously polite, but she could tell he was irritated and feeling neglected.

She didn't have the mental energy to soothe him. "I just heard a friend has been murdered," she said. "I'm sorry to cut the evening short, Will, but I have to leave." If she stayed, she was likely to end up provoking a fight that he didn't deserve.

"*Murdered?* Are you sure?" Will stared at her askance. He was probably thinking that her friends weren't any more respectable than her family, Kate reflected ruefully. First her bigamist father disappeared in scandalous circumstances, now a friend had been murdered. By this time tomorrow, he would undoubtedly be grateful that she'd removed herself and her squalid associates from his life.

"Yes, I'm afraid I'm sure. My friend was mugged. He was robbed and then killed at O'Hare airport."

"I'm sorry to hear that. What a dreadful way to lose a friend, or anyone for that matter." Will showed genuine regret and sympathy, but then his alderman reflexes kicked in. "It's surprising, too, because O'Hare actually has an excellent safety record. Their crime statistics are on the low side, given that it's the world's busiest airport. Law enforcement there is extremely efficient—"

"I'm sorry. I have to get home." At this precise moment, Kate wasn't up to sitting through a lecture on the wonders of civic life in the Chicago area.

"But the waiter just brought our desserts!" Will's smile wavered between pained and exasperated. "There's nothing you can do for your friend or his family right at this moment, so we might as well finish our meal, don't you think?"

Will couldn't help being an idiot, Kate reflected, and she should control her impatience. It was her own fault for having agreed to go out with him when she'd spent most of their previous date with her teeth gritted so that she wouldn't accidentally tell him what she really thought about ninety percent of the stuff he rambled on about.

"I guess I would really prefer to skip dessert," she said. "Sorry, but I'm just not in the mood for making small talk right now. Maybe they could put your chocolate cake in a box to take home?"

"Of course," Will said stiffly. "If you feel you must leave, I'll make the arrangements." It was now his turn to grit his teeth. They definitely needed to stop seeing each other or they'd both be paying a fortune for restorative dental work.

Kate gave a giant sigh of relief when Will dropped her off at her front door and they survived the parting without either one of them being actively rude to the other. She said good-night, thanked God she would never have to see him again and walked into her narrow row house, eager for the rush of comfort and solace that usually greeted her the moment she unlocked her front door.

Tonight there was no solace to be had. Her bright living room looked jarringly out of synch with her bleak mood and she paced between the sunporch and the kitchen, not sure what she wanted to do, or even why the news of George's death had struck her so hard.

She would have to let her mother know what had happened, assuming Paul didn't make the call. But not tonight. Avery had never actually met George Klein, so she would be sorry to hear of his death, but it would be an impersonal sort of grief. It would be pointless to ruin her mother's night simply to quell her own feeling of restlessness. Maybe she was acquiring an unhealthy touch of her uncle's overprotective attitude, Kate reflected ruefully, but her mother had gone through so much, the desire to shield her was bound to be strong.

Luke, on the other hand, had known George quite well and needed to be told the news. The relationship between the two men had been based on professional services, but Kate had sensed they genuinely liked each other, in addition to admiring each other's business skills. Luke ought to be told what had happened before he heard some garbled TV version of the murder.

It was barely nine-thirty and Luke would almost certainly still be at work. If he was at Luciano's, he would be a mere fifteen-minute drive away. Even if he was at one of his other restaurants, it would take her no more than half an hour to get there at this time on a Saturday night.

Kate dialed the number for Luciano's and got lucky on her first attempt. According to the hostess, Luke had been there all evening and had not yet left for the night.

"Would you tell him that Kate Fairfax needs to see him urgently? I'll be there in twenty minutes or less. Please ask him to wait for me."

Unlike her visit last week, this time Luke didn't keep her hanging around in the lobby. The hostess apparently had instructions to bring Kate straight to him as soon as she arrived. Once again, Luke had decided to meet her in his office off the main kitchen. The tiny room was just as stark here as at Luciano's II or at Trattoria in Oakbrook. Tonight, though, she barely noticed the austerity.

"Hello, Kate." Luke sounded somber but not unfriendly, although he didn't step out from behind the barrier of his desk.

"You must be wondering why I've come. I'm sorry, Luke, but I have bad news—"

"Is it about George Klein?"

"Yes." She saw the sadness in his eyes. "You've already heard, then."

"That he's been murdered? Yes, I heard."

"I'm so sorry, Luke. I hoped to get here before you caught the reports on TV."

"I appreciate your efforts, but I didn't see the news on TV. Your uncle called a few minutes ago." He expelled a jagged breath. "I'm still in shock."

"Me, too. I know it's a cliché, but George seemed so alive when we saw him on Tuesday. I can't visualize him dead." She realized she was on the verge of tears and swallowed hard. "I can't stop thinking about his wife and kids."

"George and his wife had a great marriage. She's a special-ed teacher and he was so proud of her." Luke cleared his throat. "I've been trying to decide if the fact they were so happily married makes her loss better or worse."

"Worse in the short term, I'm sure, but maybe better in the long run?"

"God, I hope so."

Kate hoped so, too. "George's children are just little, aren't they?" The photos she'd seen in his office were haunting her. In the wake of her father's disappearance, she had become all too good at imagining other people's grief. The boys had looked so happy—and so heart-breakingly young. Their sorrow gnawed at her.

"They're in middle school," Luke said. "I'm afraid that's an especially bad age to lose a parent."

She shivered. "God, yes, old enough to know what's happened and too young to understand why."

"They would never be old enough to understand why their father had to die in a parking garage at O'Hare airport. There's no rational explanation for something so cruel." Luke swung away from her, running his hands through his hair. "Jesus, I hope they find the guys who did this soon."

The murderer had probably been a drug addict, Kate thought. It seemed obscene that so much grief might have been caused by some crackhead who needed a fix.

She wrapped her arms around her body, craving warmth she was unable to find. She had barely known George Klein and yet the horror of his death lurked in every mental corner.

In the wake of her father's disappearance she'd become reasonably adept at analyzing her own emotions, and she recognized that her reaction to George's murder was too intense for the degree of their acquaintance. She'd met the man only once, and their conversation had focused strictly on business. Somewhere along the line, though, her feelings toward him must have become entangled in her chaotic feelings about her father. George's murder seemed to have triggered buried feelings from the trauma of those dreadful days following Ron's disappearance. Old pain was taking on a new form.

Luke turned around again, but this time he guarded his expression. In the old days he would never have hidden his feelings from her, and Kate found herself regretting the loss of openness. Tonight she craved honesty, not politeness used as a deliberate barrier to keep her at a distance from his sadness.

"Thank you for coming in person to tell me about George." His smile underlined the formality of his attitude. She yearned for one of his real, honest smiles. "I appreciate the thought, Kate. It was kind of you."

It was a dismissal, but Kate discovered she wasn't ready to be dismissed. "I've decided to go to Virginia next week," she said. Until the words were spoken, she had no idea she'd been planning any such thing. Oddly, her restlessness quieted as soon as she verbalized the commitment.

"Somebody needs to pick up the investigation where George was forced to leave off," she said. "I want that person to be me, not just another detective picked at random from the Yellow Pages."

Luke's expression remained frozen into a decent imitation of a marble statue. "What, exactly, are you planning to investigate, Kate? As far as I can tell, George Klein's last report suggests there are no serious leads left to pursue."

"I disagree. I realize there's no point in going back to the Mercedes dealership, but there are dozens of other stores in the same plaza as the Sunrise boutique. Who knows if somebody might recognize my father in one of those stores?"

"It's a very long shot. Not to mention the fact that you'd probably encounter a fair degree of hostility from most of the clerks."

She shrugged, becoming more determined in the face of Luke's opposition, mild as it was. "The store clerks can't do anything worse than refuse to help me, and the stakes are high. I'm trying to find out if my father is alive and in hiding, or murdered and floating in the Atlantic Ocean. It seems to me that's worth the cost of a plane ticket and a couple of days off work."

Luke hesitated for a moment, then walked over to his desk. Without speaking, he swiveled his laptop around so that she could see the screen. It was open to a travel Web site, with a grid showing times and prices of planes flying from Chicago into Washington's Dulles airport. A flight for Sunday morning was highlighted.

She blinked. "I don't understand. How did you know I was going to Washington?"

"I didn't know. I'd already decided to go there myself." Luke shrugged, as if deprecating his own decision. "George's death somehow makes me even more determined to get some answers about what I saw in my cousin's restaurant."

"It's kind of you to make the effort, but there's no need—"

"There's every need. I'm the one who claims to have seen Ron Raven. I should be the one to track him down."

"I'm truly appreciative of your offer to help, Luke, but tracking down Stewart Jones is my job, not yours."

Luke's expression finally relaxed into wry amusement. "Look, Kate, we can waste time fighting about who has more right to traipse around Herndon being ignored by salesclerks, or we could quit arguing and agree to go together."

God help her, she was tempted. Kate mentally listed a dozen reasons why it would be insane to spend any more time than she had to in Luke's company. Being with him was like eating chocolate fudge torte: great while you were doing it, hideous when you had to get rid of the extra pounds.

"This is a really busy season for both of us," she said, making a final play for common sense. "It's not smart for two of us to take time off work when the holidays are just around the corner. You know how crazy November gets in our business."

He didn't reason with her, just caught her gaze and held it captive. "Don't use work as an excuse, Kate. Let's at least be honest with each other, since honesty seems to be in short supply when anyone tries to deal with Ron Raven and his legacy."

"Okay, then, here's the honest reason we should fly solo. We cause each other pain when we're together."

"We used to, back in March, but we've both moved on since then. Surely to God we can behave like civilized human beings for a couple of days."

"Can we?" The question revealed far more about the state of her emotions than she cared to have on display.

"Of course we can. The truth is, we'll be more effective if we work as a team. I really care about proving the man I saw in Bruno's restaurant was Ron Raven. You really care about finding out if your father is alive. That's a winning combination." His voice softened. "Come with me. Please."

She clearly suffered from a severe and debilitating mental illness, one that made her behave like a drooling idiot whenever she spent too much time in Luke Savarini's company. There was no other way to explain the fact that she said yes. She would go with him to Virginia, and not at some distant point in the future, either. She actually agreed to fly out tomorrow, before the trail leading to Stewart Jones went stone cold.

Mentally listing all the e-mails she would have to send before crawling into bed to catch a few hours' sleep, Kate left Luke confirming their plane reservations and hurried home. She carefully ignored the small inner voice telling her that she'd done some pretty dumb things in the past year, but that agreeing to investigate something as emotionally fraught as her father's disappearance with Luke Savarini had to be right up there among the very dumbest. It was astonishing how good it felt to be doing something so incredibly, certifiably stupid.

Twelve

The early-morning plane heading from O'Hare to Dulles was crammed with passengers despite the fact that it was a Sunday. From Luke's point of view, the jam-packed plane was fortunate since it meant that Kate got seated three rows ahead of him. He was deeply grateful for the forced separation. Last night, flying to D.C. together had seemed a reasonable plan. This morning, he realized he must have lost brain function for a crucial few minutes. In the bright light of morning, he couldn't produce a single reason why he had willingly submitted himself to the torment of spending two whole days in Kate's company.

She had arrived at the airport gate looking like every man's dream of sexual fulfillment gift-wrapped in tight jeans and a soft cream sweater. By expending a six-month supply of willpower, Luke managed not to drool. He even managed to haul his gaze away from her perfect breasts a crucial couple of seconds before she came to a halt in front of him. At which point he realized that staring into her spectacular blue eyes wasn't much of an improvement in terms of lust-control.

In the end, he mumbled a greeting with his eyes fixed grimly on a spot somewhere to the left of her ear. That meant he only had to cope with a peripheral glimpse of her, combined with the teasing allure of her perfume. She was wearing some light and haunting scent that reminded him of hillside flowers in the Tuscan village where his great-grandparents had lived. He wanted to bury his face in the crook of her neck and draw deep, intoxicating breaths. Instead, he muttered something about needing to buy a book before takeoff and retreated to lick his wounds at the nearest kiosk.

Once they boarded the plane, he could only see the top of her head, thank God. But instead of using the respite to plan tactics and strategy for finding Stewart Jones in the short time he could afford to take off work, he wasted the two-hour flight torturing himself by recalling every time he could remember that the two of them had ever had sex. His memory in this regard seemed to be crystal clear and highly specific. What's more, it seemed they had had mind-blowing sex on a hell of a lot of occasions. By the time they landed, he was completely aroused and nursing a correspondingly foul mood.

They picked up the rental car with a blessed lack of hassle, which meant that he was just able to restrain himself from snapping the head off the unsuspecting guy standing behind the counter. Kate, on her best behavior, agreed that he should drive since he was more familiar with the roads around D.C. than she was. At least that compelled him to keep his eyes away from her and on the road. Luke ordered himself to count his blessings.

He'd printed out MapQuest directions to the Reston Town Shopping Center where Sunrise was located and Kate volunteered to navigate if needed. He thanked her effusively. They were both being so damn polite they were almost guaranteed to explode from the strain before the day was over.

"Do you think we should start by questioning the Sunrise people?" Kate asked as they neared their exit from the Dulles toll road. "I know George already interviewed them, but it's the one store we know for sure that Stewart Jones shopped at. It also might give us a chance to get the details of our pitch polished before we move on to fresh territory."

"Good point. As for what story we spin, my suggestion is to stick as close to the truth as possible."

"Admit up front that we were the clients who sent George Klein to question them last week, you mean?"

"Yes." Luke swerved to avoid a kamikaze cab driver, a forcible reminder that Washington might be a smaller town than Chicago, but traffic in this area obeyed none of the mild-mannered, Midwestern rules of his home town. "We should explain that we hired George to search for your father and that he was killed in an accident over the weekend. The fact that you're looking for such a close family member might engage the store clerks' sympathies."

"And make them more willing to go over the same ground." Kate nodded her agreement. "Should we tell them George was murdered, do you think? My guess is that we shouldn't."

"I agree, definitely not. You and I both know that George's death had nothing to do with his search for Ron Raven, but if we tell people he was murdered, they might decide they would be safer keeping quiet—even if by some chance they actually know something." Luke was relieved they seemed able to discuss their mission for the day without subnotes of tension erupting to the surface and causing problems. Maybe they were going to rub through these two days without disaster after all. His mood lifted a few notches at the prospect.

Reston was a busy shopping area, they discovered a few minutes later, and parking was at a premium. Crowds thronged the upscale shopping plaza where Sunrise was located, bustling in and out of cafés and stores that lined three sides of a cobbled square. A giant bookstore anchored one arm, and a big chain restaurant on the other had a constant stream of people arriving for brunch. From their spruced-up clothes, it looked as if several of them had just come from church services.

"If they have this many people shopping here every day, there isn't much chance that anyone is going to remember a customer from two weeks ago." Kate surveyed the busy plaza with disfavor. "And look, there are tons of office buildings on the opposite side of the road, so it's probably just as busy during the week."

Luke had to agree. A regular customer would be remembered, of course. But if Ron Raven was determined to hide, he wasn't likely to make the mistake of returning often to the same store. Kate's gloomy expression suggested she'd already arrived at the same depressing conclusion.

Sunrise turned out to be one of the smaller stores in

the plaza, tucked away in a corner well removed from the main road. When they went in, there was only a single clerk on duty and two customers waiting to be served. The fact that the clerk was busy gave them a welcome chance to look around and get their bearings.

Luke chose some dark-roasted Guatemalan coffee beans and Kate wandered around the store before picking out a plump, dark-skinned angel from an enchanting selection of pottery figures. A hand-lettered sign indicated the little statues were sculpted and painted by Mayan Indians from the village of Todos Santos in northwest Guatemala. They waited until they were the only customers in the store before taking their selections over to the counter.

"Hi," the clerk said, closing the drawer of the cash register from the previous transaction. "It's a lovely day, isn't it? Perfect fall weather."

They both smiled their agreement. "We're especially enjoying it," Luke said. "We flew in this morning from Chicago and it was looking a lot like winter when we took off." He held out Kate's angel, along with his coffee and a credit card.

"I love the angel you chose. Aren't the expressions on those figurines wonderful?" The clerk smiled at Kate as she swiped Luke's card. "They're all hand-painted by the village women in Todos Santos and it's been a great new source of income for them. Usually the cash in those villages remains firmly in the hands of the menfolk."

While she waited for the transaction to process, the clerk wrapped the angel in tissue and tucked it into a sturdy bag. "There. I hope you enjoy the coffee, too. You'll find it's robust without being bitter."

"That sounds perfect," Kate said as Luke signed the charge slip. "Actually, we were hoping you could help us with some information about a personal matter."

"Personal?" The clerk appeared instantly wary, her smile vanishing.

"My father went missing more than five months ago." Kate spoke quickly, so that the clerk's remaining goodwill wouldn't have time to dissipate. "He disappeared without a trace and for a long time we had no idea where he might be. Then, just recently, we learned that he'd been seen in this area. We even have a credit card receipt from this store, signed by him, so we know he shopped here at least once. His name is Stewart Jones."

"I'm sorry, miss," the clerk said, continuing to look wary. "I wouldn't know anything about that."

"We hired an investigator to see if he could trace Kate's father." Luke took over the spiel. "The detective's name was George Klein and he was in here on Thursday or Friday morning. I understand you were very helpful—"

"Not me." The clerk denied the suggestion that she'd been helpful with as much fervor as if she'd been accused of committing a heinous crime. "I wasn't here last week. The owner of the store is always here from Monday to Friday and she might be able to help you. Her name is Alana Gomez and she'll be back at work tomorrow."

Obviously searching for an excuse to avoid any more conversation, the clerk handed over a business card from the little display rack on the counter. "Alana will be here no later than 9:00 a.m. You might want to come back then."

"Thanks, we appreciate your help," Luke said, not yet ready to give up. If this particular clerk hadn't spoken to George Klein, it might mean she had information to share that the detective hadn't known about.

The clerk clearly wished they would leave the store, but she seemed reluctant to be outright rude to a woman searching for a missing parent. Luke pressed lightly against Kate's back in a silent cue that she should take over the questioning again.

Kate not only picked up on his hint, she played the sympathy card. "If you wouldn't mind answering another question, I'd be so grateful. As you can imagine, my family has been worried for months and everyone was excited when we finally got a lead on my father's whereabouts." Kate was careful not to appear overeager or threatening as she reached into her purse for a picture of Ron Raven.

"I guess I already explained that we have a copy of a charge slip that shows my dad must have been in this store on the morning of October 3. I know it's stretching things to ask if you can remember a customer from three weeks ago, but this is a picture of the man we're looking for. As I mentioned already, his name is Stewart Jones."

Kate handed over the photo and the clerk studied it reluctantly, but with attention.

"Here's the receipt from the transaction that day." Luke passed a copy across the counter.

The clerk's forehead furrowed as she studied both the sales slip and the photo. "He does seem a bit familiar," she conceded. She stared at the picture some more and then shrugged. "I'm sorry. I think he might have been a customer of ours, but I don't remember a thing about him. He certainly isn't a regular. But Alana went to the airport to pick up her parents on the third, so I was helping out by working here that day. Not all day, of course, but for a few hours. It's quite possible that I served your father, because the man in that photo does look vaguely familiar."

Unfortunately, such fuzzy recognition wasn't going to get them anywhere. "Kate's father may have had a woman with him," Luke said, determined to explore every possible avenue before throwing in the towel. "The woman we're talking about has a petite build and she's slightly below average height. She's in her late thirties, with dark curly hair. We heard one report that her name is Heather. Does that ring any mental bells?"

"No, I'm afraid not." The clerk shook her head vigorously.

"The name Heather may not be correct," Kate said. "Her name might be Consuela Mackenzie. Consuela is from Belize." She shot a faintly challenging glance in Luke's direction. She clearly recognized that by identifying the unknown woman by the name Julio Castellano had claimed for his niece she was taking a giant leap based on nothing more than a hunch and a story woven by a convicted murderer. "Since this store features a lot of pottery from Mayans living in the area on the border between Guatemala and Belize, it seems quite likely that Consuela would enjoy coming here to shop."

The clerk's face lit up in a surprised smile. "Consuela Mackenzie? Oh, of course I know Connie! She's been in here several times. She loves the coffee and the little jars of sauce we import for cooking chicken Pepian. Alana, the owner of the store, is from Guatemala, but I'm from Belize, too, you know, or at least I was born there." She actually chuckled. "I'm old enough to remember when it was still called British Honduras."

"What a coincidence!" Kate seized on the link, however tenuous. "My uncle and his wife were just in Belize and they said it was a beautiful country."

"Oh, it is. And so unspoiled in a lot of areas. Where-abouts were they? Your uncle and aunt, I mean."

"In the southwest, mostly. And of course they visited Belize City."

"A lot of cruise ships stop in Belize City nowadays, but not so many people travel inland."

"My uncle flew in from Mexico. It was quite a journey, I believe." Which happened to be the truth, even if not quite in the way it sounded.

"Yes, we still don't have very good transportation links to get tourists in and out of Belize. Our population is too small." The clerk, increasingly mellowed by Kate's appreciation of her native land, studied the photo of Ron Raven again. "You know, now that I'm looking at this picture in context, I'm sure this man has been in here a couple of times with Connie. He's your father, you say?"

"Yes. We...his family,...think he must have lost his memory," Kate said. "Otherwise, we can't imagine why he wouldn't come home. There were no arguments, no disagreements of any sort before he disappeared. We're really worried about him."

"I'm sure you must be." The clerk hesitated for a moment, then turned away and busied herself rearranging the jar of pens by the cash register before deciding to share her thought.

She finally stopped fussing with the pens. "I don't mean to pry, but is your mother still married to your father?"

"No, absolutely not. Not for years and years." Kate smiled and Luke appreciated the irony of her entirely truthful answer. "You don't have to worry that we might be angry because my dad has found a new companion. We just want to make sure his health is good. That's all."

The clerk was visibly relieved. "Well, if I'm remembering right, I don't think you have any worries. The man with Connie didn't strike me as a person who'd lost his memory. The opposite, in fact. He struck me as one of those men who is very confident about themselves, you know? He was never rude to Connie or angry, but I sure got the impression that he was the man in charge of that relationship."

"That sounds like my dad. He always wants to be in charge." Kate deliberately made light of the clerk's comment, although Luke could see that she was holding on to her self-control by the thinnest of threads. "I'm so anxious to get in touch with him. Is there any way you could look up their address? Maybe you have a record of it for some reason. We'd really appreciate any help you can give us in contacting them."

The clerk immediately looked wary again. "Next time they come into the store, I'll be sure to let them know you're trying to find them. Why don't you write down your names and address, and then I'll have it handy to give to them?"

There was almost zero chance that Ron Raven would

come back to this store, Luke thought, watching Kate write down her contact information. Ron knew he'd been spotted and would never run the risk of returning to one of his old haunts.

"It would be a major breakthrough if you provide some way for us to contact Consuela Mackenzie," Luke said. "Even if Kate's father isn't living with her, she probably knows his current address. As you can imagine, quite apart from all the emotional turmoil, there are several legal issues pending. We would be so grateful if you could supply us with an address…."

"Oh, heavens, I couldn't give you Connie's address even if I knew it."

"How about her phone number? Do you have a phone number for her?"

The clerk hesitated, and then shook her head, her hands clasping to form a sturdy barrier. Her body language was the epitome of resistance and Luke resigned himself to the fact that they were going to get nothing more out of her.

"We talk about Belize when Connie comes into the store, but we're not friends, or anything. Even if I knew her address, it would be completely against store policy to share it with anyone." She shot an apologetic glance toward Kate. "I'm sorry."

"I can understand that." Luke hid his frustration as best he could. Store rules undoubtedly forbade the sharing of personal information, and there was no reason for the clerk to put helping total strangers ahead of her job security. That, of course, was part of the reason they'd been paying George Klein to investigate: he had years of experience developing clever techniques for persuading people to part with confidential information. Experience would have enabled George to gauge whether a hundred-dollar bill slipped across the counter was more likely to produce Connie's address or an irate demand for them to leave the store. With this particular clerk, Luke was pretty sure it would be the latter.

Kate made several more attempts to extract contact information, but the clerk became less cooperative as the minutes ticked past. Eventually, Luke decided there was nothing for it but to thank her and move on. He propelled a reluctant Kate from the store and led her into a bistro located a couple of doors down.

"We weren't going to get anywhere, Katie. We were just raising the hostility level."

"But she knew their address, I'm sure."

"Yes, I think she did. If we don't get lucky anywhere else, we can come back tomorrow and talk to her boss." He glanced at the business card. "Alana Gomez. Since Alana's the owner, she at least wouldn't worry that talking to us could get her fired."

"Presumably George already talked to her. If George couldn't weasel an address out of her, why would we?"

"Because a daughter is more sympathetic than a paid investigator?" He handed Kate the bistro's lunch menu in an effort to distract her. It was now almost two and most of the lunchtime crowd had dissipated, so they had been seated at a table by the window with a pleasant view onto the sunny plaza.

"I think I'm too angry to eat." Kate drew in a shaky breath, putting down the menu after a single quick glance. "Until now, a big part of me assumed that you'd made a mistake in believing you'd seen my father. But after talking to that clerk, it's crazy to keep pretending Stewart Jones is an Australian diplomat who happens to look like my dad. It's glaringly obvious that Stewart Jones and Ron Raven are the same person."

"More and more likely, but still not certain."

Kate gave an impatient shake of her head. "If Mr. Jones was simply a look-alike, he wouldn't be running around the D.C. area with precisely the same woman from Belize that we had already been told was in my father's hotel room the night he supposedly died."

Her logic was irrefutable, and Luke wasn't willing to soothe her with lies or platitudes. He recognized that she was more wounded than angry, which was okay, since he was feeling enough anger for both of them. This ultimate deception of her father's must hurt in the deepest and most painful way. Damn Ron Raven, he thought viciously. As if it wasn't bad enough to be a bigamist, what the hell kind of a man disappeared for months, allowing his wives and children to believe that he'd been brutally murdered?

Luke ordered bowls of homemade cream of asparagus soup for both of them, since Kate didn't seem to care what she ate at this point and soup was easy to get down. Despite the unresolved tensions that lingered from finding her in bed with his high school buddy, he wanted to make the hurt in her eyes go away. And, apparently, he was enough his mother's son to believe that hot food would do the trick.

While they waited for their meals to arrive, he asked her to fill him in one more time on the details of Adam's experiences in Belize. The fact that Ron Raven was keeping company with Consuela Mackenzie suggested it was important to learn as much as possible about her. Talking about Consuela provided the added bonus that focusing on a factual account of complicated events might stop Kate brooding over her father's multiple betrayals.

Kate seemed willing enough to talk about Consuela. She explained in more detail than before how Adam, her mother's younger brother and the president of a bank in rural Georgia, had joined forces with Megan, Ron's daughter by his Wyoming wife. Together, Adam and Megan had flown to Mexico City on the trail of three million dollars that Ron Raven owed to Adam's bank. Since the Flying W ranch, Megan's family home, was the collateral for the loan, she had at least as much interest as Adam in tracing the missing money.

The trail had eventually led them to a platinum mine in rural Belize where, they discovered, Ron Raven had invested millions of dollars. When Adam and Megan's inquiries threatened the profitable operation of a platinum smuggling ring, they had been grabbed from their beds and taken captive. Adam and Megan both swore they would have been murdered and their bodies tossed to the desert vultures if not for the intervention of Julio Castellano.

The circumstances of their rescue had left Adam and Megan with little time for chitchat, but Julio Castellano did explain that the woman in the Miami hotel room with Ron Raven was called Consuela Mackenzie and that she was Julio's own niece. Consuela Mackenzie, at least according to Julio, was in love with Ron and had been for some time. It was because of Adam and Megan's adventures in Belize that Ron's wives and children had learned the name of the mystery woman sharing Ron's hotel room on the night of his disappearance.

Julio Castellano had saved Adam and Megan from certain death by having them driven to Belize City under cover of night and arranging for them to fly back to the States. In return for the rescue, he asked them to access a safety-deposit box in Miami where documentary proof identifying the ringleaders of the smuggling operation had been stashed by Consuela.

Adam and Megan had found the documents exactly where and how Julio indicated, which proved that at least part of his story was true. They'd copied all the documents and then handed the originals over to the Belizean authorities, with yet another set of copies going to the owner of the platinum mine. Arrests had been made, prosecutions initiated, and the smuggling ring had been closed down. Since that time, however, neither Adam nor Megan had heard any word from Castellano.

"I guess that isn't surprising," Kate said, leaning back to allow the server to place bowls of steaming soup in front of them. "There's still a first-degree murder warrant outstanding for Julio Castellano in Miami. Of course, Julio insisted to Adam and Megan that he hadn't killed Ron Raven."

"Astonishingly, a statement that appears to be true!"

"Yes, it seems he was telling the truth after all." Kate gave a rueful smile. "Anyway, I guess it's not surprising that Castellano is keeping quiet. Presumably he has nothing to gain by letting Adam and Megan know where he is."

"The opposite," Luke agreed. "He has a lot to lose. Telling them his location would simply increase his risk of being extradited by the Miami cops and charged with Ron Raven's murder."

"I'm not sure Adam and Megan would feel obligated to tell the cops even if they knew where Castellano was."

"Do you blame them? When I called the Miami police, I got the impression that every detective on the force down there is bound and determined to see Castellano convicted, regardless of any evidence to the contrary that might come to light."

"My mother said the same thing. Right now, if Castellano was forced to stand trial, our family would be in the crazy position of trying to convince a jury that he couldn't be guilty of murder because my father is alive." Kate shook her head. "Good grief, the situation is insane!"

"Hopefully, it's not going to get to the point of Castellano being on trial, or anything close to it." Luke handed her a spoon. "Eat some soup. You must have left home at five this morning to get to the airport on time, and I'm sure you didn't bother with breakfast."

She pulled a face. "You're turning into my mother." But she took the spoon and ate some soup. "It's good," she said. "I'm hungrier than I realized."

"It occurs to me it would be very useful to have a picture of Consuela Mackenzie." Luke took two slices of hot, crusty bread and slipped one onto Kate's side plate. "With Consuela's photo to show around, we'd be doubling our chances of having somebody recognize either her or your father. And I suspect Consuela goes shopping a lot more often than he does."

"I agree it would be great to have her picture. But we have no way of getting one."

"Are you sure? This is a hell of a long shot, but is it possible that Adam might have found a photo of Consuela among those documents in the safety-deposit box?"

"I could call and ask. It seems unlikely, though, don't you think? Surely Adam would have told us right away if he had a picture of the woman who was with Dad the night he disappeared."

"Maybe not. My guess is Adam said as little as possible about Consuela out of deference to your mother's feelings."

"You could be right." Kate frowned into her soup. "You know, I realized last night that we've all been too protective of my mother, me included. It doesn't change reality by refusing to acknowledge it, and my mother has never been somebody who likes to ignore facts. Uncle Paul is the worst offender, but we've all followed his lead and played along."

"It's partly because she's handled the bigamy situation with such dignity that I guess everyone feels protective."

"But we need to move past that," Kate said. "There's no way to transform the twenty-eight years Mom spent with my father into a legal marriage, so we have to accept we were all duped and turn the page to a fresh start. We need to get over it already."

"I thought that was what Avery's new house and new career were all about."

Kate wrinkled her nose. "Practically, she's moved on. Emotionally, everyone is still in full protective mode. And not only of Mom, but of me, too. Adam even brought his new wife to Chicago when I was in Europe. I'm sure it's because he's tiptoeing around the fact that Megan is Dad's daughter by his Wyoming wife and he didn't want to ruffle my feelings."

"Maybe you need to take the initiative and invite Megan to Chicago. She's your half sister, after all. Ron's deceptions as a father presumably hurt her every bit as much as they hurt you."

"You're right, I should invite her." Kate finished the slice of bread Luke was sure she hadn't noticed she was eating, and absently brushed crumbs from her fingers. "I spent a lot of time when I was growing up wishing I had a sister. Now I have one and I haven't made the slightest effort to meet her."

"You probably needed these past six months to stop thinking of her as a rival and start seeing her as a fellow victim."

"You're right again. How annoying of you." Her smile softened her complaint. "Adam and Megan got married in Las Vegas, with two complete strangers as witnesses. At the time I was just relieved they didn't make things difficult for Mom and me by trying to arrange a big wedding in the hope that it would reconcile the two branches of Dad's family. Until now, I never allowed myself to wonder how the two of them felt exchanging their vows without any friends or relatives to keep them company."

Luke reached across the table to squeeze Kate's hands, the comforting gesture automatic. He stopped as soon as he realized what he was doing and picked up his spoon again. "If they're truly in love, the ceremony will have been wonderful wherever they had it."

Kate flashed him a smile that was almost affectionate. "You're such an optimist, Luke, always willing to see the silver lining lurking in the darkest cloud. Wouldn't you want to have all your brothers and sisters at your wedding?"

About to toss off a reply, he stopped to consider. "I'd enjoy having a huge party so that I could show off my new wife to all my hundreds of relatives, and the Savarini cousins could get together and sing their usual slightly drunken version of 'O Sole Mio.' But the exchanging vows part… No, I think I'd be happier if it was just me, the woman I loved, and a priest. As far as I'm concerned, Adam and Megan had the perfect wedding."

"I hope they felt the same way." Kate still sounded dubious, but she looked more cheerful. "Anyway, back to getting our hands on a photo of Consuela Mackenzie. It's definitely worth asking Adam if he has one. The answer's almost certainly no, but let's find out. I'll call him now."

She pushed away her half-empty soup bowl and took out her cell phone. Shamefully, she realized as she dialed his number that this was the first time she'd called Adam at home since his marriage. Despite the fact that he was president of the only bank in Fairfax, and she always had to negotiate her way past his assistant, she'd preferred to do that rather than risk having to speak to Megan.

Now, finally, she geared herself up to talk to the sister she'd never met, and then felt almost a moment of letdown when Adam answered.

"Kate!" Her uncle's voice was warm. "I'd say this is an unexpected pleasure, except that you almost never call me just to chat. I hope everything's okay?"

"Everyone is fine, more or less. How are you? And...Megan?"

"We're wonderful, thank you. Busy, but hoping to see you soon."

"Any chance that you and Megan could come to Chicago for Thanksgiving? I actually bought a bed for my guest room after I got back from Europe, and I can promise you the best pecan pie outside of Georgia."

Adam's voice deepened. "Thank you for the invitation, Kate. Sincerely. Megan and I would love to come and see you sometime soon, I really mean that, but we're going to spend Thanksgiving at the ranch in Wyoming. Liam, Megan's brother, is planning to get married to Chloe while we're there, so it's a pretty big deal."

"Well, I understand that weddings have to come first." Kate realized she was envious of Adam and the fact that he would be attending Liam's wedding, whereas she hadn't been invited. It was crazy to feel jealous when she'd never set eyes on her half brother and sister, but after months of studied indifference, she was suddenly impatient to meet the unknown members of her family. "Just keep in mind that Mom and I are hoping to see you both soon."

"We'll compare calendars and get back to you very soon. How is Avery? She sounded excited about her new house the last time we spoke."

"She is excited. And the renovations are going faster than we'd hoped, so she should soon have a really attractive office at home for meeting with clients. Actually, though, it's not Mom I'm calling about. It's about my father."

"Oh, Lord, I should have guessed! I got a couple of

e-mails from Paul this past week. Apparently some fruit loop thinks he saw Ron in Washington, D.C., and you've hired a private investigator to follow up—"

"Well, the fruit loop who thinks he saw my father is sitting across the table from me right now and he can hear you. His name is Luke Savarini, he's one of Chicago's premier chefs, and we're in D.C. trying to find somebody who can provide us with an address for the man Luke saw."

"Ouch! Removing my foot from my mouth…" Adam sounded more amused than contrite. "Let me rephrase. As I understand it, your friend got no more than a glimpse of this man across a crowded restaurant. They never exchanged a single word. Leaving aside the issue of whether it could possibly have been Ron, how in God's name do you expect to find an address for a man seen for a couple of seconds in a public place? And why are you doing the investigating personally? Did you fire the detective? Paul suggested he was very competent at his job."

"It's a long story."

"It's also important. I can sure make the time to listen."

Kate brought Adam up to date on the tragic murder of George Klein, and the results of their interview with the Sunrise store clerk. "It would be one thing if the clerk had simply claimed to recognize the picture of my father," she concluded. "But she did much more than that. She recognized the name Consuela Mackenzie and identified her as Belizean. Adam, it can't be a coincidence that Stewart Jones—a man who looks exactly like my dad—is doing his shopping in the company of the woman supposedly with Ron Raven the night he disappeared. That's stretching the long arm of coincidence miles beyond breaking point."

Adam was silent for a full thirty seconds before responding with a single, vicious expletive.

"Yes, that was pretty much my reaction," Kate said calmly.

"Why did you call?" Adam asked finally. "Just to keep me in the loop, or is there some way you think I can help you find the son of a bitch?" He made no apology for the insult to Kate's father.

"If you have a picture of Consuela Mackenzie you could send us, we figure it would double our chances of finding somebody who recognizes her or Dad. Apparently she hasn't even bothered to change her name, which suggests she may have been more careless than my father about handing out contact information. Maybe she assumes nobody in the States knows about her link to my father?"

"That could be," Adam agreed. "Julio Castellano implied to us that she'd never been to the States until she left Belize to meet up with Ron in Miami, so she's not likely to run into somebody who knows her from way back. Although, if she's kept in touch with Castellano, presumably he's told her Megan and I were in Belize, and that we now know she's the woman who was in Ron's hotel room the night he disappeared."

"Well, I realize that getting a picture of Consuela isn't likely to make a huge difference to our chances of finding my father, but Luke and I are clutching at mighty thin straws here and two pictures are presumably better than one. If you have a photo you can send, even if it's not clear, it has to improve our odds."

"You're in luck," Adam said, his voice still grim. "There was a photo of Consuela with Ron in the safety-deposit box. I already scanned the picture into my laptop, along with all the other documents Megan and I found. A couple of mouse clicks and I can e-mail the picture to you right now. Do you have your laptop with you?"

"I never leave home without it." Kate patted the briefcase on the seat beside her. "Thanks, Adam. This might be the break we need."

"Wait! How are you going to get prints you can show around?"

"This isn't sleepy old Fairfax!" she said, laughing. "We're in a shopping center only a few miles from the White House and Washington, D.C., is a wired city. There are probably a dozen different places right in this plaza that could run us off a copy."

"In fact, there's a print shop on the other side of the plaza." Luke intervened to point out the familiar logo.

"Okay," Adam said. "I'm attaching my picture of Consuela to an e-mail right now. You should have it in a couple of minutes."

"We'll go and find some wireless network we can access so that I can download it," Kate said. "Thanks, Adam. We'll let you know as soon as anybody recognizes it."

"I'll warn Megan that Ron Raven has apparently returned from the dead," Adam said, his voice grim again. "I'm afraid she'll take it hard. Your mutual father sure knows how to screw up other people's lives, doesn't he?"

"Yes," Kate said. "That and making money seem to be the two things he does best."

Thirteen

Sam, the young man who helped Kate hook her laptop up to one of the store's printers, was good-looking and knew it. He ran a quick, practiced glance over her body, his gaze lingering on her breasts, and she saw the immediate predatory gleam that lit up his melting brown eyes. In normal circumstances, she'd have cut him off at the knees. Today she gave him a flirty smile and made a point of letting him know that Luke was her brother, not a boyfriend.

Luke took their sudden kinship in stride and did no more than roll his eyes behind Sam's back while she played dumb bunny to Sam's superhero. Feeling like the poor man's version of Paris Hilton, she did her best to act as if she had difficulty telling the difference between her keyboard and her mouse pad. Fluttering her lashes, she expressed awe and gratitude at Sam's ability to unite her laptop with the store's photo printer.

She zipped through their story of her search for her father, keeping the tale short since it was clear that Sam had far more interest in the size of her boobs than in her angst over a missing parent. He must have been listening with at least some of his attention, though, because as the picture of Consuela and her father emerged from the printer, he gave a sudden jolt of recognition.

"Hey, I know this woman," he said, picking the photo up from the printer tray. "Is she the one you're looking for?"

Kate nodded. "Either her, or the man with her. The man is my father."

"I don't recognize the man—" Kate had a suspicion that men generally came and went in Sam's world without much notice from him "—but she's been in here a couple of times and I've helped her mail packages."

"Do you remember the last time you saw her?"

Sam scratched his head. "I dunno. She hasn't been in for a while. It's probably been a couple of weeks. Maybe three."

Her father had already run, Kate thought despondently. Ron knew he'd been spotted and he'd probably hightailed it out of the D.C. area right after selling his car. Stewart Jones, Australian diplomat, had morphed by now into some new and completely unknown identity. The chances were that any address she and Luke managed to ferret out for "Mr. Jones" would simply be another dead end.

Still, she had to try to dig up any information she could, and Sam seemed relatively easy to work on, especially in comparison to the clerk at Sunrise. He struck her as the type to blow off store policies and hand over an address for her father if he happened to feel in the mood to impress her.

She tapped the photo, indicating Consuela. "If this woman mailed packages from here, would you have a record of her address? Her name is Consuela Mackenzie, or she might have given you my father's name, Stewart Jones."

"I'm pretty sure they have an account with the store." Sam sent her an assessing glance, clearly enjoying the knowledge that he was in possession of information Kate wanted.

She blinked. "They have a personal account? Here?" She was shocked enough that this time she didn't need to fake sounding stupid.

"Yeah. That way it's quicker to mail things, you know? We'll even pick up packages at your home once you have an account with us."

She supposed her father might have risked setting up an account rather than paying cash for every transaction. These days, people paying cash ran the risk of being remembered simply because of their rarity. And, as her father had apparently calculated, giving people a false name still left him pretty well protected: he could shed the Stewart Jones identity the moment it became a problem, so it wouldn't matter too much if a few stores had records of the biographic details for a nonexistent person.

"If my father has an account here, then you certainly must have a record of his address. Could you tell me what it is?"

"Sure." Sam laughed. "If I wanted to get fired I could tell you."

She'd overestimated her seductive charms, Kate reflected ruefully. Sam was willing to flirt, but he wasn't a total fool.

Luke spoke for the first time. "We've taken up enough of your time, Sam. Thanks for your help. How much do we owe you for the copy of the photo?"

Kate glared at Luke, silently protesting the abrupt termination of her conversation, but he gave an almost imperceptible shake of his head, warning her to keep quiet.

"I dunno the exact amount until I ring up the charges. There's tax and stuff." Sam's gaze swiveled toward Luke for no more than a second before fixing back on Kate. "How would you like to pay?"

"We'll pay cash." Luke followed him to the nearest cash register, pulling out his wallet as he went. He set his wallet on the counter, and rested two hundred-dollar bills on top. Sam looked at the money and finally looked—really looked—at Luke.

"We're grateful for your help," Luke said. He made no reference to the two hundred dollars, keeping his bland gaze fixed directly on Sam.

"Er….right." Appearing unsure of himself for the first time, Sam keyed in codes and numbers and informed them their total charge amounted to seven dollars and thirty cents. Luke paid with a ten-dollar bill and dropped the change into his jacket pocket. He left the two bills sitting on the counter.

"Okay, then." Sam eyed the two hundred dollars. "I guess that's it."

Luke showed no sign he was aware of Sam's interest in the money. "Did you give me my receipt?" he asked.

"Yes."

"No, I don't think you did." Luke gave the bills a casual flick toward Sam. "I'm pretty sure we're still missing our receipt. I need it for my tax records."

Sam hesitated. He sneaked a furtive glance over each shoulder and, apparently satisfied that no managers were watching, quickly keyed a command into the computer terminal. He hit the print command and almost simultaneously scooped up the bills, shoving them into his pocket.

"Thanks for stopping by today. Come and see us again soon." Sam's voice squeaked with nerves. His role as Cool Dude apparently didn't extend very deep. He handed Luke the one-page printout, looking so guilty that if a manager had been in range, he or she would have come running. Kate could see that the sheet did at least have words written on it, but she couldn't tell if Sam had given them an address, much less an address for Stewart Jones. His nervousness boded well, though.

Sam was already disappearing through a door marked Staff. Kate was quite sure her mother would say that they'd only be getting the reward they deserved if Sam took their bribe and then failed to deliver the goods.

"What did he print out for us?" she asked as soon as they were outside the store. "By the way, I owe you for my plane ticket as well as the two hundred bucks you just used to bribe Sam."

"You can give me a check sometime. No rush." Luke handed her Sam's sheet of paper. *Stewart M. Jones,* she read, *344 Maple View Drive, Herndon, Virginia, 20170.* A Virginia driver's license number was recorded, as well as home phone, office phone and cell phone numbers.

Euphoria made her light-headed. She handed the

paper back to Luke and managed to speak with only a slight tremor of excitement in her voice. "It's not the same address as the one he gave the car dealer. It could mean that we've found him."

Luke hesitated. "We've almost certainly found where he was living up until the night I saw him at Bruno's."

Kate's euphoria deflated. "But he won't be there anymore, will he? He took off for some new hidey-hole as soon as he realized you'd recognized him."

"I wish I could believe that Ron is still at this address, Kate, but my guess is he bolted within hours of seeing me." Luke grinned and gave her a high five. "But between your boobs and my bucks, we did pretty well in there, huh?"

She smiled back. "We sure did. We make a winning team." They'd done better than a professional detective, in fact, since George Klein hadn't managed to rustle up a mention of Consuela Mackenzie, and certainly hadn't managed to find this more recent address for "Mr. Jones." The driver's license number was new, too, although probably irrelevant since her father was unlikely to use it now that his Stewart Jones identity was compromised.

She didn't mention her thoughts about George Klein to Luke, though. It seemed disrespectful to celebrate a petty triumph over a man who'd been murdered only a few days earlier.

"What's our next step? Should we try to call the phone numbers Sam just provided for us?" She shook her head, answering her own question. "No, that would only spook Dad if they still happen to be valid. We absolutely don't want to let him know we're getting close.

I guess our next step is to pay a visit to 344 Maple View Drive."

"I agree." Luke glanced at his watch. "It's already three-thirty. We only have a couple more hours of daylight. Let's make the most of them."

Maple View Drive was located in one of the older-established areas of Herndon. Its name had been acquired honestly, with mature maple trees planted along the entire length of a spacious median divide. This late in October some leaves had already fallen, but many of the trees were still a magnificent crimson, bright enough in the afternoon sun to cast a warm glow on the brick facades of the upscale villas and patio homes lining the street.

Luke drove at a sedate pace, slowing only a little more as they passed 344. Maple View Drive seemed to be a dormitory street, designed for professional couples, with none of the residents home at this hour.

"Great location if you want to hide," he commented. "I'm guessing none of these people know one another. I'll bet we could show pictures of Ron and Consuela to a dozen residents and nobody would recognize them as neighbors."

It was depressing but true, Kate thought. "You were right about Washington being a great city for anyone who wants to disappear. The short-term rental apartment where he was living back in June struck me as the ideal situation for somebody who wanted to be anonymous, but this is even better. No doormen, no communal lobby, nothing at all to cause anyone to remember him." Animosity seeped into her voice. "He's really good at hiding, isn't he?"

"Yes, but we only need him to have been careless once. Just once, and we've got him."

"Not necessarily. We may only have Mr. Jones, who probably doesn't exist anymore."

"Think positive thoughts, kiddo." Luke turned around at the crossroad and parked the car across the street from their target. Number 344 seemed to be a standard patio home, with its own front door, a pocket-size individual front yard and no other humans anywhere in sight.

They both spotted the For Rent sign in a corner window at the same moment. "There's a phone number for the rental agent. Sunday's a busy day in real estate. Let's hope the office is open." Luke squinted against the sun to read the numbers and then keyed them into his cell phone.

"Is it even worth calling?" The rental sign had confirmed Kate's fears. "If the place is for rent, it means Dad has flown the coop already. There's no way any legitimate rental agent is going to hand over information about a previous set of tenants. Not to us at least. And impersonating a police officer will get us arrested."

"I'm not going to ask the rental agent about Ron, at least not directly. I'm going to get us inside the house where your father and Consuela were living and hope to God we find something to provide our next lead. We have slim pickings, Kate, and we have to pursue all of them. The first thing is to be very friendly on the phone so that we've established a level of rapport before the agent even unlocks the front door."

The rental office responded to Luke's call with a seemingly endless menu of choices. He worked his way through four irrelevant options and finally gave the thumbs-up sign: he'd reached a real, live human.

"My wife and I are looking for a furnished town-home in the Herndon area," he informed the gushing Southern voice on the other end of the phone. "I've just been transferred here and we need a place to rent for six months while my wife finishes out the school year back in Chicago."

He paused for a moment to listen to a question. "Oh, no," he answered quickly. "We don't have kids of our own. My wife is a schoolteacher and I'm a chef. In fact, we're sitting outside one of your properties right now. It's on Maple View Drive. The location's ideal for me. How much is the monthly rental? I'd only want a six-month lease."

He listened again. "Hmm…that's right at the upper end of what we can afford, but it's doable. Could somebody bring over the keys so that we can take a look inside?"

He listened some more, said yes several times, and then hung up. "Mary Ellen Robell is on her way over." He grinned. "Hold on to my right hand at all times, Katie-love, or I just might find myself signing a rental agreement. Beneath her Southern charm, Mary Ellen sounds a tad on the aggressive side. Visualize a piranha that hasn't eaten in a while."

Luke's comment about holding on to his hand had slipped out too easily, Kate reflected. She'd almost responded that it would be a pleasure. Worse, Luke didn't even seem to notice that he'd used one of his old endearments. Katie-love. It didn't mean anything, of course. Except that it would be disastrous if they allowed the camaraderie of today's search to create the illusion they could safely become friends. There was nothing about her feelings for Luke that fell under the heading of friendly, much less safe.

"Let's take a walk around the outside of the property while we're waiting." She needed to get out of the car; her awareness of Luke's physical presence suddenly seemed suffocating. "What are we going to be looking for once we're inside?"

"I wish I knew. Anything at all that might lead us to Ron. I'll try to keep Mary Ellen occupied. Since I told her I'm a chef, I'll say I do a lot of cooking at home and display an obsession with cupboard space for all my specialized equipment. That'll give me an excuse to open every drawer in the kitchen area. Meanwhile, you can whiz through the house and see if you can find anything at all that Ron and Consuela might have left behind. If I get even a whiff of a chance, I'll ask her about the previous tenants, of course."

"Bet she tells us they've gone back to Australia."

He gave a regretful nod. "I bet you're right."

Kate was willing to follow up every lead, especially one they'd worked so hard to acquire, but she was beginning to accept that finding her father might be a task beyond the capabilities of a couple of amateurs, however motivated. And, God knew, she had plenty of motivation. Still, she and Luke had already confirmed almost beyond the possibility of doubt that her father was alive—something that would have seemed inconceivable only a couple of weeks ago. Even if they found out nothing else, their trip had been worthwhile. Maybe they had even gathered sufficient circumstantial evidence to interest the police in reopening the case. It was a possibility at any rate.

Mary Ellen, lacquered and buffed to perfection, greeted them with a welcoming smile as artificial as her makeup. "You came at just the right moment," she said. "We sent in the crew to clean up after the last tenants only a couple of days ago. Our cleaners are the best in the business and you'll find everything is spotless."

If only Mary Ellen knew what bad news she was delivering, Kate reflected wryly. The last thing she and Luke wanted to hear was that the property had been cleaned to perfection. Her father would have taken care to leave nothing behind, and on the remote chance that he'd been in such a hurry that he'd slipped up, an efficient cleaning crew would have taken care of any odd scraps of paper he might conceivably have overlooked.

"Did the last tenants cause problems?" Luke asked. "Is that why you needed to send in the cleaning crew?"

"Oh, no, that's standard practice. At McMasters Realty we pride ourselves on handing over our properties in pristine condition. But it's true that the last tenants did leave unexpectedly. Mr. Jones was an Australian diplomat and he got transferred back to Sydney on such short notice that he had to mail the house keys back to us from the airport."

"I thought Canberra was the capital of Australia," Luke said. "I wonder why Mr. Jones was going back to Sydney? Diplomats usually work in their foreign ministry and that's always located in the capital city."

"Maybe he just stopped off in Sydney. Maybe he has a home there." Mary Ellen clearly was a woman who focused on the deal ahead and she had zero interest in

idle chatter about tenants who were no longer providing rent to her company. She'd probably only mentioned Mr. Jones because *diplomat* sounded like an
impressively upper-class profession.

"Now, Mr. Savarini—"

"Call me Luke, please."

"Then, Luke, you must come and look at the terrific
kitchen. This particular model is one of our most
popular rental homes and I think you'll be very pleas-
antly surprised with the features. We replaced all the ap-
pliances eight months ago and now they're stainless
steel, top of the line." Mary Ellen siphoned him off
from Kate and propelled him into the kitchen. A Marine
Corps general couldn't have executed the maneuver
with more efficiency.

You could only admire her father's efficiency as a
deceiver, Kate thought, heading in the opposite direction. Not for him anything as clumsy as leaving his
rental accommodations without notice, even if he was
running away at top speed. He'd actually taken the time
to invent a convincing lie and mail back the keys from
the airport so that Mary Ellen and her colleagues would
have no reason to remember him anything but kindly.
Of course, he had almost thirty years of experience of
inventing lies on the fly. No wonder he was so damn
good at it.

Mary Ellen talked as though her company had learned
very recently of Mr. Jones's departure. Kate assumed her
father had actually packed and left within twenty-four
hours of seeing Luke at Bruno's restaurant. Then, when
he was safely out of reach and living under a new name,
he tied up the loose end of this rental and returned the keys.

With hindsight, it was all too easy to see that they'd conducted their investigation at far too leisurely a pace, as if it didn't matter whether they followed up Luke's initial sighting the next day, or a month later. Still, there were few things more useless than regretting missed opportunities, and since Luke was valiantly chatting up Mary Ellen in the kitchen, Kate did her duty and quickly walked through the rest of the two-bedroom, two-bath villa.

She opened every closet door, checked the dressers in the master bedroom and even peeked under the king-size bed. The cleaning crew, as promised by Mary Ellen, had done an excellent job. There wasn't a dust ball in sight, and the drawers had all been freshly lined with scented paper. The closets contained plastic hangers and nothing else.

The villa was designed to accommodate a childless couple—presumably the most desirable category of renters—and the second bedroom had been furnished as a combination guest bedroom and office, with a daybed against one wall, and a built-in desk against the opposite wall. Bookshelves, currently empty, framed the window, and a leather armchair completed the furnishings. It was a pleasant, usefully designed room, as was the rest of the villa, and Kate could imagine that her father and Consuela would have been quite comfortable there.

She sat at the desk and switched on the hotel-style lamp, which had electrical and phone outlets built into the base for easy Internet access. Apparently rental property owners had finally figured out that nobody enjoyed crawling under the desk to set up their laptops.

There was also a leather folder on the desk, filled with printed instruction sheets from the property company. Kate searched through it with high hopes—it was the only thing she'd found so far worth searching—but there were no convenient scraps of paper tucked by Ron Raven between printed cards and forgotten.

Sighing, she pulled open the two file drawers, the very last thing left for her to check out. A few empty folders hung crookedly from the metal frame, but once again there wasn't a single scrap of paper to be seen. Giving way to a moment of extreme frustration, Kate slammed the drawer shut. The drawer responded with a slight, intriguing rattle.

Kate damped down a flare of excitement. The sound had probably been nothing more than a file falling off its runner. Opening the drawer again, she pushed all the hanging folders toward the back. Resting on the dusty bottom of the drawer was a tiny flash drive, smaller than a stick of gum. She'd finally managed to find a place where the cleaning crew hadn't been busy. Heart thumping, she reached into the drawer and palmed the flash drive.

She smelled Mary Ellen's perfume even before she registered her voice or the sound of her footsteps coming up the stairs. Kate quickly pocketed the tiny device. She walked across to the window and was staring out, apparently transfixed by the view of the street, when Luke and Mary Ellen came into the room.

Mary Ellen noticed nothing amiss in her demeanor, but Luke realized at once that she was almost bursting with excitement. He got rid of the agent by the simple method of announcing that he didn't think the villa would work for him, citing the lack of a separate dining room. Not one to go down to easy defeat, Mary Ellen assured them as she escorted them out into the street that her company had several other great rentals to show them.

"What have you got?" Luke asked Kate as soon as they were back in the car. "That place was cleaned so thoroughly, I thought we'd be totally out of luck."

"Maybe we *are* out of luck. It might be nothing. What I found might not even be my father's. Or we might have hit pay dirt." Kate opened her hand and showed him the flash drive. "This was in the desk file drawer."

"Holy shit!"

"Yeah, that, too." She laughed, giddy with unexpected success. "If it is my father's, it *could* have all his active files on it. It says right on the casing that it's a two-gigabyte drive, so it's got tons of storage space." Reality returned, sharp enough to pierce the bubble of her enthusiasm. "Except if he'd lost something as important as his backup drive, he'd presumably have gone back to the house to reclaim it."

"Not if he was afraid I was closing in on him. And he might not have known where he lost it. Something that small could have been dropped anywhere. In the rush of packing up, he could easily have lost track of when he last had it." Luke leaned over the back of the car seat and grabbed his laptop from the backseat. "Anyway, there's no need to guess what's on it. We can take a look."

Kate held his computer balanced on the arms between the front seats and waited impatiently for it to boot. Luke slotted the flash drive into a USB port and adjusted the screen so that they could both see the results.

The drive contained two files, RR21 and RR22. RR21 was almost three hundred kilobytes in size. RR22 was significantly smaller. "That's several dozen pages of data in total, isn't it?" Kate tried to visualize some of her recipe files and their size in kilobytes. "We have more than twenty pages of data in RR21, I think."

"Yep, maybe as many as thirty."

"And the file names suggest we've found something that definitely belonged to Ron Raven. RR21 and RR22. Those initials can't be a coincidence, not on top of everything else we've discovered today."

"It would be astonishing if they don't belong to him. Hot damn, we could finally be closing in on your dad's trail. Okay, here goes. Drum roll, please." Luke sent her a cheerful grin before clicking on one of the files. Kate held her breath while the screen flickered. She exhaled in a disappointed gust when, instead of opening up to pages of text, the screen produced a dialogue box, informing them the file was password-protected and requesting the password.

"Damn." Tight-lipped, Luke closed the box and clicked on the second file. Another box appeared with the same message as before.

"Any suggestions as to what your father's password might be?" Luke asked. "Wait, there are seven stars, so we need something with seven letters."

"Try Dad's middle name," Kate suggested. "It's Howatch. That has seven letters." She supposed there was a slim chance Ron had been careless enough to use something as obvious as his own name to protect his files. Although, the more she learned about her father, the less appropriate *careless* seemed to be as a word to describe his behavior.

Luke keyed in *Howatch* and was informed it was an invalid password. They tried Ron's initials, combined with the year of his birth, and then the names of both his wives and all three of his children. They even tried various seven-letter combinations of Consuela Mackenzie and Julio Castellano. Nothing worked. The unpalatable fact was that she didn't know enough about her father to have the remotest clue what he might choose as a locking code on his file system, Kate reflected grimly.

"Let's leave it until we've had a chance to call Mom," she suggested finally, when the frustration level inside the car was becoming palpable. "We should call Uncle Paul, too. He's Dad's business partner, so he might know more about the passwords Dad favored for business deals than Mom or me. Maybe it's a strictly numerical combination." In which case the possibilities were virtually infinite.

"You're right." Luke straightened, flexing cramped muscles. "It's crazy to sit here, balancing a laptop on the car's armrest, when we could check into a hotel and have our very own desk to sit at." He removed the flash drive and shut down his computer.

"Since you already believe I'm a pie-eyed optimist, I'll look on the bright side," he said, clicking on his seat belt and turning on the ignition. "At least Ron's files weren't programmed to self-destruct if the wrong password was keyed in more than a couple of times."

"Yep, that's really great news." Kate gave a wry laugh. "Since the files apparently won't self-destruct, that means there's no end to our torment. We can spend the rest of our lives trying to guess which out of a thousand gazillion possibilities Dad might have chosen for his password."

"Don't let a temporary setback get you down. You'll feel better after a hot shower."

"You should pat my knee when you say that, otherwise I might not grasp how totally patronizing you're being."

Luke grinned. "You always get grouchy around this time of day. I saw a fancy-looking hotel right on the main road in Reston, near the shopping center. Want to splurge and try it?"

"Sure." Kate turned to look out of the window, alarmed by the way they kept toppling over into old, familiar ways. Instead of thinking how glad she was to have Luke with her on this quest, she ought to be remembering that the last time they'd had a serious relationship, she'd ended up feeling so inadequate that she'd almost blown the most important competition of her professional career.

That miserable place was a destination she would take great care never to arrive at again. One trip to the wrong side of the rainbow could be excused. A second trip down the same path was plain stupid. She needed to remember the pain of those last few weeks back in the spring. All the more so because being with Luke eased an ache deep inside that, until this past week, she hadn't been willing to acknowledge was there.

Fourteen

When Kate joined him in the hotel restaurant for dinner, Luke could see she was determined to be on her best and most formal behavior. Her smile as she greeted him was charming and meaningless. Even her clothes—changed from jeans and a sweater to dress pants and a blazer—shouted the message that the rapport they'd enjoyed during the afternoon wasn't going to lead to anything more intimate for the remaining time they would be spending together.

Her tendency to hide behind cool politeness had mystified Luke when they were dating. Now he understood so clearly where she was coming from that he wondered why he'd ever found her behavior puzzling. He had felt an insidious closeness to Kate this afternoon, something more than mere sexual attraction, and she'd probably felt the same thing. She wouldn't want that closeness to develop any more than he did, but since she always tried to avoid confrontation, she wouldn't say anything directly to him.

Instead of discussing the problem, she'd retreated behind a facade that practically stood up and tap-danced to make sure he grasped her silent message: keep your distance.

In the bad old days at the end of their relationship, Luke would have pushed hard against the barrier of her seeming indifference, oblivious to the fact that with Kate, formal behavior was a prime sign of vulnerability and that pressure was precisely the wrong tactic to employ. Tonight, though, he had no intention of forcing emotional honesty from her. God knew, he wanted nothing to do with Kate's emotions. Right this moment, his chief reaction to her changed clothes and formal manner was relief that she was taking steps to prevent their physical attraction propelling them into a sexual encounter they would both regret. However badly Kate wanted to avoid getting involved again, Luke was sure he wanted it even less. He was sorry Ron Raven was turning out to be such an asshole, but he wasn't going to confuse sympathy with compatibility. The bottom line was that he and Kate couldn't be together for long without generating sparks, and in their case, those sparks always turned into a conflagration.

He recognized that his emotions were almost as battered as Kate's and that he badly needed to talk and think for a while about something other than Ron Raven. There was a lot of unresolved anger swirling around the fraught subject of Ron's disappearance and some of it had rubbed off on him. He had realized as they learned of Consuela Mackenzie's continuing presence in Ron's life that he was furious on Kate and Avery's behalf. That anger was becoming more intense, not less, as they uncovered each new hint of how Ron had been occupying himself for the past six months.

On top of his anger, Luke was nursing an uncomfortable burden of guilt concerning George Klein's death. It was because of the search for Ron Raven that George had ended up in O'Hare airport. Now George was dead and Luke had a widow and two orphans on his conscience. He knew the guilt was irrational, but that didn't help to dissipate it.

Their profession, thank God, provided a safe topic for both of them to retreat into. They talked about food as they made their dinner choices, and they both worked hard to keep their comments impersonal. They discussed the increasing influence of Asian cuisine and commented on the trend at a few upscale restaurants toward "small plate dining." Some innovative restaurants, especially on the coasts, had started to offer tiny portions, so that customers could order a seven- or eight-course meal, enjoy a variety of flavors, and actually eat everything that was brought to their table.

Having spent much of the summer in Europe, Kate had plenty of experience with multicourse, small-portion meals. Their discussion was wide-ranging and often technical, but by the time their entrées arrived, the impersonal had somehow started to slide into the personal. Luke recognized what was happening, but he experienced a what-the-hell moment and chose not to draw back.

Kate was a good listener and her comments were so insightful that he found himself explaining that he was working on the idea of introducing a six-course, fixed-price menu at Luciano's on Chestnut. Three of the courses would be no more than a couple of mouthfuls, and only the entrée would be anything approaching substantial. He'd already discussed his ideas with his sous-chefs, but there was nobody else in his life right now who could begin to appreciate the problems and opportunities inherent in such a radical menu change. His last two girlfriends had been bored to death by the subject of food, which was probably why he'd chosen to go out with them, Luke realized with a jolt. It was only now, talking to Kate, that he recognized how much he'd missed this sort of free-ranging professional discussion in the months since he'd broken up with her.

Kate was genuinely fascinated by his plans and wanted to hear every detail. Part of her interest sprang from the fact that she was in the process of developing her own line of bite-size desserts, something that was nowhere near as easy as it sounded. The science of many sweet dishes required certain minimum quantities to be cooked in a single pan in order for the texture and consistency to be correct, and not every great confection lent itself to being cut into three-centimeter squares or wafer-thin slices.

The coincidence of discovering they were both working on downsized portions led by natural progression to a discussion of Luke buying some of Kate's bite-size desserts to include with his new six-course dinners. Since he would still be offering normal à la carte choices, as well, preparing top-of-the-line mini-desserts had been a major stumbling block to his plans, chiefly because it would have required a new hire. Buying the desserts from Kate would not only be cost effective, it would provide better quality since she was arguably the best baker in the Chicago area. He was aiming to introduce the new menu in January, when smaller portions would seem a tempting counterbalance to the holiday excesses of November and December. Kate promised to have a variety of samples ready for him to taste within the next two weeks.

The last traces of her formality vanished as they considered and discarded options. Her eyes sparkled and her hands wove intricate patterns as she searched for words to describe her latest creations. Her whole body seemed in movement. Kate loved her profession and her passion was on full display.

It was ironic, Luke reflected, that now, when it no longer mattered to him, he'd finally discovered how to break through Kate's touch-me-not facade. Why in the world had it been so hard for him to grasp that Kate retreated when she felt pressured and stepped forward when she felt he was leaving her space? Leaning back in his chair, he sipped the Spanish red wine they'd chosen to accompany their grilled pork and thought how incredibly beautiful she was when she was animated.

Perhaps he'd fumbled their relationship because his own family handled intimacy so differently from Kate. His parents and siblings weren't big on subtlety. When they wanted to know something about you, they asked. When they were happy or sad or angry, you were left in no doubt as to their feelings. He'd always assumed such casual, exuberant honesty was the best way to deal with personal relationships. Growing up, he'd been grateful for the fact that in his family there might be arguments and shouting matches but there were no horrible, simmering feuds. Best of all, in his family even the noisiest arguments were quickly followed by hugs and sincere apologies.

Still, it had dawned on him years ago that he was the odd man out in his family for more than his gray eyes and six-foot frame. He sometimes found his family's honesty brutal and their demands for inclusion oppressive. His brothers and sisters, even Anna, were quite content to live their lives in the family spotlight. For them the light seemed to provide a warm glow; for him it more often cast a punitive glare. In his search for the privacy zone he needed in order to stay sane, he'd retreated from the onslaught of their love in a myriad of subtle ways.

He'd always been aware of what he was doing and why he was stepping back. Somehow, though, he had never analyzed how his relationship with Kate had been affected by his feelings toward his family. Now he understood. He'd fallen in love with her at least in part because she was the perfect, soothing contrast to the constant drama of his family's boisterous relationships. And then, having been attracted to her differences, he'd spent a fair amount of time wondering why in the world she wasn't more like his parents and siblings.

Tonight, Luke could see with crystal clarity where he'd gone wrong. Sometimes he'd been too determined to get close when Kate needed breathing room. On other occasions, he'd stepped back too far in an effort to avoid duplicating his family's well-meaning interference. Even something as simple as not taking her to the infamous Savarini Sunday dinners demonstrated his ambivalence: he'd wanted to protect Kate from his family's high spirits, but he'd never stopped to consider that she might have felt excluded. By failing to introduce her to his family, he'd kept her shut away from people she knew were vitally important to him. He should have trusted both his family and Kate more, Luke reflected.

Still, however badly he'd messed up, the bottom line was that Kate could have found a million or so ways to end their relationship that would have been less hurtful than sleeping with Michael Rourke. Not only had that been an incredible betrayal of her relationship with him, she had managed to destroy his fifteen-year friendship with Mike in the process.

"What is it?" Kate asked. "Luke, what's wrong?"

"Nothing. Everything's fine."

"You looked positively ferocious for a moment."

"I was thinking about your father and those files locked up on the damn flash drive. That's guaranteed to produce a scowl." There was zero point in raking over the past. On the contrary, it was time to focus on the reason why they'd come to Washington in the first place. Luke saw that Kate had finished her coffee and signaled to the waiter for the bill.

"Did you manage to reach your mother earlier this evening?" he asked.

"Yes, I called, although I almost chickened out at the last minute and contacted Uncle Paul instead. Then I remembered that I'd decided only this afternoon that it was time to stop protecting Mom, so I told her the truth."

He smiled wryly. "Do we know what the truth is? I hadn't realized we'd made so much progress."

"Well, we know some of it. I told Mom we're almost positive my father is alive and that we've probably found the place he was living until very recently." She hesitated for a moment. "It was…a difficult conversation."

"It must have been. Your mother has every reason to be upset with Ron."

"She was angry. I'm not sure about upset." Kate reflected for a moment. "To be honest, I don't think she was all that sad, or even surprised by the deception. When we heard Dad was dead, she really grieved for him, even though it was such a shock to discover he'd been a bigamist. For a few weeks after we heard the news of his death, Mom was utterly lost, but so much has happened since May that she's almost a different person now. I understand why this latest development seems to be leaving her more angry than sad. The bottom line is that we didn't know my father and you can't mourn somebody you didn't know."

"Maybe not. But you can mourn the relationship you thought you had. Deception always hurts. Don't assume your mother isn't grieving just because she sounds angry rather than devastated."

"You're right, I need to remember that." Kate thought for a moment. "Besides, based on my own reactions, I would guess anger and grief can be almost interchangeable emotions where my father is concerned."

Because she looked sad and he wanted to get up and put his arms around her, Luke delivered a brisk change of subject. "Did your mother have any suggestions for a password Ron might have used?"

"None that we hadn't already thought of. After I

talked to Mom, I called Uncle Paul and he suggested a few more possibilities. He sounded rather harried, actually. He's in Denver, checking on his development project there, and I got the impression he wasn't entirely focused on what I was saying. I wrote down his suggestions, though, and we can try them after dinner if you like. Unfortunately, most of the security codes they use at Raven Enterprises are numerical, and if my father carried on that tradition there's almost no chance we'll be able to hit on the correct password." Her expression turned disconsolate. "I'm beginning to think finding that flash drive wasn't the great breakthrough I'd hoped."

"Jesus, what an idiot!" Luke struck himself on the forehead.

"Why? What did I say?"

"Nothing. I was talking to myself." Luke laughed. "But I'm willing to let you share the blame. We both got obsessed with the individual trees and totally forgot the forest. It's just occurred to me that we don't have to guess Ron's password! We can bypass it."

"How? Isn't that the point of passwords? They're put in place so that you can't bypass them."

"I can't and you can't, but there are people who can. My sister, Anna, is a physicist and she hangs out with a bunch of scientists. She has a good friend who's a computer geek. His name is Seth Bedinsky. She and Seth were in grad school together and she told me once she was surprised he wasn't arrested for hacking. I know he broke into the systems at a couple of major banks, just to prove he could. At which point, according to Anna, he realized he was likely to get himself into a heap of trouble if he didn't change his ways. So he got himself hired by the Defense Department, and when he decided government technology wasn't cutting edge enough to amuse him, he set himself up as an independent security consultant. Unless your father used a really sophisticated protective device, Seth can probably get us into those two files in a matter of minutes."

Kate smiled, her spectacular eyes glowing with excitement. "That's fantastic, Luke. I can't believe we didn't think earlier about bypassing the security lock on the files! It's such an obvious solution. Will we be able to talk to Seth tomorrow before we have to catch our flight back to Chicago? We don't have to be at the airport until around three."

"In normal circumstances I don't believe we'd have a chance of getting in to see him at such short notice. We're talking major high-powered Washington insider here. However, I'm fairly confident he's either sleeping with my sister or wishes like hell that he was." He grinned. "If Seth's in town, I'm guessing a phone call to Anna would get us an interview first thing tomorrow morning."

"Great. I'm already psyched."

"Three cheers for sisters. I'll call her as soon as I get back to the room." Luke raised his coffee cup in a salute to Anna.

Kate looked at him, her attention visibly caught.

"What is it? You're staring at me."

"Nothing." She looked a little wistful. "Except…when you say your sister's name, your eyes smile."

He was taken aback. "Do they?" He shrugged. "Anna's only thirteen months older than I am. I guess we got into a lot of mischief together when we were growing up and we're still close. We exchange e-mails almost every day."

"I'm jealous. You've no idea how hard it is to invent interesting mischief when you're an only child."

He sensed there was genuine regret behind Kate's casual words. "I'll be happy to lend you one of my brothers anytime you feel too sorry for yourself. Ben would be a good choice. Trust me, a couple of hours in Ben's company and you'll be on your knees, offering up prayers of gratitude that you're an only child."

"Your eyes are still smiling. You love Ben, too."

"Well, he's a complete pain in the ass, but he's my pain in the ass, you know?"

"I don't know yet, but I hope to understand one day soon." Kate's smile brightened. "Anyway, thanks for the offer to loan out Ben, but I have a brother and sister of my own now, and I'm going to make sure I meet them sometime soon. It's time the three of us got to know one another."

"Good. And speaking once again as your officially certified optimist, at least that's one positive thing to come out of your dad's bigamy—the fact that you have the brother and sister you always wanted."

She agreed, her moment of melancholy banished. "I was so shocked when I first learned of Liam and Megan's existence that I didn't realize just how glad I was to have siblings at last. Now the shock has worn off and I've hurtled past mere acceptance. I'm becoming more and more impatient to meet them."

The waiter arrived with their bill and they bickered amicably about who should pay it. Kate won the argument since Luke had shelled out two hundred bucks to bribe Sam at the print shop in addition to paying for their airline tickets. The bill signed, they made their way back up to their rooms in harmony with the world and with each other.

The ease and harmony both fled when Luke stopped outside Kate's room to say good-night. Sexual awareness always flowed dangerously close to the surface whenever he was around Kate and tonight was no exception. Despite all his dire admonitions to himself about keeping his distance and not repeating past mistakes, he could think of nothing he wanted more at this precise moment than to have sex with Kate.

The overhead light shone on her hair, turning it from ash-blond to magical burnished-gold. Her light floral scent enveloped him, intoxicating in its power to evoke memories of other nights when they'd barely been able to wait to open the door to his condo or her house before tumbling into each other's arms and searching out the nearest horizontal surface. She glanced up at him, smiling as she said good-night, and the final set of floodgates opened. Desire erupted from the dark, subterranean place where he had it contained, drowning common sense in primitive emotion.

"Kate." He murmured her name, leaning toward her. He could have resisted the urge to touch her, of course, but suddenly his painful efforts at self-control seemed crazy. He wondered why on earth he was struggling so hard to resist something so uniquely pleasurable.

She stepped away from him, her back flattening against the wall. "No," she said, her voice husky. "We can't get involved again, Luke. We'll only hurt each other in the end."

She dipped her head, avoiding his eyes, but she didn't go into her room. He put his hand under her chin, compelling her to meet his gaze. She tried to hide what she was feeling, but they'd been lovers for six fulfilling months and he could read the signs. She wanted him as much as he wanted her.

"Don't think about the end," he whispered. "Who cares about the end? Just think about tonight and how great we are together."

She closed her eyes. "Don't do this to me, Luke."

"Don't do what?" He bent his head and kissed her lightly, teasingly on the mouth. "Not this?" He pulled her close and kissed her harder. "Or this?"

"Neither." Her voice was husky. She put her hands on his chest and pushed him away, but she made no attempt to move once she was free.

He stroked his fingers across her cheekbones in a caress that was almost more about tenderness than it was about sex. "I didn't know how much I'd missed you until I saw you again. Did you miss me, Katie?"

She started to answer, and then abruptly spun inside the circle of his arms, pushing her key card into the lock with hands that were visibly unsteady. She spoke without turning to look at him. "Good night, Luke. You'll thank me in the morning."

He laughed without mirth. "No, Katie, I won't. The way I feel right now I can guarantee that I'll still feel like hell in the morning." He drew in a deep breath and grasped the lifeline thrown by her moment of sanity. "Okay…you're right. This isn't smart and we'll end up wishing we hadn't done this. Good night, Katie."

Although he spoke with reluctance, he honest to God

intended to step back and let her walk alone into her room. But somehow he was dragging her into his arms, twisting her around and kissing her with all the force and intensity of seven long months of deprivation. And she was kissing him back, her mouth moving hungrily beneath his. Her body curved against him, provoking conflicting sensations of the forbidden and the familiar. Her breath came in short, sharp gasps and her hands ripped at his shirt, reaching eagerly inside.

The sensation of her fingers against his bare skin literally took his breath away. He had to stop kissing her long enough to breathe in a gulp of air. As he broke away from Kate, she tilted her head back and stared at him for a dazed, silent moment. Then she once again shoved her key card into the door. This time she pushed the door open and held it ajar. "I have to go. We can't do this. *I* can't do this."

She disappeared into her room and slammed the door. Luke lifted his fists, ready to pound and demand entry, but better judgment won out. Kate was right and he was a fool. They couldn't do this.

He repeated the mantra all the way into his own room and through the twenty-minute cold shower that did not do a single damn thing to help his state of arousal. Kate was right and he was a fool. They couldn't do this.

God, he wanted her.

Fifteen

She should enter herself in the Moron of the Month Contest, Kate thought acidly; she would bring home the grand prize for sure. Leaning against the closed door, she waited for her legs to stop trembling. When her miscellaneous body parts felt more or less under control she staggered to the center of the room and ripped off her clothes, leaving them where they fell.

Once she was naked she had no idea what to do next, so she took herself off to the bathroom and stood under a hot shower for the best part of fifteen minutes. While shampooing her hair, she made a mental list of all the reasons why Luke was totally wrong for her.

It was a long list, but somehow the reasons had seemed a lot more compelling back in April than they did now. Yes, she'd felt that their relationship came in a distant second to his career and an even more distant third to his family, but so what? Holding second place in Luke's life was a hell of a lot more interesting than being first in, say, Willy-the-Councilperson's life.

Kate shook herself hard, sending water droplets flying. For God's sake, she needed to get a grip, or she would convince herself it was okay to walk back into a relationship knowing you were of secondary importance to the man you loved. She needed to keep in mind that Luke had made her feel so worthless that she'd not only come close to blowing an important contest, she'd actually ended up trying to recapture her self-esteem in Michael Rourke's bed. That particular catastrophe had taken an escape to Europe and seven months to overcome—and she still wasn't sure she'd recovered. She didn't need a repeat disaster to reinforce the lesson.

Wanting physical activity, she blow-dried her hair with a lot more attention than usual. Then she filed her nails and even plucked her eyebrows, but she felt no better at the end of her impromptu beauty session. Her idiotic body still wanted to be in bed with Luke and her sensible mind was doing a lousy job of convincing it otherwise.

She stopped pacing long enough to check the bedside alarm clock. It was almost eleven, an hour past her regular bedtime. She was in the habit of going to bed early since her job demanded a crack-of-dawn start and she ought to be tired. Maybe her subconscious would go to work while she slept, providing answers to all her problems by morning. It was a nice fantasy and she decided to run with it. She climbed into bed, pulled up the covers and willed herself to sleep.

Willpower was apparently no match for hormones. Why couldn't Willy-the-Councilperson be a good kisser, or even a decent one? Or how about all the Willy-the-Councilperson clones she'd dated? Why did it have to be Luke who raised goose bumps and curled her toes? She hadn't felt the faintest quiver of sexual attraction for any man since that awful, botched experiment with Michael, and yet Luke just had to look at her in that certain way and her entire body thrummed with desire. True, Luke was good-looking…well, okay, he was exceptionally good-looking. But she'd met other good-looking men and managed to survive without developing an overwhelming urge to fall into bed with them. What was it with this bizarre, unwelcome Luke obsession?

By eleven-thirty she was tired of mulling over questions to which she could find no answers. She gave up on the idea of sleep and switched on the bedside light, propping herself against a stack of pillows. She turned on the TV and tuned to the Science Channel, a reliable standby. She watched a couple of galaxies collide and then blow themselves up in brilliant HD color. Unfortunately, Luke wasn't in either galaxy. Even more unfortunately, he was still in the next room, waiting to be dealt with.

The phone rang and she stared at it in mute reproach. Nobody would be calling her at this hour except Luke, and she wasn't even slightly in the mood to speak with him. The phone continued to ring. She snatched the receiver. Her voice icy with reproach, she informed him—with self-evident lack of truth—that she was sleeping.

Her caller cut across her complaint, riding roughshod over her comment. "Listen up, because I'm only going to say this once." The masculine voice was achingly familiar, but it wasn't Luke's.

"Looking for me is a fool's errand. It's also hazar-

dous to your health. Be smart, for once in your life, and
stop looking. Oh, and by the way, just so you know—
if by any remote chance you did manage to track me
down, you'll wish you hadn't. That isn't a threat, it's a
promise. A certified, Ron Raven promise." The man
gave a short, amused laugh, as if aware of the irony of
his final comment.

"Dad? *Dad!*" Kate finally gathered her wits enough
to speak, but she was too late. The buzz on the line told
her that the call had already been disconnected.

For a long time she sat on the bed, holding the phone
and listening to the buzz. Eventually, when a recorded
message instructed her to hang up the phone, she attempted to return the receiver to the cradle. Her movements were so clumsy that the phone fell onto the floor.
She bent down and picked it up, her mind blank. She
sat down again on the end of the bed, staring at yet
another supernova igniting on the TV screen. She
finally patted the covers and found the remote so that
she could switch off the television.

The sudden cessation of lights and sounds propelled
her out of her trance. She blinked, looking all around
the room to reassure herself it was still as she would
expect. There was some comfort to be derived from the
knowledge that the walls remained cream-colored and
the furniture exactly where it had been a few moments
ago. She wasn't crazy, then, or hallucinating. She really
had taken a phone call from her evidently-not-dead
father.

Still not properly coordinated, she pulled on her
slacks and searched through the crumpled clothing discarded on the floor until she found her camisole. Then

she left her room and walked blindly to the room next door. To Luke. She thought she might feel a little better if she could just talk to Luke.

Kate rapped her clenched fists against the panels of his door, but she was shaking so badly that her wrists were flaccid and she made almost no sound. She raised her arm and pounded again with more determination. After a few moments, the door swung inward and Luke stood in the opening.

He began to say something but checked himself as soon as he got a good look at her. "What is it? Katie, for God's sake, what's happened, sweetheart?"

"He phoned me. Just now. A couple of minutes ago."

"Who phoned?" Luke put his arm around her unresisting shoulders and ushered her into his room.

She was grateful for the solid feel of him, for the strength and for the warmth radiating from his body. She was freezing cold, she realized. A chilled-to-the-marrow, deep-in-her-bones cold.

"Talk to me, Katie. Tell me what the problem is. Who phoned you?"

She looked up at him, but his face appeared blurred and she rubbed her eyes, trying to clear her vision. "My father. He just called. A few minutes ago."

"Your *father* phoned you?"

"Yes, he did. The one and only Ronald Raven." She laughed and heard the wild edge to the sound. She recognized she was barely in control of the hysteria fighting to be let loose, but at this moment, she didn't really care. "The best of it is, I think he was threatening to kill me."

Sixteen

Kate was so pale that Luke was afraid she might pass out. He quickly walked her to the bed and sat down next to her. She neither resisted nor cooperated, apparently too much in shock to make conscious choices. She gave the appearance of somebody not far removed from a trance and Luke wondered if she might have been dreaming. Could she have been so deeply asleep that she imagined the call from her father? The horror of a powerful nightmare could linger quite a long time.

He tossed the idea of a bad dream almost as soon as it formed. Kate was a practical sort of person who confined her flights of fancy to spun sugar and sculpted chocolate, and tended to relieve stress through physical activity. In all the time they'd been together, she'd never had a nightmare that was severe enough to wake her, much less one vivid enough to send her into a state of shock. If Kate said her father had phoned her and made threats, he almost certainly had.

First things first. Luke pulled on a T-shirt and boxers,

although he was pretty sure Kate hadn't noticed he'd been naked except for a towel when he opened the door. His hope that she'd changed her mind about having sex and come to find him seemed almost offensive in the circumstances. She was still sitting on the end of his bed, staring into space, so he grabbed a spare blanket from the closet and wrapped it around her shoulders, holding it in place until she stopped shivering.

"Do you want some water? Something hot to drink?" He kept his arm tightly around her. "We can call room service if you'd like tea."

She shook her head. "No." She paused for a long moment, searching for words. "Thank you."

She leaned against him willingly enough, but her body remained rigid except for the occasional convulsive shudder. He decided to wait another few moments before pressing her about precisely what Ron Raven had threatened. For now, he simply concentrated on holding her close, stroking her hair and murmuring the occasional word of comfort.

She finally drew in a long, slow breath and sat up so that she could look at him. "I'm sorry. I probably woke you. It was such a surprise to hear his voice, that's all."

"You didn't wake me, and of course it was a shock for you. If you're feeling up to it, can you tell me what he said?"

"That we would never be able to find him."

"He's been wrong about other things. We'll make sure he's wrong about this, too." If it took him the rest of his life, he would find Ron Raven and punish him for what he'd done tonight to his own daughter. The man was a monster.

Luke took Kate's hands, cradling them between his and rubbing gently. She was still ice-cold. "We can wait a while longer before we talk about him, you know."

"It's okay. I'm over it now and I want to tell you what he said." She looked less punch-drunk, but she left her hands in his clasp, something she would never have done if she'd been feeling anywhere close to normal.

"Did you talk for long?" Luke asked.

She shook her head. "Not at all. Actually, he cut me off the moment I started to speak." Kate's smile was wan. "That was in character, at any rate. My father always liked the sound of his own voice better than he liked listening to other people."

"Take it step by step, word by word." Luke wanted to capture exactly what Ron had said before her subconscious started to rewrite the memory. "The phone rang. You picked it up and he said…"

"*Listen up.* That was one of his favorite expressions when I was growing up. As soon as I heard those words I knew it was him. Then he said that looking for him would be hazardous to my health."

"Those were his exact words?"

She nodded. "He said there was no point in looking for him because he was too well hidden to be found and, anyway, the search was hazardous to my health. Then he added that if by any chance I did ever manage to find out where he was, I'd regret it. And that wasn't a threat, it was a certified Ron Raven promise. Those were his exact words. A certified Ron Raven promise."

A chill ran down Luke's spine, followed by a flash of white-hot rage. There was no way to interpret that final remark other than as a cruel, frightening joke. It was bad enough for Ron Raven to threaten his own daughter, but it struck Luke as truly obscene that the son of a bitch had taunted her with his lifetime string of lies and broken promises. For the first time he could ever recall, Luke experienced an intense desire to smash his fists into the face of a fellow human being.

For Kate's sake, he forced himself to put the rage aside. She had claimed a few minutes ago that her father had threatened to kill her, but from what she'd just recounted, it seemed as if the threat had been implicit rather than explicit. Unfortunately, he wasn't sure that made the danger any less real. Kate obviously felt the threat had been serious, however delivered.

He tightened his grip on Kate's hands, trying to provide the reassurance of friendly human contact as he asked the brutal but essential question. "Did your father actually say the words that he would kill you if you continued to look for him?" He could hardly believe he was asking her something so far outside the bounds of normal parameters.

She flinched at the question, but answered calmly enough. "No, he only said that if I didn't stop searching for him, I would regret it." Kate thought for a moment, her forehead wrinkled in sudden puzzlement. "I guess that could mean almost anything, couldn't it? Why did I immediately jump to the conclusion that he was threatening to kill me?"

Because the combination of Ron's tone of voice, choice of words and general attitude had made that a logical conclusion. And because he'd warned her that looking for him was hazardous to her health.

"You were scared and shocked," Luke said. "Your

fear affected what you heard." And he hoped like hell that his relatively benign explanation was true.

"That's true. Hearing his voice was so unexpected that the impact was intensified." She frowned. "Maybe his call was so shocking because everything he said seemed out of character. He was absent a lot of the time when I was growing up, but he was always kind and affectionate when he happened to be around. Did he manage to put on an act for all those years? Or has something radically changed him in the past few months?"

"Perhaps neither," Luke suggested. "From what we're learning, Ron isn't much into long-term planning. He seems to go with whatever is most convenient at any given moment and worry about the consequences later. When you were growing up, for some reason he found it satisfying to play the indulgent dad. You weren't mistaken—he really did enjoy your company. Now that he's in a different place, he has different needs."

He *really* hoped those needs didn't include trying to kill Kate. She seemed lost in contemplation, and judging from her expression, the memories she was pulling up weren't happy. Luke decided to distract her with a more practical and less harrowing question than the true nature of Ron's intentions toward her. "Have you thought about how your father managed to reach you?" he asked. He was puzzled as to how Ron Raven had known where to find his daughter. "Did he call on your cell phone?"

"No, he called on the regular hotel phone. To be honest, when the phone rang, I assumed it was you."

Luke didn't much like her answer. Not surprisingly

with all she had to cope with, Kate hadn't yet stopped to consider just how strange it was that her father had known where to reach her. Luke, however, wondered how in hell Ron Raven had known his daughter was spending the night in this specific hotel.

"I'm going to call the operator and see if there's any way they can tell us where your father's call originated. Heck, everyone has caller ID these days. Maybe the hotel does, too. We might even learn what alias Ron is using these days." Luke leaned across the bed and picked up the phone as he spoke.

The operator responded at once. "Good evening, sir. How may I help you?"

"Is there any way you can trace phone calls coming into this hotel?" he asked.

"I'm sorry, sir, our system isn't set up to provide that service."

"Your system doesn't have caller ID?"

"No, sir. Not on the system we use for guest calls."

"Maybe I could speak to the operator who took the call I'm interested in. How many operators are on duty at this time of night?"

"After 11:00 p.m. we route all phone calls through the front desk. Right now, I'm the only person on duty here."

"Then maybe you're the person who can help me. Somebody called room 820 about thirty minutes ago. The guest's name is Kate Fairfax. Did you put that call through?"

"I must have done, but I'm sorry, sir, I don't remember anything about it. There have been more calls than usual tonight. To be honest, they're all a bit of a blur."

Luke pressed hard, but the desk clerk's answers remained the same: she didn't remember the call and there was no way to trace its point of origin without a court order to the phone company. Luke thanked her and hung up, controlling his frustration. He wasn't surprised that Ron Raven had once again managed to game the system. Although perhaps it didn't matter much that they couldn't pinpoint Ron's exact location. Ron would have covered his ass by calling from a bar, or an airport or some other public place. And wherever he called from, he would have been somewhere else within seconds of hanging up the phone.

While Luke talked to the front desk clerk, Kate had walked through to the bathroom and poured herself a glass of water, but she'd heard their conversation. "My father knew we'd never be able to trace his call," she said as she walked back into the bedroom.

"I'm afraid so. Even if the hotel had caller ID, Ron probably uses a blocking technique so that nobody can see the number he's calling from."

What interested Luke at this precise moment was not the fact that Ron's call couldn't be traced but the fact that Ron had known Kate was spending the night in a hotel in Reston. The decision to stay here had been made *after* they visited the house on Maple Drive, a mere thirty minutes before they checked in. There was only one way Luke could think of for Ron Raven to know where they were: he'd been following them. That unpleasant thought sent another couple of nasty chills chasing down his spine.

"I'm not going to tell Mom or Uncle Paul about Dad calling me," Kate said. There was more color in her cheeks and she was no longer visibly numb with shock, but she looked so sad Luke ached in sympathy.

He was pretty sure she'd want to revisit that judgment, because her family obviously needed to be in the loop. But he wasn't going to press the issue tonight. What she needed now was to get some sleep, to be oblivious for a few hours to the fact that her own father had threatened her life, or at the very least her safety.

"There's no reason to disturb your mother or your uncle tonight," he said. "In fact, the only thing we need to decide right now is whether we're going to keep our appointment tomorrow morning with Seth Bedinsky. It's your call, Kate, and in view of your father's threats, nobody will be surprised or upset if you decide to back off. If the rest of your family knew the whole story, I'm sure they'd beg you to stop searching."

"I'm not backing off." Kate's voice was low, hard and intense. "I definitely want to keep that appointment with Seth Bedinsky. If my father thinks he can scare me off with threats and spiteful jokes about his own string of broken promises, then he's about to discover he's mistaken."

"I'm glad you feel that way," Luke said softly. He took her hand and held it for a moment against his cheek before turning it over and dropping a deliberately casual kiss in her palm. "Personally, I think it's past time we found your father and held him accountable. He'll only cause trouble until we run him to ground."

"Do they put bigamists in prison?" Kate asked.

"Probably not. But Ron faked his own death, and that's definitely a crime."

"If you'd told me six months ago that I'd be quite

happy to visualize my father behind bars, I'd have assumed you were crazy."

"Six months ago, you didn't know the man your father really is."

Kate pulled a face. "Ignorance is definitely bliss."

"Maybe." The trouble with unfounded bliss, Luke thought, was that truth could intervene and rip away your happiness at any moment, which was exactly what had happened with Ron Raven and his two families.

"Anyway, about the meeting with Seth," he said. "I called my sister after I got back to the room from dinner, and we're supposed to be seeing him tomorrow morning at nine-thirty. Seth's office is in Georgetown, on Q Street, so we need to be out of here by eight-thirty. Will you set your alarm or would you like me to wake you?"

Kate didn't respond directly. She patted her hips and registered that she was wearing pants that had no pockets. "I forgot to grab my room key when I came to talk to you. I can't get back into my room."

"I'll go down to the front desk and pick up a duplicate for you." Luke hoped the receptionist wouldn't demand that Kate request the key in person.

"Could I...do you think...would you mind if I slept here with you tonight?" Kate turned away from him, apparently finding it easier to talk to the wall. "If I go back to my own room, I'm afraid I'll lie awake all night waiting for the phone to ring again." She swung around to face him, her cheeks flushed. "I understand if you'd prefer not to have me here with you. I know it's an imposition."

"Of course you can sleep with me." Luke winced, but somehow—God knows how—managed a smile. He wondered if there could be a better definition of torment than the prospect of having Katie in his bed when he was obligated to keep his hands entirely away from every part of her.

"Thank you." She tried to return his smile, but she couldn't hold on to it. "This isn't a good night to be alone."

"Fortunately, there's no need for you to be alone." Luke turned back the covers on the king-size bed and Kate climbed in. She flipped over onto her stomach, her favorite sleeping position, and Luke's gut twisted into a tight, heavy knot. Between anger at Ron Raven and suppressed desire for Katie, his stomach—not to mention various other portions of his anatomy—seemed destined to have a long and uncomfortable night.

He followed her into bed, careful to avoid touching her. Kate reached out and took his hand, twining her fingers through his. He knew there wasn't an ounce of sexual invitation in the gesture; she was simply searching for the comfort of human contact.

He squeezed her fingers. "Good night, Kate. Try to sleep now." Excellent advice. For his part, he had about as much chance of sleeping as of levitating three feet above the bed.

"Good night, Luke. I'm glad you're here. Thank you for being so kind."

Her voice was husky and definitely sleepy. The aftermath of shock was taking a toll. Luke hoped like hell that Saint Peter was watching and had his heavenly ledger for recording noble deeds wide open to the page marked *Luke Savarini*. By the time this night was over, he would have earned at least a dozen gold stars.

Seventeen

"Why do you keep checking the rearview mirror?" Kate asked.

"I'm trying to see if we're being followed." Luke turned his gaze back to the road ahead. "Since it's Monday morning and there are approximately ten thousand other vehicles traveling on the same stretch of road, it's tough to decide."

"Who do you think is tailing us? My father?" Last night the issue of how her father had known where to find her hadn't crossed Kate's mind. This morning, almost as soon as she woke up, she'd realized the only way Ron could have known where to call her was if he'd been following them the previous afternoon.

"I guess we have to accept the possibility," Luke conceded. "Either Ron was tailing us in person yesterday or he hired a surrogate. I can't figure out any other way he could have known where to call, can you?"

"No. We only chose the hotel a few minutes before we booked in. Nobody knew where we would be." The image of her father pursuing them as they made the rounds of the print shop and the villa on Maple Drive left Kate feeling nauseated. She not only hated to imagine herself under surveillance, she was cross that neither she nor Luke had noticed their tail.

In some ways, their amateur status had worked to their disadvantage, Kate acknowledged. She and Luke had enthusiasm, but in the same way plenty of good home cooks would nevertheless be lost in a commercial kitchen, an investigator such as George Klein would have had his own valuable repertoire of tricks of the detective trade. George would have noticed if he'd been followed for an entire afternoon, whereas she and Luke had been blithely unaware. The possible risk hadn't occurred to either of them until after the damage had been done.

Luke glanced once more into his rearview mirror and then shook his head in frustration. "If anyone is tailing us this morning, I'm damned if I can spot the vehicle."

She snapped out of her melancholy, diverted by memories of past outings with Luke. His sedate driving habits had amused her when they were dating, partly because they had always struck her as so out of character.

"It's no surprise you can't spot the tail," she said with mock severity. "As usual, you're driving like my great-aunt Jessica."

"So speaks the woman who drives like she's channeling Sam Hornish."

"I wish! In the meantime, you need to switch lanes a few times, do a U-turn, zigzag through the intersection and watch to see who follows."

"Great plan," Luke said. "Except for the minor fact that we're in the middle of three lanes of traffic, all inching toward the Potomac at approximately fifteen miles an hour. Zigging and zagging are only slightly less possible at the moment than sprouting wings and flying."

"Don't be defeatist. Think Matt Damon and *The Bourne Identity.* Now, that's how you shake a tail."

"Matt Damon was smart enough to use stunt drivers and his producers cleared the city before they filmed those car chases. We, on the other hand, are sitting in bumper-to-bumper rush-hour traffic. And do you see that cop car over there, just longing to pounce?"

She rolled her eyes. "You always did have a tendency to get hung up on minor technical details."

"That, and there's also my odd dislike of contemplating life from inside a jail cell."

"I'd bail you out." She grinned. "Probably."

"You're all heart. Thanks."

"You're welcome." She thought how amazing it was that Luke could make her laugh about the possibility of being followed, especially after what had happened last night. "So what's *your* plan for shaking our tail, if any?"

"You'll consider it boringly low-key. I suggest we park the car a couple of blocks away from Seth Bedinsky's office and then proceed on foot. That way, it should be easier to make sure we're not being followed. We can dodge in and out of a few buildings if you're experiencing an extreme need for drama."

"Dodging in and out of buildings doesn't exactly meet my standards for high drama." She gave his arm an affectionate squeeze. "Face it, Luke, you're a repressed, law-abiding citizen at heart."

"Damn right." He was untroubled by her accusation. Without taking his eyes from the road, he reached out and covered her hand with his. For all that they were both making light of the situation, he was aware of how emotionally fragile she felt. It was no fun driving in heavy traffic, wondering if your father was pursuing you with murder on his mind.

"Why do you think he called me last night?" Kate asked, giving voice to the question that had haunted her dreams. "Until he called, we had no clue he was still somewhere in this general area. For all we knew to the contrary, he might really have decided to start a new life in Australia. My father may be a risk-taker, but why did he call unless it was absolutely essential to warn me off? Do you think we're getting too close for his comfort?"

"I wish." Luke sighed as they drew to a halt behind a truck belching black exhaust fumes. "The truth is, though, that Ron didn't actually reveal very much."

"He revealed that he'd been following us through northern Virginia! That seems major to me."

Luke shook his head. "He didn't reveal anything about his location at the time of the call. In fact, he didn't even reveal that he'd been in Reston earlier in the day."

"Because he could have hired somebody to follow us, you mean?"

"Right. And even if he personally tailed us all afternoon, six or seven hours passed between the time we checked into the hotel and Ron's call to you at midnight. During those six or seven hours, he could have driven five hundred miles from Virginia in any direction. Alternatively, Dulles airport is less than thirty minutes from the hotel and has flights taking off to cities around the world. When Ron spoke to you, he could have been five minutes away from boarding a flight to China for all we know."

"Still, his phone call proved he's alive, so he must have had a reason for making it. And I can't figure out what that reason might be."

"We're overanalyzing again," Luke said. "My best guess is that we should take the phone call strictly at face value. He told you to stop looking for him and that's what the call was about. He's given up on pretending to be dead but he still doesn't want to be found, and on the slight chance you could succeed in tracking him, he hoped to frighten you into quitting."

"What about the other part of the message he delivered? The part where he informed me I'd regret it if by any chance we did manage to find him. Are we supposed to take that at face value, too?"

The traffic slowed to a standstill and Luke turned his gaze from the car ahead long enough to look searchingly at her. "Now that you've slept on it, do you still believe Ron threatened to kill you?"

"I don't know." Now that it was morning, and the sun was shining on a normal, everyday scene of people hurrying to work, it seemed overdramatic to believe that her father had been threatening murder. After all, he might have been warning her that she'd regret finding him because he was involved with another woman, or for a dozen relatively benign reasons she didn't have enough information to grasp. And yet, if she replayed his words in her head, the overtones of menace were still present. Sleep had not removed any of the sting from her memory. She still believed her father had been threatening to physically harm her.

She forced herself to speak lightly because if she allowed her emotions full play, she might easily find herself paralyzed by a mixture of fear and rage. "As far as I'm concerned, the jury's still out on exactly what my father was threatening. But let's just say I'd like to make damn sure we aren't followed before we go into Seth Bedinsky's offices."

They parked the car two blocks away from Q Street and then dodged and wove their way to Seth Bedinsky's office, arriving there with some degree of confidence that nobody had pursued them. Seth turned out to be the quintessential techie nerd. He was a short man, a little on the plump side, with thinning hair and rimless glasses. His baggy khakis and white shirt looked as if they had been pulled from the dryer after days of lying there untended, guaranteeing maximum wrinkles.

Apparently humans didn't rate much higher than clothes in Seth's grand scheme of things. He greeted them with an abstracted air, as if his attention had only reluctantly been pulled from the half-dozen computer monitors that lined his wall-length desk. Only when his gaze lighted on Anna did his eyes come fully into focus.

Luke's sister looked nothing like the way Kate had imagined her. Anna was dark, petite and vivacious, with clear olive skin and brown eyes. Only the bright intelligence of her expression reminded Kate of Luke.

"I'm delighted to meet you," Anna said, shaking Kate's hand. "My brother told me the two of you were dating for a while, but he forgot to mention that you're drop-dead gorgeous." She smiled, somehow managing to sound entirely sincere while delivering the extravagant compliment.

"And Katie makes the world's best chocolate fudge cake, too." Luke wrapped a surprisingly possessive arm around her shoulders. "Not to mention the most exquisite raspberry torte, and croissants so light they melt in your mouth. Et cetera, et cetera, et cetera." He gave his sister a teasing grin. "That should really intimidate you, Annie."

"I can't cook," Anna explained to Kate, looking entirely untroubled by her lack of ability. "I can't sew, clean house or grow houseplants, either. My mother is a domestic goddess and she swears I'm a changeling. She wasted years of her life and endured dozens of ruined saucepans trying to teach me to make spaghetti sauce. When I hit thirty, she acknowledged it was a lost cause. She's convinced my inability to prepare a decent family meal is the major reason I'm not married. Except on the days when she decides it's because I'm such a lousy housekeeper."

"I should fill her in on all the other reasons," Seth murmured, startling Kate, who hadn't realized he was listening.

Anna didn't seem in the least offended by Seth's acerbic comment. She bent down and whispered something into his ear which made him turn bright red. She laughed softly when she saw his blush and rumpled her fingers affectionately through his thinning hair.

Luke had suggested earlier that Seth wanted to sleep with his sister. Watching the two of them, Kate was pretty sure Seth had succeeded in his goal and that Anna was very content with the resulting situation.

Seth swung around on his chair. He glanced at Kate, blinking several times behind his glasses. She suspected he was searching for her name and not finding it. "I'm Kate," she reminded him, putting him out of his misery. "And this is Luke."

"Yeah, great. Thanks." He cleared his throat. "Well, let's get down to business, okay? I understand you have a couple of password-protected files you want me to open."

"Yes, please." Kate took the flash drive from her purse and handed it over. "The files we need to open are both on here."

"Just so I know what I'm getting into, do you have any legal right to be opening these files?"

"It's possible," Kate said. "We hadn't thought about that, to be honest."

Seth didn't look happy with her response, so she tried again. "The flash drive was abandoned in an empty house. In addition, we believe it once belonged to my father. Since he's officially missing, presumed dead, I can't see how there would be any legal problem with us trying to open those files. The lawyers had us searching through all my father's other personal papers, so these files shouldn't be any different just because it's digital information rather than printed."

"Great. Glad to hear it." Seth slotted the drive into a USB port. "It's always nice to know I'm not breaking the law." He grinned. "Rare, but nice."

He worked in silence for less than five minutes, and then gave a satisfied grunt when the first of the files opened. Columns of numbers flashed onto the screen with no headers to explain what they might mean.

"What is it?" Luke asked. "It looks like strings of gibberish."

Seth gave another grunt before remembering he had to use real words when conversing with pesky non-techies. "The passwords aren't the only security lock on these files. Your father used an encryption program before he applied his password protocol. The encryption isn't very elaborate, though. Enough to stop random corporate predators from hacking in and stealing your data but not much more. Still, these programs are marketed as the last word in security, so you have to figure your dad *really* didn't want anyone to see this information."

"Can you decode the files despite the encryption?" Kate asked.

Seth looked up at her, clearly startled by the question. "Of course. As I said, it's a standard commercial product and I already wrote my own program for rendering the encryption in clear text…." His voice tailed off as he walked over to a shelving unit and searched through a row of filing boxes designed to hold data disks.

He found the one he needed surprisingly fast. For all the coiled wires, stray cables and discarded scraps of paper, Seth apparently had an organizational system that worked. He slipped the small data disk into one of his computer drives.

"This is going to take a few minutes," he said. He glanced at the screen and read the message. "Seven minutes and change, to be precise."

Anna turned to Kate. "I really come here for the coffee. Seth has a fancy machine set up in the storeroom and it makes heavenly espressos. Would you like one while we wait?"

"Yes, thank you. That would be great."

"Luke? You, too?"

"Sure, I could use another shot of caffeine. Do you need help?"

"I'll take Kate." Anna turned to her. "If you don't mind lending a hand?"

"Of course not." Kate smiled politely, although Anna was pretty transparent in her maneuvering. She wanted to discuss Kate's relationship with her brother a lot more than she wanted help brewing a few cups of coffee.

Her guess turned out to be correct. Anna might not be able to cook or clean, but she was a whiz with the espresso machine and needed no assistance from Kate or anyone else.

"My brother is in love with you," she said without preamble, as the first cup hissed and steamed its way to completion.

"No, he really isn't," Kate assured her. "We were…dating…but that's been over for months. Luke is just helping me out on this trip. As a friend, you know? He feels responsible because he's the one who started off this whole chase when he saw my father in your cousin's restaurant."

"All of that may be true. Luke may be helping you out because he feels responsible, and he may be treating you as a friend on this trip. None of that changes the fact that my brother is head over heels in love with you. I know Luke well and his heart is in his eyes each time he looks at you."

"In this case, though, I'm sure you're mistaken." But for the first time, Kate allowed herself to wonder what would happen if Anna were right. If Luke loved her—as opposed to simply desiring her—would she want to get together with him again?

The answer was blindingly obvious: of course she would. She was determined not to get involved again because she didn't believe Luke had ever loved her. Lusted for her and admired her professional talents, yes. But loved her in a make a commitment, buy a house, have babies kind of way? Until now, she'd been pretty sure the answer to all those questions was a resounding no. And despite Anna's confidence in her ability to read her brother's emotions, Kate doubted if a mere sister, however close, was a reliable judge of whether or not a man was in love. Maybe there really was a gleam in Luke's eyes when he looked at her. But there was little chance that Anna could distinguish between a spark of lust and the glow of true love.

Anna deftly switched out cups, refilled the basket with fresh coffee and pressed the lever. Then she looked up, her gaze troubled as she met Kate's eyes. "Are you going to hurt him, Kate?"

"I already did hurt him," she admitted. "We hurt each other. A lot." The truth was that her split from Luke, followed so rapidly by the news of her father's disappearance, had sent her into an emotional tailspin from which she was still recovering. As for Luke, whether or not his deeper feelings had been involved during their affair, she knew his pride had been devastated by her sexual encounter with Michael Rourke. She'd counted on that in starting the affair.

She'd regretted that particular act of vengeance almost from the moment she accepted one of Michael's persistent invitations to join him for dinner. She'd *really* regretted it by the time she ended up in Michael's bed. Even so, the pain of her relationship with Luke had become so overwhelming toward the end that she'd deliberately chosen to stay on a path she'd recognized from the beginning as viciously destructive.

Since she had never seen or spoken to Michael after Luke found the two of them in bed, she had never confirmed her suspicion that Michael had set the whole situation up, with every intention of having Luke discover them together. For all Michael's success in his career, Kate guessed he was jealous of his so-called best buddy. He had struck her as especially jealous of Luke's ability to attract women and then to keep them as friends once the sexual liaison ended. Michael had wanted to be sure that at least this one relationship ended in disaster, and she had been regrettably willing to help him along.

Luke had walked into Michael's bedroom, brought to his friend's penthouse condo in the middle of the night for reasons that had never been clear to Kate. The resulting nightmare played out at lightning speed. Kate retreated to the bathroom before Luke could say anything. Once there, she'd thrown up as if she'd caught some virulent, deadly virus. She was splashing her face with cold water, trying to control her nausea, when she heard the slamming of the front door. Luke had left the condo less than five minutes after finding her in bed with his soon-to-be-ex best friend.

The sound of the door slamming had vibrated throughout her entire being, drumming the message that she and Luke were over. Done. Finished. And that, presumably, was what she'd wanted. Why else had she been in Michael's bed? Funny that success could feel so very much like the most terrible sort of failure. She'd leaned against the coolness of the tiled wall and wondered if hearts really could break. At that moment, it seemed entirely possible the answer in her case was yes. Her heart had felt poised on the verge of exploding from sheer misery, but eventually she'd recovered enough to get dressed, call a cab and get herself home.

None of this was information she planned to share with Luke's sister, however, not even in censored form. Kate busied herself grinding some more beans and waited to speak until she was sure she could keep her voice steady.

"You needn't worry, Anna. Luke and I are both too smart to get involved again. We have a lot in common, professionally speaking, so the first time around we were in over our heads before we quite realized what was happening. This time, we're all too aware that it takes more than great sex and a shared profession to make a relationship."

"Does it? Great sex and a shared interest in science are what Seth and I have going for us, and it seems pretty terrific to me."

"I expect you trust him, too."

"Of course."

"Luke doesn't trust me."

"Why? Does he have cause to distrust you?"

Kate drew in a deep breath. Luke had warned her that his family asked what they wanted to know, but she wasn't used to blunt discussions like this. Her own family was masterful at keeping a collective stiff upper lip, and painfully inadequate at expressing deep feelings. She felt exposed just listening to Anna's questions, let alone answering them.

To Kate's overwhelming relief, Luke stuck his head around the door and she was granted a reprieve from interrogation. There was too much going on in her life right now and she wasn't ready to confront difficult questions about her feelings for Luke. Everything that had happened over the past couple of weeks in regard to her father had been guaranteed to knock her off balance, which made this an especially unwise moment to start wondering if her old relationship with Luke could be resurrected in a new and less hurtful form. Any answers she came up with were likely to be dangerously skewed by emotional overload.

"Is the coffee ready?" Luke asked. "Seth's almost done decoding the first file."

"And we're done, too. Good timing. Here's your coffee. Black, one sugar." Anna handed him a cup and passed another one to Kate. "Help yourself to sugar if you want it, Kate. If you take cream, Seth has the real stuff in the minifridge over there."

"No, I'll drink it black. Thank you." Kate carried her coffee and Seth's back into the office. Seth took the cup with a distracted mumble, possibly meant to be interpreted as thanks. He pointed to the computer screen where the decryption program had just finished working its magic. File RR21 was now revealed as a document thirty pages long, divided into five separate subfiles, each one headed with a different name: Russo Enterprises, Romney Enterprises, Rausch Enterprises, Reinhard Enterprises and finally Roanoke Enterprises.

"It's printing out now." Seth jerked his head toward a large printer that was spewing out pages at a fast clip. "Why don't you start reading those pages while I get to work on the other file."

Eighteen

Kate and Luke drew up chairs and began to read. Each six-page document provided details of a potential deal where stock would be exchanged for an infusion of cash, making five profiles and five potential deals in all. The five companies were located in the general vicinity of Washington, D.C.: three in the densely populated suburbs of northern Virginia, and two in Maryland.

The first sheet for each subfile provided basic information, such as the company address and phone number, along with the names of the principal officers. The next three pages contained financial data, together with Ron's concise personal assessment of that individual company's strengths and weaknesses.

All five companies appeared to be modestly sized and family owned, and each had new products they were trying to bring to the market. The products varied widely, from a medical gadget aimed at making life easier for aging baby boomers to an environmentally friendly insect repellent and a collection of upscale-looking furniture that could be ordered from a catalog or Web site and put together by home owners with nothing more than a screwdriver and small wrench.

This last company was the one which had garnered the most favorable comments from Ron. A deal for his financial support seemed imminent. The company, Millbank Woodworks, had been inherited by the current president from his grandfather. The new president was having a tough time persuading the banks to take his ideas seriously, probably because he'd barely turned twenty-five.

Her father had always been especially good at spotting twentysomethings with guts, drive, ambition and a great business plan, Kate mused. That was exactly the category Luke had fallen into, and her father's investment in Luciano's had doubled in value within three years. Millbank Woodworks was in the mold of many previous success stories.

The fifth sheet in each section was headed More Contact Information and provided names, extension phone numbers, e-mail addresses and informal bios for each person that Ron had dealt with at that specific company. The bios listed educational backgrounds and professional achievements, but the emphasis seemed to be on personal data. Spouses or significant others were always listed, along with notations such as *Recently divorced* or *Avoids talking about his partner.* The number of children, favorite restaurants and hobbies were also listed, as well as one-sentence reminders of what had been discussed in addition to business.

Fanatic supporter of Ohio State Football, one typical comment read. Another comment was highlighted in red:

Warning!!! Don't forget Brad was born in Casper, Wyoming. Presumably, with less than half a million people living in the entire state of Wyoming, Ron was afraid the usual six degrees of separation might be decreased to two or three. The exclamation points were most likely a reminder to himself never to say anything that would enable Brad to connect his potential business partner to the Flying W ranch and the town of Thatch, Wyoming.

Her father had come up with a system that avoided almost any chance of arousing suspicion in the minds of his clients, Kate reflected. He had notes about every danger point. After a lifetime of living as a bigamist, he must be an expert at compartmentalizing his relationships so that he never slipped up and said the wrong thing to the wrong person.

The final sheet of each subfile was a photograph of a middle-aged man, each labeled with a name. Robert Russo, Richard Romney, Raymond Rausch, Ralph Reinhard and Ramsey Roanoke stared unsmilingly into the camera. The shots were full face, with no attempt to flatter.

Kate realized at once that all five names shared initials with her father, and that they must be pseudonyms, but she actually wasted a few seconds wondering how her father had managed to recruit five middle-aged men willing to work as fronts for him before she did a double take and realized that she was looking at five pictures of Ron Raven.

"My God, these photos are all of my father," she said to Luke, staring at the shot of black-haired, black-eyed Robert Russo. "I wouldn't have recognized him in any of them! What's the purpose of including them in the files, do you think?"

Luke picked up the photo of gray-haired, gray-eyed Richard Romney and compared it with the other four. "I think he must have wanted a quick and easy reminder of exactly how he looked when he dealt with each company. When absolutely everything about your life is a lie, you might need a few concrete physical reminders to help you keep straight which set of lies you told to which set of people. Ron doesn't want to arrange a meeting in the guise of one of his fake characters and realize too late that he's left home without his brown contacts, or his black toupee or whatever."

That made sense, Kate supposed, although the vision of her father as a quick-change scam artist did nothing to quell the renewed queasiness in the pit of her stomach. "I suppose he has to use disguises if he wants to build up a successful business again. There was so much TV coverage of his disappearance that he couldn't just turn up looking like Ron Raven. The risk of being recognized would be too high."

"He's certainly taken care of that problem," Luke commented. "But I wonder why he has a different disguise for each company."

"The business world is surprisingly small," Kate suggested. "I guess he doesn't want the CEO of Millbank Woodworks to talk to the CEO of Senior Empowerment at the local chamber of commerce dinner and realize that they're both being financed by the same man. Dad can't afford to build a reputation anymore. If he wants to stay hidden, each deal he makes will have to be a one-off."

"Makes sense," Luke conceded. "Although it begs the question as to why he wasn't disguised the night I spotted him in Cousin Bruno's restaurant."

"Those disguises can't be comfortable. Besides, what my father seems to have done is to live his private life as Stewart Jones, and conduct his business life under various pseudonyms, with disguises to match." Kate stared at a photo where, in addition to donning a curly brown toupee, her father had substantially padded his waistline and added a pair of thick-rimmed glasses. The disguise was effective enough that if she had seen him in this outfit in real life, she doubted if she would have recognized him.

"Your father seems to have made fewer changes in his work habits than in his appearance," Luke commented. "Judging by these files, he's spent the past six months working exactly the same sort of financial deals that he put together so successfully before he disappeared."

"In a way, that's only to be expected, don't you think? Whatever else we've learned about my father, none of it has changed the fact that he has a near-genius for spotting small- and medium-size businesses that are poised on the verge of success and just need an infusion of cash in order to grow. It seems only logical for him to continue doing what he does best."

Luke frowned in thought. "Logical up to a certain point, I agree. Except that if I'd gone to as much trouble as Ron in order to disappear, I'd want to make more of a change in my life than moving someplace new and then working exactly the same sort of deals."

"Maybe having a new lover and no kids was all the

change he needed." Kate sounded more resentful than she'd intended and she quickly amended her answer. "Actually, I'm not doing him justice. We shouldn't forget that as far as his initial disappearance from the Miami hotel is concerned, my father deserves the benefit of the doubt about his motives."

"How so?" Luke didn't look in the least forgiving.

"Well, according to everything Adam learned in Belize, my father didn't disappear because he woke up one morning and decided it would be nice to get rid of his wives and children. He disappeared because he was warned people had been hired to murder him. His life was at risk."

"You're right." Luke made the concession reluctantly, obviously unhappy about cutting Ron any slack. "I guess whatever we conclude about Julio Castellano's honesty, it does seem clear by now that people really were trying to kill your father."

Kate traced a finger over the mustache sported by "Ramsey Roanoke." "That could be another reason he's using all these disguises and why he's so desperate to avoid contact with us and the rest of his family. Maybe he still feels his life is in danger, so he wants to remain officially dead. His enemies aren't going to waste time and energy targeting a dead person."

Luke nodded in grudging agreement. "The smugglers at the platinum mine have been arrested by the Belizean police according to Adam, but nobody's captured Julio Castellano as far as we know, right?"

"The cops haven't heard a word about him or from him," Kate said.

"That suggests there's a hell of a lot we still don't

understand about your father's dealings with Castellano. I guess it's even possible that Ron warned you off last night because he was afraid you were putting yourself in the path of danger aimed at him."

It was a possibility Kate hadn't considered before. She was still mulling the idea over, wondering if she was too anxious to latch on to any excuse for her father's miserable behavior, when Seth scooted his chair across the tile floor and handed her another slim stack of papers.

"That's the printout for the second file," he said. "RR22."

This file had only a dozen pages and the significance of the content was much harder to understand. A word or two, all in capital letters, was centered on each page. Charts, containing four columns with a sprinkling of numbers in each column, made up the rest of the content. On all twelve pages, the first three columns were without headers. The final column was topped by a dollar sign, suggesting that the figures in that column represented sums of money. However, there was no way to tell if the sums were debts, bills, receivables or money paid into a bank account somewhere.

"Is it an accounts ledger?" Kate asked.

"Could be." Luke finished leafing through the sheets. "If so, it's a very simple one, though."

"The first column might be a date." Anna had joined them and leaned over Luke's shoulder to scrutinize the mysterious pages. "Look, there's always a slash between the first and second number—4/22, 5/31, 6/17 and so on."

"There's nothing higher than 10/2." Kate skimmed

quickly through the pages. "Or I guess I should say there's no entry later than the second of October, if these really are dates."

Anna gave a satisfied nod. "That October 2 date would tie in with the fact that Luke spotted Ron at our cousin's restaurant on October 3. Presumably Ron made some entries on Tuesday the second, after which the record—whatever it is—stops."

"Because Ron was on the run after the third," Luke said. "That sounds plausible." He spread the pages over the table for easier side-by-side comparison. "You're both right, there's nothing noted after 10/2 on any of these sheets. That could mean we're seeing a date in column one and a payment or charge in column four, separated by two columns that represent…we have no clue."

"Mathematically speaking, the numbers are random." Anna stared at the columns as if willing them to make sense. "I can't detect any pattern at all."

"They're small numbers," Luke pointed out. "There's nothing higher than three hundred, not even in the money column."

"But we have no way of knowing if Ron mentally added a bunch of zeroes to some of these entries," Anna said. "Is he really talking about three hundred bucks here, and a hundred and fifty there? Or should we add a couple of zeroes and call it thirty thousand and fifteen thousand?"

"Or add four zeroes and call it three million." Kate grimaced in frustration and then pointed to the headers at the top of each page. "And what about these? Are they words, or are they initials?"

"I think they're words," Anna said. "A few of them even seem vaguely familiar, but I can't for the life of me remember the context where I heard them." She read a couple of the headers out loud. *"Chaac. Yumil Kaxob."* She frowned. "Not star systems. Not galaxies. Where the hell have I come across those words before?"

"It doesn't even look like a real language to me," Kate said. "I'm not convinced they're words. Seth, is it possible the headers are still encoded?"

He swiveled his chair around and squinted at the headers. "It's possible, but they weren't encoded as part of the computer program. I can tell you this much for sure, the headers were originally numbers, and they converted to those groups of letters when I applied my decryption protocol. They could have been doubly encoded, of course."

"I've got it!" Luke interjected with visible triumph. "I know what they are! They're Mayan gods and goddesses. "Chaac is the Mayan god of rain and thunder. Kinich Ahau is the sun god. Yumil Kaxob…I don't remember who he is. Maybe he's the god of farming, or maize and crops or something. I don't have a clue about the others, but it seems likely they're Mayan deities, too. Oh, wait, I just remembered who Kukulcan is. He's the big boss, the feathered serpent who likes to have virgins cut up on his stone altars."

"Okay, I'm impressed," Anna said. "How in the world did you know that, little brother?"

He grinned. "Remember Liz Griffiths?"

"Oh my God, the dreaded Liz Griffiths!" Anna laughed and expanded for Kate and Seth's benefit. "Liz was a girlfriend of Luke's—"

"*Briefly* a girlfriend," Luke interrupted.

"Okay, briefly a girlfriend," Anna conceded. "She was a good person, really nice in fact, but she was a graduate student in archaeology and she couldn't stop talking about the glories of the Mayan civilization. I mean, she literally couldn't stop."

"When I started dating Liz, she had just spent the summer in Mexico's Yucatan Peninsula, excavating an ancient temple," Luke explained. "She came to our Savarini family dinner one Sunday and spent two hours giving us a nonstop lecture on the religious and cultural history of the Mayan civilization. I thought she would be talked out after that marathon, but on the next Sunday, she said she'd like to drive to my parents' house by herself because she'd be coming in from Lake Forest. It was only when she arrived at the front door that we discovered she'd brought slides, all taken at the excavation site."

"She insisted on making a presentation while we were eating dessert," Anna said, laughing. "There were a hundred slides, and she had something to say about every damn one. Lots of the slides were taken in tunnels of dirt, showing pieces of rock with squiggles on them, which didn't seem to fascinate any of us nearly as much as it fascinated Liz. It's the only time I remember my family being stunned into absolute silence."

Luke laughed. "Trust me, Annie, if you thought dinner and the slide show were bad, I promise you it got worse. Liz could work those damned Mayan gods into every imaginable and unimaginable situation. Especially the unimaginable ones, come to think of it. I'm surprised I didn't recognize the names sooner. I'd have sworn those gods were etched into my memory for all eternity."

Kate decided that Luke and his sister were too busy reminiscing about Liz Griffiths to have noticed that identifying the page headers as Mayan gods and goddesses hardly solved the mystery of what the columns of figures actually meant.

"I'm thrilled to know what—who?—Chaac and Yumil Kaxob are, but why would my father have chosen to name these pages in honor of Mayan gods?" she asked.

"Maybe he just needed headers and pulled something out of Wikipedia," Anna suggested.

"That doesn't make much sense." Luke frowned. "If Ron wanted identifiers, what's wrong with heading the pages A, B, C, and so on? Why mess with something as out of the ordinary as Mayan gods? Surely they have to carry some real meaning?"

"It can't be a coincidence that Consuela Mackenzie comes from a family that has Mayan ancestry," Kate said.

"So he named the pages as a tip of the hat to his new girlfriend, you mean?" Luke nodded. "It's possible."

"I think it's something more complex than that." Kate rubbed her forehead, trying to tease out a buried memory. "I'm remembering what Adam told us about his time with Julio Castellano—"

"Who's he?" Seth had apparently found their conversation interesting enough to stop working and had joined them at the table where they were poring over the printouts.

"Castellano is the man who was accused of murdering my father," Kate said. "A warrant for his arrest was issued back in June. But the cops here in the States have Castellano's bio and life history all wrong. His arrest record describes Castellano as an illegal Mexican immigrant. In fact, he was born and raised in Belize, and his ancestry is mixed Hispanic and Mayan."

"I guess my response to that is something along the lines of, so what?" Luke said. "I agree that Consuela and Julio both have ties to the Mayan community. They're related, so obviously their ethnic roots will be similar. But how does the fact that Julio Castellano has Mayan ancestors provide a reason for Ron to use the names of Mayan gods to head up his charts?"

"You have to think of the bigger picture," Kate persisted. "Step back and work from the premise that Castellano has links to my father beyond the fact that Consuela is his niece. I'd say the weight of evidence suggests Castellano is an ally of my father's, not his enemy."

"Agreed," Luke said. "And that implies—"

"Wait, I'm sorry to interrupt, but if Castellano and Ron Raven are allies, how do you explain what happened in Miami the night Ron disappeared?" Anna perched on the edge of the table, putting her hand on Seth's shoulder, the gesture revealing in its casual intimacy. "I'm genuinely curious," she added. "I'm not just poking holes in your theory."

Kate realized how far her views of that night had changed in the past couple of weeks. The scenario she'd finally arrived at bore no resemblance to the police theory of the crime. "I believe my father and Consuela decided to fake their own deaths and Julio Castellano agreed to help them. Castellano was crucial to the success of their deception. He made the whole blood-spattered, empty-hotel-room scenario more credible simply by providing a few drops of his own blood to spread around the scene of the supposed crime."

"It's amazing how finding Castellano's blood changed everything," Luke said. "Law enforcement in Miami withheld judgment as to whether Ron Raven was alive or dead until the police labs announced they had a DNA match on Castellano's blood. Then everyone's attitude within the department changed instantly. Castellano was a convicted murderer, so— according to the cops—it was obvious that he'd killed Ron Raven. Kate's father went from being missing to being presumed dead in the blink of an eye."

"And don't forget the most important part," Kate added, "at least from my father's point of view. The moment a warrant was issued for Castellano's arrest, the cops basically stopped all other investigation of the case. Nobody was looking for my father anymore because everybody's attention was focused on finding Castellano, the wicked triple murderer. Except the cops were searching for him in South Florida's Mexican community, so it's not surprising they didn't have much luck finding him."

"All that misdirection from a couple of blood splatters," Seth murmured. "Pretty impressive planning on your father's part. He took the current obsession with forensic evidence and manipulated it to provide a completely false picture of what had happened."

"I agree," Anna said. "It's brilliant planning on Ron Raven's part if we accept that his goal was to disappear. Do we accept that?"

"I do," Kate said. "I think he wanted to be dead so that his enemies in Belize would stop trying to kill him. Julio Castellano was hired by my dad's enemies to do the job, but my father thwarted their plans by recruiting Julio to his side. That way he achieved two goals in one fell swoop—he was able to fool *both* the smugglers back in Belize *and* the cops in Miami. Everyone accepted he was dead—"

"Leaving him free to do whatever the hell he wanted." Seth sounded admiring. "Man, this is a guy who knows how to pull off a scam."

"But why is he still hiding?" Luke picked up the printout of the file labeled RR21. "These are all legitimate business ventures, which means your father could pursue them openly if he'd step forward and acknowledge he's alive. We just agreed the smuggling ring in Belize has been shut down and your dad isn't at risk from them anymore. Why is he still running? Why is he putting on wigs and false beards and assuming fake identities to do something entirely legal?"

The answer seemed glaringly obvious to Kate. Some of her father's activities might be legitimate. Others, it seemed likely, were not. She hesitated to express her suspicions in front of Anna and Seth, but she realized they were both sympathetic and smart, a combination likely to generate a lot of good advice, so she overcame her reluctance.

"My father's choice of Mayan gods at the head of each page must have real meaning. I don't know much about the world of international art, but I do remember reading a magazine article about Mayan cities, lost for centuries in the jungle, and the fabulous treasure trove of art and historical objects waiting to be found in the temples there. Don't you think it's at least possible that Julio and Consuela are helping my father to smuggle ancient Mayan artifacts out of Belize and into the United States?"

"Bingo!" Anna sat bolt upright in her chair. "Finally an explanation that makes sense."

"I don't know that it does." Luke gestured to the thick printout of companies Ron Raven had contacted as potential investment opportunities. "Kate and I were agreeing just a little while ago that among the many amazing things about her father, one of the *most* amazing is his talent for spotting entrepreneurs and businesses that are going to succeed. Over the last twenty years, Ron earned millions of dollars legitimately. There's every reason to suppose he could earn millions more dollars over the next ten or twenty years. Why would he devote hundreds of hours to generating honest new business opportunities if he's decided to launch a new career as a criminal smuggling Mayan art out of Central America?"

"Why don't you ask him?" Seth suggested softly.

Kate wondered if Seth had been too caught up in his techie stuff to grasp the most important point. "We don't know where my father is," she said patiently. "We don't know how to find him."

"Sure you do." Seth smiled slightly. "Fortunately, you have all the information you need to find Ron Raven right here."

"Of course!" Anna exclaimed. "Look, Ron has an address and phone number listed for each of his identities and the addresses are all the same. It's an office plaza in Leesburg, which is in Loudon County, right on the border between Virginia and Maryland. He must maintain some sort of a presence there, otherwise he wouldn't be able to conduct any business."

Seth shook his head. "Unfortunately, that's not true. He can have all his calls routed to wherever he happens to be, which could be hundreds of miles away from Leesburg. The technology's simple."

"Okay, but somebody must collect mail on a regular basis. This isn't a post office box, it's a street address."

Seth shrugged. "A so-called 'street address' can be arranged at almost any store that rents mailboxes these days. Besides, nobody does important business by mail anymore, so most of what's getting delivered to that address will be junk. On the off chance there's something that needs to be picked up, Ron could either make a quick trip once a week to his Leesburg office or, more likely, send in a temp with instructions on how to handle any first-class mail."

"Then how do you suggest we find Ron Raven? You were the person who said we had all the information we need to track him." Luke glanced at his watch. "Kate and I are supposed to be flying back to Chicago in less than four hours, so if you have any brilliant ideas, now would be a good time to share them."

"It's simple," Seth said. "Your father will be suspicious of anyone trying to contact him through his Leesburg address and phone number. But he won't be in the least suspicious if somebody calls him from one of the companies he's negotiating with. You need to pick the company you think your father sounds most enthusiastic about, and then decide how you're going to persuade somebody from that company to set up a meeting with him. You don't have to go out and find Ron Raven. You can get him to come to you."

Anna gave Seth an exuberant hug and a kiss. "You're such a clever man."

"I know." Seth grinned. "That's why you love me."

Nineteen

October 22, 2007

The darkness was so intense that it penetrated Kate's dreams. Or perhaps it was some tiny, out-of-place sound that set her interior alarm bells jangling. She woke with a start and needed a moment to remember that she was back in Chicago, safely tucked into her own bed. For some reason, her heart continued to pound even after she oriented herself, so she rolled over, reaching for the switch on the bedside lamp. She clicked it on, but nothing happened.

The darkness, she realized belatedly, was total. The face of her alarm clock wasn't illuminated and the night-light by the doorway wasn't casting its usual friendly pink glow. A blown fuse, then, or maybe a power failure. She really needed to keep a flashlight in the drawer of her nightstand so that she wouldn't have to stumble and fumble her way to the fuse box when this sort of thing happened.

Then she remembered: her alarm clock ran on batteries. Even if there had been a power failure that should have no effect on her clock. Why weren't the digital numbers shining brightly? Kate patted the surface of her nightstand, feeling for her clock.

It wasn't there.

She pushed back against rising fear. Had she become disoriented by travel and made a mistake about where she was? Maybe she was still in the hotel in Virginia. She rubbed her fingers over the distinctive fluffy surface of her comforter and felt the lacy edge on her favorite pillowcase. Everything was familiar, which meant that she was at home, this was definitely her bed and the clock was missing. Perhaps the tiny sound that penetrated her sleep had been made by the clock falling from the nightstand.

A creak of the floor warned her of another human presence in the room. Her fear metastasized into a giant cancer, eating away at her ability to think. She instinctively dived toward the edge of the bed, away from the sound, but it was already too late for evasive action. A cloth was thrown over her head and drawn tight, cutting off air and demonstrating the terrifying fact that what had seemed pitch darkness only a few seconds before had just become several degrees darker yet.

It was instinctive to struggle, to fight against the inevitable horrors to come. But her captor was prepared and she'd been caught sleepy and off guard. The roughness of his grip warned her it was a man, although she hadn't even glimpsed his outline, much less seen him. He quickly taped her wrists together, covering her hands and most of her fingers, too. The darkness transformed the zip of unraveling tape from an everyday sound into a riff of terrifying menace. Her attacker wound the tape around her neck, securing the covering he'd thrown over her head into a makeshift hood. The folds of the thick cloth pressed against her mouth, making breathing a chore and talking impossible.

She could feel looped fibers brushing against her lips and caught a disorienting whiff of her own lavender shower gel. The cloth covering her head must be a towel, she realized. Apparently her attacker hadn't arrived already equipped with a blindfold. He'd simply purloined a towel from her bathroom as he passed by en route to her bedroom.

Perhaps by accident, perhaps because he didn't have murder on his mind, her attacker didn't lash the tape around her neck tightly enough to cut off her breathing. Kate tried to be grateful for that one small spark of hope. She willed herself not to get hysterical, not to pass out. If she was going to be raped, most experts warned it was safer not to fight back. She hung on to her sanity by promising herself she would remember every detail about the assailant that sound and touch could provide. She made herself a promise that she would see him brought to trial if it took the rest of her life to find him. He'd taped her fingers, so there was little hope of scratching him and getting a sliver of skin under her fingernails that could be tested for DNA. His preparations, she thought bleakly, seemed depressingly well planned. Despite that, she could still fight him. She would use her mind, the only weapon he'd left her, and, by God, she would defeat him.

"I warned you to stop looking for me." The whisper

was harsh and barely audible through the towel tied over her head.

Chills shook her body. So this was what it had come to. She wasn't about to endure the horror of rape by a stranger. She was going to end up killed by her own father. The prospect of rape had been terrifying enough; this was something worse. Kate wanted to feel anger, but her terror was so all-consuming that it left no room for any other emotion, not even the rage her father so richly deserved.

"You're my daughter, so I'm giving you one more chance." His whisper held more menace than a shouted threat. "Stop looking for me, Kate. Don't corner me, or I'll become like any other trapped animal. I'll lash out. I can't afford to give you any more warnings after this. Keep searching and you will die. You're leaving me with no choice."

She couldn't talk, and she had no intention of humiliating herself by making pathetic grunting sounds, but she probably wouldn't have deigned to answer him even if the towel hadn't made coherent speech a physical impossibility. She could move her legs, though, and rage suddenly liberated her from the paralysis of fear. She twisted out from under the covers and kicked as hard and as fast as she could.

She connected with flesh, but the blow didn't make much impact, enough for a brief moment of pain, perhaps, but no more. She kicked again, but this time her father sidestepped and her foot merely brushed against the side of his hip. Still, she heard the gratifying hiss of his indrawn breath and felt a split second of triumph that she hadn't allowed him to escape totally unscathed.

"Keep still, or I'll hit you."

For the first time in her life, she wished she had a gun. A rational part of her recognized that since she was blindfolded and handcuffed, introducing a gun into the picture was as likely to get her killed as it was to injure her father. At this moment, though, she would have traded her certain death for the hope of inflicting injury on him.

She didn't doubt that he meant exactly what he said, and since she didn't want to add a blow to her head to the woes already afflicting her, she sat quietly, no longer fighting.

The whispering began again. "Kate, you're my own flesh and blood and I admire your feistiness and your will to live. I don't want to hurt you. I love you, I really do. Don't force me to do something we'll both regret. You know the last thing I want is to be left with no choice but to kill you. Take this warning, Kate, for both our sakes. Please."

He was claiming to *love* her? Even if she hadn't been tied up, blindfolded and barely breathing, his whispered words would have left her speechless with disgust. As it was, she couldn't do anything more constructive than turn her back to the direction of his voice and force herself to remain calm so that she wouldn't throw up behind the heavy weight of the towel. How was it possible that she and her mother had both lived with this man for almost three decades without understanding anything about him?

He didn't react to her pathetic gesture of defiance in any way that she could detect. In fact, he'd never touched her at all once he finished tying her up. Rigid with tension, she waited for what would happen next. More verbal threats? A physical assault of some sort?

Nothing happened. Silence and darkness spread their thick, oppressive cover.

After a while, she wasn't sure how long, it occurred to her that she no longer had any sense of another presence in the room. However hard she strained to hear, she could detect no sound. Even though the towel over her head filtered out several levels of awareness, she gradually became confident that she was once again alone.

She was alone, but blinded by a towel and severely hampered by the tape wound around her hands. There was a phone on her nightstand, but with her fingers bound together, she couldn't even hold the phone, much less dial out and summon help, even if she could somehow find the correct numbers. She wriggled her wrists, but the tape was strong and she felt almost no give in the sturdy bindings. It could take hours—days— to loosen the tape to the point that she could break her hands apart.

Panic returned. She lived alone, and although she and her mother normally exchanged phone calls every couple of days, Avery wasn't the sort of person to hover. Unfortunately, Kate had stopped by to see her mother on her way home from the airport, so it wasn't as if Avery would be waiting anxiously for news about what had happened in Virginia. Kate had already filled her in on at least the general outline of everything she and Luke had discovered. She had promised to be in touch with her mother very soon, so that they could decide exactly when and how to pursue her father, but if Kate didn't call, her mother might assume she was snowed under at work and leave it at that.

If Avery didn't raise the alarm, how long would it take before somebody else got worried and came looking for her? She would be missed at work, of course, but it could easily be a couple of days before anyone actually became concerned enough to jump through the hoops of getting possession of a house key and physically searching for her.

Luke? He might call—she hoped he would call for reasons that went beyond her need to be set free—but they'd parted company at the airport without making any definite plans. Would he keep calling when she didn't pick up?

"I'll be in touch," Luke had said. He'd sounded as if he meant it, but she'd responded with a careless smile and a casual wave because God forbid that he should guess how badly she had wanted to invite him to come home with her.

Get a grip, Kate informed herself grimly. *If nobody's going to come looking for you, then you have to escape. It's that simple.*

She wasn't tied to the bed, she reminded herself. If worst came to the worst, she could slowly feel her way along the walls, down the stairs and to the front door. There had to be some way she could get the door open, even if she couldn't imagine right at this moment how she would twist the handle and actually open the door.

The prospect of wandering into the street blindfolded, and with bound hands, wasn't appealing, but it sure beat the alternatives. She should count herself lucky that she happened to be wearing pajamas tonight, as opposed to the skimpy tank top and panties that she usually slept in. She might even be able to locate a pair of shoes she could scuff into before she walked outside. The low temperature tonight had been forecast in the thirties, which wouldn't make for a happy prospect if she was forced to end up meandering blind and barefoot along the sidewalk.

Removing the blindfold would open up a world of possibilities, Kate realized. It might, in fact, be a better key to making a swift escape than trying to get rid of the tape binding her wrists. With her sight restored she could quickly and easily find a knife. She could put the knife in her mouth and quite possibly saw through the layers of tape to free her hands.

Okay, so she'd work on the blindfold, not on freeing her hands. At least she now had a plan and a goal. Resting against the headboard to provide herself with balance, she retracted her chin tightly against her neck and scrunched her head, trying to insert her chin beneath the tape that held the towel in place. Her hope of instant release proved a fantasy, but she refused to give up. The tape wouldn't stick anywhere near as efficiently to rough toweling as it stuck to her skin; she only needed to pop one fold, and she would be free.

She worked doggedly, pushing her chin down, edging it beneath the folds of the towel and then pushing outward. She started to get some traction and heard the sound of tape splitting. Unfortunately, there were multiple layers of tape and the other layers continued to hold the towel in place. Still, the fact that she'd succeeded at all gave her fresh incentive to carry on.

A minute later she realized that every time she maneuvered with her chin, she'd simultaneously been wriggling her fingers beneath their duct-tape binding. The movement had been instinctive, no clever planning involved, but the results were glorious: the tip of her left thumb and index finger suddenly burst free of their constraints. Her wrists and hands were still tightly bound, but two fingertips were free!

It was all the leverage she needed. She hooked her index finger behind the tape in the place where she could feel give from the layer she'd already managed to split. Then she ripped with all the force of her combined anger and fear. The tape tore away from the towel. Within moments, the towel was on the bed and she could see again.

Her clock had been put back on the nightstand, and the night-light near the bedroom door provided what seemed like a blaze of light in comparison to the utter darkness she'd just escaped from. Presumably her father had flipped the breaker on the electric panel, restoring power as he left the house. She wondered why he'd been so anxious to keep her in total darkness as he whispered his threats. Did he simply want to increase the level of her fear? Or was there something about his appearance he didn't want her to see?

In fact, question crowded upon question now that she wasn't too panicked to think. Why had he never raised his voice above a whisper? Yes, it had been eerie to hear powerful threats issued in a menacing whisper, but something about his decision never to speak in a normal voice was nagging at her. It was important, she thought, but she couldn't quite grasp why. Not yet, but she would get there. She would understand and hold him to account eventually.

Kate got out of bed, chagrined to discover that she was literally shaky around the knees.

She ordered herself to put some steel in her flabby muscles since she couldn't afford to waste valuable time indulging in a panic attack. She needed to set herself free, not wallow in the aftermath of shock.

She crept down the stairs, elbow on top of the banister to provide orientation, but mentally she visualized herself storming to victory. Once in the kitchen, she flipped on the light and then used her mouth, along with her bound hands, to extract her razor-sharp boning knife from the storage block on the counter.

She had anticipated that it would be difficult to insert the point of the knife into the tape in a place where she wasn't also piercing her own skin. In fact, though, there was a convenient hollow made by the angle of her wrists, and inserting the knife turned out to be easy. The difficult part was moving the knife in a cutting motion so that the tape split and her skin didn't. In the end, after a lot of uncomfortable trial and error, she realized that the trick was to hold the knife absolutely still and move her hands.

Once she'd figured out the mechanics, making the first crucial cut became relatively easy, or at least not impossibly hard. And as soon as she managed to cut the tape sufficiently to pull her hands somewhat apart, making a bigger cut in the remaining tape took only seconds. She'd done it!

Freedom was glorious for about two seconds. Then the adrenaline that had been fueling both her ingenuity and her stamina abandoned her. Her knees went back to wobbling and she staggered over to the kitchen table, collapsing into the nearest chair. For a few minutes she didn't even try to control a severe attack of the shakes.

Finally, she found just enough strength to get up again and walk over to the kitchen phone. She dialed the number that would bring help and waited for an answer.

"Hello."

Her breath expelled in a relieved sigh. Luke was there, and she didn't feel even a twinge of guilt that he sounded groggy with sleep. "It's Kate. I need you, Luke. Please come." She gave a laugh that immediately degenerated into a sob. "He came to my house."

"Who came, sweetheart?"

"My father. This time he spelled it out. He threatened to kill me. Please come."

Her message delivered, she hung up the phone. It was only then that she realized she hadn't waited for Luke to respond. She wasn't worried. He would come; she knew she could count on him.

She sat down again and stared into space, thinking and waiting. Waiting for Luke.

Twenty

It was a good thing the predawn streets had been almost free of traffic, Luke thought as he pulled up at the curb outside Kate's house. He had no conscious memory of making the drive over here, but he was pretty sure that even Kate wouldn't have been able to complain about his speed on this occasion. He ran up the steps and rang her doorbell, banging the knocker for good measure when she didn't respond within thirty seconds.

Kate opened the door and walked straight into his arms. He was so relieved to find her at least superficially unharmed that seven months of separation and hurt vanished to a burial ground in the furthest reaches of his mind, interred by overwhelming sensations of love and longing. He murmured her name and folded her against him, nestling her head against his down jacket in an embrace that seemed both inevitable and utterly right.

She was icy cold, her fingers so chilled they were almost bloodless. He unzipped his jacket, pulling it apart and wrapping her inside its warmth. She gave a little sigh of contentment and rested with her cheek against his sweatshirt, huddling close and wrapping her arms around his waist as she soaked up his body heat.

She didn't speak, and he refrained from bombarding her with demands for information, offering her instead the silent reassurance she seemed to be seeking. There were at least a dozen questions that would require answers sometime soon, but right now he didn't care about the precise details of what had happened here tonight. He already knew Ron Raven had invaded her home and threatened her with harm and that was enough for the time being. Soon, very soon, he could start the inquisition, but for a while it was enough to know that he was the person Kate had turned to when she needed to feel safe. He kicked the front door shut behind them and leaned against it, cradling her protectively. He stroked her hair and gently kneaded her shoulders, intent only on providing warmth and comfort, helping her to rebuild her emotional defenses.

It was Kate who changed the nature of what was happening between them. At one moment she was soft and pliant, almost docile, in his arms. The next instant, she reached up and held his face between her hands, pressing her lips against his and kissing him with fierce hunger. He kissed her back with equal fierceness, his tongue thrusting deep, his hands tangling in her hair, holding her body pressed tightly against his. When he was with Kate, it took a lot less than passionate, open-mouthed kisses to send him into a state of instant arousal and tonight was no exception.

"Make love to me, Luke." It was the first time she'd spoken since she opened the door. She murmured the words against his mouth, her hands raking down his spine, her breasts thrust against his chest.

"God, yes." He was only too happy to oblige. Thrilled, delighted and ecstatic to oblige, in fact.

He'd already started to propel her toward the living room couch, mouths and bodies locked together, when the cold wash of reason intervened. His desire for her was spiraling upward at breakneck speed, but for once when they were together he was more in control than Kate. Enticing as it was to throw away restraint and seize her invitation with both hands, there was no way to ignore the fact that her father's visit must have been a devastating experience. The fact that she was physically unharmed was almost irrelevant. Her choppy, truncated phone call was evidence of her mental turmoil, not to mention the silent intensity of her behavior since she opened the front door. Luke's conscience—his infuriating conscience—sent out a loud warning that only a major league asshole would take advantage of her vulnerability.

Even so, since he'd spent most of the past three weeks fantasizing about having Katie in his bed again, he struggled with temptation before gulping in air and stopping their progression toward the couch a scant few seconds before they toppled onto its welcoming cushions. The effort of calling a halt left him panting as if he'd run a fast three miles. He consoled himself as best he could with the thought that having sex now would surely kill any chance of rebuilding a long-term relationship with Kate, and he was finally ready to acknowledge that he wanted her back in his life even more than he wanted to have sex with her right this second. And God knew, that was saying a lot.

He pushed her hair out of her eyes and tilted her head

back so that he could look straight into her eyes. They were as startlingly blue as ever, but stormy with emotion. And the hell of it was, he couldn't be sure precisely what emotion.

"Kate, you know I want to make love to you."

She smiled slightly. "Yes, I kinda figured that."

He was relieved to see that she could smile, even joke a little. "Smart-ass." He dropped a light, friendly kiss on her forehead, although the restraint damn near killed him. "Look, as you can tell, I'm totally in favor of us spending the next several hours having down-and-dirty sex. The next several days, in fact. But first, we need to talk about what happened with your father."

"No, we don't. Not now. It's not relevant."

"It's very relevant, Katie."

"No." She made a short, impatient gesture and her smile became rueful. "You're doing your noble thing again, Luke, but you don't have to. You're afraid I'm reacting to stress, but that's not what this is about. Or at least not in the way you think. I'm not looking for a quick and easy way to forget what happened. I want to make love to you, but that's because of how I feel about *you,* not because of how I feel about my father."

He wished he could believe her. "Katie-love, how can you be sure you know the difference right now?"

"It's easy." She sounded surprisingly confident. "While I was waiting for you to arrive, I realized I never even considered calling anyone else for help before dialing your number. I didn't call 911, or one of my girlfriends, I didn't call my uncle, or even my mother, although I love her and admire her a lot. It was you I called. You were the person I wanted, the person I trusted to make me feel safe again."

Somehow he managed to say the honorable thing. "And because you trust me, that's why I have to do what's right, not what I want."

"Making love to me *is* what's right, as well as what we both want." She made another impatient, sweeping gesture. "I understand we have to talk about my father sometime soon. I understand we have to talk about what happened between you and me back in March. If you like, we can even have a serious conversation about ways to make our relationship work despite the fact that we're both ambitious workaholics with impossible schedules. But not right now. None of that matters right now. At least not to me."

He was afraid she was underestimating the impact of her father's cruelty, but she was stroking her hands over him as she spoke, and he was a man, not a eunuch or a saint. Nevertheless, he raked up the pathetic last few dregs of his willpower and gave resistance one final shot.

He grabbed hold of her hands and stepped back so that no part of his body touched any part of her. "I can't believe I'm fighting to convince you that you don't want to have sex with me. I must be insane! But I'm doing it because I don't want to wake up tomorrow morning and discover that you hate me."

She smiled a little wryly. "There's no chance I'm going to hate you tomorrow morning. I tried hating you for seven months already and it didn't work worth a damn." She moved into his arms again, linking her hands at the nape of his neck. "I'm glad you're an honorable man, Luke. I'm sure I'll appreciate your integrity many times in the years to come. But right at this moment, you're driving me crazy. Your honor isn't what I need. I need your passion." Her smile flickered, elusive and impossibly erotic. "I need you to shut up and kiss me, for God's sake."

Luke gave up the fight he had never wanted to win and kissed her with all the fire and longing he'd been holding in check. She responded with a passion hot enough to burn away the last frail threads of his resistance. He swung her up into his arms and carried her the final few steps to the couch. They tumbled onto the cushions, scattering clothes, ending up in a tangle of limbs and desire. He'd wanted her for so long that the mere touch of her bare skin worked on him with an impact that hovered just a fraction on the ecstatic side of torture. She writhed beneath him, her hips rising off the sofa, their bodies rocking in unison, slick with sweat, pulsing with seven months of mutual, unsatisfied yearning.

He'd assumed he remembered what it was like to make love to her, but he'd been mistaken. Self-preservation had required that neither his memory nor his imagination could allow him to dwell on the enormity of his loss during the time they'd spent apart. He'd had sex with other women; he'd liked all of his partners, even cared about a few. He wondered what kind of an idiot he was that it had taken him so long to understand that he didn't want or need other women. He wanted and needed Kate. Only Kate.

He drove into her and she arched beneath him, her arousal feeding his as they raced together toward climax. Her orgasm was powerful enough to leave her shuddering in his arms, gasping for breath, her fingernails digging into his shoulders. Moments later he climaxed, and for a few seconds he had no coherent thoughts at all, only sensations of consuming, shattering pleasure.

Making love to Kate had always been an amazing experience, he thought as he gradually sank back down to earth, but tonight they'd experienced a level of intimacy that had changed spectacular sex into something new, something that had left him emotionally filled as well as physically sated.

When he could summon the energy to move, he sat up, giving her breathing room on the narrow couch. She sat up, too, and then twisted around so that she could rest her head on his shoulder. It was a while before she said anything, and when she spoke her voice was still husky from the intensity of the sex. "Last night, in the hotel, you asked me if I'd missed you while we were apart."

"I remember." His hands stroked with lazy contentment across her breasts. "You didn't answer me."

"Yesterday I wasn't ready to deal with how big a mistake we'd made when we split up. Now I am. The truth is I missed you every single day."

He looked down at her, smiling softly, his hands still cupping her breasts. "Nah, you just missed the great sex."

Her gaze held steady. "No, I missed you." She gave a faint smile. "And the sex, too."

His gut tightened with a sensation he reluctantly identified as love. Even now, the thought of being this much in thrall to another human being had the power to make him squirm. For once, though, he overcame his instinct to retreat into the safeness of isolation. "You realize you've sealed your fate, don't you? There's no way I can ever let you go again. Not after this."

"That's good news, because I was planning to stick around for a while anyway."

Instead of setting him on edge, the idea of having Kate around left him absurdly content. He trailed his hand down her body until his finger rested right on the tip of her tattooed dragon's fire-breathing nose. "Puff tells me it's been tough taking care of you without me around."

She smiled, her eyes laughing, too. "For once Puff isn't exaggerating."

He hugged her, just because he could, and realized that she was getting cold again. Her favorite brightly colored throw had fallen from the couch onto the floor. He picked it up and wrapped it around her shoulders, then pulled on his own sweatpants. Instead of returning to the couch, he sat on the coffee table, which left him looking straight at her, their knees touching.

He took her hands, needing the physical contact. "What happened to us last time, Katie? Where did we go wrong?"

She thought for a moment before answering. "You were afraid to commit and I was afraid to trust. That's it in a nutshell."

It seemed a pretty accurate assessment to him; such a simple explanation for such a cataclysmic outcome. "Why were you afraid to trust me? I didn't as much as look at another woman when we were dating, Katie."

"Until a couple of weeks ago, I never admitted to myself how much the fact that I grew up not trusting my father affected my relationship with you. My suspicions about Dad's integrity were never strong enough to provoke a confrontation between us, but some part of me was always afraid that if I ever relied on him to catch me, he would fail and I would fall." She hesitated for a moment. "In a lot of ways, you know, you remind me of him."

"Jesus, Kate, that's not exactly a compliment!"

"Actually it is, because the similarities between you aren't important in comparison to all the ways the two of you are different. You have the same drive and ambition as my father, and you've learned to cloak some of your intensity behind a friendly, low-key manner, just as he does. You have his charisma, too, not to mention his great looks. It took me those months apart to realize that's where the similarities between the two of you end, thank God. You're transparently honest and loyal. And kind, too. My father was…is…indulgent but he was almost never kind."

Luke raised her hands to his mouth, kissing her knuckles before folding her hands against his chest and holding them there. "You can always trust me, Kate, you know that, don't you? I would never betray you the way your father betrayed your mother and the rest of his family. God knows I have a thousand faults, but I'll never lie to you."

"I understand that now. I'm just sorry I put us both through so much to discover something so obvious."

For seven months, Luke had done his best to avoid thinking about Michael Rourke, much less talking about him. Avoidance had never worked too well and it was no longer even a semiviable option if his relationship with

Kate was going to flourish. "We have to talk about Michael," he said, and his voice sounded harsh despite his best efforts. "We'll never be able to move on unless we do."

"It's really difficult for me to talk about him." Her cheeks flushed dark red. "Going to bed with Michael is one of the few things in my life I'm truly ashamed of."

"Did you imagine you were in love with him?" Luke prompted when she didn't say anything more.

"Never," she said quickly. "Michael wasn't about being in love. He wasn't even about sex. Not really. It was about revenge, and restoring my sense of self-worth. It was a terrible revenge to take, but I fell in love with you almost as soon as we met and I was never sure you felt the same way. Yes, you were friendly and fun to be with and the sex was great, but there was a barrier between us that you never, ever took down. It felt sometimes as if I was throwing my love at a brick wall and watching it bounce back at me, untouched by a human hand."

"God, Katie, I never meant to be so unreachable."

"The odd thing is that you weren't unreachable at first. The opposite, in fact. You were so much more approachable and open than anyone in my family and I loved that openness. Then everything began to change. It was as if the more time we spent together, the further you retreated. In the end, when our relationship was coming apart at every seam, there seemed to be nothing left at the center of me except a great big gaping hole where my self-esteem used to be. Having an affair with Michael was my desperate last-ditch effort to fill that hole. Although God knows how sex with a man I didn't much like was supposed to achieve that particular miracle."

His grip on her hands tightened. "What happened before we broke up was my fault, as well as yours. Not Michael, but everything that led up to him." Luke had never before allowed himself to admit as much. "I know I wasn't always there for you and you're right that I had commitment issues. Intimacy scares the hell out of me. I love my family, but their demands can get overwhelming. I've learned to cope by keeping part of myself walled off in a safe place where they have no access. There was an invisible line in our relationship that I had no intention of crossing, and when I felt myself getting too involved or needing you too much, I pulled back. Hard. It scared the hell out of me when I saw how close you were getting to places I'd been guarding since I was a kid."

"Are we going to do better this time?" For the first time, Kate turned away, unwilling to meet his gaze. "I don't believe I could handle another breakup like the last one."

"We're going to do much better this time." Luke was surprised at how strongly he believed that. "This time we're going to be terrific. I love you, Kate."

"You're laughing."

"Because I never could say those words to you before. Why the hell not? What's so difficult about telling the truth? I—love—you—Kate. I need you. I want you to be with me now and when I'm old and gray and have nothing better to do than potter around the yard nagging you to come and admire my vegetable garden."

"I love you, too. And I'd be happy to admire your vegetable garden anytime. Even before you get old and gray."

He stood up, pulling her into his arms, wondering if the grin plastered all over his face looked as sappy and wonderful as it felt. "You're beautiful, and I love you, and if you don't get some sleep soon, you'll keel over where you stand. You look exhausted and I sure as hell feel exhausted. Let's go to bed, Katie."

She stopped in her tracks, her smile vanishing. "Maybe we should sleep down here tonight...." She shivered. "I don't want to go upstairs."

There was real dread in her voice and he realized how crazy it had been to imagine they could put off talking about her father's invasion of her home until the morning.

"Why would you want to sleep on the couch when you have a great bed upstairs?" He asked the question although he was pretty sure he already knew the answer.

She didn't reply and he tilted her head back so that he could see her expression. What he read on her face confirmed his guess. "Your father came into your bedroom."

She gave a reluctant nod of assent. "I woke up and...he was there."

"How did he get into the house without waking you?"

"I suppose he used a key. He's always had a spare key, ever since I moved into the house, and I guess tonight proves he still has it." She shrugged. "I never changed the locks after he disappeared—there was no reason to. He must have let himself in while I was sleeping."

"How did he look? Did he seem changed to you? To me, he looked as if he'd lost a few pounds, but that was about it."

"I never actually saw him, only heard him."

Luke frowned. "I don't understand. He came upstairs and went into your bedroom, but you never saw him?"

"I couldn't see him because it was already pitch-black when I woke up. He'd doused every light. He's been in this house dozens of times so he knows the main electrical panel is in the laundry room, right off the kitchen. Apparently he flipped the circuit breaker to cut off the electrical power before he came upstairs. He even got rid of my alarm clock, which is glow-in-the-dark and battery operated. Presumably he wanted to make sure there wasn't the faintest glimmer of light anywhere."

Luke frowned. "Why the hell would he do that?"

She shook her head. "I don't know. To inspire fear, maybe?"

"Total darkness is disorienting—literally you can forget which way is up," Luke said. "But would your father want you to be disoriented? Presumably he had a message to deliver and wanted you to pay attention."

"Something about his whole visit is bothering me. I tried to put my finger on the problem while I was waiting for you to arrive, but all I could come up with was how out of character it was for my dad to do something like this. But that's ridiculous, because clearly I have no idea what his true character is. Anyway, after his phone call in Virginia, this visit tonight isn't out of character at all. It's just more of the same, except worse."

She had grown paler as she spoke, but her voice remained steady, and Luke was so full of admiration for her courage that he ached with the weight of it. "What happened when Ron realized you were awake?"

"He blindfolded me, despite the dark, which strikes me as a really odd thing to have done. He taped my hands together, too, tightly enough that I couldn't move them. He told me I was forcing him into a corner and this was his last warning. If I kept on trying to find him, he'd have to kill me. I was leaving him no choice. Then I guess he walked out of the room. He didn't hit me or hurt me or anything."

She seemed to feel that small gift of moderation on Ron Raven's part was cause for gratitude. Luke considered it less than a drop in the bucket of good deeds when compared with the ocean of Ron's sins. He was going to track down the son of a bitch, he swore silently, and make sure the bastard spent the rest of his miserable life in prison.

He put his arms around Kate, holding her tight, willing her to feel the comfort he was offering. "Let me guess. He didn't untie you before he left."

She shook her head. "No. He didn't remove the blindfold, either. The only thing I can think of is maybe he was afraid I would follow him if I could see. Otherwise, why mess with a blindfold? It can't be because he didn't want me to recognize him, since that was the whole point of the exercise. He wanted me to know exactly who it was threatening to kill me."

It made sense that Ron Raven wouldn't want Kate to follow him, and perhaps a blindfold was marginally less cruel than any other precautions he could have taken. Tying her to the bed, for example, might have resulted in leaving her imprisoned for days until somebody came to the house in search of her. Luke gave up trying to second-guess Ron's motives because thinking about the terror the man had inflicted on his own daughter left him homicidal with rage.

"You were very clever to escape." Luke managed to filter most of the rage out of his voice, in itself a minor miracle. He suspected Kate needed kindness at the moment, not rage and bombastic threats of retribution. He'd save those for tomorrow morning, when he could start planning how to turn the threats into a realistic plan of action. "How did you manage to get rid of the blindfold? It must have been difficult with your hands taped together."

"My father used my own bath towel to cover my head and the duct tape didn't stick to the pile all that well. Eventually I managed to pop the tape around my neck and get rid of the towel. Then I went down to the kitchen and held a knife in my mouth so that I could cut the tape off my hands." She produced a wan smile, but it tore at Luke's heart to see the effort behind it. "Once I could see, it wasn't too bad. Still, as you can imagine, my bedroom isn't exactly my favorite place right now. It's as if…as if I can feel his presence up there, menacing me."

He wanted to bring Ron Raven to her in handcuffs, with steel chains around his waist and shackles on his ankles. Then he would compel the asshole to kneel down and plead for her forgiveness. Unfortunately, there was no way to make the fantasy real, so all he could do was hug her and offer advice that might help to limit the harm the monster had caused.

"It's easy to understand why the idea of going back upstairs bothers you, Kate, and we can sleep on the sofa if you want. Except I hate to give your father that much power. You worked so hard to fix this house up and you've always loved it. Don't let him destroy your pleasure in your home. Come to bed in your own room and reassert possession of the space."

She managed to hold a smile for a couple of seconds before it slipped away. "Like a dog marking its territory, you mean?"

"Exactly like that." He squeezed her tight, his heart swelling with emotion. "We'll make love and stamp our presence on your bedroom, and obliterate any trace of Ron and his visit." He kissed her gently on her mouth. "I'll be there, Kate. I'll keep the demons away."

"Yes, you will for tonight, but the demons will be lurking just beyond the horizon, waiting to pounce when I least expect them." The expression on her face was resigned, but it turned to determination as he watched. "There's only one way to banish the demons forever. We have to find my father. I'm going to do it, Luke. I'm going to find him. I won't let him scare me off."

Twenty-One

October 23, 2007

The phone rang, waking Kate from a deep and refreshing sleep. For a couple of seconds she was so afraid the call might be from her father that she had trouble drawing breath. Then she realized Luke was in bed next to her, his hand resting casually on Puff, and the paralysis vanished. The power of movement restored, she checked the caller ID and, with a sigh of relief, picked up the phone.

"Good morning, Uncle Paul. How are you doing?"

"Oh, you're home. I called the bakery a few minutes ago expecting to reach you and they said you hadn't come in today. I was a little worried to learn that you hadn't let them know you would be late. I hope you're feeling well, Kate?"

She glanced at the clock and saw it was nine-fifteen, more than three hours past her usual time for getting to work. "Thanks for the reminder, Uncle Paul. I need to call and let them know what's happened. I had a…disturbed night and turned off the alarm before I went to sleep. I didn't expect to be this late waking up, though."

"I'm sorry to hear you had a rough night." Her uncle's usually pompous voice softened. "There's a nasty stomach virus making the rounds, so if you're feeling sick you should stay home. Shall I call your mother and ask her to stop by your place?"

"No, I'm fine, thanks. My only problem was lack of sleep, and since I didn't wake up until past nine o'clock, I've pretty much taken care of that!" She would explain about her father's visit later, when they were face-to-face. Her uncle tended to fuss and he would be round here in a flash if she told him what had really happened last night.

"There must be a reason you're trying to reach me, Uncle Paul. I hope nothing's wrong?"

"Oh, no, nothing at all," he said with heavy sarcasm. "I'm just fine and dandy, except for the minor fact that your mother called last night and explained what you and Luke Savarini discovered while the two of you were in Virginia. It's a definite shock to the system to realize we've wasted six months grieving for a man who is very much alive. I'm stunned, Kate, simply stunned. I don't know what to say, much less what to do."

"He planned a convincing death, didn't he? I wonder how long he spent preparing that particular little scam."

"Less time than either of us would imagine possible, I expect." Paul sounded bitter. "Ron's been creating illusions for the past thirty years, and this was just one more. He always thought fast on his feet, that's for sure.

What mystifies me is how he got away with deceiving us all about his basic character for such a long time."

"Have you come up with any good answers?"

"I sure haven't, but I've managed to work up a fine head of steam mulling over the possibilities."

Kate could certainly sympathize with her uncle's attitude. "I guess I've given up asking myself that sort of question. My plan is to find my father and then we can demand answers directly."

Her uncle snorted. "I'm sorry, my dear, but that's a bit like asking a dog why it wags its tail or asking a monkey why it likes bananas. They're physically and mentally incapable of answering you. So is Ron."

Kate was afraid Paul might be right. Her father had deceived so many people for so long that deception had become his standard mode of operation. She breathed every day without stopping to wonder how or why. Apparently her father deceived people on a daily basis with identical lack of thought.

"Was my mother upset when she talked to you, Uncle Paul? When I stopped by on the way home from the airport, she seemed okay with the news that Dad was definitely alive."

"She sounded fine to me, too. My sister…your mother is a remarkable woman. I had moments during our conversation yesterday evening when it seemed to me she was coping with the news of Ron's return from the dead better than I was. And while I'm handing out compliments, you and Luke deserve several. I'm truly impressed by your ingenuity. I'd never have expected you to run down so many leads in such a short time. That was well done, Kate."

"Thanks. We were lucky that Luke happened to

know exactly the right person to help us open up the files on that flash drive we found, otherwise we'd have been no further forward. Hopefully those files are going to provide us with a solid way to track my father. With so many addresses and phone numbers to work with, it should be a snap. Relatively speaking." She scooted under the covers, snuggling against Luke as she talked. Somehow, even discussing Ron Raven didn't seem quite so bad with Luke's arm around her and her head resting on his shoulder.

"I sure hope so," her uncle said. "But, as all the self-help books tell you, luck is what happens when opportunity meets preparation. You and Luke weren't lucky, you were well prepared."

She bit her lip to contain a giggle. Her uncle was so predictably patronizing she'd learned to be fond of his quirks. "Thanks for the praise, Uncle Paul."

"I always like to give credit where credit is due. Anyway, you and Luke did a great job—in such a short time period! Now we need to discuss how we're going to handle this new information. I understand from your mother that you believe you've come up with a way to smoke Ron out of his hiding place? She didn't explain how, though."

"It's a bit complicated. It would be easier to explain if we talked about the situation face-to-face so that we can show you the files on the flash drive."

"I certainly agree it's complicated. In fact, it occurred to me as I was driving into work this morning that we might be getting in over our heads. We're amateurs, all of us. Maybe it's time for us to call in the police."

"I don't know, Uncle Paul—"

"A major step like going to the police needs to be thoroughly discussed beforehand." Her uncle was clearly in no mood to waste time listening to her comments. "I'm hoping to arrange a little get-together with you and your mother as soon as you finish work this afternoon. I'll call Luke Savarini once we've agreed on a time and place for the meeting and see if he can join us. On the one hand, I usually don't like the idea of sharing intimate problems with someone who's outside the family. On the other hand, Luke already knows what's going on, so his input might be valuable. A well-informed outsider sometimes has a better grasp of the big picture than those of us struggling to view the situation from the inside."

"I agree we need to arrange a meeting, and the sooner the better." Kate spoke quickly, before her uncle could go off into another peroration. His tendency to deliver monologues richly dotted with *on the one hand, on the other hand* was a family legend. "If I go to the bakery for a few hours, just to catch up on any crises, we could meet in the early afternoon at my mother's house. That way, Luke could join us before the evening rush starts at his restaurants."

"Shall we say two o'clock, then, at Avery's house? She tells me her office furniture arrived at the end of last week, so we'll have somewhere comfortable to sit while we talk, and her house is conveniently located for both you and Luke." He delivered this information as if it were news to Kate.

"I'll be there at two," she confirmed. "I'll take care of filling Luke in on our plans."

"And I'll let your mother know we've volunteered

her house for our meeting. I'm glad to hear you sounding so well, Kate. When the girl at La Lanterne said you hadn't gone in or called this morning, I got a bit worried."

Kate ignored the reference to the "girl" at the bakery. There wasn't a woman working at La Lanterne who was less than forty, but her uncle was too set in his ways to change them now. She smothered a sigh and reassured him one more time that she was healthy, with no sign of any bugs or viruses about to launch an attack on her health. Her uncle ended the call after what was, for him, a relatively short goodbye.

"What have you volunteered me to join?" Luke asked as she hung up the phone.

"Mom gave my uncle Paul the news about my father being alive and Paul is not a happy camper. He thinks we should have a meeting to discuss what to do next."

"I agree with your uncle, especially since you need to let both him and your mom know about Ron's visit here last night. That's information you need to share, Kate, however reluctant you might be to tell them about Ron's threats."

She pulled a face, but she knew Luke was right. She hated to be responsible for delivering a mortal blow to any shreds of affection her mother might still hold for her bigamous husband, but it couldn't be helped. Ron's visit was proof positive he was alive, and that was knowledge to be shared, not kept secret.

"Uncle Paul and I agreed to get together with my mother this afternoon. Two o'clock at Mom's house. I know how busy you'll be today since we just got back into town, but I figured the middle of the afternoon would be the easiest time for you to break away for an hour. If you can join us, that would be great."

"I'll make the time," Luke said. "Sometimes I need to remind myself that I hired executive chefs for my restaurants so that I wouldn't have to be physically on the premises 24-7." He reached across the bed and took her hands, lacing his fingers through hers. "Before you get up, tell me what your plans are for the rest of the morning, Kate."

"I'm going to call the bakery right now, before I shower. I need to apologize for being late and let them know I'll be coming in for a few hours, at least—long enough to catch up on anything urgent left over from the time we spent in Virginia." She shrugged. "Apart from work, I guess I'm not doing much, at least until the meeting at my mother's place."

"There's something else you should consider taking care of this morning," Luke said. "This is important, Kate."

"What's that? You're looking very somber."

"I guess I feel somber. You need to make an official police report about your father's visit here last night. What he did was criminal and the cops need to know."

"Maybe." She wrinkled her nose. "I wish I trusted the cops more."

"Why don't you trust them? Do you think they're corrupt, or just incompetent?"

"Neither," she said. "I think mostly they're overworked and have too few resources. On top of that, the ones I've encountered seem to suffer from severe tunnel vision. What happened with Julio Castellano and the investigation of my father's disappearance is a classic example of how they get their teeth into a theory and won't let go."

"My sympathy is with the cops." Luke shrugged. "Your father went to a lot of trouble to have them believe Castellano had killed him."

"Unfortunately for us, his ploy worked too well. At this point I think it would take the equivalent of a nuclear explosion to blast the police out of their preconceived notions about this case."

"Your father's visit here last night almost counts as a nuclear explosion. It was one thing for detectives to ignore me when all I could tell them was that I'd glimpsed Ron Raven across a crowded restaurant. They can't ignore the fact that your father invaded your home last night, tied you up, and then threatened to kill you. Tying people up and threatening murder are serious crimes—felonies, not misdemeanors. They're obligated to investigate."

She gave a sigh that turned into a yawn. Between her father's phone call and his nocturnal visit, she was running several hours short on sleep over the past two nights. "If I talk to the cops, I'm worried somebody inside the department will leak to the press that Ron Raven is alive. The media will instantly go wild, my father will be spooked and we'll never be able to smoke him out of hiding. Right now, if we're careful how we set up the sting, there's no reason for him to suspect that we're so close to catching up with him. But it only takes a few careless words from some clerk to the media and we'll lose the edge we have right now."

Luke frowned, his silence an acknowledgment of the problems. "Your uncle is a fixture in the Chicago business community. Maybe he has a high-level contact or two inside the police department. If you make your report to somebody really senior, there's more chance of keeping the information confidential. I agree, media hype is a problem, but the cops have resources we don't for tracking people on a national scale, especially since 9/11."

"But why do we need to launch a massive manhunt? Thanks to Seth and your sister, we decoded my father's files and we have a way to trick him into showing up at a time and place we can control. I'm not clear what we gain by involving the cops right now."

"Increased safety for you, at the very least."

She laughed. "You're joking, right? The cops are as likely to parade naked down Michigan Avenue whistling 'Dixie' as they are to waste manpower guarding me from a man they're not a hundred percent sure is alive."

"You have a point," he conceded. "And if the cops aren't going to protect you, I guess the negatives of talking to them outweigh the positives. Ron is obviously spooked, or he wouldn't have risked coming here last night to threaten you. If he gets any more alarmed than he already is, he'll bury himself so deep in a new identity that we'll never pick up his trail. Realistically, all he has to do is drive across the border into Mexico, and we haven't a hope in hell of tracking him down."

"At least if he's in Mexico, I don't have to worry about him killing me." Kate laughed without any humor at all. "It seems every cloud truly does have a silver lining. Don't you just love the old clichés?"

"There are others I like better than that one," Luke

said grimly. "How about *what goes around, comes around?* I'd really like to see Ron Raven get his. And as for him killing you, he isn't going to get the chance because you're not going to be alone anymore. You need to move in with me, Katie, starting tonight. My building has street-level security doors that can only be accessed if you know the code, plus my condo is on the fifteenth floor. Unless Ron turned into Spider-Man during the past six months, once you're with me, he can't do a repeat of last night's performance because there's no way for him to gain access to my condo."

"You don't have to work so hard to convince me. I don't want to be alone at night any more until after we've found him." Kate couldn't quite suppress a shudder.

Luke noticed, of course. He leaned forward and kissed her. "If by any amazing chance Ron did find his way into our bedroom, he would soon realize he'd made a giant mistake. Because I'd make damn sure he didn't leave again, except wearing handcuffs and with a police escort."

Kate really liked the sound of that.

Twenty-Two

There was so much demanding her attention at the bakery for the few hours she was there that Kate didn't have time to mull over her father's threats, the renewal of her relationship with Luke or even the relatively minor problem of whether or not to go to the police with the news that her father was alive and threatening her safety. Rushing to help the apprentice baker prepare some of the day's more complicated pastries, she worked till the last second and arrived at her mother's house a few minutes after two.

Both her uncle and Luke were already there. Her heart gave a little skip when she saw Luke, and then another one when he smiled at her. Avery, insightful as ever, looked from one to the other with sudden alertness. Fortunately, she also remained as tactful as ever and made no personal comments. Her uncle, typical middle-aged male, remained blissfully unaware of any silent undercurrents.

Avery was an accomplished hostess and the offers of

refreshment were dealt with in short order. As soon as they were all sitting down and sipping tea, Kate decided to get the unpleasant chore of telling her mother about Ron Raven's nighttime visit out of the way.

She kept her account as dry and factual as possible, a task made easier by the discovery that she could no longer recall exactly what her father had said. She remembered her fear; she clearly recalled the odd sensation of disorientation, a disorientation that went beyond the confusion caused by darkness and the blindfold. But her mental images had become jumbled, like one of those pictures that seem to depict a butterfly until you blink and realize it's actually two people kissing. Stress had apparently blanked her memory of crucial details, leaving only the bare bones of the event. So much for eyewitness accounts, she reflected. No wonder they often led to accusations against the wrong person.

When she finished her story, neither her mother nor her uncle spoke for at least thirty seconds. Then Avery got up and enveloped her daughter in a tight hug. "I'm sorry," she said, her voice crackling with anger. "Kate, I'm so very sorry. There are no excuses I can make. I failed you."

"You're not responsible for his threats, Mom."

"But I ought to have seen through his facade. How did I live for almost thirty years with a man I apparently knew nothing about?"

Paul set his cup on its saucer, making a loud rattle. "My God, this isn't a time to be worrying about why we never noticed Ron was a criminal lunatic! He's threatening your life, Katie. *Your life!* Can we focus on what really matters here?"

Avery turned white. "You have to move in with me, Kate, at least for a week or two. We simply can't risk the possibility that your father is serious in his threats."

"Kate already agreed to spend the next few nights at my condo." Luke placed a casually possessive arm around her shoulders, and this time even her uncle looked at the pair of them with suddenly narrowed eyes.

Luke continued as if he hadn't noticed the stares. "The entrance to my building is permanently locked and it needs a code or a key card to open it. Plus my condo is on the fifteenth floor. Of course, neither of those things totally guarantees Kate's safety, but it makes her a lot safer than she would be alone in her house."

"Promise me you'll take care when you go to work, Kate." Avery's brows remained drawn together in worry. "You start so early in the morning that it's still dark when you leave home. Anyone could be lurking in or around your car."

"She can keep her car in my garage space," Luke said. "I'll escort her down to the garage each morning."

Kate was appalled. "Don't be crazy, Luke. I leave hours before you get up."

"Yeah, you do, and I'm going to be cranky as hell." He grinned. "If you're a smart woman, you won't talk to me. I'm definitely not a nice person in the wee hours of the morning."

"Luckily for both of us, I won't be putting your claim to the test, because there's no reason for you to play bodyguard."

"Unfortunately, there's every reason." The kiss he dropped on her cheek broadcast the intimacy of their relationship by its very casualness. "This is one argument you're not going to win, Katie-love, so save your breath. Don't worry. I plan on going back to bed the moment I know you're safely in your car and en route to the bakery."

Paul's initial shock had given way to anger. Slamming his clenched fist into the palm of his hand—the equivalent of a wild leap in the air for a less conservative man—he declared his intention of immediately calling the police. As Luke and Kate had suspected, he personally knew one of the precinct captains and he insisted that he would demand instant action to track down Ron Raven, arrest him and put him in prison.

"They'd better call in the FBI," he muttered, picking up the phone. "Or they're going to answer to me, and I'm not going to be listening to any excuses."

Kate and Luke had to use all their powers to convince Paul to sit down again and delay calling the police, at least until he heard their plans. He seemed unpersuaded by their argument that Ron might flee to Mexico or Belize the moment he realized that nobody believed anymore that he was dead. He stubbornly insisted that the FBI would put out an all-points bulletin and pick Ron up in a very short time.

"For heaven's sake, Paul, I really think you're exaggerating the powers of the police." Avery paced, more restless than Kate could remember seeing her. "Some of the criminals on the FBI's Most Wanted List have been there for ten years! And I imagine Ron is twice as smart as many of the people on that list, so he's even less likely to get caught than most of them. You need to back off and listen to Kate and Luke."

Avery wasn't in the habit of expressing irritation with her older brother and Paul didn't look at all pleased by this breach with tradition. Luke came to the rescue. Kate had noticed many times that Luke had a pitch-perfect instinct for working with other people, probably because as one of six siblings he'd learned his compromising and negotiating skills early. He managed to soothe her uncle's ruffled feelings and distract him from his determination to call the police by the simple device of asking for his help.

"We urgently need your advice," Luke said, guiding her uncle toward the table where he'd just finished spreading out printed copies of all the information contained on Ron's flash drive. "As you can see, Kate's father is apparently considering signing off on deals with these five different companies. Which of them do you think we should approach for help in smoking him out of hiding?"

"And we need input about the best techniques for approaching them, too," Kate said. Her uncle would be much easier to work with if he had the illusion that all the important decisions were his. "We'll have to tell them at least some part of the truth, don't you think? I don't see how else we'll convince them to help us. What's your opinion, Uncle Paul?"

She was sincere in asking for his input, but as she'd expected, the side benefit was that her uncle got so caught up in holding forth that he forgot all about calling the police.

"Is this everything you collected while you were in Virginia?" Paul asked, adjusting his reading glasses.

"Yes, and we made those copies for you to keep."

Paul murmured thanks. He skimmed through the files, expressing mystification as to why Ron had chosen to use the names of Mayan gods as headers on his accounting sheets and shaking his head as he came to each new photo, with its accompanying fake ID. He paused at the shot of "Raymond Rausch," visibly wincing as he took in the droopy mustache, horn-rimmed glasses and dark brown hair.

"He's laughing at us," he said tautly, jabbing his finger at the image. "I'm telling you these disguises are nothing more than another of Ron's sick jokes."

Kate wasn't sure how Paul reached that conclusion, since her father had never expected them to see any of his alter egos. But her uncle was entitled to feel resentment. Rather than dispute the point, she simply shifted the conversation to a discussion of how and where they might be able to tempt Ron into setting up a meeting.

They were working through a variety of complex plans, not happy with any of them, when Luke suddenly snapped his fingers. "Got it!" He beamed, first at Kate and then at the other two, clearly pleased with himself. "Here's what we have to do. It's simple. Kate, you must call each of the companies and pretend to be Ron's assistant. Tell them Ron's PalmPilot malfunctioned, or got lost…whatever…and you want to confirm the date of Ron's next meeting with them. He probably has meetings already scheduled with one or two of these companies, possibly with all five of them. After all, he's in the middle of negotiating deals with these people."

"Hey, that's brilliant. What did you put in your oatmeal this morning? And you're right, it's simple, which is always best."

Luke tried to look modest, but then gave a huge grin. "It does seem to answer our problems. If none of the companies already has a meeting scheduled with Ron, we'll have to think again, of course. But let's hope we get lucky."

Paul voiced a few objections, probably because he was annoyed at not having come up with the plan himself, Kate thought, silently amused by her uncle's inevitable wish to be seen as the person in charge. Luke politely countered Paul's objections, one by one, until Avery surprised them all by stepping in to take charge.

"Enough already, Paul. Kate, you should call Millbank Woodworks first, since everyone seems to agree these are the negotiations that Ron has pursued most actively. That presumably means they provide the highest probability of a face-to-face meeting already being scheduled with Ron."

Paul subsided in the face of Luke's determination, although he didn't look happy. Kate quickly reread the salient points in the Millbank file. According to his notes, her father had always dealt directly with Ethan Millbank, the young owner who'd recently taken over management of the company, so she would try to talk with Ethan's assistant. The assistant's name was Jodie, and Ron had written himself a reminder that Millbank's phone system was old-fashioned enough that Jodie also acted as the telephonist, a 1980s relic carried into the twenty-first century world of voice mail.

Drawing a deep breath, trying not to notice that Luke, her mother and Paul were hanging on her every word, Kate dialed Millbank's number. Her call was answered on the first ring. "Millbank Woodworks, Jodie speaking. How may I direct your call?"

"Hi, Jodie. This is Raymond Rausch's assistant, from Rausch Enterprises."

"Oh, hi, how are you? But this isn't Connie, is it?"

"Er...no. This is Lisa. I'm...um...new to Rausch Enterprises."

"Hi, Lisa." The young woman sounded friendly and not in the least suspicious. "Do you want to speak to Raymond? He's still walking the factory floor with the boss, but I can connect you."

For a split second, Kate's mind blanked. Then, with a flash of dismay, she realized what Jodie meant. Her father was actually visiting Millbank Woodworks right at this moment! She searched feverishly for an excuse to avoid speaking with him.

"Hello?" Jodie, not surprisingly, sounded puzzled by the long pause. "Are you still there, Lisa?"

"Yes, I'm here." Kate hoped she didn't sound as panicked as she felt. "Thanks so much for the offer, but I just wanted to check that Raymond hadn't left already. No problem. I appreciate the help. Talk to you later. Take care now." She hung up the phone, her palm sweaty with nerves.

Her mother, uncle and Luke were all staring at her. "What's going on?" Luke asked. "You look poleaxed."

"My father was there—right there on the premises!"

"At Millbank Woodworks?" Paul sounded suitably appalled.

"Yes." Kate gave a laugh that shaded toward the hysterical. "As soon as I said I was Raymond Rausch's assistant, Jodie asked me if I wanted to be put through to him!"

"That was a narrow escape," Paul said grimly. "Good Lord, talk about unfortunate coincidences."

"How did Ron get to Virginia already?" Avery asked. "He was invading Kate's home and threatening her life in the middle of last night. Now he's at Millbank Woodworks. How did he manage to get back to the Washington area so quickly?"

"There are plenty of flights between Chicago and Washington, D.C." Paul sounded more than a little impatient with his sister. "If Ron flew out of O'Hare on the first flight this morning, he'd have landed in Dulles with hours to spare. Millbank Woodworks isn't more than an hour from Dulles."

"At least there's an upside," Luke said, once again intervening to soothe the irritation between Avery and her brother. "If Ron is at Millbank Woodworks, he can't be at any of the other companies." He gave Kate's shoulder a reassuring squeeze. "You'd better place the other four phone calls fast, in case Ron plans to drive straight from Millbank to his next meeting!"

Her heartbeat finally slowing to normal, Kate made the remaining calls without any mishaps and without, as far as she could tell, arousing any suspicion that she might not be who she claimed to be. At two of the companies, Ron had no meetings currently scheduled. At Innovation Lifestyles, which happened to be located only ten miles away from Millbank Woodworks, he had a meeting scheduled for 8:00 a.m. the next morning. At Focus Health, he had a meeting scheduled for Friday afternoon at two-thirty.

"At least that makes it simple to decide where we need to intercept him," Luke said. "The meeting at Innovation Lifestyles is too soon. We couldn't get there without scrambling like hell and possibly screwing up.

So it has to be Focus Health, on Old Ox Road, in Loudon County, Virginia, on Friday afternoon at two-thirty."

Kate understood why Luke was repeating the information in such detail. The idea that they could name the date and time at which they would be able to confront her father and demand answers was mind-blowing, even though they'd worked so hard to arrive at this point.

Avery had retreated to a seat in the corner of the room by the window. She was staring out into the small backyard, seemingly oblivious to the discussion taking place around her. She didn't look sad, but she looked abstracted, as if her attention were turned inward. Even her exquisite makeup couldn't hide the fact that she was very pale.

"Mom, are you okay with all this?" Kate asked, although the question was redundant. Clearly her mother *wasn't* okay. As Luke had pointed out earlier, just because her mother was angry with Ron, it didn't mean she wasn't also coping with feelings of sadness and loss along with the betrayal. Kate had reached the point where she was more than willing to see her father behind bars, but her mother might well be ambivalent at the prospect of watching Ron face imminent arrest and possible incarceration.

"What?" With visible effort, Avery turned her attention to her daughter. "Sorry, sweetheart, I wasn't paying as much attention as I should. Did you ask me something?"

"I asked if you were okay with the plans we've made."

"Oh, yes. I'm sure they'll be fine."

Paul chuckled as he gave his sister an indulgent, older-brother hug. "Don't be fooled by Avery's little show of confusion, Luke. I know my sister well. When she goes off into one of these reveries of hers, she's plotting something remarkable. You mark my words, she's about to drop a bombshell." From his amused tone of voice, Kate assumed her uncle wasn't taking his own comment seriously.

"Is he right, Mom? What deep thoughts have you been mulling over in that corner seat of yours?"

Avery gave herself a shake and her pensiveness vanished, but she appeared no less worried than before. "I was thinking about your father's strange visit to you last night and the threats he made," she said. "That set me to thinking about George Klein. His death haunts me—that poor wife, and those young boys."

"George's death haunts all of us," Luke said. "It's a tragedy that shouldn't have happened."

"Yes, but I've been troubled for days now about Mr. Klein's murder...."

Her voice trailed away and Kate prompted her. "Is there something specific about his death that's bothering you, Mom?"

Avery gave a reluctant nod. "I'm afraid so. As soon as I heard the news of his murder, it occurred to me that Mr. Klein's death was amazingly convenient."

"Convenient?" Paul asked, sounding bewildered. "Convenient for whom?"

"For Ron, of course. Who else? When Kate told us about Ron's threats against her... Well, it got me thinking. And I began to wonder if Mr. Klein's death had merely been convenient...or if Ron was responsible."

"For killing George Klein?" Kate's stomach swooped toward her feet. "Mom, you can't be serious!"

Paul looked shell-shocked by his sister's suggestion. "For goodness' sake, Avery, that's a bit over-the-top! I know there have been a lot of unpleasant revelations about Ron over the past few months, but surely you don't believe he's capable of committing *murder?*"

"Ron has threatened to kill his own daughter," Luke reminded them. "Why are you so sure he couldn't be responsible for George Klein's death?"

"Well, I know Ron has made some outrageous threats, and I realize we have to take precautions to keep Kate safe, but I can't believe Ron has any real intention of killing his own child." Paul appeared to have forgotten that earlier he'd been the person warning them to take Ron's threats seriously.

"Based on past evidence, I think we can safely assume that Ron doesn't have the same attitude toward family as the rest of us," Luke said dryly. "I don't believe the fact that Kate is his daughter provides her with much protection. We'd be fools not to take Ron at his word. He's said he'll kill Kate if she continues to pursue him. For all our sakes, we need to believe he'll do just that if he gets the chance. Our job is to make sure he doesn't get the chance."

Paul spluttered and then subsided into silence, helping himself to another cup of tea, apparently in the hope that drinking something would help to wash the bad taste from his mouth.

"We're getting off the subject of George Klein's murder." Kate rubbed between her eyes, where a splitting headache had begun to throb. "I don't see what motive my father…" She stumbled over the word *father* and then forced herself to continue. "I don't see what motive he had to murder George Klein."

"To stop you looking for your father," Avery said promptly. "Or at least to increase the chance that you wouldn't find him."

"There are dozens of private investigators in Chicago, maybe hundreds. Getting rid of George Klein wouldn't stop us looking for my father."

"That's true and Ron would have to realize that, I suppose." Avery appeared a little more cheerful at the thought.

"Absolutely." Luke nodded his agreement. "Ron couldn't have guessed that Kate and I would decide to pursue him ourselves, but he would have to realize that taking George out of the picture wouldn't stop the investigation. Obviously, we'd hire somebody else. Ron could hope that the new investigator wouldn't be as experienced and hardworking as George, but he would have known we wouldn't select anyone flat-out incompetent. Anything George discovered, his successor was likely to uncover, too, sooner or later."

"Exactly," Paul said. "Let's not have our imaginations run away with us here. The police suspect random robbery was the motive for George Klein's murder, and there's every reason to assume they're right. Ron may be a really unpleasant man, but there are no grounds for us to attribute such a heinous crime to him."

To Kate's surprise, her mother didn't seem willing to abandon her suspicions. "What if George Klein had already found out something important about Ron? Something Ron couldn't afford to have reported to us."

"How would my father even know what George discovered?" Kate asked. "How would Ron manage to stay hidden from us, negotiate deals with five companies and still find a way to fly to Chicago to murder George? It's impossible. Or darn near it, anyway."

"Besides, killing George wouldn't keep the secret," Luke interjected. "Ron would be going to all that trouble for nothing. If George could discover something, presumably any other investigator could discover the same thing."

"But not until several days later," Avery persisted. "Maybe Mr. Klein discovered something Ron desperately needed to keep quiet just for a few days. Killing George Klein would buy time, even if Ron realized we'd immediately hire somebody else."

"But this speculation is silly because we know George *hadn't* discovered anything important," Paul pointed out. "He'd sent me his report, remember? I showed you the memo. He was coming back to Chicago on Friday night precisely because he needed fresh instructions. And in the end, because George was dead, Kate and Luke decided to investigate personally. And they turned up more information than George, the so-called professional whiz kid. So if Ron killed George Klein in order to stop our investigation in its tracks, he sure didn't succeed!"

"That's true." Color finally returned to Avery's cheeks. "And Ron would realize that with e-mail and cell phones, Mr. Klein would report anything important the moment he discovered it. Which, I suppose, leaves Ron with no motive to get rid of George Klein."

"None that I can think of," Luke said. "I'm a hundred

percent in favor of taking Ron's threats against Kate seriously. We'd be fools to ignore the possibility that he might be capable of murder. Still, let's not pin crimes on him just for the hell of it."

"I'm with you, one hundred percent," Paul said. "Stop torturing yourself, Avery. George Klein's murder is tragic and we're all sorry for his family, but it's got nothing to do with Ron."

"I hope you're both correct." Avery shrugged. "The truth is, I no longer trust coincidences where Ron is concerned. I spent too many years believing his excuses when I should have questioned every one of them. I guess I've moved from naive belief into a state of permanent doubt." She gave a small, rueful smile. "I obviously need to work on finding a spot somewhere in the happy middle between credulity and constant suspicion."

"I see you looking at your watch," Paul said to Luke, clearly deciding the discussion of George Klein's murder had already wasted too much time. "You need to get out of here and I do, too. Can we agree on our plans for Friday afternoon? I'm flying out of here tomorrow afternoon. I need to be in Denver on Thursday and my meetings are likely to run all day. I'll catch the last flight out of Denver International back to Washington and probably spend the night at a hotel near Dulles airport. That leaves me all morning to rent a car and drive to Focus Health. Are all three of you going to fly to Virginia and join me in our attempt to confront Ron and force him to admit what he's done?"

"I wouldn't miss it," Avery said grimly.

"Absolutely, I want to be there," Luke said.

"And me." Kate turned to look at her mother. "The three of us will fly together, right, Mom? Luke?"

"I'd like that," Avery said. "Airports are such miserable places these days. Companionship helps."

"We just need to agree on a place to meet up with you in Virginia, Uncle Paul."

"We also need to agree on exactly what we're going to do when Ron turns up in the parking lot of Focus Health," Luke said. "We've come this far. We sure don't want to blow it at the last minute. Based on my experience at Bruno's restaurant, if Ron catches so much as a glimpse of us, he's going to get straight back into his car and drive away like a bat out of hell."

"Very true." Paul nodded. "We should all check out the location for Focus Health on MapQuest, and then we can e-mail each other with suggestions about precisely where we should get together. Some nearby coffee shop would be ideal. As you point out, Luke, at a minimum we need to make sure Ron can't just drive off the moment he catches sight of us."

"If Focus Health has a lobby, maybe we need to wait inside?" Kate suggested. "Then Dad wouldn't see us until it's too late."

"Yes, once he's inside, he can't run back to his car," Paul agreed. "At least not so easily. However, we can't finalize anything until we see exactly how the parking lot around Focus Health is configured."

"How does one-fifteen sound for our get-together?" Luke asked. "Even if Ron arrives a bit early for his meeting, that gives us at least an hour to make sure we all know exactly what we're going to do when we see him drive up."

"Right now, it seems almost too easy," Avery said, and Kate silently agreed. "He's avoided us for so long. Is it really going to be this simple to catch him?"

"Knock on wood, it is." Paul rapped the nearby table. "Let's start praying that the reality turns out to be as easy as the planning."

Twenty-Three

October 25, 2007

"It was a very smart move on my part to come over right at cocktail time." Avery settled into the chair across from Kate and sampled one of Luke's famous mushroom caps, stuffed with artichokes and sun-dried tomato pesto and topped with pecorino cheese. "These are yummy. When on earth did Luke have time to make them with all that's been going on around here?"

"He brought them home from the restaurant last night." Kate uncorked a bottle of wine and lifted two glasses down from the cupboard next to the fridge without needing to stop and think where the wineglasses were kept. She'd spent so much time in Luke's condo when they were dating the first time around that moving in with him yesterday had felt almost like a homecoming.

"How fortunate for me." Avery took another luxurious bite of mushroom. "Really, from my point of view, you and Luke make the perfect couple. He's the best cook I've ever met and you're the best baker. It's a killer combo. The only problem I see is that the two of you are never home at the same time to enjoy each other's cooking."

Kate laughed and handed her mother a glass of wine. "Mom, you're usually more subtle than that. Are you asking me if Luke and I are dating again?"

"Oh, no, dear." Avery gave a bland smile. "It's perfectly obvious that the two of you are dating—if that's the current euphemism for having wildly satisfying sex. What I'm curious about is whether the two of you can make your relationship work long-term this time around. When you were apart from him this summer it was a little hard for a mother to watch. I'd hate to think of you going through that much grief again."

"We're pretty sure we can make it work this time." Kate sat down cross-legged on the sofa. "We love each other and we understand what went wrong before, so now I guess we just have to straighten out the logistics."

"It seems a bit ridiculous for me to offer advice on relationships, given the muddle I've made of my life thus far, but I can't resist offering some anyway. Luke is a good man, Kate, a keeper. Find a way to make the logistics work."

"Advice noted." Kate reached for her wine. "I'm glad you like him, Mom. He's a really great guy."

"To be honest, I was sad when you broke up. Not just for you, but because I enjoy his company. He's smart and fun to be around. Best of all, my integrity meter, which is very sensitive these days, continues to register high on the approval scale."

"Mine, too." Kate raised her wineglass in an affectionate salute. "Okay, Mom, before you can ask me a ton of questions I don't want to answer, let's change the subject from my love life. Do you want to stay and veg out with a movie? I was thinking about eating popcorn for dinner and watching *Hocus Pocus*. With Halloween just around the corner, a story about witches seems appropriate."

"Normally, I'd be thrilled to stay, but not tonight. I have to go shopping for a couple of Halloween costumes before we leave for Virginia tomorrow. I volunteered to help out at the homeless shelter next week, and their supply of costumes is sadly depleted, especially for the boys."

"What are this year's hot-ticket items?" Kate asked, smiling. "Spider-Man? Batman?"

Avery gave an airy wave of her hand. "Those are both so yesterday, my dear. This year the Pirates of the Caribbean are totally cool, and the X-Men still have some devoted followers. There's one little boy at the shelter who has bright red hair and freckles and, truth be told, is a tad on the pudgy side, but he's determined to be Wolverine on Halloween night. Because, he informed me, he's a cool dude who looks exactly like Hugh Jackman!"

Kate laughed. "Little boys pretending they're superheroes are very cute."

"Yes, they are. It only gets annoying when they refuse to grow up and accept they're never going to be Johnny Depp or Hugh Jackman, so they'd better learn to make the most of the person they actually are."

A frisson of alarm ran down Kate's spine, but as soon as she tried to identify what had bothered her, the alarm dissipated, leaving her with nothing to track. Why in the world had her mother's comment concerning men refusing to grow up generated an itch in her subconscious? What the *hell* was bothering her? There was something about her father's attack lurking just on the horizon of her peripheral vision, but it wouldn't come into focus, and every time she reached for it, it danced out of sight. The occasional, distorted glimpses were driving her crazy.

"Kate, honey, are you okay?"

"Yes, of course. I was just remembering the Halloween when Dad took me trick-or-treating and I dropped my entire sack of candy." She pulled the memory out of nowhere, simply to have something to say to her mother, but suddenly she had a vivid mental image of her father, down on his hands and knees, helping her rescue Snickers bars and Tootsie Rolls from the sidewalk. He had laughed and joked as they chased errant candies, doing a silly little happy dance when they managed to capture most of them before they could land in the gutter. How in the world had that father—that *affectionate* father—turned into a monster who whispered death threats in the middle of the night? She couldn't draw a line to connect the two radically different mental images.

"I remember that Halloween." Avery's smile was wistful. "We had some good times with your father over the years, didn't we? Sometimes, though, I wonder if I'm just inventing all the happy memories, or at least polishing past reality out of all recognition."

"You're not inventing the memories," Kate said quietly. "There were good times and plenty of them.

That's what makes me so sad when I think about Dad now. He's definitely one of those larger-than-life people and he was a lot of fun to be with when I was growing up. He wasn't a bad father—an absent one, maybe, but not a bad one."

"Well, before we drown in nostalgia for a man who betrayed both of us, let me get to the point of my visit." Avery spoke with unusual tartness directed, Kate suspected, entirely at herself. "What I really came over for was to let you know that I talked at length with Adam yesterday, filling him in on the details of your father's latest threats. Adam was furious with Ron, of course, and asked me to pass on an invitation to come and stay with him and Megan in Georgia. I told him I was sure you'd be grateful for the offer, but we had you well protected here."

Kate nodded. "I appreciate the invitation, but I don't believe it would be any safer with Adam and Megan than it is here. I'd expose the two of them to unnecessary danger, and presumably Dad could track me in a small town even more easily than in a big city like Chicago."

"I agree." Avery nodded. "Speaking of tracking, that's something I've been puzzling over since you got back from Virginia. How in the world does Ron manage to monitor your movements so closely? How did he know you were in Herndon over the weekend? How did he know you had returned to Chicago on Monday evening? He must have a hundred other balls he's keeping in the air right now and yet he can keep tabs on you almost to the minute, apparently."

"He's got years of experience in juggling multiple deceptions at the same time," Kate said acidly. "We're watching a master at work."

"Still, following someone is labor-intensive and energy-consuming." Avery smiled faintly. "At least according to the cop shows on TV."

"Presumably he's not trailing me in person. There are a ton of private investigators out there who are nowhere near as decent as George Klein was. Actually, come to think of it, Dad doesn't even need to hire someone with dubious ethics. He's so brilliant at spinning credible lies, he's capable of persuading anyone he hires that world peace will collapse into nuclear disaster unless I'm under constant surveillance."

Avery nodded in reluctant agreement. "Have you and Luke noticed anyone following you?"

Kate shook her head. "Not a twitch of a sign, although Luke is convinced that Dad must somehow have tracked us through our rental car. We know he isn't using an electronic monitoring chip attached to our shoes, or clothing, or anything high tech like that."

"Good Lord, such an idea never even occurred to me!"

"Nor to us, at least not at first." Kate smiled ruefully. "Fortunately Luke's friend, Seth, is so paranoid about all the high-tech-surveillance possibilities that he insisted on checking us out before we left his office on Monday. We were squeaky clean, both of us. On top of that, Seth suggested Dad might be tracking our rental car with a GPS device attached to the bumper or the wheel rim, but we couldn't find anything." Kate shrugged. "I admit I don't understand how Dad is tracking me. Still, the bottom line is that he knew I was back in Chicago on Monday night, which means he's found some way to keep tabs on us."

Avery fell silent for a moment, but then pulled herself out of her reverie with a brisk shake. "Well, there's much more to report from my conversation with Adam. I thought you'd be interested to know that as soon as he saw those sheets of paper with the names of Mayan gods as headers, Adam had a theory about what they might mean."

"He did?" Kate sat up straighter on the couch. "I'm fascinated to hear it. Since he and Megan have actually been in Belize, their theory is a lot more likely to be correct than anything we could come up with." She smiled ruefully. "Not that we came up with anything even halfway coherent. The best I could do was to guess Dad might be smuggling valuable ancient artwork out of Belize."

"I think you'll like Adam's theory better, since it paints your father in a more flattering light. Although, there's no light flattering enough to obliterate the shadows cast by his threats to you."

"I'm not letting his threats depress me." Kate shrugged. "I've decided to go with Uncle Paul's theory that my father intends to scare me, not to kill me."

"I admire your ability to look on the bright side, provided you never let down your guard. Don't put yourself in danger, Kate, because you'd prefer not to think ill of your father."

"Don't worry, Mom. I'm a lot less vulnerable than Dad imagines. His threats make me sad, but they don't frighten me nearly as much as he seems to think they will."

"I'm happy to hear it." Avery leaned forward and squeezed Kate's hand. "You always were incredibly strong and purposeful, even as a child. I'm so proud of you, Kate. You know that, don't you?"

"The feeling is definitely mutual," Kate said, resisting the urge to drop her gaze and change the subject. The Fairfaxes were so inhibited it was almost laughable, and she'd inherited her full share of repressive genes. Avoiding confrontation in a family could be a good thing, but she'd come to realize over the past six months that her father would never have been able to get away with his lies if she and her mother had occasionally forced an honest conversation and to hell with the fallout. Instead, they'd behaved as if the main goal of human life was never to let anyone know what you truly felt. Perhaps they shouldn't be surprised that they'd ended up paying a high price for years of silence and unasked questions.

Avery turned pink, embarrassed but also pleased by Kate's praise. "Anyway, back to Adam's theory about what that file of Ron's might mean. Apparently he and Megan have been trying to renew contact with Julio Castellano ever since the two of them got back from Belize. They haven't succeeded, but they've talked to a lot of Belizeans in the process, including the owner of the platinum mine where they were taken captive. The mine owner told them that Julio and his sister are impossible to find because they're deeply involved in a semisecret political movement that aims to create greater economic opportunities for the Mayan people. It's allied with similar peasant liberation movements in Guatemala and the Zapatistas in Mexico. Julio is trying to raise social awareness among Mayans of all ages, and foster pride among Mayan teens in their cultural heritage and their ancient religion."

"Their gods and goddesses!" Kate exclaimed.

Avery smiled. "Yes, you're exactly right, their gods and goddesses. The ancient religious myths are very significant in Mayan culture, which is closely tied to agriculture and the land itself. Unfortunately, everything Julio Castellano wants to achieve is problematic for the Belizean government. The government considers him a tiresome fanatic who is wasting his time and talents trying to revive eighty-year-old theories about social justice and peasant liberation, all the while getting in the way of real progress."

Kate grimaced. "The Miami police will be happy to hear Julio is officially considered a troublemaker by his government, even if he isn't a murderer. Still, he sounds kind of noble to me. Misguided, maybe, but noble."

"Adam said the same thing. He also says it would probably be more accurate to call Julio a political activist rather than a revolutionary."

"What's the distinction?"

"According to Adam, even Castellano's enemies admit that he tries to work within the legitimate political structure. However, he and his followers are secretive about their activities, and one of the ways they hide what they're doing from the government is to utilize a cell system for communications. They avoid telling one another their real names and they use the symbols of ancient Mayan gods and goddesses to identify themselves. Adam thinks the file you found on Ron's flash drive, the one labeled RR22, is actually an accounting record of money that your father has sent to Castellano. It seems your father is actively supporting Julio Castellano's efforts to establish agricultural communes and rural cooperatives."

"Adam's explanation fits perfectly with everything we know," Kate said. "Except for one problem. Can you imagine my father—the original Mr. Conservative— funneling money to a secretive rebel movement that wants social justice for an oppressed ethnic minority? Good grief, he's about as likely to donate to the Save Fidel Castro fund or the Revive Communism in Europe committee."

"Six months ago I would have agreed with you." Avery lifted her shoulders in a gesture too elegant to be termed a shrug. "Now I would simply remind you that we know nothing at all about the real Ron Raven. Maybe during the years we lived with him he preached right-wing, conservative politics but actually went into the booth at election time and voted socialist. We have no idea what really made him tick all those years, much less what he might feel right now. Or maybe he's changed into a left-wing radical only since he became involved with Consuela Mackenzie. After all, she's half Mayan and apparently passionate about her cultural heritage. Maybe her passion has rubbed off on Ron."

The image of her father as a left-winger was so bizarre that Kate had to laugh. "Don't tell Uncle Paul about Castellano," she said. "He'll have a heart attack if he thinks someone associated with his family is helping to support peasant revolutionaries."

Her mother actually laughed out loud. "He would, wouldn't he? It's even worse than Ron being a bigamist. Don't worry, I'll spare my brother's sensibilities."

"Poor old Uncle Paul, he's such a stick-in-the-mud."

"He always has been, too. Adam and I never quite fit into the Fairfax family mold, but Paul would have been happy to travel back a hundred years in time and live as the owner of the Fairfax plantation." Avery drew in a deep breath, as if seeking fortitude. "One final thing, Kate, and then I absolutely must go. It's already later than I planned to be out and the rain makes driving nasty."

Avery cleared her throat, clearly not quite at ease as she would have liked to pretend. "I'm sure I mentioned to you that I spoke with Ellie Raven a few days ago."

"Yes, you wanted her to know we'd hired George Klein to investigate Dad's disappearance."

"Isn't it amazing to recall that it's only three weeks since most of us still believed Ron was dead and Luke was imagining things?"

"It's astonishing," Kate agreed. "I was furious with Luke for bothering you with his hallucinations."

"Thank goodness he did! Anyway, as I've mentioned, I've been keeping Adam updated as our investigation unfolded, and Megan has been passing our news along to her mother and brother, so their whole family has been kept in the picture. It's a roundabout way of communicating, to put it mildly, but it did avoid a lot of phone calls that I felt Ellie Raven might find as difficult to handle as I do. However, Adam pointed out that now we're certain Ron is alive, we…I…owed Ellie Raven the courtesy of telling her in advance what we're planning to do. He even suggested we should ask Ellie if she wants to join us tomorrow in Virginia."

"I'd thought about that myself," Kate said quietly. "I didn't know how you would feel about her joining us, though."

"I'm fine with it." Avery lifted her hands in a gesture of bafflement that still managed to appear graceful. "It's only six months since your father staged his disappearing act, but it's amazing how much can change in six months. When I first heard about Ellie, I was determined to hate her. In fact, it's humiliating to recall how I instantly blamed her for everything, without a shred of evidence. But the more I've learned about Ron, the more I realize Ellie wasn't a scheming villain, she was simply another of his victims. Now I've reached the point where I genuinely feel that if she wants to be with us in Virginia, why not? She seems a really nice woman. Anyway, I called her yesterday morning and she was very grateful for the call. She definitely plans to be there. In fact, she must already be en route. It takes a long time to get from Thatch, Wyoming, to Washington, D.C."

"Are you certain you can trust her not to reveal our plans to anyone?" Kate asked. "It would be a disaster if she blew it after all our efforts."

"I think she can be trusted with anything we care to tell her. Ellie strikes me as a very practical, down-to-earth sort of person and she's got no interest in protecting Ron."

"You're sure of that, Mom? She was married to him even longer than you were."

Avery put down her empty wineglass. "True, but Adam mentioned that Ellie has started divorce proceedings."

"Against Dad? Why would she want to do that? More to the point, how can she divorce him when everyone thinks he's dead?"

"Her lawyers are working on that problem. Remember Liam, her son, was a divorce lawyer, although he's gone back to the practice of criminal law recently. I'm sure he's offering her lots of good, practical advice."

"But why is Ellie going to so much trouble to achieve something so symbolic? A divorce makes no real difference to her legal status, does it?"

"A big difference, since apparently she'd like to get married again. To the sheriff of Stark County, no less."

"No!" Kate was briefly shocked, and then realized how absurd it was to assume Ellie owed even a smidgen of loyalty to Ron Raven. "I hope she and the sheriff are very happy. She certainly deserves it after surviving all those years of deceit and betrayal." She smiled at her mother. "How about you, Mom? Are you about to blindside me with the news that you're preparing to become Mrs. Somebody or Other? I'm sure you've had dozens of proposals since Dad disappeared."

"I've had a few," Avery agreed. Then she chuckled. "And I think some of the men even hoped I would say yes *after* they discovered I have very little money."

"I'm sure all of them did. You're spectacular wife material."

"Hmm, I'm not sure about that. But it's beside the point, because there's nobody I have the slightest desire to marry. At the moment, finding a life partner is way down on the list of things I'm eager to do."

"Maybe that's just a reaction to what happened with Dad. Your attitude might change more quickly than you expect once we've found my father and forced him to acknowledge how badly he betrayed us."

"Could be, but somehow I don't believe so. When I

lived with Ron, my energy was entirely focused on being a good wife. When he disappeared, died as we thought, I was truly devastated. And yet, now I feel…liberated, there's no other word for it. I'm having the most fun of my entire life getting my new business off the ground and doing things to suit myself, rather than to suit Ron. I've no interest in being one half of a couple again."

Kate was surprised at how confident her mother sounded in her newfound independence. "I never really thought about it before, but Dad being such a forceful personality cut both ways. Somebody larger than life can make a fascinating father for a kid, maybe, but it's not so great for a spouse. Looking back, I can see how you were sometimes smothered by the sheer force of his personality."

"I was more than willing to be smothered," Avery said. "I realize now that one partner in a relationship can only dominate if the other partner is willing to submit. Did you notice how prickly Paul was getting yesterday because I wasn't willing to agree with everything he said? I've submitted to him all these years, as well as to Ron, but becoming more assertive with the males in my life is among my resolutions for self-improvement now that Ron is out of the picture. It's taken me a while to grasp the amazing idea that it's crazy to live by rules concerning feminine behavior that were out of date before I was born, let alone now that I'm heading toward fifty."

Kate grinned. "Way to go, Mom. Watch out, world! It may have taken you a while to hit the barricades, but now I can see you'll soon be storming over them."

"I hope so." Avery rose to her feet with such grace that Kate smiled inwardly. When her mother stormed the barricades, she'd probably do it in white gloves and wearing panty hose.

Avery leaned across the coffee table to give her daughter a goodbye kiss. "I'm going to call Ellie tonight when she gets to Washington. I'll let her know that we've arranged to meet in Lucinda's Café at one o'clock tomorrow." She gave a tiny smile. "I confess I'm looking forward to seeing Ron's face when he steps out of his car and finds both of his wives waiting to greet him!"

"I can't believe I heard you say that!"

"Well, as we just agreed, I'm now a liberated woman."

"Our confrontation with my father seems to be turning into a cross between a family reunion and a tailgate party," Kate said, accompanying her mother to the front door. "It's surreal."

"Yes, it is a little. But then, most things about your father seem to end up being impossible to believe unless you've lived through them." Avery gave a laugh that sounded amused rather than bitter. "I suppose, given his past history, we should never have expected Ron to do anything as normal and boring as staying dead."

Twenty-Four

Kate ate popcorn, watched the movie and finished packing an overnight bag. Then she took a long, luxurious bath, prepared a cup of herbal tea with the promising name Sleepytime, and climbed into bed.

It took less than five minutes to accept that she might be exhausted and facing an early-morning flight, but there was no way she was going to fall asleep anytime soon. For the past two nights, Luke had insisted on coming home from the restaurant by ten. Falling asleep with him beside her had been easy, so this morning, anxious not to drag him away from work, she'd assured him she would be fine going to bed alone.

Apparently, she'd lied. The moment she switched out the light, her entire body stiffened into a parody of relaxation that would have been comic if it hadn't been so painful. Lying in Luke's king-size bed, snuggled beneath his soft, European down comforter, she felt about as comfortable as if she'd been stranded on the ledge of a cliff, with a thousand feet of jagged rock between her and safety. The phone beside the bed had become the enemy, and each time she closed her eyes, she froze in expectation that it would start ringing, ready to attack her with its latest installment of hideous threats.

Reluctantly surrendering to the inevitable, she sat up in bed and switched the light on so that she could read until Luke arrived home. She flicked through the pages of her favorite gourmet cooking magazine, longing for sleep and yet too hyper to let herself succumb.

In the end, her wait for Luke wasn't as long as she'd feared. He came into the bedroom shortly after midnight and greeted her with a smile that melted her heart. He sat on the bed, folding her into his arms and kissing her hard.

"I hoped you'd be sleeping," he said when they finally broke apart for air. "But I'm glad you're not, even though we have such an early start in the morning."

"I was waiting for you." The phone was once again an ordinary, everyday object and not a bare-toothed monster waiting to pounce. "Did you have a busy night?"

"Insane, but no special crises, thank God. The Trattoria actually did the most business tonight, both volume and dollar receipts." He lay down next to her, still fully clothed, cradling her against the length of his body. "No phone calls? No unexpected visitors?"

"My mother stopped by for a quick visit." Kate smiled. "She was very impressed by your stuffed mushrooms."

"I'll send her a batch the next time we make them." He grinned. "It's always a smart idea to suck up to your future mother-in-law."

Her heart performed a somersault. "Gee, I must have forgotten the occasion when you and I talked about getting married. How absentminded of me."

"I was waiting until we found your father before I asked you to marry me, but right now I can't for the life of me remember why that seemed such a great idea." He brushed his knuckles over her cheek in a caress tender enough to set her pulses racing. "It feels good to come home to you, Kate." His hand slid across her hips and his eyes warmed with laughter. "And to Puff, of course."

"We both missed you." She could feel herself relaxing, muscle by strained muscle, as she soaked up the balm of his presence. Succumbing to an overwhelming urge to be closer to him, she unfastened the buttons on his gray chambray shirt and rested her cheek against the soft white cotton of his T-shirt.

He'd changed out of his chef's uniform, but the smell of rosemary and basil still clung to his skin, mingling with faint traces of soap from his morning shower and the subtle woodsy scent of his cologne. There was something wonderfully familiar and comforting about the combination of smells, something that was more than merely erotic. Together they made up a package that was quintessentially Luke. Even with her eyes closed, she would recognize him, she mused, finally relaxed enough to feel sleepy. Her thoughts drifted along in drowsy disorder and she floated with them.

The image of butterflies had suddenly transformed into a crystal-clear picture of a man and woman kissing.

Kate shot up in bed, rigid with shock. *He'd covered her head with a towel to cut off her sense of smell. Of course! He knew that she was almost as likely to identify him by smell as she was by sight or sound.* Good God, how had she ever believed she was looking at butterflies? What a fool she'd been to allow herself to be tricked!

Luke grabbed her upper arms. "Kate, what just happened? Open your eyes! Talk to me."

She obediently opened her eyes and stared at Luke, the familiar, strong contours of his face providing a sense of security while the world around her cracked and shuddered into a new form.

"It wasn't my father," she said, her teeth chattering in delayed reaction. "He didn't come here. He probably never trailed us when we were in Reston…never left Virginia. That's why he had to blindfold me. Not just to frighten me, but so that I wouldn't get even a glimpse of him."

Somehow, Luke disentangled the gist of her garbled explanation, realizing she was talking about more than one *he*. "Are you telling me it wasn't your father who invaded your house on Monday night?"

She managed to nod, struggling to impose order on a tumult of impressions that suddenly all needed to be realigned. "It wasn't my dad. I realize that now. Of course it wasn't. Part of me always recognized it was a trick. But I was scared and disoriented and I fell into the trap he set for me."

"Kate, sweetheart, it's been a rough few days and you're tired. It's understandable that you'd prefer the person who attacked you to be somebody other than your dad. But…are you absolutely sure about this?"

"I'm sure. At some level, I never really believed it

was my father. Tonight, when I was lying next to you and thinking how I could recognize you anywhere, even with my eyes closed, everything just clicked."

"All right, but if it wasn't your father, then who the hell was it?"

She could hear the lingering doubts in Luke's voice although he was trying to be supportive. "I wish I knew." She thought for a moment and realized that she didn't have a clue as to who had threatened her. The darkness and the blindfold had done their work too well. "All I know is that it was a man. When he tied me up, his arms and hands definitely felt masculine."

She was having trouble catching her breath, as if the towel had been thrown back over her head and she was once again suffocating from the weight of it. For a moment Kate was afraid she would choke, but then she pressed her hands against her rib cage and drew in a deep, calming breath. Dammit, her attacker had wanted to terrify her to the point that she wouldn't be able to respond rationally. She wasn't going to let him win that battle twice.

"He did everything in his power to convince me he was my father. That's what the towel was about, that's why it had to be pitch black."

"But you heard him speak!" Luke gathered her back into his arms, stroking his hands gently up and down her spine. "You'd have recognized if it wasn't Ron's voice, sweetheart. Nobody could have fooled you into believing it was your father talking to you if it wasn't. You know Ron too well to be deceived."

"But I *didn't* hear him speak. That's the whole point. Whoever it was never spoke out loud. He only whispered."

"You never mentioned that before."

"Didn't I? I should have, because it bothered me a lot. In some ways, it made the whole experience more frightening, because the whispering combined with the towel over my head made everything feel disconnected from reality. That's how the attacker was able to convince me he was my dad. He claimed to be my father and I took his word for it because there was nothing else to hang on to. But I never recognized his voice because I never heard it."

"Katie-love, are you sure you're not recollecting something that isn't true?"

"I'm sure. I'm a hundred percent sure." She moved away from the comfort of his arms so that she could look straight into his eyes. "Luke, you have to believe me about this. I'm not retrofitting the facts to fit my wishes. I've finally realized why that assault has felt so disorienting ever since it happened. Part of me always rejected the idea that my father was the man attacking me."

"You were the person who went through it, so you know what happened." Luke leaned back against the pillows, taking her with him and tucking her head against his shoulder as they talked. "Then I guess the next question is obvious. If it wasn't Ron invading your home on Monday night, then are you sure it was Ron who phoned you while we were in Virginia? Were those threats whispered, too?"

"No, they weren't." She shook her head. "He spoke in his regular voice and it was definitely my father."

Luke frowned. "Doesn't it strike you as very strange that your father called and threatened you while we were in Virginia, but then somebody else, pretending to be Ron, invaded your house as soon as we got back to Chicago? Are Ron and somebody else *both* threatening you?"

"It's very strange, I agree, but that's what must have happened. I'd recognize Dad's voice anywhere and it was unmistakable. I'm positive..." Her voice died away again, lost in a jumble of speculation.

"You're positive of what? What did you just think of?" Luke asked. He rolled over, propping himself on his elbow so that he could see her more clearly. "Kate, your whole expression just changed. What is it?"

"Wait, don't talk. I have to remember." She rubbed her forehead, desperately trying to pull up an accurate memory of everything her father had said during his phone call.

Looking for me is a fool's errand.... Be smart, for once in your life.... If you should happen to find me, you'll regret it. The ugly snippets all surfaced on demand, etched unpleasantly into her subconscious.

Be smart, for once in your life. It was her father who had spoken those words, she was sure of it, and he had sounded as if he was repeating a frequent complaint. Yet now that she was thinking rationally instead of wallowing in self-pity, she realized that from the time of her earliest childhood memories until the day he disappeared, her father had never once hinted that he considered her dumb. The opposite was true, in fact. His nickname for her as a little kid had been smarty-pants, and he'd been lavish in praising her academic success in high school and equally lavish in praising her creative skills when she attended culinary school.

Her father had concluded his phone call with his chilling warning that he wasn't offering a threat, but a certified Ron Raven promise. Their conversation had ended right there because he'd cut her off as soon as she tried to speak to him. His call had been a monologue, albeit a short one, with no greeting and no goodbyes.

"Kate, talk to me. Tell me what you're thinking."

"He never said my name." She heard the confusion in her own voice, which mimicked the bewilderment churning in her gut. "When I tried to talk to him, he ended the call. My father never responded directly to anything I said."

Luke's expression was grim. "Precisely what are you suggesting, Kate? Spell it out for me."

The last of the haze shrouding her thoughts vanished and she could finally speak with confidence. "Okay, here's what I think. It was definitely my father speaking—but I don't believe he was speaking to me. I believe I was listening to a recording, a snippet from a longer conversation that somebody replayed to terrorize me. Yes, it was my father who made those threats, but not to me. He made them to somebody else. And that somebody took advantage of an earlier conversation when he wanted to frighten me."

"Holy Mother of God." Luke expelled a long, slow breath.

She gave a tight smile. "My thoughts exactly."

Luke ran his hand through his hair, leaving the short strands standing upright. He looked like a comic book parody of a man in shock, Kate thought, and she felt pretty much the same.

"Somebody is going to a hell of a lot of trouble to

make it appear your father will kill you if you continue to search for him."

"Yes." Her brain tumbled in chaos; her body felt uncoordinated. "Who is doing this to me, Luke? Who could be so unspeakably cruel?"

"I sure as hell wish I knew the answer to that. More to the point, *why* is he doing it? What is he trying to achieve?"

"There must be a rational motive. It can't be a crazy stalker. It's too much of a coincidence that he's making these threats at the same time as we're on the brink of making contact with my father."

"I agree. Obviously, the phone call was made by somebody who doesn't want your father to be found. And he followed up with a personal visit to reinforce his message that you should stop looking for Ron Raven."

"It's not true that the attacker doesn't want my father to be found." Kate got out of bed and started to pace, too restless to remain in one place. "He just doesn't want *me* to find my father."

"How do you reach that conclusion?"

"Because of the message my father delivered in Virginia," she said. "We don't know who my father was talking to in that recording, but we know he was demanding that someone should stop looking for him. Logically, if my father was ordering someone to back off, that same someone must have been searching long enough for Dad to have noticed."

"Well, that insight narrows the field of suspects right down," Luke said with heavy sarcasm. "As far as I can see, half the people who knew Ron Raven are anxious to find him—chiefly so that they can kill him."

She and Luke stared at each other, the impact of his statement hitting them both at the same time. He had intended to be sarcastic, but his comment was quite possibly true, Kate reflected grimly. Somebody was desperate to find her father in order to kill him.

She bit back a bubble of hysterical laughter. When Luke had walked into the bedroom shortly after midnight, she'd considered her father a violent criminal. She'd been impatient for tomorrow to arrive so that they could confront him, tie him up if need be and bundle him off to the nearest police station. Now she was worried about how to keep him safe from a would-be murderer. The revolution in her emotions was leaving her dizzy.

"I need to identify the man who attacked me," she said, perching on the edge of the bed before jumping up and resuming her pacing. "I really need to know who's doing this. I may be angry as hell with my father, but I don't want anyone to kill him." She smiled wanly. "Except maybe me."

"We can't narrow the list of suspects by looking for motives," Luke said. "There are way too many people who have reasons to kill Ron. But we can sure narrow the list by considering how many men there are who could gain access to your house without needing to break any locks or smash any windows."

"In other words, we're looking for somebody who has a key."

"Exactly."

Kate considered Luke's point with surprising calm. In comparison to believing that her father intended to murder her, almost any other possibility was a major improvement.

"My father had a key, which is another reason I believed he was the person who'd attacked me. I knew he had a way to get into the house. You had a key, but you mailed it back to me after we broke up. My mother has one." She shrugged. "There's nobody else."

"Nobody else has a key that you've *given* him," Luke corrected. "There could be a lot of people who have been able to make copies of the keys owned by your father, or even your mother for that matter. Let's change the definition slightly. We're looking for a man able to obtain a copy of your house key who also knew you were back from Virginia. Who do we know that fits the description?"

"Nobody. I went straight from the airport to my mother's house, and as soon as I'd filled Mom in on everything we found out in Virginia, I came home. Mom said she'd pass on all the news to Uncle Paul, so I didn't call anyone, or speak to anyone."

Luke stood and captured her hand, halting her march up and down. "Listen to what you've just said, sweetheart. You went straight from the airport to your mother's house, and *she called your uncle.* Your uncle, who was Ron's business partner and presumably had almost unlimited access to your father's keys and your mother's, too. Your uncle, who already knew which flight you were planning to take home from Virginia. Your uncle, who has been aware of every move the two of us have made ever since this investigation started— because we've been calling him on a regular basis to keep him informed, for Christ's sake!"

Kate stared at him, speechless. *"Uncle Paul?"* she said, when she could finally speak. "You think *Uncle*

Paul attacked me?" She intended to protest against Luke's conclusions, but almost as soon as she uttered her uncle's name, she experienced a sickening realization that Luke was right. There was no more likely suspect than her uncle.

"Paul is far and away the most logical suspect," Luke said, echoing her thoughts. "He could make copies of the keys to this house more easily than anyone else. As for the phone call when we were in Virginia, he's one of the few people in the world who knew which hotel we were staying in."

"Because I'd told him," she said bitterly.

"Yes. And it's just occurred to me…if Ron wasn't responsible for the attack on you, it answers the question your mother keeps asking about how he managed to track your movements so accurately. He didn't. We weren't followed. We weren't monitored. We were personally keeping your attacker informed!"

"Mom was right to be puzzled." The details of the attack, which had never seemed rational when she believed it was perpetrated by her father, suddenly made sense.

"That's why Paul had to ensure my bedroom was pitch-black before he came into the room. I know him so well that I'd have needed only a quick glimpse in order to identify him. That's why he got rid of the clock—even the glow from the digital numbers might have been enough. It's why he used one of my own towels to blindfold me. He knew he would have to move in really close to tie me up and whisper his threats. He must have been afraid I would recognize the feel of him, or even his smell. With my bath towel over my head, I was breathing in the scent of my own shower gel, totally blocking my impressions of the outside world."

Luke's mouth turned down. "Paul is not only cruel, he sounds like a pretty sick puppy to me. You could have been tied and blindfolded for days."

"Actually, he wasn't planning to leave me tied up indefinitely. Remember how he called me first thing on Tuesday morning? He'd already contacted the bakery and that gave him a valid excuse to call the house and check on me. If I hadn't managed to escape under my own steam, I bet he planned to play the hero and come rushing to the rescue."

"Hypocritical asshole." Luke put his arm around her shoulders, shielding her from the ugliness of what they were contemplating. "Want to make a guess at the reasons Paul might be so desperate to find your father that he was reduced to attacking you?"

"Specifically, I haven't the smallest clue. In general?" Kate shrugged. "He and Ron were partners in Raven Enterprises. That leaves plenty of scope for double-crossing and betrayal."

"Yeah, I guess it does. If Ron Raven had no problems screwing over his two wives and three children, he'd presumably have even less trouble screwing over his business partner. I can think of a ton of reasons why Paul might be frantic to find his former partner—all of them with dollar signs attached."

More puzzles began to unlock. "My uncle has always claimed that Dad left Raven Enterprises in great financial shape, barring a few trivial cash-flow problems mostly caused because of the lawyers putting holds on various parts of the business. But how would we know if he's telling the truth? It's a private partnership and Paul's in complete control of all the records."

"In fact, if your father cleaned out the company accounts before he disappeared, that would explain why Paul is so anxious to find him." Energized by their insights, Luke joined her in pacing. "When Ron made the start-up loan for my first restaurant, he flat-out stated that he was the person with a nose for sniffing out potentially exciting deals and the person who had the final say as to which projects would go ahead and which wouldn't. Paul was just the guy who handled legal and financial matters. In other words, Paul was never much more than an in-house accountant. Without Ron there to guide him, Paul might easily have made a couple of terrible investments and left himself seriously strapped for cash."

"And if Dad cleaned out the company coffers, it would explain why Paul went looking for my father as soon as he was reported missing," Kate said. "If the money was gone, Paul would have cause to suspect right from the start that my father had faked his own death and was taking money from Raven Enterprises to fund his new life."

She paused for a moment, her flow of insights grinding to a halt. "Still, despite all the motives Paul might have for needing to find my father, I don't understand what he expected to achieve by threatening me."

Luke hesitated. "There's one reason that occurred to me…." His voice tailed away.

"For heaven's sake, don't try to shield me, Luke. My family has come to the very edge of disaster because we all avoid telling one another even vaguely unpleasant truths. I can cope with harsh facts a lot better than tactful silences." She sent him a tiny smile. "Don't fall into bad Fairfax family habits before you're even a member of the family."

"You're right and I'm sorry. It's just that my thoughts were gruesome—"

"I can handle gruesome. Trust me, it would be hard for you to come up with any scenario that's more gruesome than believing your father is willing to kill you if you get in his way."

"Okay, here's a possible motive for Paul's attack. If you had been found dead or injured before we had this conversation, your mother and I would have had a prime suspect to hand over to the police."

"My father," Kate said flatly.

Luke nodded. "Until ten minutes ago, if anything had happened to you, I'd have been on the front lines demanding the cops find Ron Raven and throw him in prison for murder. After all, I believed Ron had viciously assaulted you and threatened your life on two separate occasions. If you were hurt or killed, it would have been inevitable for me to assume he'd made good on his threats."

"In other words, you're suggesting Paul is impersonating my father to provide himself with an alibi for my murder."

Luke tilted his head in bleak acknowledgment. "It would be a brilliant piece of misdirection to have everyone out there hunting for your father, wouldn't it?"

Kate considered for a few moments, but however hard she thought, she couldn't see why her uncle would want her dead. "What reason does Paul have for killing me?" she asked. "The two of us have no links beyond the accident of birth, no business dealings, no shared secrets. He's not going to inherit my money, even if I had any. Killing me doesn't achieve a darn thing from Paul's point of view. No financial gain, no release from an unhappy relationship, nothing."

"It gets your father arrested for committing murder! That's a pretty good revenge."

"If Paul wants to see Dad behind bars, he doesn't have to kill me to achieve his goal. It's already pretty much guaranteed Dad will be arrested as soon as we find him. The moment we can present proof that he's alive, the cops will go after him, no holds barred. He faked his own death, he committed bigamy, he defrauded the First Bank of Fairfax of three million bucks, and Lord knows how many other offenses there are to pin on him. And the cops are going to be totally pissed that he managed to deceive them about Castellano, so there will be a personal vengeance angle, too. Dad isn't going to get off the hook."

"Murder is going to earn Ron a much longer sentence than bigamy and fraud."

"True, but I can't believe Paul would risk killing me in the vague hope that my father would spend twenty-five years locked up instead of ten. Not to mention the fact that Dad might never be convicted of my murder. What if he has an iron-clad alibi for the time of my death?"

"If you're right, then we're left with no reason for Paul to threaten you," Luke said.

"Perhaps we're being too subtle, too twisted." Kate

shook her head, running her fingers through her hair, combing it into place as if that might somehow help to reduce the chaos inside. "Paul ordered me to stop looking for my father. Why not assume he meant what he said?"

"It's possible," Luke conceded. "When you think about it from Paul's point of view, the phone call required almost no effort on his part and the payoff was potentially huge if he succeeded in scaring you off. He could have placed the call from any phone, anywhere in the country, and the chances of the call being traced back to him are close to zero."

"And if there's no way we could prove he was responsible for placing the call, it was a very low-risk proposition for him."

"But the invasion of your home was a lot riskier. If you'd recognized him, Kate, it would have been a disaster for Paul. There are lengthy prison sentences waiting for men who tie women up and whisper death threats."

"He wasn't running as much of a risk as you might think," Kate disagreed. "He knows my neighborhood, he knows the house and he knows I go to bed quite early. He would have known the best place to park his car so that it wasn't noticed, and if the lights had been on in my room, I guess he wouldn't have come upstairs. Presumably he wasn't carrying any sort of weapon. Even if I'd woken up and seen him, he'd have been able to invent dozens of at least semiplausible excuses for being at my house. In fact, the more I think about this from Paul's point of view, his attack on Monday night makes perfect sense—it was low risk for him and devastating for me."

Luke raised her hands to his face and pressed her palms against his cheeks. "Except that Paul seriously underestimated you. Instead of causing you to back off, his attacks made you more determined than ever to find Ron."

"Paul never was very good at judging character." Kate yawned and plopped onto the bed. The rush of adrenaline that had kept her going was fading fast, and she was suddenly almost falling-down tired. "Finding Dad seemed easier when we thought he was the only bad guy we had to deal with. Have you by any chance noticed, Luke, that if we do get married, you'll be infiltrating yourself into a family of crooks?"

He laughed. "No, I hadn't considered that."

"Maybe you should."

"Maybe. And then in exchange I'll open a few of the Savarini closets and show you some of our family skeletons. We have our fair share, you know."

"Nothing that comes close to my father, I'm guessing. Or dear old Uncle Paul."

"I'm not so sure of that. I have a couple of cousins who are definite contenders. They were animal rights activists who kept sneaking into college science departments and—quote—liberating all the oppressed animals. Unfortunately, on their last excursion they liberated a saw-scaled viper, one of the most poisonous snakes in the entire world. It bit a lab assistant, who died before anyone could administer antivenin."

"Oh my God."

"Yep, that's what all three hundred or so Savarini cousins said when we heard the story. The Morons, as they're not-so-affectionately known within the family, are currently serving time for second-degree murder. So don't think you have a premium on crazy relatives."

She looked at Luke, her heart melting with love. "Thank you," she said softly.

He squished the tip of her nose. "For what?"

"You know for what. For making me feel that I'm not the weirdest person in the world to have Ron Raven and Paul Fairfax as members of my family."

"You'll need to come up with a much better excuse than horrible relatives if you want to avoid marrying me." He tugged her backward and she tumbled against the pillows, her head ending up very conveniently on his shoulder.

"We could talk some more about Uncle Paul," he said, turning toward her. "Or we could make love and worry about Uncle Paul tomorrow."

She sighed, forcing herself to be sensible. "We need to discuss what we're going to do. Paul must be planning to sabotage our arrangements to meet up with my father—"

"We have an entire flight to Washington, D.C., with nothing to do except discuss our options." Luke leaned down so that he could kiss her. "Puff votes for making love," he murmured, his lips almost touching her. "So do I, and that makes two against one. Besides, Puff is a very powerful dragon, and you'd be smart to surrender to his command. His revenge could be terrible."

Kate surrendered. Only a fool would argue with a dragon.

Twenty-Five

October 26, 2007

Avery stared at the busy airport scene around her without actually seeing any of it. Listening to Kate, she struggled to absorb the latest twist in the nightmare that had started to unfold on the day Ron disappeared and had ever since staggered with drunken exuberance from one incredible event to the next.

Sadly, Kate's accusations against Paul were distressingly easy to believe, for more reasons than Kate knew. A couple of weeks ago, when it had become clear that Ron was more likely to be alive than dead, Avery had felt an overwhelming compulsion to organize her life. She'd worked on refurbishing her new home with manic energy, as if to make sure that she had a secure new nest before Ron exploded back into her life. Then at night, when she was too exhausted to scrub and clean and sew any longer, she'd hauled out boxes of neglected bank documents, legal notices and

IRS forms, determined to take charge of her finances once and for all.

For once, she'd cut Paul out of the loop, not telling him what she was doing and certainly not turning to him every time she didn't instantly understand a document. It was way past time, she had realized, to stop relying on her brother and take full responsibility for both the nitty-gritty details and the big picture.

Her search through her financial records had been enlightening, to say the least. For over a week now, she had known that the mysterious three-million-dollar mortgage on her penthouse had actually been taken out by her brother and not by Ron. That mortgage alone, with its accompanying forged signatures and falsified documents, provided Paul with three million good reasons to prevent her meeting with Ron.

But there was another, much darker cloud looming on the Fairfax family horizon, and that was the death of George Klein. After twenty-seven years of believing Ron's lies, and accepting strings of coincidences as part of the natural fabric of life, in the wake of his disappearance Avery had switched mental gears and become a complete skeptic. George Klein's death fell slap-bang into the middle of her new skepticism.

For several days, she'd suspected Ron of being the murderer. Then Kate and Luke had convinced her that Ron wasn't responsible. But as she heard her daughter recount the list of Paul's horrific acts, her old suspicions returned in new form. It occurred to Avery that her brother had not only known precisely when George would be arriving at O'Hare airport, he also might have reasons for wanting the detective to die. According to her brother, one of the best detectives in the state of Illinois had uncovered nothing of interest about Ron Raven during three days of intensive investigation. And yet Kate and Luke, with no special training, had managed to find Ron's latest address within a couple of hours of arriving in Virginia. Had George Klein been incredibly careless? Had her daughter been incredibly lucky? It seemed to Avery that a more likely explanation was simply that her brother had lied. George Klein had been making his reports directly to her brother. Who knew what he'd really said? It seemed quite possible that he'd reported information Paul didn't want pursued and her brother had doctored those reports before passing them on. Was her brother capable of killing a man with no better reason than the need to silence him and put an end to a crucial investigation?

Avery shied away from answering that question. Still, she was convinced the motive existed. There was no way Paul could have foreseen that Kate and Luke would immediately take up where George had left off, and Paul certainly couldn't have guessed two amateurs, better known for their creativity than their logic, would be so successful in their endeavors. If her brother had merely wanted to shut down the investigation of Ron's whereabouts for a few days so that he could get to Ron first, killing George Klein would have seemed to be a clear route to success. Hence her brother's frantic efforts to scare Kate off by making threats while pretending to be Ron.

Aware that she teetered dangerously close to hysteria, Avery quelled a gurgle of inappropriate laughter. She wondered if it was worth suspecting that your brother was a vicious criminal if the reward was to learn that your bigamous husband had no plans to murder your daughter. The answer in her case seemed to be yes. Now that the terrible suspicion against Ron was lifted, she recognized what a heavy weight of guilt and depression it had imposed. She no longer loved Ron—his betrayals had been too many and too deep—but it was a huge relief to know that she had merely been blind and credulous during the decades they spent together, as opposed to utterly and totally moronic. Ron was undoubtedly an unfaithful rogue. That, thank God, was several steps up from being a cruel, murdering psychopath.

Avery brought her full attention back to her daughter. "We're sure Paul must have some plan up his sleeve to disrupt our meeting with Dad," Kate was saying. "Luke and I have tried to second-guess what he's intending to do, but we're coming up empty. There are three of us, four counting Ellie Raven, and only one of him. How in the world does he expect to keep us away from Dad?"

"Paul doesn't know Ellie will be in Virginia," Avery said, her thoughts still a little scattered. "I haven't spoken to him since she decided to make the trip. I've no idea if that would affect anything he might be planning."

"Even so, even if he doesn't know about Ellie, he knows it's at least three against one," Kate said. "How is he expecting to get around that?"

"Paul has no clue we've uncovered what he's been up to," Luke added. "That might be important. Considering how much trouble he's taken to divert our attention away from him, presumably he's anxious to keep up the facade of good friend and loving family member."

"Is it important to know precisely what Paul is planning?" Avery made an apologetic gesture. "I'm sorry, Kate, your revelations this morning were so un-expected, it's taking me a while to grasp the conse-quences and pitfalls."

"Yes, I think it's important," Kate said. "We need to have some inkling of how Paul intends to prevent us meeting with Dad. If we're totally unprepared, anything could happen."

"And there's an excellent chance Ron will take ad-vantage of the confusion and disappear, never to be seen again." Luke looked as grim as he sounded. "We're not going to get two chances with Ron, that's a certainty, so we need to get this right."

"We considered calling Paul and telling him we know he's the person who attacked me. He would probably answer his cell phone if we called, since there's no reason at the moment for him to be suspicious of us." Kate had folded and refolded her boarding pass so many times that it was in danger of shredding. When she saw what she'd done, she put the pass in her pocket and linked her hands in her lap. It took a visible effort for her to keep them there.

"The trouble is, we don't know if telling him what we know would inspire Paul to retreat or to attack. I keep remembering what he said on Monday night when he was pretending to be my father. He begged me not to push him into a corner. If I did, he threatened to behave like any other cornered animal and lash out. I'm afraid he may have been expressing his own feelings under the guise of impersonating Dad." Her voice dropped. "I'm *really* afraid that if Paul lashes out, someone will get hurt. Badly hurt."

The solution to the problem of what her brother planned to do seemed so clear cut to Avery that she decided she must have missed something. Which wouldn't be surprising given the current jumbled state of her brain, she reflected with rueful self-mockery.

"Let me see if I have everything straight," she said, ticking off her thoughts on her fingers. "My brother probably never believed that Ron was dead, and he's been searching for Ron for several months now. However, my brother had no success in smoking Ron out of hiding. Then Luke spotted Ron by sheer chance at his cousin's restaurant. The minute that happened, Paul was left with a double problem—he still desperately needed to make contact with Ron, but he wanted to find him first, without any of us around. For some reason, undoubtedly money related, he's so anxious to stop us talking to Ron that he faked a threatening phone call and invaded your home on Monday night, Kate, in the hope that he could terrorize you into backing off from the hunt for your father. Have I got everything right so far?"

"Well, you've done a grand job of explaining our theory of what's going on," Kate said wryly. "Unfortunately, we have no proof for any of this."

"Leaving aside the question of proof, that brings us to right now, this morning. Our flight, knock on wood, is currently scheduled to depart on time, and we'll be landing in Dulles airport around eleven. Meanwhile, if Paul stuck to the schedule he told us about, he flew into

Dulles airport last night from Colorado. He doesn't know this, but Ellie Raven is already in Virginia and I have her cell phone number, so we can talk to her if need be. Coming from Wyoming, there was no way for her to arrive at Focus Health by two-thirty unless she flew in yesterday."

"Mom, they're going to be calling our flight at any moment. Are these scheduling details important?"

"Yes, as it happens, I think they are. Very important. Bear with me a little longer. Paul has arranged for all of us to meet at a place called Lucinda's Café, about two miles up the road from Focus Health. Lucinda's Café exists, because we all checked it out on the Internet. Given all those facts, how is Paul going to stop us meeting up with Ron? He can't prevent us catching our plane—we're here and we're going to board. He can't prevent us renting a car at Dulles airport, or driving to Focus Health. Even if he was willing to risk injuring us, he can't plan any unfortunate 'accidents' because he's not in a position to make them happen."

"So what the hell is he going to do?" Luke demanded.

Avery spoke with a calm she didn't entirely feel. "He's going to change the time of Ron's meeting at Focus Health, of course. When we all get there at two-thirty, Ron will already have gone."

"Oh, my God," Luke said. "Shit…I mean, shoot, that's so simple. Why the hell didn't I think of it?"

Visibly stunned, Kate didn't say anything for several seconds, at which point the counter clerk announced that the flight for Washington's Dulles airport was now boarding. "How could Paul change the time of the meeting?" Kate demanded, scrambling to her feet. "In the first place, we have no current phone number for Dad, so we have no idea how to reach him. And second, the reason we went through Focus Health was precisely so that Dad wouldn't become suspicious. Paul can't just call and demand that Dad should arrive two hours early. It's a dead giveaway."

"We'll be lucky if Paul only moves the meeting up by a couple of hours," Avery said bleakly. "We'd have a slight chance of getting there if that's the case. As for how my brother can change the meeting schedule... Well, obviously he won't phone Ron himself. He'll get Focus Health to make the call."

"How will he do that, for gosh sake?"

Avery shrugged. "He just has to invent some persuasive tale for the Focus Health people. Remember, he has all Ron's files and notes on the company. He can read through those and come up with something convincing, I'm sure." Avery joined Kate and Luke in the line of passengers waiting to board. "I may not have the details precisely right, but I'm sure the general theory is correct. There's no other way for Paul to prevent us seeing Ron, so he has to find a way to make this work."

Conversation was impossible as they filed onto the plane, but the few minutes of forced preoccupation with mundane matters like finding their seats and stowing their three small carry-on bags provided Avery with just enough time to realize there was only one sure way to thwart any plan Paul might have to kidnap Ron before any other members of the family could arrive. The moment they were seated, she pulled out her cell phone, quickly scanning the list of phone numbers.

"What's up, Mom?" Kate searched for the ends of her seat belt. "Who are you calling?"

"I can't explain. No time. They're going to tell us to turn off our cell phones any minute now. And then it will be too late." Avery found the number she'd been searching for and dialed fast, sending up a quick prayer of gratitude when Ellie answered.

"Hi, Avery. Where are you calling from?"

"Hello, Ellie, how are you?" Impatient with her own inability to dispense with the courtesies, even in an emergency, Avery rushed on, giving Ellie no time to speak. "I'm on the plane at O'Hare, about to take off, so I need to make this fast. Are you in Virginia? Please tell me you're already in Virginia."

"Yes, I'm here. At the Courtyard Inn about five miles north of Focus Health."

"Thank God. Ellie, we have reason to believe Ron may turn up at Focus Health much earlier than we expected. It's too complicated to explain what's going on, but there's no way for the three of us to arrive there before noon. Twelve-thirty is more realistic. Later than that if the traffic is as terrible as everyone always claims it is. Could you possibly get over to Focus Health right now—as soon as possible—and wait there to see if Ron arrives? I'm sorry to assign you such a boring task, but otherwise I'm afraid we're going to miss him."

"Don't apologize. It's not boring at all if the end result is a chance to give Ron a piece of my mind! Do you have any special instructions?"

Avery mentally blessed her for not asking useless questions. "Remember, Ron is going to be disguised as Robert Russo, which means he'll be wearing a black wig and dark contacts. Also, you need to watch out for my brother, Paul Fairfax. We're pretty sure he'll be there and, unfortunately, we're afraid he may be up to mischief. Paul is in his fifties, tall—"

"I've met him, remember? He was at your penthouse when I came to visit you after Ron disappeared."

"Oh, yes. Thank goodness you'll be able to recognize him! Be sure to look out for him. Whatever you do, Ellie, don't put yourself in danger. I have no idea what my brother might be planning, but I'm quite sure he loathes Ron."

"It's a public place, and broad daylight. Even if he wants to get up to mischief, there's not too much he can do."

Avery hoped she was right. "Thank you, Ellie. What a relief that you had already arrived in Virginia! You may just have saved the day."

Twenty-Six

The events of the past ten days had been so extraordinary that Ellie almost wasn't surprised to find herself sitting behind the wheel of her rented Pontiac, waiting for her returned-from-the-dead husband to put in an appearance in the parking lot of Focus Health in Loudon County, Virginia.

The news that Ron wasn't dead had been huge, of course. But the fact that Harry Ford had asked her to marry him—and she'd accepted!—struck her as even more important in her personal scheme of things. Harry was her future, and she was looking forward to their life together with an enthusiasm that she'd once assumed was gone from her life forever. Her heart raced like a teenager's when she thought about them setting up house together and working to turn the Flying W into one of Wyoming's premier vacation resorts. By contrast, being here today to confront Ron was no more than a necessary chore, something that needed to be done to tidy up the loose ends of her past.

She'd originally planned to ask Harry to come with her to Virginia. Then she'd realized what a big mistake that would be. Through thirty-five years of marriage to Ron, she'd basically allowed him to make all the decisions except those connected to the running of the ranch. She'd never really taken responsibility for her own life: she signed their tax returns without even flicking through the pages; she managed her own bank account, but never questioned the larger financial picture. On an emotional level, she'd never demanded that Ron step up to the plate and either commit fully to their marriage or end it. She'd been too cowardly to risk the consequences of forcing a confrontation. Now, finally, she understood that she had to stand on her own two feet. Ron was her past and she needed to deal with him by herself. Only then would she be strong enough, and independent enough, to make Harry the equal partner he deserved to be. In a strange way, it felt good to be sitting behind the wheel of her rental car, knowing that Avery Fairfax and a bunch of other people were all depending on her to hold down the fort until they could get here.

Focus Health turned out to be located in a strip mall, lined up alongside a dentist's office, a dog-grooming parlor, an insurance broker and a store selling hot tubs. It was eleven-thirty, and she'd been waiting here for more than two hours now. Unfortunately, that meant at least another half hour would have to pass by before there was even a slight chance of Avery, Kate and Luke arriving from the airport. She *really* hoped the three of them would get here before Ron put in an appearance.

The strip mall wasn't exactly a hive of activity,

although there were enough cars, minivans and trucks around that her rented Pontiac wasn't conspicuous. So far, the most exciting thing to have happened was the brief escape from its leash of a bad-tempered poodle en route to the groomer. The little swirl of activity as the owner and various other people chased the poodle around a cluster of parked vehicles was the closest to high drama that the strip mall had managed to generate this morning. That was fine with Ellie, who suspected she wasn't the stuff heroines were made of and didn't need a scrap more drama in her life than she'd already had.

Time to move to a new parking spot in front of a different business, Ellie decided. She rolled down her side window both for fresh air and to give herself a clear view of her surroundings. Then she drove for a second time around the perimeter of the lot, carefully scrutinizing all the cars to make certain she hadn't slipped up and overlooked one that was occupied. Unless Paul was hiding beneath a blanket, or on the floor, the cars were empty. Somehow, Ellie just couldn't picture snooty Paul Fairfax squashed onto the floor of a car, ruining his two-thousand-dollar suit. He might loathe Ron Raven, but judging by her brief acquaintance with him, she'd guess he would loathe getting dust on his clothes even more.

Once she reached the service alley, she stopped and got out of the car so that she could stretch her legs. She didn't want to risk sitting behind the wheel for so long that she ended up with a cramp when she most needed to be quick and agile.

Jogging in place for a minute, she stretched her arms

over her head and did a couple of quick knee bends. She smothered a giggle, aware of what a sight she would look if anyone bothered to notice her: a middle-aged woman in her best new Ultrasuede travel suit, doing knee bends behind the Dumpster.

She did a final big stretch, closing her eyes and tilting her head up to the sun. It was a beautiful fall day, sunny enough to make the temperature comfortable, with plenty of colorful leaves still clinging to the branches of the trees. If you had to hang around a parking lot waiting to tell your bigamous husband that he was a loser, you despised him and you were getting a divorce, it was a pretty day for the job.

Ellie got back into the car and chose a new parking spot with a clear view both of the road and the entrance to Focus Health. Her rental car still hadn't attracted a lick of attention. She'd thought at first that anyone parked for too long would create suspicion for sure since the various businesses all had beveled glass doors and windows facing out to the lot. Now she realized the glass was frosted, so that it let in light, but the people inside had only a blurred view of the parking lot.

It was good that she hadn't been told to move on. Still, that was only the first of the hurdles she needed to overcome this morning. Ever since Avery's phone call, she'd been worrying about how she was going to prevent Ron running away if and when he finally turned up. He'd made a dash for it the moment Kate Fairfax's friend spotted him in his cousin's restaurant. Why wouldn't he do the same as soon as he noticed her? Based on his past behavior, Ron sure wasn't going to feel he owed her the courtesy of an explanation for his years of deception and betrayal.

Two hours of mulling over the problem hadn't yet provided any answers. Avery Fairfax had trusted her to do this right, and Ellie didn't want to mess up. Some of that was due to pride and some of it was due to an odd feeling of kinship. She had grown up on a ranch in rural Wyoming and Avery Fairfax was an aristocrat of the old South; on the surface they couldn't be more different, but Ellie really liked the woman, despite all the obvious reasons why she shouldn't.

As far as she could tell, she only enjoyed one advantage over Ron this morning: she was expecting to see him, whereas he had no reason to pay special attention to a white Pontiac parked between a Ford pickup and a Toyota minivan. But even the element of surprise wasn't as big an advantage as it might have been. After so many years of anticipating the unexpected, Ron must have developed a sixth sense for danger. To a regular person, she would be invisible. Ron, on the other hand, was quite likely to turn and look the moment he heard the car door open.

Ellie allowed herself the luxury of a sigh. Truth was, she couldn't prevent Ron running away, at least while she was on her own and the two of them were out here in the open. Even catching the fleeing poodle had required a posse of four women. She wouldn't have a hope of corralling six-foot, one-hundred-and-ninety-pound Ron while he had the entire parking lot to run around in. He'd be back in his car and driving off, Lord knew where, the first glimpse he got of her. For a moment, she wished that Harry was with her. His strong muscles and rock-solid common sense would sure have been welcome right about now.

She gave herself a shake, squaring her shoulders. *No falling back into bad old habits, Ellie my girl.* She wasn't going to free herself from Ron only to start clinging to Harry. It was her job to find a way to keep Ron pinned down until Avery, Kate and Luke could arrive.

Think positive, she commanded herself. *Concentrate on how you're going to do it, not how difficult it's going to be.*

It would be a whole different story once Ron was inside Focus Health, Ellie mused. There was no exit from the lobby except through the front entrance, and she could block that easily enough, just by standing right there and closing the door behind her.

Wait, that was it! She smiled triumphantly. She'd finally hit on a solution, and a simple one at that. All she needed to do was to remain out of sight until Ron stepped into the Focus Health lobby. The second he was inside, she would have him cornered. He surely wouldn't manhandle her in front of witnesses, so the disparity in their sizes wouldn't matter once he was safely inside. If need be, she'd tell the folks at Focus Health the truth: that Ron was her missing husband, supposedly dead, and wanted by the police on charges of bigamy. It would be embarrassing to involve the Focus Health employees in her problems, but the circumstances were out of the ordinary and she couldn't worry about social rules at this point. Etiquette would have to surrender to justice.

More relaxed now that she'd come up with something that almost deserved the name of a plan, Ellie leaned back in her seat and took a small sip from the bottle of water she'd brought from the hotel. She couldn't drink too much or she'd be searching for a restroom before she knew it. Who could have guessed that surveillance was so darn complicated? she thought, sneaking another look at her watch. Only fifteen minutes had passed, drat it. Still not a chance in the world that Avery Fairfax would be arriving from the airport for another little while.

A small panel van drove up and parked a couple of spaces down from the entrance to Focus Health. The logo on the side announced Snow White Linen and Uniform at Your Service. Ellie waited for the driver to get out and make a delivery, but ten minutes ticked by and nothing happened.

A deliveryman who didn't make deliveries warranted a second look, but it was difficult to get a clear view of him behind the tinted glass of his window. She could see nothing more than that he was a middle-aged man of medium build, wearing a cap. He wasn't eating or drinking, so he hadn't parked to enjoy his lunch. He wasn't checking a clipboard, leastways she couldn't see one. He was just sitting there, looking around the parking lot. Could this possibly be Paul Fairfax?

It seemed to her that the man's gaze came to rest on her a couple of times, but he apparently wasn't curious enough to get out of his van and check on her. If the driver *was* Paul Fairfax, she had the same advantage with him that she had with Ron: neither man was expecting to see her. It was a pity that she couldn't just walk over and introduce herself, since cooperating with Paul would surely double their chances of success. Still, Avery had clearly warned her to stay away from Paul, and she could only assume Avery knew what she was talking about. The man was her brother, after all.

Ellie picked up the magazine she'd put on the front seat and pretended to read. She tipped the water bottle against her mouth, although she didn't actually drink. Hopefully, she looked like an office worker taking a break and eating lunch in her car. From behind the cover of her magazine, she kept a close eye on the van.

The driver finally turned his face so that she could see him almost full on and she studied him intently. She had always been lucky enough to have good eyesight, and although she needed glasses for close work these days, her distance vision remained twenty/twenty. She couldn't say for sure that she was looking at Paul Fairfax, but she was ninety-five percent positive.

Her cell phone rang and the caller ID displayed the name Avery Fairfax. Ellie flipped the phone open so fast she almost dropped it. *Please God, let Avery say she would be here within the next two minutes.* "Yes, Avery, I'm so glad you called. Where are you?"

"We're about to pick up the rental car and we hope to be heading out of the airport in the next five minutes. Are you at Focus Health, Ellie? What's going on?"

"I'm at Focus Health," she confirmed. "Well, in the parking lot outside, actually. Not much is going on, although I think your brother is here. I can't be sure because he drove up in a delivery truck and he hasn't gotten out. Just before you called I was wondering if I should maybe walk over and let him know I'm here.

Otherwise, it seems to me, there's a risk whatever he's intending to do when Ron arrives might interfere with my plans. Plus if the two of us cooperated, there's less chance Ron could make a dash for it—"

"Ellie, listen to me." Avery's normally musical voice was harsh with strain. "Whatever you do, don't let Paul know that you're there. Don't approach him. Try to keep out of his line of sight. Above all, *don't trust him!*"

Ellie was taken aback by Avery's vehemence. "All right—"

"Luke says we'll be at Focus Health in thirty minutes or less." Avery must be really stressed to cut in while somebody was speaking, Ellie thought. "Hang in there, Ellie, and with luck we'll be able to tackle Ron and my brother together."

Another car turned into the parking lot. It was a dark blue Mercedes, and as it drew closer, Ellie saw that the man behind the wheel looked to be about fifty, with black, straight hair and a solid, muscular build. "I don't think we're going to get that lucky," she said. "I think Ron just drove into the parking lot right now."

"Ellie, take care! Remember, the most important thing is that you avoid getting hurt."

"Yes, I understand, I have to go." Ellie's palms turned sweaty and her breath came twice as fast as normal. She closed the phone and watched as Ron parked the Mercedes directly outside the entrance to Focus Health. She was quite sure it was Ron, even though he was wearing a wig. After he disappeared and all his lies were exposed, she'd wasted a lot of time wondering if she'd ever really known him at all. Seeing the man at the wheel of the Mercedes, she realized that she might not know Ron Raven the man, but she could recognize his outward appearance, even when he was disguised. There wasn't a doubt in her mind that she was looking at the man who'd lived with her for thirty-five years, telling her he loved her for each and every one of them.

The deliveryman had finally gotten out of his van and was standing by the rear doors, just waiting. From where she was parked, she could see him quite clearly, and she was more than ever convinced she was looking at Paul Fairfax. Height, body build, stance—everything fit. From where Ron was parked, Paul would be invisible until he started walking into Focus Health. She supposed that was a good thing, but the fact that she had no idea what Paul planned to do bothered Ellie. She could only hope that his plan for confronting Ron wouldn't interfere with hers.

She was surprised at how hard it was to stay quietly in her car and bide her time, even though she knew full well that lying low offered her the best chance of successfully cornering Ron. Adrenaline was rushing through her, urging her to jump out of the car and shout insults at Ron until she could rid herself of all the hurt and anger piled up inside. Taking deep breaths, she forced herself to be sensible and not let pent-up anger ruin her chance of success.

Ron got out of the car, slipping his sunglasses into the breast pocket of his jacket in a gesture so familiar that for a moment Ellie's heart stopped. He reached into the back for his briefcase. At the same instant, she saw Paul Fairfax emerge at a fast run from behind the shelter of his van and raise his hand to take aim—

"Oh my God, no! Ron, look out! He's going to shoot you!" She hurtled out of her car just in time to see Ron swing toward her, his face displaying an expression of utter astonishment.

Paul was running, as well, but there had been no sound of a shot and Ron was still on his feet. Hadn't Paul been aiming a gun, after all? Had he missed? She was still a couple of yards away when Ron seemed to freeze. The next minute he doubled over and fell to his knees.

Paul was already there when she arrived at Ron's side. She doubled over to cut a stitch. "Oh God, you shot him!"

Ron's face was contorted with pain, and he seemed to be struggling to speak, moving Ellie to an unexpected tenderness. She discovered that imagining vengeance and actually seeing the injured body of a man you had once cared about were two very different things. She knelt beside Ron, searching for a wound, but there was no blood that she could find, no gaping bullet wound.

"Of course I didn't shoot him," Paul Fairfax said. "I used a Taser, that's all." As he spoke, Ron started to get up, but he fell back to his knees when Paul pushed the Taser against his chest and once again pulled the trigger. Ron collapsed onto the ground, literally stunned, his body freezing in a rictus of pain.

"What did you just do, for heaven's sake? There was no need to Taser him again."

"It's set on low." Paul sounded disdainful rather than apologetic. "Help me get Ron to the van before we attract a crowd."

"He can't walk!"

"Then help me! There's someone coming out of the Hot Tub Emporium. We need to get Ron on his feet and out of sight." Paul looped Ron's arm around his neck and started walking, dragging Ron at his side. Ellie draped Ron's other arm over her shoulders, wondering if she ought to be calling to the passerby for help instead of concealing what Paul had done.

"Ron will be fine in a few minutes. You look disapproving, Mrs. Raven, but you should know your own husband by now. I had to think of some method to prevent him running away and this was the best I could come up with."

Using a Taser struck Ellie as a brutal way to achieve that goal, but she had to admit it was effective. There had been no noise to attract attention, Ron was unable to flee the scene, and the long-term effects on his health would hopefully be nil. She realized she was paying scant heed to Avery's warning to keep away from Paul, but in the circumstances she didn't see what choice she had. It was a little late to walk away and pretend she wasn't there.

They covered the short distance to the van without mishap and Ellie helped Paul lift Ron's limp body into the spacious rear compartment. "He's not a young man," she said, worried that Ron showed no signs of recovery. "He's going to need medical attention."

Paul made a dismissive gesture. "I doubt it, but we'll check him out when we're somewhere more private."

"Where are you planning on taking Ron exactly?"

"To a local café," Paul said curtly. "I'm not sure that I owe you any explanations, Mrs. Raven, but I'm waiting for my sister and niece to arrive from Chicago. Once we've had a chance to talk with Ron, we'll arrange for the police to come and arrest him."

"Avery invited me to join you all," Ellie said. "I appreciate her invitation. As you can imagine, I have plenty of questions I'd like my ex-husband to answer."

"If you're joining us at Lucinda's, then you need to hurry up and get in the van." Paul slammed the rear doors of the van, hiding the interior mere seconds before another car passed within a yard of where they were standing.

"Look, we can't stand around here talking. We need to get out of here before anyone starts asking questions."

It was one thing to ignore Avery's advice and confront Paul when she'd thought Ron was about to get a bullet in his back. It was another thing to voluntarily deliver herself into the hands of a man whose own sister had warned her to stay away from him. But Paul was still holding the Taser, and she was very much afraid that if she refused to get in the van he would simply pull the trigger, leaving her unable to resist. With Avery's warnings ringing in her ears, most of Paul's explanations struck Ellie as falling far short of the truth.

"Thanks for the offer of a ride." She smiled at him guilelessly, as if she were truly the gullible country bumpkin he imagined her to be. "I always hate trying to find new places, even when I have directions, and the traffic around here is the worst."

She turned her back on him and walked away as if meekly going to the passenger side of the van. She prayed that he wouldn't bother to follow. Tasers had a short range, she knew that much, and once she got on the other side of the van, she would run like hell—and shout for help while she was running.

Her plan would never have worked if Paul Fairfax hadn't considered her a dowdy, unintelligent nobody. As it was, it didn't seem to cross his aristocratic mind that she might be tricking him. She walked around the van and then, protected by its bulk, ran like hell toward her car.

"Help! Help! He has a gun! He's going to kill me!"

Paul was chasing her, she could hear the pounding of his footsteps, but she had a significant head start and it seemed she was out of range of the Taser because no terrifying jolt of electricity stopped her in her tracks. Out of the corner of her eye she saw somebody had appeared in the doorway of Focus Health. Thank God, a witness!

"Help!" she shouted again. "He has a gun!" Not true, of course, but yelling that he had a Taser might not produce the desired effect.

"Call the police!" She collapsed against the side of the Pontiac, shaking, panting and totally petrified. Another person arrived in the doorway of Focus Health and somebody was coming out of the Hot Tub Emporium, too. Paul wouldn't be able to Taser her now.

Then she realized that Paul had reached the same conclusion. He'd not only given up the chase, he was climbing back into the van. She heard him start the ignition. Drat it, darn it and double darn. She'd saved herself, but in a moment, Paul would be gone, taking Ron with him. God knew what his plans were, but they almost certainly didn't bode well for Ron.

Almost without conscious thought, Ellie threw herself into her rental car. The keys were still in the ignition and she reversed out of her parking space at a speed she hadn't attempted since she was in high school and suffering from teenage delusions of immortality. She knew there was almost no chance she could follow the van through the nightmare of Washington, D.C., traffic. Besides, if she did by some miracle keep up with Paul, what would she do when they arrived at their destination? Paul had a stun gun for sure and possibly even a gun that fired real bullets. She had nothing.

She revved the engine and shot past half a dozen parked cars. The van was cumbersome and Paul was still maneuvering it out of its parking space. It was now or never. Ellie drew in a deep breath, took her foot from the accelerator and rammed her rental car straight into the hood on the passenger side of the Snow White Linen delivery van.

Twenty-Seven

Avery's worst fears were realized when Luke turned into the Focus Health parking area and she saw the crowd gathered around a white Pontiac that had apparently crashed into a delivery truck.

"I'm afraid we didn't get here in time," she said, and she could hear the dread in her own voice.

Luke slammed their rented Taurus into a parking space and shot out of the car. Kate jumped out almost before the car stopped moving, Avery following hard on her heels. The police hadn't arrived, she noticed, and there were no paramedics, which must mean that the crash had occurred within the past few minutes. She hoped—she really hoped—that her decision to ask earlier this morning for Ellie's help hadn't led to Ellie being injured. Or worse.

As they approached the crash site she saw that the crowd was smaller than it had appeared as they drove in. No more than a dozen people were milling around, with nobody doing anything very useful for the victims.

"Let us through, please. These are our family members." Luke spoke with authority and he had the advantage of being tall, so that he looked commanding. The crowd parted, allowing him access to the cars. He and Kate headed in the direction of the van, so Avery made her way toward the Pontiac.

As she walked, she could hear a woman babbling to anybody who cared to listen. "She crashed her car into the van! She did it on purpose! One minute she was yelling for help. The next minute she turned around and was trying to kill him!"

Avery didn't waste time wondering whether the claim was true or not, but she did wonder where Ron was. What a disaster it would be if they'd put themselves through all this and Ron had somehow slipped through their fingers yet again. As for her brother…he was presumably behind the wheel of the delivery van and she was more than happy to leave Kate and Luke to deal with him.

Steeling herself, Avery made her way to the driver's side of the Pontiac, dreading what she might see. The air bag had deployed, but it had already deflated and a fine mist of cornstarch or talcum powder had settled over the car's interior. Ellie, looking incredibly petite and fragile, was slumped in the driver's seat. She wasn't wearing a seat belt, Avery noticed, her stomach plunging. Petite women not wearing seat belts could be killed by the air bag, let alone by the impact that caused the bag to deploy in the first place.

There was no blood, however, at any rate none that she could see, and although the hood of the car was ominously crumpled where it had crashed into the right front side of the delivery van, there didn't appear to be any reason why she shouldn't attempt to open the car door. Nothing seemed on the point of bursting into flames, but if the car did, it would be all the more important to rescue Ellie.

Gingerly, afraid that movement might cause the air bag to redeploy if it hadn't been fully extended the last time, she slowly opened the door. The air bag, thank goodness, remained quiescent, and there was still no sign of blood. That had to be positive, surely?

It had been a very long time since she'd earned a Girl Scout badge in first aid and she was reluctant to move Ellie. Still, nobody else was taking charge, so she'd better do it. "Could somebody please bring me some drinking water and a towel? And has anybody called 911?"

"I called. I called as soon as I saw them crash." A woman clutching a small cocker spaniel stepped forward and peered into the car. "She's not moving. Is she…is she all right?"

"I'm not sure. I have no medical training. But she's breathing and her pulse seems steady."

"That's a relief," the woman said.

As Avery watched, Ellie's eyelids fluttered. After another moment, she opened them and seemed to recognize Avery. "Oh, hello. My…ribs…hurt."

Avery rested her hand very lightly against Ellie's forehead, just so that she would have the reassurance of human touch. "The air bag deployed and it probably winded you. You may even have some cracked ribs. Don't talk if it hurts."

"Paul…was getting away…with Ron. Didn't know how else to stop him."

"You did the right thing. Thank you."

"You asked me to…save the day. I think maybe I did."

"Absolutely, you did. If you hadn't been here, Paul would have driven off with Ron and we'd have lost him."

Kate came up at that moment. "Is this Ellie? How is she doing?"

"Yes, it's Ellie and she's doing well, I hope. How about Paul?"

"He's unconscious. He doesn't seem to have any bleeding wounds, but we're afraid to move him in case there are internal injuries."

"I think I hear sirens," Avery said. "Let's hope it's the paramedics and not the police."

"Yes, I hear them, too. Mom, we found Dad in the back of the van. He doesn't seem badly injured and he's asking to speak with you. Can you come?"

"If you'll stay here with Ellie."

"Of course."

Kate knelt down so that she was at eye level with Ellie inside the car. "Hello, Ellie. I'm Kate, Avery's daughter. I'm going to stay here with you for the next couple of minutes. I expect you can hear the sirens, which is good news. It sounds as if help is on the way."

Avery left her daughter to take care of Ellie and made her way to the delivery van. The rear doors had been thrown open and Ron was sitting up, his back supported by the wall of the van, his legs dangling over the edge of the loading platform. He looked pale, with two small and unhealthy blotches of color on his cheeks, but he gave Avery a smile of vintage charm when he caught sight of her.

"My dear, how have you been? I must say, you look simply wonderful."

"I wish I could say the same for you." Avery had no intention of allowing Ron to direct the conversation to some level where they ended up exchanging pleasantries as if they were old acquaintances reunited at a high school reunion. "What happened here today, Ron?"

"Paul obviously was afraid I'd make a run for it as soon as I saw him."

"Was Paul wrong?" Avery asked dryly.

Ron actually laughed. "Probably not. Anyway, Paul wanted to make damn sure I couldn't escape and so he used a Taser on me. The bastard had the Taser set on high stun, I'm sure of it. I'm damn lucky I didn't die of a heart attack."

"Paul may not be a prince, but he has legitimate cause to be angry with you, Ron."

"Like hell he has legitimate cause. Your brother's a complete fraud, Avery, just like Ellie's brother. They're two of a kind. Paul was so damned incompetent I'd have fired him in a heartbeat, except he blackmailed me to keep him on the job."

"Which particular ethical lapse did my brother choose to blackmail you about?"

"He found out about Ellie when Kate was in high school and he threatened to tell you I was a bigamist if I didn't keep paying him off." Ron gave a tight smile. "In retrospect, I can see I should have told the son of a bitch to fuck off. That would have called his bluff, because he damn sure needed me a hell of a lot more than I needed him."

"Why did Paul need you so badly?"

"Because your brother has the world's worst business judgment, that's why. If Paul invests in a project, you can just about guarantee it'll go belly up within a couple of years. He never had any money and he was a constant drain on our partnership. Without me, he would have spent his entire life two steps away from bankruptcy."

This wasn't the moment to mull over the incredible truth that Paul had known for years about Ron's bigamy and chosen never to tell her about it. The men in her life had not exactly been noble cavaliers, Avery thought acidly. She drew in a deep breath and focused on the real issue. She wasn't going to let Ron shift the blame for his sins, even if her brother was a lying, deceitful lowlife.

"My brother wouldn't have been able to blackmail you if you hadn't been a bigamist. Why did you do it, Ron? Why did you lie to me, and to Ellie, too, for that matter? Why did you fake your own death? And why have you been hiding from us all these months?"

"You know why I faked my own death," he said, sounding weary. "Ellie's brother was trying to kill me."

"Ellie's brother has been dead for five months, which means that particular excuse hasn't been valid for equally as long."

It was silly of her to have expected honesty from him when she'd never received it before. "God, I have the world's worst headache." Ron rubbed his hand across his forehead in a convincing portrayal of a man suffering.

Avery discovered to her astonishment that she didn't

care anymore about Ron's evasive tactics. Didn't even care whether or not he really had a headache. She had no particular desire to stay and listen to Ron weave clever, or not-so-clever, explanations for unforgivable behavior. Looking at him, she realized with a surge of an emotion pretty close to happiness that her liberation was truly complete. There was no reason to waste time asking in a hundred different ways why he had deceived her for so many years. The simple answer was that he'd lied because he was, at his most fundamental core, a liar.

She sent him a look that was more of pity than of anger. "I can hear the paramedics arriving. I'm sure they'll take good care of you. Goodbye, Ron. I don't believe we have anything more to say to each other."

She turned to leave and he called after her. "Avery, wait! Wait up!"

She paused and half turned back. "Yes?"

"I'm sorry, Avery, for everything. Truly. I never meant to hurt you. I stayed with you all those years because I loved you."

Avery felt her mouth curve into a smile. "Did you, Ron? And Ellie? Did you love her, too?"

He didn't even have the grace to look embarrassed. "Yes," he said earnestly. "I did. You're wonderful women. Quite different, but equally wonderful. I loved both of you."

"By your standards, perhaps. By my standards, you didn't love either of us."

"You have a narrow definition of love, Avery. That's what comes from being raised by such old-fashioned, inhibited parents."

"You know, Ron, insulting my family probably isn't

the very best way to make me think more kindly of you. Although, I'm afraid there probably aren't any methods left to achieve that goal."

"You've changed," he said sorrowfully. "I'm surprised at you, Avery. You never used to be this hard."

"I'm pleased to hear that I've changed. And I don't think I'm hard, just confident in my own abilities. But let's talk about you for a moment, Ron. I see a police squad car arriving right now. The police are going to arrest you, you know that, don't you? You committed bigamy, you faked your own death, you stole money from Adam's bank—"

"I can explain everything." He sounded supremely confident.

"I hope for your sake that you can, although bigamy is a little hard to explain away, I would have thought, and theft even harder." She held up her hand. "No, please don't make your excuses to me. I don't care, so save it for the police. You'd better hope that your son, Liam, is willing to defend you, because you're going to need a really good lawyer."

Ron was silent for several seconds. "Look, Avery, I want you to understand," he said finally. "I've done some things I'm not proud of, but I'm a different man since I met Consuela Mackenzie. Until I met her and she showed me how much the Mayan people have been forced to suffer at the hands of invaders and conquerors, life always seemed something of a game to me. Could I prove I was better than the competition? Could I win in this negotiation? Make more money than my rivals? Those were my main motives a lot of the time." He shrugged. "It's different now. Julio Castellano is a really good man, and Consuela Mackenzie is a really good woman. I want to help them. I want to help the Mayan people win freedom from their economic servitude."

He sounded genuine, earnest even, but Avery didn't really care if he was being honest or not. "I've no idea how you'll help the Mayan people from a prison cell, Ron, but I wish you luck in your endeavors. Sincerely." She turned to go once again.

He spoke from behind her. "Consuela is pregnant," he said. "It's my child."

It was almost the only thing he could have said that had the power to hurt her. Ron had always resisted the idea of having another child after Kate, despite the fact that he'd known Avery badly wanted more children. It was painful to think that with Consuela he'd been willing to embrace the notion of fatherhood when he'd denied her another baby for a decade after Kate's birth. If there had been any thread of affection left for him in her heart, nothing could more effectively have severed it.

Avery waited until she was sure her face displayed nothing beyond impersonal courtesy before she once again turned to look at him. "I wish Consuela and her baby only the best. Good luck to all three of you." She said nothing more, just walked away from him at a fast, steady pace. And this time when he called her name she didn't look back.

The paramedics arrived as she joined Luke at her brother's side. "Paul's regained consciousness," Luke said. "But he really doesn't look too good."

"How are you feeling, Paul?" Avery's voice softened

as she saw the pain etched on her brother's face. "What happened? How did you get so badly hurt? Ron has barely a scratch."

"Taser," he said, his voice a thin and reedy rasp. "Multiple stuns."

Avery looked inquiringly toward Luke. "I thought Paul was the person aiming the Taser at Ron. Is he claiming it was the other way around?"

"I don't think so. We found him with a Taser resting in his lap. It must have discharged when the car crashed. Maybe it even discharged several times, if that's technically possible. My guess is Paul's suffering more from an adverse reaction to the Taser shots than from the aftereffects of the crash. For some people, especially if they have weak hearts, a blow from a Taser can have quite an impact."

Avery switched her attention to her brother. "Just so you know what's going on, Paul, we're all aware that you're the person who invaded Kate's home and made those terrible threats. I also know you forged the documents so that you could take out an illegal three-million-dollar mortgage on my penthouse."

"No, you're wrong—"

"Paul, save your energy. I don't believe your denials." She looked directly into his eyes. "I'm also sure that you killed poor George Klein. What was his offense, Paul? That he'd found Ron and was about to tell all of us how to contact him?"

"Don't know…what you're…talking about." But she'd seen the horror in his eyes when she mentioned George's murder and knew he was lying.

"There's probably no way for the police to make a

case against you for George's murder that will stand up in court. But I *can* provide the evidence that will enable the state's attorney's office to charge you with fraudulently obtaining three million dollars in loans on my penthouse. That should get you at least a couple of years behind bars, and rest assured, Paul, I'm going to make it my personal mission to see that you get them. With any luck, they'll throw in another couple of years for threatening to kill Kate. It's not much in payment for George Klein's life, but it's something."

"You can't send…your own brother to jail."

"Watch me do just that. You've had your run, Paul, but now it's over. You…Ron…the whole sordid web of lies. It's finally over."

Epilogue

December 26, 2007

The marriage of Luke Savarini to Kate Fairfax took place on the day after Christmas, a traditional date for Savarini weddings. Their wedding celebration also followed tradition by providing the guests with lavish and wonderful food, catered in this instance by the groom's own restaurants. The dazzlingly gorgeous wedding cake, baked by the bride herself, was acknowledged to outshine those even at the best of previous Savarini weddings.

The attendance of 302 out of a possible 314 Savarini uncles, cousins, aunts and assorted in-laws marked a new record. Copious numbers of Savarini children were in attendance and spilled the usual number of drinks in a variety of extraordinary places. The band was one of Little Italy's best, and thirty of the male relatives, aspiring Andrea Bocellis to a man, got together and delivered the usual impassioned but slightly off-key rendition of "O Sole Mio." Not to be outdone, Luke's brothers delivered the requisite doses of sentiment and embarrassment when they made their toasts to the happy couple.

It was impossible to avoid noticing, however, that not every aspect of the wedding was entirely in keeping with the best Savarini traditions. To start with, the church service had been private, with only the parents of the groom and the mother of the bride in attendance. Although the bride was wearing a lovely white lace gown in a traditional style, she'd arrived at the party from the church wearing a cloak of scarlet velvet.

The Savarini clan considered themselves tolerant folks. The scarlet cloak could be considered a fashion statement, or even an acknowledgment of the holiday season, but there were a few of the cousins who wondered if it might not have been Kate's way of metaphorically flinging down the gauntlet.

There was no getting around the fact that Kate had some mighty strange relatives, and she'd invited several of them to the wedding. Liam Raven, her half brother, was there, along with his new wife, the notorious Chloe Hamilton. Chloe was the widow of the murdered mayor of Denver. She'd only lost her first husband sometime in August and here she was, married again. While it was true that Chloe had been officially exonerated of any suspicion that she was responsible for her husband's murder, it was too much too expect people to ignore the titillating truth that she had originally been arrested for the crime.

Another interesting guest was Megan Raven, the bride's half sister, who was married to Adam Fairfax, the bride's uncle. This complex relationship caused several elderly Savarinis to scratch their heads and mutter dark comments about incest and other undesirable practices. The actual truth was less Gothic—there was no blood relationship at all between Megan and her husband, not even a distant one—but the Savarinis decided not to let truth get in the way of entertainment.

These two notorious marriages were merely line items among the many fascinating scandals clinging to the bride's family. Avery Fairfax, the bride's mother, could lay claim to being one of the leading lights of the Chicago social scene. However, she had for twenty-eight years been the bigamous wife of Ron Raven, a man once proclaimed dead, who was now wanted by the police for skipping out on his bail. It was rumored that Ron Raven was hiding out in Central America, in one of those countries nobody ever heard about until the army marched into the presidential palace and everyone had a revolution before taking the weekend off for another fiesta.

As if that weren't enough, Ron Raven's other wife, the one he'd kept hidden away somewhere out in the Wild West, was already remarried—to the local sheriff of all things! The Savarinis had always suspected that law enforcement out on the range was more about protecting your own than bringing criminals to justice, and this seemed to prove it.

To crown it all, the bride's uncle, Paul Fairfax, had died recently in mysterious circumstances. Details about that particular event were really hard to come by, suggesting it might be the most interesting gossip of all.

Bruno Savarini, who seemed to know more than most people about the event, insisted there was no mystery at all about Paul Fairfax's death. He'd died of heart failure following a car crash in Virginia. Since Bruno lived in Virginia, this seemed to add weight to his pronouncements. Other Savarinis, however, muttered about suicide in the face of pending felony charges for grand theft and attempted murder.

Be that as it may, Kate's Fairfax grandparents had nothing to look so darn snooty about, all the Savarinis agreed. They might be blue bloods, but they were darn lucky to have their granddaughter marrying into solid Italian immigrant stock. Apparently blue blood after a while needed to be mixed with ordinary red if you didn't want to create a heck of a lot of problems. And since Luke was about as red-blooded a man as you could find, Kate should count her blessings.

If Kate's relatives were cause for gossip, it had to be admitted that Kate herself was just about the most beautiful woman any of the Savarini cousins had seen outside the pages of *Playboy* or *Bride* magazine. The cousins' choice of comparison depended, naturally, on whether they were male or female. When you saw the way Luke looked at her, not to mention the way she looked back at him, you could almost believe the two of them loved each other enough to make the whole unlikely union work. And their children would probably be gorgeous, as Luke's mother made sure to tell anyone who cared to listen. The Savarini clan hoped that Kate would set about the business of having babies as soon as possible, and leave the scandals to the other members of her family.

Mellowed by champagne and the best handmade

chocolates they'd ever tasted, the Savarinis waved goodbye to Luke and Kate as they left the reception for the start of their honeymoon. Rumor had it that they were flying to an island in the Caribbean where the entertainment consisted chiefly of sailing during the day and long walks on the beach at night.

The Savarini clan hoped the newlyweds would have a wonderful time. One thing seemed clear. With nothing better to do for ten days than walk and sail, Luke's parents should be able to count on another grandbaby by next October.

The clan looked forward to the christening.

NEW YORK TIMES BESTSELLING AUTHOR

STELLA CAMERON

'Tis the season to be wary....

Christmas is coming and all is far from calm in Pointe Judah, Louisiana. Newcomer Christian DeAngelo—Angel to his friends—is at his wit's end trying to manage Sonny, the hotheaded nineteen-year-old everyone believes is his nephew.

Angel has been commiserating with Eileen Moggeridge, whose lonely son Aaron has latched on to Sonny and gotten into deeper trouble than ever. But nothing could prepare Angel and Eileen for the boys' latest crisis: as they are horsing around in the swamp one afternoon, a shot rings out....

A COLD DAY IN HELL

"If you're looking for chilling suspense and red-hot romance, look no farther than Stella Cameron!"
—Tess Gerritsen

Available the first week of November 2007 wherever paperbacks are sold!

www.MIRABooks.com

MSC2495

ICE STORM

REQUEST YOUR FREE BOOKS!

2 FREE NOVELS
FROM THE ROMANCE/SUSPENSE
COLLECTION PLUS 2 FREE GIFTS!

YES! Please send me 2 FREE novels from the Romance/Suspense Collection and my 2 FREE gifts. After receiving them, if I don't wish to receive any more books, I can return the shipping statement marked "cancel." If I don't cancel, I will receive 4 brand-new novels every month and be billed just $5.49 per book in the U.S., or $5.99 per book in Canada, plus 25¢ shipping and handling per book plus applicable taxes, if any*. That's a savings of at least 20% off the cover price! I understand that accepting the 2 free books and gifts places me under no obligation to buy anything. I can always return a shipment and cancel at any time. Even if I never buy another book from the Reader Service, the two free books and gifts are mine to keep forever.

185 MDN EF5Y   385 MDN EF6C

Name _____ (PLEASE PRINT)

Address _____ Apt. #

City _____ State/Prov. _____ Zip/Postal Code

Signature (if under 18, a parent or guardian must sign)

Mail to **The Reader Service:**
IN U.S.A.: P.O. Box 1867, Buffalo, NY 14240-1867
IN CANADA: P.O. Box 609, Fort Erie, Ontario L2A 5X3

Not valid to current subscribers to the Romance Collection,
the Suspense Collection or the Romance/Suspense Collection.

Want to try two free books from another line?
Call 1-800-873-8635 or visit www.morefreebooks.com.

* Terms and prices subject to change without notice. NY residents add applicable sales tax. Canadian residents will be charged applicable provincial taxes and GST. This offer is limited to one order per household. All orders subject to approval. Credit or debit balances in a customer's account(s) may be offset by any other outstanding balance owed by or to the customer. Please allow 4 to 6 weeks for delivery.

Your Privacy: Harlequin is committed to protecting your privacy. Our Privacy Policy is available online at www.eHarlequin.com or upon request from the Reader Service. From time to time we make our lists of customers available to reputable firms who may have a product or service of interest to you. If you would prefer we not share your name and address, please check here. ☐

BOB07

JASMINE CRESSWELL

32477 SUSPECT	___ $6.99 U.S.	___ $8.50 CAN.
32467 MISSING	___ $6.99 U.S.	___ $8.50 CAN.
32066 FULL PURSUIT	___ $6.50 U.S.	___ $7.99 CAN.
66712 DEAD RINGER	___ $6.50 U.S.	___ $7.99 CAN.

(limited quantities available)

TOTAL AMOUNT	$ _____
POSTAGE & HANDLING	$ _____
($1.00 FOR 1 BOOK, 50¢ for each additional)	
APPLICABLE TAXES*	$ _____
TOTAL PAYABLE	$ _____

(check or money order—please do not send cash)

To order, complete this form and send it, along with a check or money order for the total above, payable to MIRA Books, to: **In the U.S.:** 3010 Walden Avenue, P.O. Box 9077, Buffalo, NY 14269-9077; **In Canada:** P.O. Box 636, Fort Erie, Ontario, L2A 5X3.

Name: _____

Address: _____ City: _____

State/Prov.: _____ Zip/Postal Code: _____

Account Number (if applicable): _____

075 CSAS

*New York residents remit applicable sales taxes.
*Canadian residents remit applicable GST and provincial taxes.

MIRA®

www.MIRABooks.com

MJCI1107BL